Praise for *The Search for Maggie Ward*
and Andrew M. Greeley

"A fascinating novelist . . . with a rare, possibly unmatched point of view."
—*Los Angeles Times*

"I enjoy reading Andrew Greeley. He spins wondrous romances."
—*The New York Times Book Review*

"Unabashedly romantic . . . Impossible to resist . . . That is the singular magic of *The Search for Maggie Ward*."
—*Orlando Sentinel*

"He has mastered the art of suspense and of drawing living, breathing men and women with whom you quickly become involved. . . . Keeps you turning the pages to find answers at the end of the book—and then leaves you feeling wistful because the last page has been turned."
—*Arizona Daily Star*

"Greeley has that elusive ability to tell a story so that you want to find out what happens next."
—*The Atlanta Journal-Constitution*

"A master storyteller."
—*The Cincinnati Enquirer*

"In the tradition of James T. Farrell, Father Greeley writes with passion and narrative force about the parishes where he grew up."
—*Chicago Sun-Times*

"A genius for plumbing people's convictions as well as their opinions. That and his rich literary imagination make him truly exceptional."
—*The Cleveland Press*

THE Search FOR Maggie Ward

Andrew M. Greeley

A Tom Doherty Associates Book
New York

THE SEARCH FOR MAGGIE WARD

Copyright © 2018 by Andrew M. Greeley Enterprises, Ltd.

A Forge Book
Published by Tom Doherty Associates
175 Fifth Avenue
New York, NY 10010

www.tor-forge.com

Forge® is a registered trademark of Macmillan Publishing Group, LLC.

The Library of Congress has cataloged the Warner Books edition as follows:

Greeley, Andrew M., 1928–2013.
    The search for Maggie Ward / Andrew M. Greeley.—First edition.
        p. cm.
    ISBN 978-0-446-51476-7 (hardcover)
I. Title.
    PS3557.R358 S4 1991
    813'.54—dc20

                                                    90050282

ISBN 978-1-250-17516-8 (trade paperback)
ISBN 978-1-4299-4675-9 (ebook)

Our books may be purchased in bulk for promotional, educational, or business use. Please contact your local bookseller or the Macmillan Corporate and Premium Sales Department at 1-800-221-7945, extension 5442, or by email at MacmillanSpecialMarkets@macmillan.com.

Originally published by Warner Books, a Time Warner Company

First Forge Trade Paperback Edition: December 2018

Printed in the United States of America

0 9 8 7 6 5 4 3 2 1

THE Search FOR Maggie Ward

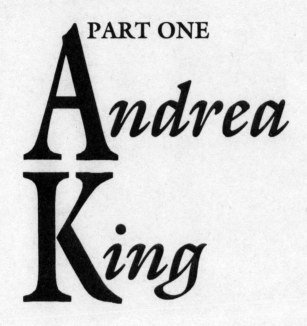

PART ONE

Andrea King

CHAPTER 1

THE FIRST TIME I SAW HER I THOUGHT SHE WAS A GHOST.

Her appearance and my instinctive reaction to the uncanny vibrations I felt are as vivid in my imagination as though it all happened yesterday instead of forty years ago.

Bing Crosby was singing "Ole Buttermilk Sky" on a wheezy jukebox in the railroad station café in Tucson. I'll never forget the date—July 22, 1946. The station smelled of steam, stale water, dried human sweat, and burned bacon. There were only a handful of weary people sitting in the sticky café, all of them surely wishing they were somewhere else.

"She's dead." I put down my faintly sour grapefruit juice and stared.

Like a good group commander, I tried to analyze my reaction. It made no sense at all, I informed the intelligence officer lurking in the back of my brain.

"You're alive today, sir," he replied, "because you pay attention to your instincts."

My impression that she was unearthly passed quickly. I disregarded it because it had been recorded in a brain dazed by habitual depression, a lifetime of bizarre romantic fantasy, months of terrifying nightmares, and a night-long drive across the desert: milk-white skin, pale-blue eyes, slender ethereal body, brown skirt, white blouse, already wet at the armpits. She slipped through the chairs and the tables dragging a heavy piece of cardboard luggage in one hand, somehow making the effort seem both insubstantial and elegant, like a minor but very responsible angel gracefully changing the location of a mountain range.

As I watched her (covertly, I thought), the girl approached the counter and sat down across from me so quietly that no one seemed to notice her. She had to order her coffee twice before the waitress was aware that she was sitting at the counter.

She looks like she's from beyond the grave: the premonition pushed back into my brain. I dismissed it as if it were an immoral desire. Grudgingly it slipped into an unused closet in the dark corners of the basement of my brain, promising that it would sneak out again, perhaps after dark.

I had been thinking about the dead that morning—a pretty common activity for me at that time, even though the war had ended eleven months before. The dead on my mind that morning, however, had not been the millions who were killed in the war (while I lived); rather, since I was planning a visit to Tombstone after my breakfast, I was thinking of the Earps and the Clantons, the legendary figures from Tombstone in 1881. The hot, dirty adobe station with a red tile roof was not the one to which Earp had escaped from Cochise County to Pima County sixty years before. But it was on the same spot. Wyatt Earp had once eaten breakfast in this very locale.

Now he was as dead as the Clantons. And Doc Holliday. And this tarnished little waif?

She was too young and too pretty to be a ghost, I told myself. Ghosts don't have dark red hair shaped like crisp halos around high, intelligent foreheads. They don't have gracefully swelling breasts and they don't have lithe young bodies that move with unselfconscious grace.

Why not? my gloomy imagination wondered.

I no longer believed in God or life after death. I had lost my faith on the *Enterprise*, not in a dramatic crisis but rather in a process of slow erosion. One Sunday when I could have gone to Mass on the hangar deck, I simply did not get out of my bunk. I realized I no longer took seriously the simple pieties with which the chaplain tried to prepare us for the possibility of death.

In my letters home I continued to assure my mother that I never missed Mass except when I was on duty or in the air in my F6F.

A few years later, during the Korean War, it was a matter of debate whether or not there were atheists in the foxholes. There were, however, atheists in the air crews in the western Pacific.

I was one of them.

In principle, then, I had to reject the possibility of ghosts, particularly in the hot, dirty, enervating murk of a railroad-station café early in the morning.

Loss of your faith does not mean, I told myself, that you lose your superstitions. Or your imagination. Especially when the ghost was so pretty.

It was an early morning fantasy, nothing more. I would not even speak to her.

Rather to my surprise I discovered that my imagination had already begun to undress her and to enjoy what it found —a fine, serviceable young-womanly body, ripe for play and love.

I twisted uneasily on my counter seat. I had not given up sex quite as definitively as I had given up God, but somehow I had lost interest in it. As we would say today, I put sex on hold after Leyte Gulf. Women continued to exist and to be admirable and desirable, but more as a theoretical option than one with any practical consequences for me. I assumed that eventually I would regain my interest in them.

But not quite so dramatically and in such an unpromising place.

This winter, when I began to work on my story about Andrea King, I finally showed my wife the journal I kept in those days. "That dreadful girl," she observed tartly, "was the first woman you permitted close enough to you so that you could feel lust for her."

I pointed out the passage in my journal where I described my almost irresistible urge to peel off her sweaty clothes and devour her before I had even spoken to her.

My wife sniffed. "If young women, like that poor girl, did not excite such emotions in young men, neither you nor I would have come into existence."

"Such reactions go away when you get older," I demanded, reaching casually for the zipper of her dress.

"Stop that." She pretended to push my hand away. "And stop mooning over that dreadful girl."

On that morning so long ago in Tucson the indifferent waitress slapped a coffee cup down in front of the dreadful girl with such vigor that some of the dismal liquid sloshed into her saucer. Meekly she laid a dime on the sloppy counter next to it.

Her eyes flicked in my direction, as though she had heard my obscene thoughts. Quickly she looked away, embarrassed but not totally displeased at my erotic fantasies.

It is, my wife told me many years later when she caught me staring at a particularly enticing young woman, totally offensive to strip a woman in your imagination. "They always know what you're doing and they don't like it. So don't do it, at least not so obviously, unless the woman approves."

"How do you know that?"

She patted my thigh approvingly. "Someone like you, darling, with wavy black hair, broad shoulders, a dimpled smile, and Irish charm, almost always is approved. That hussy loves it. And you must respect the woman's modesty too."

"How do you mentally undress a woman and still respect her modesty?"

"You know the answer to that. Now please stare at me."

"Why should I imagine undressing you in public when I do the real thing in private?"

"It's different."

So I devoured her with my eyes. She gasped, ordered another martini, and forbade me ever to do anything like that in public again, an injunction I did not take seriously.

"Did I forget to respect your modesty?"

"What? Oh, you poor dear sweet man, of course not. You can't help yourself. You always respect women."

By that time in our intimacy I was half ready to believe her.

I looked away from my ghost child, filing for reference my imagination's observation that, while indeed it was an excellent young body, it was also very thin, almost paper thin. Virtually transparent.

Why can't ghosts be gorgeous? I asked myself, not quite ready to give up my grotesque fantasy despite the intensity with which I stared at my coffee cup. Why shouldn't you lust after a ghost? Maybe they are better in bed than living women; they have less to lose.

That perverse thought, which I remember quite distinctly, gives you some idea of the emotional condition I was in. Most young men at war don't expect to die and are astonished in that last millisecond when they discover that they are dying. I had expected to die and was astonished to find myself still alive. Instead of rejoicing over my new prospects, I had turned morose and melancholy. I was driving from San Diego to Chicago in one last romantic binge before I settled down to college and law school and River Forest affluence. What would be more appropriate than to meet a pretty ghost on the first leg of the trip?

From the perspective of four decades I can understand why someone would think I was asking for trouble. A less melancholy young man would have either dismissed the fantasy and walked away from the counter without looking back at this rather slovenly apparition or confidently made what would have probably been a transient pickup.

Not this gloomy Celtic Don Quixote. Without realizing it, I had been looking for an obsession on which to become hooked. This kid (she couldn't be any more than eighteen) was Dulcinea.

I glanced up from my coffee cup. A bedraggled and perhaps frightened Dulcinea.

Ah, frightened. There's the rub. Find a woman who seems to need protection and you have perfect bait for Jerry Keenan, USNR (ret.).

Especially when the woman has such lovely breasts, my imagination noted triumphantly.

"The Irish have a fixation on breasts," my son the Ph.D. in Irish literature (and a Freudian) remarked once in, you should excuse the expression, the bosom of our family. "When Cuchulain was threatening to attack a town in Ulster, the women of that town came forth naked to the waist, and the hero fled in terror. He jumped into a pond and it sizzled for three days."

"Some hero," his sister remarked cynically.

"Typical Irish male," his mother observed.

"Maybe the reason," his father said tentatively, "for the obsession, which I do not in fact deny, is that Irish women have such, you should excuse the expression, outstanding tits."

Then I could afford to joke about the subject—not that my compliment was invalid. At twenty-three, with little sexual experience, damn little, it was not a matter for laughter that my neighbor had left open one more button on her blouse than was absolutely necessary. My imagination began an exploration of the area with the same vigor with which I had once flown search missions off the *Enterprise*.

"It's fifteen cents," the slovenly waitress said, wiping the counter indifferently with a dirty towel.

"Fresh young breasts," the search mission reported, "not large but compact, neat, and inviting the firm but delicate fingers of a man."

Already obsessed.

She glanced at me again, mildly annoyed but not uninterested.

I was too innocent of the mysteries of the reproductive strategies of the species to consider the possibility that she might have been considering me in a roughly analogous process. Women (as I would complain later to my wife) are so much more deceptive about it.

"They have to be," she replied. "What would happen to me if I stared at you all the time?" I made some appropriately obscene suggestion that led her, as usual, to challenge me to go ahead and try.

That morning I knew none of these secrets. If there was seduction to be done, I would do it and she would either resist—in which case I would run for cover, or submit—in which case I might also run for cover.

Certainly I would not be seduced. Not by a shabby child.

Is she a virgin? I wondered. Then I saw the thin wedding ring on her finger. No engagement ring. Well, that ends that.

Maybe it doesn't. If you don't believe in God . . .

Nonsense, I told myself sternly. Now is the time to leave. You don't want to become involved with a bimbo you meet in a railroad station. Not even if that is a very fortunate brown scapular hanging between her breasts where I wanted my inquiring lips to be.

There are Catholic bimbos too.

Even Irish Catholic ones?

Is she Irish?

Would you notice any other kind of bimbo?

Brave Quixote.

It was already hot in the station. My guidebook said that in summer the usual thirty-degree variation in Tucson temperatures continued—between 80 and 110 degrees. And during the monsoon, it added helpfully, humidity added to the discomfort caused by the heat. Monsoons, I thought, happened in India. And whoever heard of a humid desert?

I had a lot to learn about this country I was exploring for the first and probably the last time.

The young woman reached into her worn purse and almost furtively searched for another coin. She withdrew a second dime, one of the tarnished "war dimes," and laid it next to the first. The waitress scooped them both up and replaced them with a nickel.

An elegant hand reached out to reclaim the nickel and then, it seemed to me shamefully, retreated, leaving the tip for the waitress, who would certainly not be grateful.

Shabby, tarnished, but with bodily movements of unself-conscious elegance. Maybe a serviceman's widow.

An eighteen-year-old widow—which, from the heights of my almost twenty-four—made her virtually a child. She was dead-tired, lonely, a little frightened, and broke. I had ten crisp hundred-dollar bills in my wallet and a checkbook which could duplicate that many times over. Perhaps I could help.

Her brown skirt and white blouse were wrinkled—all night in coach—and worn. The leather on her low-heeled shoes was cracked. Her hair was disheveled. Yet she drank the coffee (black the way it should be) as though she were in an expensive restaurant, with natural elegance.

A child's innocence softened the lines of weariness on her gently curving face. And a hint of pain that no child ought to have suffered.

Four decades later I can still feel the sting of need that accompanied my sentiments of tenderness. And can't sort them out. Immediately after I lost her, I tried to sort them out. Now I know that it was a pointless exercise.

I think, as I type these words, of my own daughters at eighteen, especially of Brigid (Biddy), who is just eighteen now. I'm not sure they were capable of riding the train into the Loop without getting lost. Looking back, I wonder how a child could be crossing the country by herself.

One does what one must do. My mother's older sister went to work at Sears when she was fourteen. Sixty-hour week.

In the next few days I would learn, viewing the events from the perspective of the present, that Andrea King was an intricate and complex young woman—less sophisticated than Biddy and yet more experienced than my oldest, who is now a professional woman with an eighteen-year-old daughter of her own.

Then all I did was to consider my options, as we would say now, and decided that I would leave without uttering a word. Pickup searched and rejected. "No enemy vessels in this area, sir. Should I pass on to the next search quadrant?"

"Roger. Proceed as indicated."

I signaled for my check. Pay for the second cup of coffee and leave.

"Your husband in the service?"

Startled, she glanced around, uncertain that I was speaking to her.

"He was on the *Indianapolis.*"

A sentence of death. No wonder the terrible pain in her soft blue eyes.

"I'm sorry."

She nodded, accepting my sympathy. "I hope he died on the ship, before the sharks got to them."

"What did he do?" Navy talk to cover the awkwardness and the sorrow. Somehow my intentions became, if not completely honorable, at least more respectable than they had been.

"Radar/tech/first. He said that electronics training"—she reached into her purse—"would guarantee a job after the war. Even better than civil service." She opened a cheap wallet to show me his picture. A husky towhead in high school graduation pose. "He was only nineteen."

"Classmate?"

"Two years ahead. I was a junior when I married him. The nuns said we were too young." She shrugged her shoulders. "Maybe we were. I don't know."

Just barely legal age. In some states. Probably had not graduated from high school. Pregnant?

"I'm sorry." What else could I say?

"What kind of plane did you fly?"

It was my turn to be startled. How did she know that I was a pilot?

"F6F."

"Hellcat. What ship?"

"*Enterprise.*"

She raised an auburn eyebrow. The *Big E* was a legend. "Lieutenant?"

I spread my hands in fake humility. "Gold oak-leaf type. Silver one when my reserve term is up next year."

Hope that impresses you, kid.

She smiled and Tucson disappeared for a couple of moments. "Impressive."

"Survival."

I wanted to tell her everything. She would understand. I hated the killing and the dying. I missed my friends who had crashed into the Pacific—Saipan, Leyte, Yap, all those other places that had even now blurred in my memory. But I also missed the roar of engines, the surge of power as my Grumman lifted off the deck, the sky dark with our fleets of planes, the excitement of battle, the triumph of return, the fierce yank of the arresting gear as I touched down on the deck, then the horror of counting noses and vacant bunks.

"A trip across the country before you settle down?"

"And begin to grow old." Did she read minds?

"Real old-timer." She smiled again; her teeth were fine and even, like her delicate facial bones. She was a natural beauty, needing neither makeup nor expensive clothes to strike at your heart.

"The war made us all grow up too soon." I pushed aside my plate of soggy pancakes. "I wish . . . I don't know what I wish."

"I wish," she said as she finished her coffee, "I had my husband back."

"Let me buy you a real breakfast." I stood up from the counter and walked around to the other side.

"That isn't necessary." She clutched her purse. "I'm not hungry."

I picked up her suitcase. Heavy, probably all her worldly goods. "Yes, you are. I don't have any . . . well, bad ideas."

I did too. Just a few minutes ago. But I'd banished them.

She considered me very carefully, her eyes probing at my soul like a doctor's exploring scalpel. "You do, too, Commander, but you won't act on them, will you?"

"Not at the breakfast table."

"Nor with an enlisted man's widow. All right, sir." Yet another smile. "I'll admit I'm starved."

Four times she had read my mind. I thought it odd, but not frightening, much less dangerous. Only later would I try to fit it into the whole strange picture of Andrea King, if that really was her name.

CHAPTER 2

"YOU KNEW I'D ASK?" WE WERE WALKING UP SIXTH AVEnue, past the Congress Hotel. My guest thought I would take her there. I said that when I take a young woman to breakfast it was in the best hotel in town. She had flushed, her skimmilk skin turning a lovely pink.

"I thought you might." She smiled again—dear God, what a wonderful smile. It really does turn out the other lights.

"You hoped I would?"

"I told myself that I'd decline politely."

"I told myself that I wouldn't ask."

We laughed together, as we would many times despite the turbulences of the next several days.

"You figured out that I was a serviceman's widow, didn't you? That's when you made up your mind."

"Eighteen is too young to be a widow."

"Almost nineteen."

"How much almost?"

She hesitated. "Well, eight . . ." She paused, considering perhaps the obligations of truthfulness that the nuns had taught her. "Almost nine months."

"Eighteen."

"Yes, Commander."

"Jerry Keenan."

"Yes, Commander, sir."

When the vibrations were good between us during the next few days—and sometimes they were very good—she made gentle fun of me. It was like being bathed in warm, sweet-smelling, healing water of an imaginary South Pacific.

Had she come from San Diego? I had wondered as we left the station. Not necessarily. The Southern Pacific tracks ran in all directions outside of Tucson. And the Greyhound depot was right across Sixth Avenue.

We turned into Congress Street, the "main" street of Tucson then, long before shopping malls, and walked by the Palace Theater, where *The Lost Weekend* was playing a year late. Tucson was not much more than a small town in those days, thirty thousand people. East of the railway there were blocks of adobe houses, slums for Mexicans. In the other direction stretched neat lines of bungalows with withered grass lawns —home designs transplanted from New England or the Middle West. Why would anyone want to live in this furnace? I wondered. Humid furnace at that. As I had driven in at sunrise on Highway 86, I had passed the sleepy red brick University of Arizona. It would be on the bottom of my list.

Yet the desert mountains all around—the Catalinas looming to the north, the lofty Santa Ritas on the south, the Tanque Verdes to the east, and the Tucson Mountains to the west— held my attention: barren desert mountains, not a bit like Fuji. But American mountains, thank God. And hence dear to a man who had decided after Yap that he would never live to see America again.

"And your name is?" I was tempted to link my arm with hers, but rejected the idea. Too soon. What would come after breakfast?

Wait and see.

"Do I have to tell you?" It was a factual question.

"As a payment for breakfast? No. Certainly not."

"Andrea King."

"Lovely name. Fits somehow."

"Thank you. . . . Clever mick."

"The question is whether we received the Blarney stone because we needed it or deserved it."

"You've been there?" Her wondrous blue eyes widened. "Kissed it?"

"Before the war."

So I had established my family as rich. Traveled to Europe during the Depression. Not Joe Kennedy rich, but still well off indeed.

"How wonderful. On the *Queen Mary!*" She linked her arm with mine as though it were the most natural movement in the world. "What was it like?"

No trace of envy. A remarkable young woman.

"More comfortable than the *Enterprise.* Greta Garbo was with us—I mean, on the same crossing. Not exactly a neighbor."

"Wow! What was she like?"

"Radiant."

"Wow!"

I was feeling light-headed and happy. I wanted to sing.

"Where are you from?"

"The East. You?"

"Chicago. Well, a suburb called River Forest. My father is a lawyer. Inherited the firm from my grandfather. I'm supposed to follow the family tradition."

"Do you want to?"

"Mostly."

From the "East." Where in the "East"? I was too busy displaying my own accomplishments to ask.

At that age in life, my daughter the doctor informs me, the bloodstream of the human young is suddenly soaked with enormous amounts of endocrine secretions. From being incapable of reproduction only a few months or years previously, both the male and the female surge into their most fertile years. The evolutionary process has selected for those genotypes which can rapidly reproduce replacements at the earliest possible age.

So sex is an obsession, often the only thing they can think about.

"One may," she continues, "deny that sexual outlet for several years and obviously do so without causing any great deal of personal harm to the individuals. The species is plastic. It can, for good and useful purposes, or sometimes not so good and useful, modify its own reproductive strategies. But one must realize that the compulsion to couple in both the physical and psychological sense is enormous."

"What is objectively sinful," adds my brother the priest, "often in circumstances loses most of its malice."

"Sacramental marriage," continues my son Jamie the priest, "is not merely an exchange of vows but the result of a long process of exploration and experimentation which begins long before."

"Kids will fuck," I add intelligently.

"Hush," says my wife, laughing tolerantly at me.

"They are under enormous biological constraint to do so, especially in times of social disorganization," the daughter continues. "They can cause great harm to themselves because they do not have the experience or the maturity to cope with the demands of the rather intense and complex intimacy that surrounds human mating."

"Amen," agrees her husband.

"Hush," she says.

"I don't notice the compulsion diminishing, do you dear?" I say to my wife.

"Hush," everyone says. Amid laughter.

"Sense increases," the wife says. "In some people."

So Andrea King and Jerry Keenan, strolling arm in arm under the desert sun that day in the summer of 1946, were under enormous biological constraint to couple. The loneliness they both had been experiencing and the sudden, rapturous release from that loneliness was nothing more than a biological imperative that disapproved of a young man and a young woman their age being alone. They were acting out a scene that seemed utterly unique to them even though it is a commonplace for the species.

There were other imperatives at work, however, not biological in the ordinary sense, but profoundly sinister. Even now I'm not sure what to call them.

We passed Steinfeld's Department Store. She glanced in the window, reacting to a display of summer clothes the way all women do—roughly the same way a little boy reacts to a drinking fountain.

Poor kid, she didn't have any money to buy new clothes.

"V-5?" she continued the conversation, asking about my navy training.

"A year at Notre Dame. I had two years there altogether. With a little luck and some paternal clout, I can go straight into law school."

"Football?" She considered my six-foot-one frame carefully.

"Only in high school. Fenwick, a Dominican place in the neighborhood."

"I had Dominicans too. Quarterback?"

"Tailback. We didn't play the T-formation."

"Passer?"

"Not very good, I'm afraid." One male of the species preening his modesty. "My brother is the athlete in the family. Basketball. He's studying for the priesthood."

"How wonderful!" She sounded as if she meant it.

"My parents think so. He's a pretty good guy actually, for a younger brother, that is. Do you have brothers or sisters?"

"No. Iowa preflight?"

"Yep." I nodded. "Then Pensacola. Carrier training back home at Glenview. Landing and taking off on a converted Great Lakes excursion ship called the *Wolverine* on Lake Michigan. Most dangerous landings ever." I tried showing off my historical knowledge. "It was the excursion boat *Eastland* on which hundreds of people died when it tipped over in the Chicago River. I always thought it was haunted."

Especially the cold day in January when a flight of four Wildcats was lost in snow flurries over Lake Michigan. We were running low on fuel, but the jaygee in command insisted that we would find the *Wolverine* regardless. We might have made it back to Glenview and we might not. Fortunately some instinct of mine told me where the carrier was and I kind of conned the jaygee into finding it.

We landed quick and then hightailed it off to Glenview.

"How did you *know?*" one of the other ensigns asked me afterward.

"Luck," I said. It was a lie. I *knew.*

Andrea shivered when I mentioned the *Eastland.*

My historical expertise hung there in still air like a tasteless joke.

We crossed the street at the corner of Congress and Stone and approached, somewhat warily, the very elegant Pioneer Hotel, surely the most impressive building in Tucson, a kind of vest-pocket version of the Blackstone in Chicago. Would they let us in this red brick palace with two-story arched windows above the entrance and penthouses on the top floors? She looked like an underage waif and my expensive sport jacket and slacks hadn't been pressed in several days. I decided I would rely on my Irish smile, usually a pretty good strategy.

"Were you in the Islands?"

She meant the Solomon Islands campaign, a conflict in which we lost a lot of ships and a lot of air crew.

"I arrived later, or most likely I wouldn't be about to walk into this hotel with you."

"Thank God," she said fervently, not so much in gratitude that I was there to buy her breakfast as that one life had somehow been spared.

"I don't believe in God," I said, stupidly parading my atheism.

"Really?" She seemed astonished. "Why ever not?"

I didn't answer her because we entered the hotel and were directed by the bell captain with notable lack of enthusiasm to the dining room, an elegant place with patterned carpets, mirrors, and sparkling white tablecloths, and a primitive but effective air conditioner puffing away.

The elderly and very proper waitress, gray hair knotted in a severe bun, was immune to Irish charm but not to the piquant appeal of my little waif (she was lucky to measure five two). "Right this way, dear," she said as she beamed an approving smile.

"Thank you very much." Andrea sounded like an obedient little girl.

The waitress considered me again and apparently decided that I was a proper protector for my charge.

Two things I had learned about Andrea King: people liked her instantly, and she fit into any environment, railroad station or hotel, like one who belonged.

"This town will never amount to anything," I proclaimed as I held the chair for her.

"Until they put air-conditioning in every home."

"That will never happen." I sat next to her and picked up the menu.

"How can people live in brick houses in this weather?" She reached for the menu like a kid grabbing for a box of Christmas candy.

"Did you notice the homes with the walls all around them? I suppose that's the Spanish emphasis on privacy. You wouldn't have to wear much behind those walls."

"I bet they do." She blushed lightly and my heart beat faster.

She ordered orange juice, bacon and eggs, pancakes, and coffee, and demolished the meal with quiet efficiency.

"Not hungry, huh?"

"Very hungry, Commander. Are you married?"

Direct, right down to business. Moreover, her pale skin was a screen on which multiple shades of red played back and forth as her emotions and her intelligent, mobile features changed with them. Light pink meant enthusiasm, a darker rose indicated embarrassment (when I mentioned wearing clothes or not wearing them behind the walls), scarlet suggested anger. And a faint but suggestive crimson hinted discreetly at sympathy and affection, especially when combined with a smile. I would learn during the next three days to wait desperately for that combination.

There was no flush at all when she asked about my marital status.

"Jerry. No."

"Engaged?"

I hesitated.

"More or less?" She smiled at me, as if to say that it was all right, she didn't expect me to be unattached.

"Oh, no. No prospects even. I was almost engaged once. But it didn't work out. She's married now."

"Oh." She dug into her pancakes.

"Grammar-school sweetheart. Her father is a partner of my father. She went to Trinity, the Dominican women's high school in our neighborhood. We went to proms and dances together all through school. There was never anything official, but our parents were pleased. They kind of expected that we would marry."

She nodded above a large slab of syrup-soaked pancake. How could anyone gobble food so quickly and yet keep her dignity?

"When I was at Pensacola we wrote back and forth, pretty intense stuff. Then, while I was doing the carrier landings out of Glenview, she gave me the ultimatum: marry before I left for the Pacific or all bets were off. She might wait and she might not."

"Why did you say no?" She scooped up more pancakes.

I realized that the answer might be painful to her, but I was telling truth (and she was evading it, but I hardly realized that until later).

"I knew about the casualty rates in air crews. I didn't want her to be a young widow."

"Shouldn't she have had the choice?" She put down the fork and watched me intently, her blue eyes probing and intelligent, a wise old woman pondering a callow lad.

"That's what she said. And she had a point. Our families were both in favor of marriage, although they thought we were terribly young, which we were."

"But you weren't sure?"

"I wasn't sure. Odd, isn't it? Parents and bride ready to take a risk. Groom being cautious and prudent?"

"No, I don't think it's odd." She returned to the pancakes, dousing them first with yet more maple syrup. "Unusual, but it looks like you're an unusual person. . . . So she sent you a 'dear John' letter?"

"I can't call it that. She made it clear that she considered herself free."

"And you were unhappy at first, but not anymore?"

"I had dinner with Barbara and her husband—a supply officer from the ETO—when I was home last. They already have two kids. I feel like a pilot who found his carrier just before dark. A close call. I mean, she's a wonderful woman. But she doesn't want the same things out of life that I do."

"And what do you want out of life, Commander Jeremiah Keenan, USNR?" Her eyes twinkled with amusement.

"I don't know, Andrea King." I leaned back and sighed. "I haven't the faintest idea. I know only what I don't want."

"And that is . . ." She nodded for more coffee to the elderly waitress, who doted on her like a loving mother. "Thank you very much."

"What Barbara and her husband already have . . . that doesn't make much sense, does it? I suppose I mean a dull, ordinary life. Maybe I'm a kind of Don Quixote . . . I don't know."

"Searching for windmills?" Her voice, light and musical, hinted at both amusement and sympathy. I was too elated with the self-disclosure (as I would call it now, having learned the phrase from my wife and kids) of the conversation to notice how much progress I had made with her. Already she felt sorry for me. "And Dulcinea?"

"Especially Dulcinea!"

We laughed together and she smiled and all the other lights went out again and I was hopelessly in love.

"How can you not believe in God?" She was deadly serious now. "Aren't you afraid of Him?"

"How can you believe in Him?" I was serious too. "He took your husband away from you, didn't he?"

She put down her coffee cup. "Maybe"—she would not look at me—"I deserved to be punished. Maybe I wasn't good enough for him."

"You want to believe in a God who plays tricks like that?"

"I often wish I could not believe in Him," she whispered, bowing her head, "then I would not have to be afraid. I . . ."

"Yes?" I snapped.

"Well." She stumbled over the words. "I wouldn't have to live suspended between earth and hell."

Those were her exact words. I felt a tremor of ice slip through my body. A touch of the uncanny.

"That's an odd thing to say."

"Is it?" Her eyes were cold now. Glacial and hard.

"I mean"—it was my turn to grope for words—"shouldn't you say 'between heaven and hell'?"

"Should I?"

"Everyone has a chance at heaven. . . . I mean, that's what the priests and nuns taught me in school."

"Did they?"

"You're not damned until you die. If you believe in God, that is, you believe that you have chances for forgiveness up to the last second of your life, don't you?"

"Do you?"

An exchange like that certainly extinguishes the fires of passion in a hurry. So I changed the subject.

"You haven't said much about your family."

"There's not much to say."

"Say what there is to say."

"I don't really have a family." She moved her coffee cup around in a little circle in its saucer. "I was raised by my mother's sister and brother-in-law—my aunt and uncle. Mom died of TB when I was a little girl. Dad . . . he sort of disappeared."

"Disappeared?"

She nodded. "Became a hobo, I guess. He was . . . is . . . I don't know . . . a lawyer, like your father. He couldn't find work during the Depression. After Mom died he must have given up hope."

"You think he's dead too?"

"I'm not sure." She hesitated, her eyes narrowing in pensive calculation of the odds. "Maybe. Maybe not. I hope not

... sometimes I think he'll reappear tomorrow and I'll be happy again like I was when I was a little girl."

"And you still believe in God?"

"Oh, yes. I have no choice." She made a mark on the tablecloth with her knife. "No choice at all."

"I don't want to argue theology with you, Andrea King," I said cautiously.

"No arguments." She put the knife down. "Just tell me your reasons and I'll drop the subject."

"I've killed a lot of people in the war. Hundreds, maybe even thousands. . . ."

"Thousands?"

"In a way. Some of them were enemies. Young men my age. Probably a couple of them planned to return home and be lawyers with their father, just like I do. Why am I alive while they are dead?"

"War . . ."

"Why does your God permit war? And why does He grant me life when so many of my friends had to die? More than half my class from Pensacola are dead, many of them, the majority, I think, in accidents—crash landings, splashing after takeoff, running out of gas, engine failures. The Japs didn't kill them." I was shouting at her now and the waitress was glaring at me. "We didn't kill them. God killed them!"

"We all die sometime. . . ."

"But you and I have a chance to live out our lives. They didn't."

"Do we?"

I ignored her question. "It isn't fair. A God who isn't fair is no God at all."

"Do you mean"—she leaned forward, reminding me of my father in the middle of a legal argument—"that you don't believe in God because He is unfair? Then He really exists, but you don't like Him?"

"*If* He really exists"—I was confused by her argument— "He's not worth believing in. So His existence is irrelevant."

She nodded again. "How often I have wished that I could feel the same way."

It was an invitation to probe, which I foolishly rejected.

"God is a murderer!" I pounded the table. "He ought to be put to death in the electric chair!"

She pulled back, now genuinely frightened of my anger. So was I. Frightened and astonished.

"Sorry, Andrea." I used words that both of us would repeat often in the next few days. "My mother, who is a wonderful, dear, understanding woman, says I'm having trouble read-justing. I think she read the word in a magazine somewhere."

"I'd say your mother is right." She touched my hand. "It's okay."

"I didn't buy you breakfast," I said, holding her hand momentarily, "to make you an audience for my atheist harangue. You do make a pretty audience, though."

"Thank you. I don't feel harangued. But I do understand why you're driving around the country before you return home. Where are you going next?"

Had I told her about my tour, my windmill-hunting, Dul-cinea-seeking tour? I couldn't remember that I had.

"Down to Colossal Cave and over to Tombstone, then up to Phoenix, probably by way of Superstition Mountains."

"What are those?"

"Where the Lost Dutchman Mine is supposed to be. I'm curious."

"Yes. I know. Is that any relation to the *Flying Dutchman?*"

"Who's he?"

"An opera about a sea captain who is doomed to roam the world forever without ever finding port."

"I don't know much about opera."

But she did. And she hadn't graduated from high school. How had she learned so much?

"Where are you going?" I asked.

"Phoenix. I know someone who thinks she can find me a job. Waiting on tables in one of the winter resorts. They call it the Arizona Biltmore."

"Can I give you a ride?"

"I don't think . . ." She drifted off, considered me again, even more cautiously, over a fork of syrup-drenched pancake. "That would be very nice. I don't have much money."

I was not a total innocent. I asked about insurance and a pension. But the Navy Department was slow. She'd run out of the money she'd saved from John's family allowance, which had been sent routinely while he was still alive.

I didn't pry. It was none of my business why she had left San Diego or why she had been unable to find a job there.

A thin but not improbable story. I was not inclined to question it. An hour before I'd been an ex-naval officer struggling with depression and wondering what point there could be in the rest of my life. Now I had a beautiful young woman to protect and care for.

At almost twenty-four that is enough. Even if the young woman is smarter than she has any right to be.

And even if there is something just a little strange, almost uncanny about her.

That was the right word. Uncanny. Andrea King was not quite of this world. In the back of my head even then I think I knew that. I did not want to pay any attention to what I knew.

No, she didn't mind if we detoured to the Cave and Tombstone before driving up to Phoenix. The job, she had been told, was waiting for her whenever she came. Thank you very much for breakfast.

I glanced at the *Arizona Daily Star* on the newsstand in the hotel lobby. SEVENTY-SIX DIE IN JERUSALEM HOTEL BLAST! I bought the paper. Zionist terrorists had blown up the King David Hotel. I no longer asked when the killing would finally stop. I knew it would never stop. Damn God.

I bought the *Star* and *Time* and *Life* (the latter two cost fifteen cents), even though they were banned at my parents' house because of what my father claimed was their anti-Truman bias. Vivien Leigh, hauntingly lovely, poor woman, was on the cover of *Life* for her film *Caesar and Cleopatra* with Claude Rains. Salazar of Portugal was on the cover of *Time*.

We walked up Stone toward Toole Street, paper and magazines under my arm; her quick eyes were drinking in everything about this sleepy little city.

"Is this the place where the movie was made?"

"You mean *My Darling Clementine?*"

"I *loved* it."

"The yards down the street next to the station are the spot where Wyatt—Henry Fonda—and Doc Holliday—Victor Mature—caught up with Frank Stilwell, the man who shot Morgan Earp. He was a deputy in Cochise County and under indictment here in Pima County for cattle rustling. It was pretty hard to tell the good guys from the bad guys in those days."

"Really?"

By unspoken agreement we had paused at the corner of Toole and Fourth while I gave my Tombstone lecture. It was made more memorable because of what looked like admiration in her gentle blue eyes.

"You see, in the real world, Wyatt had taken a woman away from Johnny Behan, the sheriff at Tombstone—Cathy Downs in the movie. So Behan came over one night to beat up on Wyatt and instead was worked over by Morgan Earp. Then Behan arranged to have his deputy, Frank Stilwell, kill Morgan. Doc Holliday was even closer to Morgan Earp than Wyatt was. So Doc got liquored up, as they say, and went gunning for Johnny. Wyatt had to stop him because they really didn't have enough evidence to kill a sheriff. Then, when they brought Morgan's body into the station here on the train from Tombstone to ship back home to California, they caught Frank skulking around the yards, perhaps with instructions to kill Doc. They both emptied their guns into him. Which was safe here in Pima County because he was a wanted outlaw here."

"How terrible!"

"The Wild West was not a nice place. And it was not so long ago. Josie Earp, Wyatt's wife—she started out as Josie Marcus, a rich Jewish kid in San Francisco, and ended up as a high class prostitute in Tombstone before she linked up with Behan and then Wyatt—died only two years ago. Same for

General Custer's widow. Doc Holiday died of TB, as you know, and became a Catholic at the last minute in response to the prayers of his cousin, who was a Sister of Charity and the only woman he really loved—not Linda Darnell like in the film."

"Do you know everything?"

Definitely admiration, almost awe. My face was pleasantly warm.

"I saw the earlier film, *Frontier Marshal* with Randolph Scott and Cesar Romero—you know, the Cisco Kid—on the carrier. And there was one in the early thirties called *Law and Order* with Walter Huston. There isn't much to do in an air crew when you're not flying and if you don't like to play cards. So I did a lot of reading on the American West. That's why I'm going to Tombstone."

End of lecture, but not end of admiration.

"How wonderful. But why?"

"I want to know more about my country." We started to walk toward my car again. "And it's something to do."

"I see."

"You think I'm crazy."

"No, not at all. Just different . . . Why did they give you the Navy Cross?"

The humidity had already laid a thick soggy curtain on Toole Street.

"Philippine Sea. I saved some TBF pilots that were in trouble."

"Does that help your conscience?"

"Some American women are not widows—if the TBF men made it through the rest of the war. Some Japanese women are."

Immediately I regretted the harshness of my reply. It did not, however, seem to bother her.

"We didn't start the war."

We turned down Toole, almost as though she knew where my 1939 Chevy ($799 FOB Detroit) was parked.

There were three million autos in America at the end of the war. Now, a year later, there were six million. That said a lot about 1946.

"How did you know I got the Navy Cross?"

"I guess"—she tilted her head to glance at me ruefully—"that I'm a pretty good guesser."

She stopped next to a battered blue car before I did. "Roxinante?"

"Damn good guesser." My beloved Chevy, the first car of my very own, was a humpback bug, longer and less appealing than the later VWs. Kids today don't fall in love with their first cars the way my generation did.

"Only car on the street." She laughed, a pure, open laugh which hinted that long ago she might have been the life of the sophomore hops at her high school.

A long, long time ago.

"Yeah, but you knew the street."

She laughed again and waited till I opened the door for her. "Thank you. Yes, I'm a very good guesser. It scared the nuns at my school."

"I bet it did, Dulcinea." I bowed her into the car, noted that she had excellent legs, accepted her smile as a reward for my courtesy, and staggered, I think, around to the driver's side of the car.

Nuns, I thought. Catholic high school. I bet they expelled her when they found out she was married. Pregnant? Lost a child?

I rolled down the window of the Chevy and turned to the sports section.

"Do you mind if I catch up on the news?" I had already buried my head in the paper. The Cubs had lost again. A long way down from the World Series last year.

"The schedule is up to the tour guide."

"Hmn . . ." Maybe the Bears would redeem the year.

Then the comics. *Terry and the Pirates, Smilin' Jack, Dick Tracy.*

I looked up. Andrea was smiling at me, a mother watching a funny little baby. Navy Cross and *Smilin' Jack.* I suppose I was funny.

Her smile quickly faded. "I had a miscarriage after John

sailed. I don't know whether my letter ever caught up with him. I hope it didn't."

She was replying to the thought I had had as I'd walked around the car, several minutes before. I ought to have worried about that, but she was so fragile and sweet that I couldn't have been afraid of her. Not then anyway.

"I'm sorry."

She nodded again.

"Does God provide, Andrea?" I asked weakly.

"It's not God I'm worried about."

CHAPTER 3

DO YOU REMEMBER 1946?

Chances are pretty good that you weren't even around then. It was a big turning point for America; how big is hard to explain unless you were alive before then.

The Depression didn't return.

We started on a roll of prosperity that has gone on, with some ups and downs, without interruption for forty years. Despite inflation, real income (real standard of living) has doubled at least twice since 1946. Not everyone has benefited equally or all the time. But unemployment has never gone beyond 8 percent. It was 25 percent during the Depression.

In 1946 we began to draw the outline of the matrix for permanent prosperity.

None of us knew that then. Most of us expected the Depression to come back. But in that first postwar summer, all who could were treating themselves to a vacation, maybe the first in ten years, and maybe, we thought, the last for the next ten years.

There were still shortages—cars, soda pop, tires, roads, summer-resort rooms, meat (especially meat) were all in short supply for our vacations. We grumbled about the difficulties of finding a new house or buying a new Philco radio or installing a new phone or having a new refrigerator delivered.

We blamed it, not unreasonably, on the government and contended that the only reason those idiots had won the war was that the leaders on the other side were dumber.

There were four big news items that summer, only one of which mattered to us—OPA, Office of Price Administration. We were of mixed mind about OPA, we resented the vast, incomprehensible, and seemingly inequitable structure of its rules; we blamed it for shortages; and we also feared that if it should die, prices would skyrocket. So President Truman was blamed both for sustaining OPA and for not eliminating it.

The Luce magazines, that very day I was indulging in delicious fantasies about the nubile body of Andrea King, were having a field day, coming at poor Truman from both sides. He was an incompetent bungler who was to blame for the failure of OPA and also for its demise. *Life* said that there was no great cause for alarm so long as Americans restrained their impulse to purchase the things they wanted.

That was, looking back on it, the worst possible advice. If the flood of consumer demands was not released, production would slump and we would indeed crash back into a depression. Fortunately no one paid any attention to Mr. Luce. Americans were no longer as poor as they had been in 1939. Most of them were making good money, and many had considerable savings from the war years. So we went on a buying binge and caused prices to skyrocket and, happily, production to do the same thing. The surge in production and jobs more than canceled out any negative effects on the standard of living that inflation might have caused.

None of us had the economic wisdom to know that that

would happen. We always, I guess, have the wisdom of the last economic crisis and not of the present one.

So in 1946 we still had our fingers crossed.

We were rushing off to schools in vast numbers, much to the astonishment of the college administrations, who had been wondering where students would come from now that wartime military training programs were ending. Everyone seemed to want to go to college—returning veterans, kids out of high school from families that had never even considered college, even girls. We were also marrying in record numbers. And getting pregnant. And looking for places to live.

Married veterans were filling up the slumlike "vetvilles" around every major college. Education, family, home, a car, a vacation—that's what we all wanted in the summer that OPA died, almost by mistake (only to be revived partially in the autumn, again by mistake).

Well, the others wanted those things. I didn't. I was in no hurry to marry, I didn't particularly want to go back to school, and I had no plans for a home or kids, though I didn't exclude them in principle.

What did I want?

Adventure, God help me.

And Romance.

And a Woman to share both.

And on that morning of July 22, 1946, it looked as if I had found all three.

As it turned out, that would be an understatement.

There were three other major events: the Paris Peace Conference, the Bikini (atoll, not swimsuit) atom tests, and the "invasion" of Palestine by Jewish refugees in blockade runners from Cyprus.

The Peace Conference confirmed what was no longer a secret: there was no trust between Russia and the West. Trieste was divided into two sections, one Italian, one Yugoslavian; the Danube was opened to shipping of all nations; Bessarabia and upper Moldavia were taken from Romania by the Soviet Union; in return northern Transylvania—and presumably the ghost of Count Dracula—was taken from Hungary and given to Romania. Russia grabbed Carpatho-Ukraine from Czechoslovakia. That was it, and it made little difference to anyone unless you happened to live in Bessarabia, Moldavia, or Carpatho-Ukraine. And you weren't used to having a say in your own fate if you lived in those places anyway.

We blasted the hell out of the carriers *Independence* and *Saratoga* and the battleships *Nevada* and *New York* with our atom bombs at Bikini, and properly scared all the world and maybe ourselves a little too. We also caused radiation damage to some of our own men, which we kept a deep dark secret.

And the Jews with utter dedication to their cause continued to try to run the blockade. A war between them and the Arabs in Palestine was inevitable after they blew up the King David Hotel. Everyone with any sense knew the Arabs would win. Jews are not good fighters, right?

General Marshall was in China trying to make peace between the Nationalists and the Communists; *Time* reported the Nationalists were winning great victories. Ethel Merman was starring in *Annie Get Your Gun;* the B-35 "flying wing" and the B-36 bombers were on test flights; Howard Hughes's "Spruce Goose" was being assembled. DC-6s and Constellations were poking their way across the Atlantic, with stops at Gander in Newfoundland and Shannon, Ireland, and for $310 underselling the *Queen Elizabeth* by $65 and giving a hint of the future.

Slogans and jingles were blaring at us from the radio: LS/MFT (Lucky Strike Means Fine Tobacco), ABC (Always Buy Chesterfield), Fight gingivitis (sounds terrible, doesn't it?) with Ipana, Vitalis Sixty-Second Work-Out, Poor Mirrian suffered from a lack of Irrium in her toothpaste. Spic and Span, Dentyne, Camay, Grape-Nuts Flakes—all had their irritating and insidious commercials that seemed to live forever. It would take time for the ad men to learn about overkill.

Princess Elizabeth danced with Guards officers, Margaret Truman danced with Navy officers, Greta Garbo went home to Sweden; the great movie stars were Hedy Lamarr, Lana Turner, Rita Hayworth, Linda Darnell, Ginger Rogers, Esther

Williams, and Maureen O'Hara. Guy Madison and William Holden, still in the service, were the promising male leads.

It was a summer of painted jeans, two-piece swimsuits, the first underwire bras, California-versus-Florida bathing-beauty contests, the Ted Williams shift (all the fielders to the right side of the field) without which the man would have hit .400 every year, Loretta Young modeling nightgowns (chastely but not unattractively), the canonization of Frances Cabrini, albums by Bob Hope or Woody Herman or Lauritz Melchior for $3.50, a nice dress for $10.50, a straw hat (did I say I was wearing one in the station? I won't mention it again, so shocked will be my kids) for $3.00.

Europe had barely survived the winter, mostly because of UNRRA grain. American farmers, however, had produced the biggest harvest in history and would save the world from starvation next winter (not the last time that would happen). Berlin and Vienna and the other great cities were struggling out of the ashes, but people thought it would take decades for them to be reborn. In fact, it required a few more years.

The U.S. Army had established an elite "constabulary" force with yellow scarves to hunt down Nazis and prevent an underground resurgence of Hitler supporters (which many predicted was certain to occur). In Japan, General MacArthur (damn his eyes!) had replaced the Emperor as God.

We were trying Nazis at Nürnberg, and a place in Denver called the National Opinion Research Center reported that half the American people did not support the Bill of Rights in practice. Gene Talmage, a gallus-snapping redneck who had once grazed pigs on the state house lawn, was again elected Governor of Georgia. Fellow rednecks celebrated by lynching (with shotgun blasts) two black veterans and their wives. Joe Louis mauled poor game Billy Conn. The *Normandie* was refloated and towed away for scrap.

And a young PT-boat hotshot named Jack Kennedy was running for Congress in Massachusetts.

In Chicago, Ed Kelly "rendered" his resignation as chairman of the Cook County Democratic Committee, to be replaced by Jake Arvey.

Paper dresses, bare shoulders, and buttons all the way down the front were in fashion for women (the "New Look" had yet to arrive). Surveys showed that Americans wanted big cars and wonderful houses. The Labor party, with the most generous and noble intentions possible, was destroying the British economy, Henry Kaiser was selling more Kaiser and Frazer cars than anyone thought he would; Olds was offering a "hydromatic" drive that you didn't have to shift (my father promptly and with some relief bought my mother one, a convertible, in fact, which says something, I guess, about them), for thirty-five dollars a month you could rent an "isophone" that answered your phone for you and Jeanne Crain, Teresa Wright, Mona Freeman, Donna Reed, and Lizabeth Scott were the most promising of the new actresses.

It was a summer, I suppose, of great expectations and holding your breath, of fear that if you mentioned how good our prospects were beginning to look, they would be torn away from you without warning, just as they had been eighteen years before.

Some of the books written about that period say that all the things wrong with America in the fifties can be traced to the late forties. I suppose so—flaws in our country like universal higher education for women as well as men, the beginning of substantial higher education for blacks and almost full employment; the first led, I am convinced, to the women's movement, the second to the civil rights movement and the last provided the economic underpinning for both.

That's not what the critics mean.

But most of their criticism of 1946 misses the point because, like all badly written history, it ignores the context, in this case the context of the Great Depression. We were catching up for fifteen years. It would take us fifteen more years to catch up completely. Then the young PT captain would be elected President and another turning-point year would occur.

I didn't see any of this in 1946, though I did have a hunch that the Depression was over and that we were in for many years of prosperity. And I was very well aware of the irresistible urge of my contemporaries for a degree, a spouse, a car, a house and kids.

Nothing much wrong with that.

But I wanted a hell of a lot more. Before midnight, under the full moon of July 22, I thought I might have found it.

CHAPTER

WE TOOK THE BENSON ROAD OUT OF TUCSON, ACROSS THE harsh brown desert. I tried to forget about God and death, war and peace, and other cosmic issues. There was a pretty young woman next to me in the car, who seemed, astonishingly, to find me both attractive and amusing. My fantasies about her became more respectful and respectable. She was now a person to be protected and cared for.

And hence even more appealing sexually—as I was beginning to learn. Barbara was a girl whom I'd necked with and petted on another planet.

This would be a brief tour through the desert, nothing more. I should enjoy it for what it was worth and then bid her a quiet good-bye in Phoenix at the end of the day.

Which was one of the most idiotic notions I ever had in all my life.

"My guidebook says that this was all cattle country until the end of the last century. Tombstone folded because the silver minds flooded and the ranch land dried up."

She nodded, a favorite gesture, conveying appropriately different reactions. God, she was lovely. I was glad that she would be with me for the day.

"Did you work in San Diego?"

A waitress at the Del Coronado Hotel after it reopened. She was not very good at it. Couldn't concentrate. Too many memories. Too much Navy. She thought she should start over somewhere else. They had been very nice to her, but she couldn't exist forever on pity.

"I used to drink there occasionally. I'm sure I would have remembered you."

"After how many drinks?" Her laugh, I decided, was pure magic.

"Touché. But you are the kind I would remember, even drunk."

"If we're going to exchange compliments, Commander, I think I would remember you, too."

Young and innocent, but somehow experienced and wise. I thought I might just be falling hopelessly in love with Andrea King.

How do you explain a young man who on the one hand thinks he's going to rid himself of an alluring young woman at the end of the day and on the other speculates that he is not only falling in love with her but hopelessly in love with her?

Endocrine secretions, is what my daughter the doctor would say.

And I would have remembered her if I had seen her at the Coronado.

So I didn't say much on the road to Tombstone. Just short of Benson, US 80 branches off from Arizona 86 and heads due south. We slowed down to twenty-five miles an hour on the outskirts of St. David.

"Mormon town." I glanced over at her. She seemed far, far away from southern Arizona.

Tombstone was even less impressive then than it is now. Wyatt Earp had yet to become a TV hero, and the old town had yet to discover it could squeeze a few extra dollars a year from tourism. I pulled up in front of the Post Office Café on Main Street.

"Want another cup of coffee?"

She was staring out the window, seeing neither the Post Office Café, nor 1946 Tombstone.

"Andrea?" I said gently, touching her arm, the first of what I was beginning to hope would be many touches.

"I'm sorry, what did you say?"

"Do you want a cup of coffee before we do the O.K. Corral?"

"No . . . Commander, uh, Jerry . . . Do you mind if I stay in the car? I'm afraid of this place."

She huddled against the door; her body was tense, her face tight with fear.

"Don't you want to see the real town on which *My Darling Clementine* is based?"

"I did till I realized that they were real people. Now I'm afraid."

"It's just an old Western ghost town." I took her hand.

"Please."

"Of course."

The O.K. Corral was a disappointment—merely a yard next to a house. Reality was so much more bland than story. But I explored Tombstone with a singing heart. A new challenge had entered my life to replace war, just as war had replaced flight training and chemistry and football. Pretty, haunted young women were, I told myself, the best excitement yet.

Still, as I stood at the site of the shoot-out, I had no trouble conjuring up images of Wyatt and Doc and the Clantons. One part of my personality wished I'd been there. Another part cringed in horror from the brutality of the few seconds of gunfire that wiped out the Clantons.

As a young man I was an odd mixture of competitiveness and fear of conflict. Or, as my wife would say later, fear of my own deep reactions to conflict. I was (and am, I add proudly) a moderately skillful athlete. I lacked the raw ability to be first string in college and the motivation to work hard to make up for that lack of ability. But when I played alley basketball or prairie softball, I played to win. Even today I can shoot in the middle eighties most of the time at golf without working at it too hard. So I don't work at it too hard, but I am a fierce competitor on the golf course, until someone else in the foursome becomes unpleasant about the contest. Then I lose interest.

My wife tells me I am afraid of my own anger. I was gifted at only one sport in high school—boxing; I was a quick, hard puncher and a deft dodger of the other kid's fists. The coach at Fenwick wanted to enter me in the Golden Gloves, a scheme that my father wisely vetoed. Once a boxer from another school took a cheap shot at me after the bell at the end of the first round. I was furious, maybe to the point of irrationality. I knocked him out, a rare event in high school boxing, in the first ten seconds of the next round.

And quit boxing the next day.

At Iowa preflight, there was some compulsory boxing. I had to do it, so I was freed from responsibility. They matched me against an overgrown bully from Texas who had been hassling me from the beginning of the program. He lasted fifteen seconds. (The poor guy died later in the Marianas when the Admirals turned off the lights on their carriers, although the risks were slight and most of the air crews had not landed, a bigger disgrace than Pearl Harbor.)

Even though it was not fashionable in those days among the Army of Occupation, I even messed around with some martial arts while I was in Japan because you were supposed to learn to discipline and focus your rage.

Maybe I was a pretty good fighter pilot because of restraints on rage that fighter planes imposed on you.

As I left the O.K. Corral and strolled back to my car, my head was filled with images of fighting for and protecting my appealing and fragile young charge.

Reconsidering my state of mind now, I think that, among other things, she provided me with an excuse to legitimize my deep-seated rage. So my daughter the psychiatrist might suggest if I ever told her this part of my life story.

The woman to be protected was still crouched against the door, now reading a book. *All the King's Men.*

"Good book?"

"Very. About politics and corruption. I'm sorry if I disappointed you."

"The sights on this tour are an option. We'll get you to Phoenix 'fore sundown, ma'am." I bowed like Randolph Scott.

"Silly." She grinned weakly. "And I'm not a schoolteacher either, Mr. Scott."

She was still terrified, even if she had read *The Virginian*.

"What was it like?" she asked as the Chevy plugged along on the gravel road toward Colossal Cave.

"Tombstone?"

"No." She seemed to be sitting very close to me, as close as she could with the gearbox between us. "The war . . . combat."

"There wasn't much combat." At last I had a chance to tell someone things I had never said before. "I was out there for more than two and a half years and I don't suppose there were more than thirty days of actual combat, and some of that was at the end, when it hardly counted—the Japanese didn't have anything with which to fight back. They were milk runs, which didn't mean you couldn't die from engine failure or get lost."

"The rest of the time? . . ."

"Monotony, boredom, rough seas, an occasional typhoon to scare the hell out of you and make you so sick you wanted to die. Training flights, air crew conferences, steaming back to Pearl or San Diego for refitting, waiting for mail, worrying about how you'd act in combat. Dangerous because a sub could always get you or you could die in an accident, but after a while even that danger doesn't scare you much."

"Lots of time to think." I kept my eyes on the highway, but I knew she was watching me, her blue eyes soft with compassion. Hell, I didn't want compassion.

Oh, yes, I did. The more the better.

"And even on the days of battle, most of the time is spent in preparation, changes of plans, fueling and refueling, flying to the target and coming home. The actual combat—you shooting at them and them shooting at you—sometimes it's only a few minutes. We won the Battle of Midway in a half hour when McCluskey and his SBDs found the Japanese carriers with refueled planes on their decks. I wasn't around for that, but in the Philippine Sea—'Marianas Turkey Shoot,' we called it—the Japanese lost most of their air crews—and for all practical purposes the war—in less than two hours."

"Such a short time." Her voice made me want to curl up against her breasts and sleep for the rest of eternity.

"A few minutes, a few seconds, even. When you get back—if you get back—you're astonished at how quickly it happens. You make your dive or your run if you're in a TBF, you drop your bomb or your torpedo, you turn around or pull out of it, and if you are still alive, you go home. Or, if you're in a fighter like me, you get behind him before he gets behind you, you squeeze the button, a few tracers lace over toward him, he explodes in a cloud of dirty orange, and it's all over. He's dead or you're dead."

"Were you frightened?"

"No time to be frightened. Before, you worry about losing your nerve and letting down your mates. After, maybe, you wake up at night wishing you could scream. In combat it's all too quick. On shore it's not too different. I mean, the marines are always in danger from snipers or mines, but it's mostly boredom too, much more uncomfortable boredom—dirt, smell, sickness, no toilets. The guys I met in San Diego after the war said the actual firefights, even on Iwo, were all pretty quick, finished before you realized they'd started."

"How horrible."

"Sherman wasn't strong enough about war," I said. "I tell myself there'll never be another one, but only a small minority of us were ever in combat, and we may not be making the decisions."

I thought about asking what kind of God would tolerate the combat I had described. Better not.

"You see," I went on, wildly, I fear, because in swerving to avoid an old truck I almost drove off the highway, "even the GIs in the infantry will tell you they can't be sure that they've ever killed anyone. It's impersonal, for which they thank . . ."

"Yes?"

"Their lucky stars. They rarely see the enemy. For fighter pilots it's different: you see the fellow in the cockpit of the Zero, you squeeze the trigger, he blows up. One second he's alive and the next second he's dead. You killed him." My hands clung so tightly to the wheel of the car I thought I might crush it. "Or if you're in a TBF, you put a fish into the side of a ship that's motionless in the water and see it explode out of the corner of your eye as you turn away. You know you've killed a lot of people, the only question is how many."

"Does everyone feel that way?"

"No." I thought about it. "At least they don't talk that way. But then I never talked that way before either. Don't misunderstand, my war was much better than that of the combat marines. I lucked out."

"Did you?"

"I don't know."

I drove on to Colossal Cave, alone with my thoughts, yet no longer alone.

Colossal Cave did not help Andrea. If anything, the entrance frightened her more than the streets of Tombstone. The young woman who could listen calmly while I poured out my private horrors was terrified at the sight of the entrance to a very mild natural wonder.

"I can't go in there. I'd die."

She sounded as if she meant it.

"You don't mind waiting?"

"No."

The cave was dark and slimy and disappointing.

"Not very scary at all," I said as I climbed back into the car.

"I would have died," she repeated, as she closed the book and laid it next to her—and between us—on the front seat. "I'm sorry."

"Don't be. It's nice to have someone waiting."

She didn't smile or nod. Still scared.

She did get out of the car at the old Saint Xavier Mission—the "white dove of the desert"—south of town, and walked into the quaint old church (1796) with me. She fell on her knees in the back of the dark nave and prayed fervently, like someone pursued by demons, I thought. Outside, she pleaded to be excused from visiting the tiny cemetery next to the church and scurried back into the steaming car.

"What frightens you?" I tried to keep my voice soft and reassuring as I started the old Chevy.

"Everything."

I didn't pursue the matter.

We then drove up to Gates Pass to glance for a moment at the vast acres of saguaro cactus spread out as far as you could see, an exotic, shadeless forest on harsh desert hills and rocks that might easily have been a landscape on the far side of the moon.

We left the car and walked for a few minutes. Updrafts of hot air, "sun devils," in the local term, my guidebook told me, were whipping desert dust into the sky. A pair of gambel quail were noisily hectoring each other near us. Through the dust clouds the mountains seemed to stretch forever. Just as my life did in those days. I tried to take a picture with my new Leica, "liberated" by a fellow officer in Germany, of the valleys beyond the pass. I was pretty sure that I had messed up the shot because I had the light angles wrong.

"Let me get one of you."

"I'll spoil the film." She ducked out of the camera range, but not before I had pushed the release. I was still learning to use color film (still am forty years later, as a matter of fact) and I ruined most of the pictures I took during the next couple of days. She continued to jump out of most of the shots in which I tried to capture her. Weeks later I calmed down enough to send the two rolls off to Kodak to be developed (the only way in those days). When the slides were returned, some of those in which I was sure she would appear had been ruined and some of the others showed only scenery.

On the basis of my color slides, then, I would have been

hard put to prove that I had not been alone during those days in late July.

There was one exception, however, a slide I will describe later and which I still have, next to my computer as I write this story.

We walked back to the car. She waited till I opened the door for her. "Dulcinea is becoming spoiled."

"And loving it." She bowed in response to my bow, displayed her elegant legs again, and fed me a hint of her magic smile.

Yes, the smile. How could anyone be evil with such a smile?

There are a lot of answers to that question, but they'll have to wait.

I was about to start the car again, when she put her hand firmly, almost imperiously, on my arm.

"Jerry, tell me about how you won your Navy Cross, the first one, I mean."

"What makes you think I won the star?" I shook her arm off. "I know I didn't tell you that."

"Good guesser." She was close to tears.

"I didn't pick you up in the railroad station to dump my nightmares on you," I shouted. "Leave me alone!"

"I know you didn't." She was contrite, penitent.

I stared grimly at the patient saguaros.

"What I feel is none of your damn business. Leave me alone."

"Yes, Commander." A long pause. "May I say my act of contrition now?"

"I don't give a goddamn what you say!"

"You need someone to talk to, Jeremiah Keenan, you want someone to talk to; now you have someone who somehow is able to understand." She sounded as wise as the elderly waitress in the hotel that morning had looked. "Don't be foolish and waste the opportunity."

"I suppose you think God sent you so I could cry on your shoulder?"

I did indeed want to cry on her shoulder.

"Does it matter who sent me?"

"And you just happen to be a good-enough guesser to have figured out that it was the time they gave me the Navy Cross that I realized there couldn't be a God?"

I hadn't quite figured out that myself, not till then.

"Does that matter?"

"No. I suppose not."

We were silent for a few moments, or a few eternities, perhaps. I wanted to hold her in my arms as I told the story. Instead I buried my face in my hands.

"It was the second day of the Marianas operation. I was flying back to the *Enterprise* at the tail end, looking for strays or life rafts, not exactly my job, but still what I did and what everyone knew I did."

"Dangerous?"

"Regardless. There were a lot of mists and rain showers in the area. The surface of the ocean was in and out of clouds. I thought I saw a couple of rafts and banked around to make sure, coming in only a couple of hundred feet above sea level. Sure enough, three rafts, close together, a couple or three men on each one of them. I radioed the sighting back to the *Big E*, knowing that they'd get a fix on me and send a float plane if they could find one. Just as I was about to pull up, I saw this Jap DD—destroyer—come racing out of a rain squall, headed at flank speed for my guys. I knew what they were going to do and it wasn't rescue they had on their minds.

"Even if they could slow down and pull some of them out of the water, the reason would be to chop off their heads for the entertainment of the crew.

"So dummy decides to stop them. I had the advantage because I knew they were there, but they hadn't caught on to me yet. I came at them, bow on, maybe only fifty feet above the waves, held my fire till I was maybe only a quarter of a mile away, got their bridge in my sights, and squeezed the trigger button. As I veered away I could see the heads on the bridge go down like bowling pins."

Her arms were around me and she was holding me tight.

She smelled of inexpensive scent and railroad washrooms and desert dust—aromas that now seemed erotic.

"They woke up and began to fire at me. I was crazy by then, convinced that I was immortal, that I would win the whole fucking war myself if I obliterated this DD with my fifties. I banked around and came back at them from the stern, diving straight through their antiaircraft fire. I knew I would die, but so would they."

Dear God, the woman is stroking my hair!

"I don't know how many passes I made, but I must have damaged something pretty badly. The ship slowed down and turned in a big uneven circle. Either the steering mechanism was dead, or I had killed everyone on the bridge. The last time by I emptied my guns into them. I guess I hit a torpedo or something because there was a big explosion aft of the funnel. For a couple of seconds I thought the blast would knock me into the waves, which would have served me right for being such a damn fool. They were blazing like a Christmas fire— the very image I had—as I pulled away and into another rain squall."

My head was against her breasts and I was clinging to her for dear life, the immemorial posture of a man home from the horrors of war.

"Did they save the men on the rafts?"

"Some of them. Maybe all. I didn't want to ask. Enough so the report of what I did got back to our Air Group Commander. I told them by radio about the destroyer too, but I didn't say what I'd done to it. I knew I killed hundreds of them. We never did find it the next day, so maybe I killed them all. And, Andrea . . ." I was sobbing now. "It only took five minutes!"

An enormous burden seemed to rise from me and swirl off into the desert updrafts, sun devils carrying away guilt.

"They were planning to kill those Americans."

"But don't you see," I said as I fought for control of my tears, though I was not ashamed of them, "like the Maryknoll priest told me in Yokosuka after the war, they have different attitudes. To kill the enemy for them represents a way of honoring the enemy's courage. They were happy to die for their country rather than be captured. They could not understand why we didn't feel the same way."

"You saved the lives of your fellow Americans."

"And destroyed the lives of hundreds of my fellow humans. . . . I know, Andrea, I know. I had to do it. . . ." I took a deep breath and recovered some of my self-discipline. "Thanks for listening."

"Glad to help."

I drew away from her, reached for the ignition, and paused. Acting on its own, I tried to explain to myself later, my hand reached for the side of her face, caressed her cheek and neck, slipped down to her chest and then to the remaining buttons on her blouse.

She drew a deep breath, sat up rigidly, her back against the other side of the car, neither acquiescing nor fighting me.

My fingers crept deeper, searching for, and finding, the firm, warm, reassuring flesh of her breasts. I realized that in a moment I would have to remove her bra and wondered exactly how that was done.

Gently she removed my hand. "Please, Jerry, no. Not now. Please."

"I'm sorry." I felt my face flame with shame. Stupid, clumsy novice lover. I rebuttoned her blouse, including the button she had left open.

"Don't be."

"I didn't intend to . . ."

"I know that." She smiled at me, I thought lovingly. "I'm flattered, to tell the truth. But it would not be right."

"I know."

But it would have been so wonderful.

And she had said "Not now," hadn't she? Maybe later.

I started the car and turned back onto Speedway Boulevard.

"Andrea King."

"Yes?"

"Thank you." I hoped I had said the two words with all the fervor I felt.

"Thank you for telling me."

A strange answer, don't you think?

As we drove away from Gates Pass I wondered about the run up to Phoenix. A hundred miles, three and a half to four hours in my overworked Chevy. Yes, we would have to do it. As much gratitude as I felt toward her, I wanted to be rid of her by nightfall. Already I was ashamed of my tears and my clumsy attempts at love.

Andrea grabbed my arm. "Those clouds over the mountains!"

Great black clouds were piling up behind the Catalinas; huge, ugly, threatening thunderheads building up strength for a mad rush down the side of the mountains and the foothills and a slashing attack on Tucson.

"I'd hate to have to fly through them. But they're only thunderstorms. Typical late-afternoon phenomenon here."

Her fingers dug into my arm. "Please . . ."

I pulled over to the side of the road and turned off the ignition. "Please what, Andrea?"

She turned her head and looked at me sorrowfully, tears forming in her eyes. "Please . . . do we have to drive through them?"

"Not if you don't want to."

"Leave me at the bus station. I'll go to Phoenix tomorrow."

"Do you really think I would do that?"

Her stiletto eyes considered my soul again. "No."

"There's a wonderful old resort on the edge of the city, called the Arizona Inn. We could swim and have a decent meal. . . . I forgot about lunch, didn't I? . . . Separate rooms, Andrea King, different wings of the inn."

"I trust you. . . ." She hesitated. "I'm not proud enough to say no to a place where I can take a shower. . . ."

"I'm thoroughly trustworthy." I patted her arm and started the car.

"Not thoroughly, but sufficiently." She laughed through her tears. "I'm sorry that I'm being a nuisance."

"I'm not."

The summer storm was the turning point.

CHAPTER 5

LATER, WHEN THE STORM HAD SWEPT THROUGH TUCSON, leaving big puddles on the tiles of the patio outside my room in the Arizona Inn, my imagination was excited at the prospect of seeing Andrea King in a swimsuit. I phoned my parents in River Forest.

"Darling, that's in Mexico!" Mom exclaimed in horror.

My mother was, as my brother Patrick put it, "Mrs. Panglossa." In her kindness she willed that we live in the best of all possible worlds. Since the evidence was frequently strong to support the opposite position, she defended herself with vagueness and denial. Convinced that Barbara and I would eventually marry, she still thought that somehow it would "work out," despite Barbara's balding husband and two children. Certain that I was in no danger during the war, she never mentioned my decorations to her friends. And confident that I would never be in a situation where sin and vice could tempt me, she created for herself an Asia in which Japan, Hong Kong, Korea, and the Philippines were much like the western suburbs of Chicago—not as affluent as River Forest, perhaps, but certainly as upright and virtuous as Maywood.

Somehow Mexico didn't fit this paradigm. And Tijuana was the antechamber of hell. I never went to Tijuana—even though it was as close to San Diego as Chicago was to Oak Park.

"It's in Arizona, dear," my father reassured her. "Near Fort Huachuca; that's were Black Jack Pershing began his search for Pancho Villa."

My father, despite his fame and affluence, was not on a first-name basis with the General of the Armies and certainly had not been involved in the Border War in which Pancho had led Black Jack on a merry and foolish chase. Yet Pershing was the only general and the "First" War the only war.

He had enlisted in the First Illinois—the 131st Infantry Regiment—the day Wilson asked for a declaration of war, was commissioned a second lieutenant and sent to France, and spent nine days in the line in front of Sedan before the Armistice. I am not sure that anyone ever shot at him or anywhere near him. Poor man, he desperately wanted, however, to share war experiences with me.

Yet he almost died during the war—from the Spanish Influenza—and my F6F had never even been dented by a piece of shrapnel.

What could we talk about?

"Isn't Arizona in Mexico?" my mother demanded. "Or New Mexico?"

"It's part of the United States—the last state admitted," my father reassured her.

"They even have telephones," I tried to cheer her up, "and the Arizona Inn is one of the great resorts in the West."

"Americans live there?" Mom persisted.

"Mostly."

"Well, I hope you find some nice young woman there and bring her home."

This was another of Mom's favorite themes. What would she think of the waif into whose breasts I had sobbed an hour earlier?

"I'll keep my eyes open."

"You could bring her home for the Butterfield Harvest Festival Dance, couldn't you?"

Butterfield was the "Catholic" country club in the western suburbs, founded in the late twenties because Catholics were excluded in those days from Oak Park and River Forest country clubs. My father was one of the founding members, and even after it was possible to join the "Protestant" clubs, indeed after they became mostly Catholic, he resolutely refused to have anything to do with them, a practice I am happy to say that I continue.

Well, I won't join them, but I'll certainly play at both. And take perverse delight in cleaning up at their calcutta tournaments!

Anyway, one of my mom's favorite fantasies was that I would someday appear at a Butterfield formal with a young woman on my arms so dazzling that everyone would forget about Barbara Conroy.

It was in truth a fantasy that I secretly shared.

"If I find her, I'll bring her home for the festival."

I found her but I did not bring her home for the festival.

"Hot out there?" my father asked in his man-to-man tone, which I both enjoyed and hated.

"Hundred and twelve or so. But we're up on a plateau, it changes forty degrees from day to night. So it'll be in the seventies in a couple of hours."

"Dry heat."

"Humid heat this time of the year."

I had to put him down that way. Just as my sons would do that to me when they were the same age.

We talked for a few more moments and then said goodbye—after I had promised Mom that I would be careful.

I would lose my mind, I thought, living in that house again.

I turned on the shower; the commander would not appear at the swimming pool dirty and smelly. I resolved that there would be no repetition of the scene at Gates Pass. I would not make a fool of myself either by breaking down or by making a clumsy pass.

The former would provide only temporary relief and the latter made no sense at all. There would be no sexual play between me and Andrea King during the next twenty-four hours.

Why that part of the resolve?

As a novelist wrote lately, it's not easy to stop being Catholic.

I'm not saying it was a bad resolution. There are so many "what ifs" associated with those days that I get a headache when I try to figure them out.

It was a naive resolution, however. It assumed (a) that the man made the decision about initiating sexual play and then the woman made the decision about whether to respond and (b) that there was nothing about me that would be profoundly appealing to a haunted kid like Andrea King.

It turned out to be a pleasant evening, punctuated by serious but not excessively heavy talk. It would also be the end of that part of my Arizona adventure which took place in a recognizable real world.

I walked into the swimming-pool area, a copy of the *Tucson Citizen* under my arm. Had to read the evening comics too.

Andrea King was already in the pool. She was neither a strong nor a skillful swimmer, but she cut through the water with the easy and natural grace that characterized everything she did.

I sat down in a deck chair and opened the paper, waiting eagerly for her to climb out of the pool. In a swimsuit, she would be sumptuous.

She was even more than that. Her luscious womanly body, encased in a white, corsetlike strapless suit, demanded to be embraced and loved.

Yet so thin and frail—slender, soft, defenseless. She also demanded to be protected.

A hard combination to beat.

"How many pounds underweight are you, young woman?" I demanded over the top of the *Citizen* comics page.

"What happened to my Blarney stone–kissing Irishman?" She shook the water out of her tight red hair. "Is that all you can say about me?" She dived back into the water, whirled around, splashed me.

"Hey!" I jumped up to protect my *Citizen*. "You soaked Pansy Yokum."

"Who?" She made a disgusted faced at me.

"Li'l Abner's mother."

"I am"—breathless and laughing she climbed out of the pool again—"maybe seven or eight pounds underweight, since you asked. And a few more breakfasts like this morning and the problem will be of the opposite sort."

"Actually you take my breath away," I admitted, as she spread out a towel and sat on the tiles next to my chair. The loudspeaker played "Tenderly" —just for us.

"A cliché, Commander, but thank you anyway. . . . This is a lovely place. So few people. Summer, I suppose. That man looked like he thought you were crazy when you insisted on separate wings."

"Maybe I am."

"Not really." She shook water out of her hair. "Reading comics?"

"Almost illiterate."

"You are *NOT*."

She leaned forward, arms around her legs, tops of her wondrous breasts pushed against the swimsuit.

"I want to live, Commander."

"I should hope so." I touched her shoulder, still wet from the pool. Her fingers took possession of mine, not so much to fend them off as to hold them.

"If I were better educated, I could say it more clearly. . . . Now don't tell me I'm smart. I know that. But I'm still uneducated. . . . I wanted to die. I still want to die most of the time. But inside me there's something stronger that tells me I want to live, something as powerful as the ocean or the sky."

"Will to live."

"I suppose. I've thought about killing myself." Her hand relinquished mine and her fists knotted fiercely. "I've given up so often. John . . . the baby . . . often I think I'm dead. Maybe I am. I know I'm damned. But I can't and I won't die and it's almost not up to me. . . . Do I make any sense?"

"Yes."

What would have happened if I had taken her into my arms then? I'll never know.

"I won't give up. I won't quit."

"I know that."

So in the fading daylight, while she finished Robert Penn Warren's book (which she had started in Tombstone), I struggled through a half-mile swim and wondered who she was.

And why, despite living in San Diego for a couple of years, her skin was so pale.

After I climbed out of the pool, I sat on the lounge next to her, huddling in the twilight against the rapidly cooling mountain air.

"I suppose you've figured out," she said as she closed the book, "that John and I had to get married."

"Yes." With Andrea King it was best not to pretend.

"It was only once. I don't think either of us knew what we were doing. I certainly didn't. My aunt was a lot older than my parents were. She didn't tell me much." Her head was resting on her knees, her voice calm and controlled, almost clinical. "I knew where babies came from, but I wasn't sure, not even at sixteen, how they were conceived. I was quiet and shy, good grades but not popular; you know the kind?"

"Sure."

"John was my first beau. He was shy too and very bright. We seemed a natural pair. I thought I loved him and cried myself to sleep when he left for the Navy. I was sure he'd disappear just like my parents. When he came home on leave we talked about marriage after the war. Well, he talked about it. I wasn't sure. He wanted to do ... to make love ... and ... well, I wasn't even certain what he wanted to do, but I finally agreed because he seemed so desperate. I knew it was wrong, but ... I didn't think it could be terribly wrong or John wouldn't have wanted me to do it with him. ..."

She stopped talking. A loner, innocent beyond reason, unprotected by family or teachers, an easy target for a horny kid home on leave who has been teased by his buddies because he's still a virgin.

"You think God holds it against you?"

She glanced at me. "That's not the problem."

I waited, wanting to strangle someone, almost anyone for this poor child's violation.

"It hurt and it wasn't any fun. I don't think that John enjoyed it much either. I tried to forget about it. Then I got sick a month later in school. One of the nuns asked me if I was pregnant. I told her I didn't know. A lot of them didn't like me from grammar-school days. Said I was 'too pretty' for my own good. . . ."

"Same order in both schools?"

"Sure, it was a parish high school. I guess they didn't like poor kids to be too pretty. This nun that caught me being sick said, first thing, 'It's what we'd expect from someone like you.' "

"My God!"

"In whom you don't believe." She grinned ruefully. "Anyway, it was terrible. She wouldn't even let me go back to the classroom. Sister Superior screamed at me, the Monsignor screamed at me, my aunt screamed too, my uncle beat me with his belt, John's parents screamed. They said I was ruining their son's life."

"And they all said you had to get married?"

She nodded solemnly. "I'm sure John didn't want to. He saw his college education being ruined. But he was afraid to disobey his father. His parents were immigrants and they were very strict."

"And you?"

"Sometimes I did"—there was not a trace of a tear on her smooth cheek—"sometimes I didn't. I had hoped for a college scholarship. I worried about the poor baby. I didn't want her to be abandoned like I was. I knew all along it would be a girl, you see. But I didn't know what else to do."

"And no one offered to help."

"No one."

An old story and utterly ordinary, to the point of being a cliché. And if my son the priest is to believed, not so extraordinary today. Yet when it happens to you it is not a cliché. It looks like the end of your world.

"It was decided by everyone, mostly by the Monsignor, that I would continue to live with my aunt until the war was over. But my uncle dug in his heels. He would not tolerate a public sinner in his house. So the Monsignor said I would have to live with John's parents."

"Good God!"

"Can't help yourself, can you? Well, that would have been terrible. So I became stubborn for the first time in my life. I told them all that I would not move in with John's parents. If he wanted to marry me, he'd have to take me with him to California. He didn't want to because by now he was so ashamed that he hated me—everyone blamed me. He was a fine young man who had been tricked by a cheap whore— that's what the Monsignor told his father. So I said, 'Okay, we won't be married and you can put me in a home somewhere.' "

Which would not have been a bad idea.

"So they all backed down."

"I won and it made them hate me even more. But, funny thing, once we had settled in San Diego, John and I got along reasonably well most of the time. We were on our own, but we were never lonely. He said to me one night, 'Do you miss home?' "

"I hadn't thought about it much. So I said, 'I guess not.' "

" 'Me neither,' he said, and sort of laughed. 'I guess we're free of them all.' I really loved him deeply that night."

But he would have had to return home after the war. We all do.

"It would have been hard, I suppose," she continued, "as the years went on and we'd blame each other for the chances we'd lost. Still, we were happy for a little while."

I took her hand and kissed it.

"Pretty cheap, commonplace little story, isn't it?"

"You are not a cheap, commonplace, or little person, Andrea King."

"Five feet three . . . well . . . two and a half." She giggled and pulled her hand away. "I'm getting cold and you're turning blue."

I helped her out of the chaise lounge. "Let's go see about that seven or eight pounds."

"Thanks for listening. I don't know why I had to explain. . . ."

"As I learned this afternoon," I said, opening the door to the corridor of the inn, "it's good to be able to talk."

"Even to strangers?"

"Especially to strangers." I brushed my lips against her forehead at the door to her room, swearing to myself that I would never violate her like that fat little son of a bitch had violated her.

In retrospect, I'm more charitable about him. A lonely, sensitive, and isolated young woman can send out signals of invitation to intimacy that are perfectly innocent to her but which an almost innocent young man might interpret very differently. John King, poor slob, might well have been able to convince himself that he had been seduced.

Which doesn't justify what he did. It does, however, make it a little more understandable.

Walking back to my room that night at the Arizona Inn, caught up in conflicting passions that would soon run completely out of control, I wanted to tear someone apart for what had been done to Andrea King.

No wonder she thinks You hate her, I informed the God in whom I did not believe. You're a worse bastard than that fat uncle and fat priest.

The deity in whom I did not believe did not deign to match me insult for insult.

The intelligence officer in the back of my head, assuring me that he was not necessarily in the employment of the rejected deity, pointed out that there were a number of holes in the story about which I ought to seek answers. I didn't pay any attention to him.

At supper she wore a sleeveless white dress, matching white shoes, nylons, and a tiny gold cross at her neck. There was, I suspected, an iron buried in her cardboard luggage.

The wedding band was still on her finger.

We ate steak and pan fried potatoes and drank red wine

and laughed like two people who are falling in love ought to laugh. I have no recollection of what we said at dinner, so it could not have been of any moment. She was, I thought, a charming dinner companion. Moreover, she would be a charming dinner companion on the *Queen Mary* or in the best restaurants and hotels in the world. I had no intention of bringing her home for the Butterfield Harvest Festival Dance, but she would be the center of attraction if I did. Andrea King was the kind of woman, I told myself confidently, who would be the center of attraction in any group in the world.

And she was entitled to expensive clothes and costly jewels and wealthy suitors and brilliant orchestras and elaborate backdrops for her beauty and charm.

I think I told her that after my last gulp of wine. I think she laughed at me, but she wasn't offended. And possibly not even surprised.

I don't think I promised her that I would deliver all these commodities to her, all but the other suitors. But one part of me certainly intended to do just that.

As best as I can recall those magic moments, she struck me as a dazzling blend of wide-eyed, naive child who required me as a teacher and a protector, and a mature and sophisticated woman of the world at whose feet I could learn for the rest of my life.

It was not, even from the hindsight of forty years, necessarily an inaccurate evaluation. My resident CIC was inclined to agree, though he observed that such a woman was not necessarily the kind with whom I could live for very long.

I told him that I certainly could and that I had about made up my mind—after fifteen hours—that she was the woman for me.

But she was still scary, otherworldly and, at the same time, too much this-worldly for me.

In her white dress she seemed innocent, virginal. Innocent she might be, but virginal she was not. She had slept with a husband, conceived and carried for a time a child, suffered twin losses. And was afraid of demons I did not understand.

And on any bed of love, I would be the novice and she

would be the novice mistress, I the virgin and she the experienced expert, I the student and she the teacher.

That was arousing in a perverse sort of way, but also terrifying.

What, I wondered, as we ordered our dessert, would that be like? I might once again make a total fool out of myself. Or I might have the time of my life.

I do remember the conversation over our chocolate ice cream sundaes.

"I think, Andrea King, that God sent me to take care of you."

The big spoonful of chocolate-drenched ice cream stopped in midflight and then returned to its goblet.

"It is not true." Her lips, normally generous, narrowed into a thin hard line. "I don't want to hear it ever again."

"I'm sorry if I made you angry."

"It is *not* true." Hands pressed together on her lap, she pushed her chair back from the table. "God did *not* send you."

Unaccountably she was furious.

"If you say so . . ."

"Maybe"—the steam seemed to hiss out of her anger—"I'm the one who was sent."

"I'll gladly agree to that." I reached for one of her hands.

"And maybe," she said as she pulled the hand away, "God shouldn't be blamed for that. Maybe someone else sent me."

CHAPTER 6

"WHO DO YOU THINK SENT YOU?"

There was an awkward pause. She was still angry but beginning to regret her outburst. I was baffled.

"I'm sorry, Jerry. I have an Irish temper."

"Too."

" 'Too' or 'two'?" She began to smile that wondrous, magic, light-extinguishing smile.

"Both. Don't let your ice cream melt. It's worth at least a half pound in our fattening program."

She laughed happily. "You're wonderful, Commander."

"When you smile at me that way, I think so too."

"Irish." She dug into the sundae with renewed vigor. "You're incorrigibly Irish."

"You deserve the best, Andrea King."

"The best?"

"Clothes, homes, food, drink"—I filled her wineglass again—"cars, jewelry, children, lovers, everything."

"You said that before, but tell me why?"

"As a setting for your beauty."

"That only earns you something if you're willing to sell yourself. I'm not."

"I don't mean economically." The drink, as my mother would say, had loosened my tongue. "I mean artistically. Your smile lights up the world. Even your temper tantrums— which, candidly, scare the hell out of me—are irresistible."

"If I were better educated . . ."

"You would agree with me completely."

We laughed together and the world seemed right in a way it hadn't been since St. Luke's won the West Suburban Grammar School basketball championship ten years before.

After dinner we sat alone on the terrace, in the still, dark night, and sipped tea ("Earl Grey is my favorite," she told me with happy round eyes)—and Napoleon Special Reserve brandy. I was happily in love, fantasizing about the look on the face of Barbara Conroy when I appeared with Andrea.

Her hand touched mine and remained there, not holding it exactly but not about to let it get away either.

"Can we talk about God once more?"

"If you want." I sighed.

"You have to promise not to lose your temper."

"You're the one who lost it the last time."

"You're losing it already, Commander. Drink some more of this terrible, wicked liquor with which you're trying to seduce me." She drained her own brandy glass and winked at the waiter, who, like everyone else so far during the day, hardly noticed me when Andrea was present.

"I'll promise on one condition."

"Well," she said skeptically.

"I have permission to ask one question at the end."

"Just one."

"All right, I promise."

"Well." She took a deep breath. "I want you to believe in God."

I wanted to take her in my arms and make love to her all night long, I wanted to anoint her as my teacher in the art of love, I wanted to play with her marvelous body until the end of time—and she wanted me to believe in God!

"Why?"

"Is that your one question?"

"No."

"All right. I'll tell you why anyway."

"Doesn't count against me?"

"Be quiet and listen. . . . Oh, thank you very much. It's wonderful!"

She gleefully accepted her renewed brandy snifter from the waiter, who placed it in front of her as though she were Princess Elizabeth.

So, as a matter of fact, did I gleefully accept mine, although I clearly did not rate in his book even the rank of faithful equerry to a magic princess.

"You ought to believe in God"—she hesitated, looking for a reason and then rushed on—"because of the moonlight on those desert mountains."

Quick and resourceful. To my catalog of her virtues, I must now add that she not only sized up people and situations with an agile and penetrating intelligence, she was no mean debater.

"Would it break my promise if I asked whether you were on the debating team in school?"

"It certainly would. It would even break your promise to ask about asking."

"Then I won't even ask about asking anymore."

"Better not." She sipped the brandy and giggled. "Of course I was on the debating team."

"Tell me about the moonlight on the Catalinas."

"The moon bathes the whole world, the mountains and the desert, the animals and the humans, in white forgiveness."

"If there's a moon, there has to be God?"

"Right." She leaned toward me, the enthusiastic debater about to score her point. "If there's moonlight and coyotes yapping and owls hooting and the fragrance of the flowers here in the garden . . . and the touch of your hand"—she touched my fingers with hers—"and friendship and love and kindness and the stars, and"—she laughed—"chocolate sauce on ice cream and swimming pools after hot days in the desert"—she pushed my hand away playfully—"if there are all those good things in the world, must there not be God?"

"What about Frank Stilwell?"

"Who? Oh, the man in the story."

"No, the man in real life whose town you were afraid to visit. Is God responsible for Stilwell killing Morgan Earp? Or for Doc Holliday and Wyatt killing Frank? Or for Josie Marcus stirring up the whole feud by trading Johnny Behan in for Wyatt?"

"You're asking questions."

"Making arguments."

"I'm not innocent about evil, Jeremiah Keenan."

"I didn't mean to suggest you were. But your argument is. You don't account for evil in the world. If your God is responsible for all the good, then He's responsible for Josie Earp and Johnny Behan and Frank Stilwell too."

It was a freshman natural-theology argument in Western folklore terms, I acknowledge that completely. But I was responding to the traditional argument of Saint Thomas in high school religion class format, presented, I also admit, with considerable charm and enthusiasm.

"I can't account for evil." She sighed and bent back into

her chair. "But you," she said as she jabbed a triumphant finger at me, "can't account for good, not even your own wonderful personal goodness."

"So now I'm an argument for God against myself?"

"You bet." She nodded vigorously. "If there isn't a God, how come there's such a good man as Commander Jerry Keenan?"

"I'm not that good."

"Yes, you are. Bad men I take for granted. A young widow finds out all about them in a hurry. A good man is a wonderful surprise."

"You're forgetting what I tried to do up at Gates Pass?"

"Dear God in heaven, Jerry, why do you pretend that you're made of armor plate instead of human flesh?"

There wasn't much left of my armor-plated heart at that moment.

We were both silent for a minute or two, alone with our own melted coronary muscles.

"I don't know what to do about you, Andrea King."

"What you should do about me is listen to my arguments and admit I'm right." She laughed like a woman leprechaun.

"From you the arguments are a lot more persuasive than from the ancient cleric who insisted I memorize them at Notre Dame a few lifetimes ago."

"I think that's a compliment, but I'm not sure. If it is, thank you."

"It was, and you're welcome. It comes free of charge with the Keenan white moonlight forgiveness service."

"You're not being serious." I saw her frown in the white moonlight as she finished her cognac.

"Another one?"

"You'd have to carry me to my room."

"That's part of the service. We tuck our clients into bed."

"I bet you do. And you're still not being serious."

"I am postponing it. Now let me think for a moment. . . ."

I searched for a response that would be both honest and satisfactory for my lovely teacher. "Would you consider tonight's lesson a success if I said you'd given me a lot to think about?"

Even now I am rather proud of that answer.

"Very clever." She was both appeased and unappeased, a good condition in which to keep a woman.

"But, since I am sincere about that answer, is it all right?"

"All right." She sounded dubious.

"Now do I get to ask my question?"

"If you want."

Had she really yawned?

"I am keeping you awake."

"Yes, but ask your question."

"How come you're so interested in selling me a God who you believe has suspended you, in your own words, Miss Teacher, between earth and hell? To rephrase the question, not, I hasten to add"—I finished my cognac, too—"ask another question, why are you working so hard in the cause of a God who has been cruel enough to reject you, a God who bathes everyone but you in white forgiveness?"

"It's different." She sounded listless, beaten.

"Tell me how."

"You're not only a good man, Jerry, like I've been trying to tell you all day—has it really only been a day?—you're a great man. You're important. You'll do wonderful things for many people during your life. I don't matter."

"You're crazy to think that."

"All right." She was angry. "I'm crazy."

"I didn't say you were crazy, woman." My lawyer genes had clicked into operation, like auxiliary fuel tanks. "I said it's crazy to think you don't matter."

"Not like you do."

The cognac had addled my brain. "I won't believe in a God who doesn't think you matter."

"Very clever."

"At your service, ma'am. Is the argument over?"

"For tonight."

The silent pause was longer this time. We both, I thought, had got to one another. In many different ways. Not a bad day by any means.

She rose from the wrought-iron chair, rather unsteadily. "We both need sleep. Neither of us had much last night."

"How did you know that?"

"You drove all night, didn't you? Besides, you're so old, you should get your sleep."

She weaved, a bit uncertainly, toward the door to the inn. I hadn't told her that I'd driven all night. But it didn't matter.

"I'll assist you," I said as I took firm possession of her elbow, "to your room in the other wing."

"Lest I collapse on my face and sleep in the corridor like a fall-down drunk."

"A courtesy of our service." I opened the door for her.

"That will be nice."

It took us some time and much tipsy laughter to find the right corridor.

At the door of her room, in the dimly lit and suggestive pastel hallway, I kissed her forehead. She lowered her eyes. "Good night, Commander, and thank you."

"Thank *you*," I said and prepared to depart, full steam astern, if you please.

Instead I said, "I don't think I'm finished kissing you."

She leaned back against the door and examined me meticulously. I put both hands on the door, surrounding her, so to speak.

"Well?" She tilted her jaw.

"I'm maybe not all that good at it. I don't want to say too much and I don't want to say too little. With the kissing, I mean."

That will give you some idea of what a bungler I was, Navy Crosses or not.

"Up to me to make an evaluation, Commander?"

"Right."

"You want my permission?"

"No. Well . . . no. I'm going to kiss you whether you like it or not."

"Ah."

"You don't seem ready to fight me off."

"You're bigger and stronger."

"That's true. But you could make a fuss."

"Who would hear me?"

"Someone might."

I was making a terrible mess out of it. Or maybe I wasn't. Her big blue eyes were soft and round—amusement, affection, anticipation.

She put her arms around me. "Carry on, CAG."

Commander, Air Group. She knew I had been that too.

So I carried on, gently at first, barely brushing her forehead and her cheeks, her eyelids and her earlobes, her chin and her nostrils. She put her hands, holding a tiny black purse, behind her back, the completely submissive slave.

"Very clever." She sighed.

Then her throat and the back of her neck, her sweet-smelling hair, her shoulders, down one arm and up the other, then the route back, oh, so slowly, to her lips.

"You've been practicing," she said with a sigh.

"Only imagining. Quality still passable?"

"I think so . . . no final judgment yet."

I brushed her lips back and forth, hardly touching them at first. They tasted of cognac and coffee and chocolate ice cream, savors I wanted to hold forever. She sagged against the door, absorbing all the affection I had to offer. Her eyes were open but lidded, not seeing anything. My lips became more insistent, inciting, then forcing her to respond.

She hesitated, and then matched me kiss for kiss, demanding as much as she was giving. Our lips burned into each other, our tongues tormented each other, our bodies locked in passionate embrace, her heart pounded against her tiny rib cage, her breasts thrust against my chest. I felt, or imagined I felt, hard nipples digging into me. We were rushing toward the rapids.

She gently pushed me away.

"Not too bad at all," she said, trying to sound casual, but really gasping.

"Grade, please."

"Well." She put her finger on her chin in feigned thought,

but her breasts were still moving up and down rapidly against her dress. "C plus. . . . no, maybe B minus."

"Witch." I swatted at her rear, tightly girdled as I thought it would be, not hard enough to have any impact.

She snickered. "You kiss better than you swat. Which is fine with me." She took a key out of her purse, fingers still trembling, and opened the door to her room. "Now I think I'd better head for home port. Quickly."

Uncertain lover that I was, I could not leave well enough alone.

"I'm sorry if I . . . I didn't mean to . . . if you're offended . . ."

"Oh, Jerry." She looked up at me with the adoring expression that so quickly melted my heart. "All you did was kiss me, very gently and affectionately, too. I'm not angry, only out of breath and a little bit overwhelmed. Good night," she said as she bussed my cheek, "and thank you for everything."

I hesitated at the door as it closed and then gave again the command for full speed astern. If I had invited myself into her room and into her bed, she would not, I thought on that stern run, have resisted. But we had a whole lifetime ahead of us. Why should I rush her?

I was, after all, trustworthy, if not completely trustworthy.

I undressed and, clad in my shorts, sat down wearily at the table in my room. I had learned early in my resolution that if one intends to keep a journal—as I had since I sailed for the western Pacific—one must work at it every night, no matter how tired one is.

So, my brain dulled from the Napoleon and the taste of Andrea's lips and maybe from the ingenuity of her theology, I scribbled an account of the day's adventure. It is next to my monitor as I work on this story. As is the picture I'll tell you about later.

As I wrote I paused often to look out at the full moon drenching the desert in Andrea's white forgiveness.

The moon, I thought, stands for romance and love. Or so they say. But if you were looking at it for the first time and had none of the background images our culture hands down about it, you might well think it sinister instead of reassuring or forgiving. It's cold, unfeeling, deadly. No wonder the coyotes are howling at it. It is supposed to cause madness and bring out werewolves and vampires, demons and ghosts.

Did it bring out Andrea for me?

That initial gut reaction was still with me, not lodging with my intelligence officer who didn't believe in ghosts, and completely disregarded by my poet/lover self who was, as you probably have grasped, completely enchanted.

No, the gut suspicion about Andrea was deep in the soul of Jeremiah Keenan the wild, superstitious, frightened pagan Celt. Jerry the berserker, the guy who takes on DDs with fifty-caliber machine guns.

Let me quote for you what the lover/poet wrote at the end of his journal that night:

> *I've always thought women were confusing, but not complicated. Barbara was unpredictable because she did not value consistency in the slightest, not because there was any mystery about her. My sister Joanne is the same way. The only puzzle about her is how she can live with her own erratic emotions. But Andrea King is confusing because she is complicated.*
>
> *She's bright, quick, more intelligent than I am. And probably more experienced in many ways too. Yet she is also an innocent little girl, almost untouched by the nastiness of her life. She's modest and reserved and even secretive, but also sensual, frighteningly sensual maybe. She likes me, and at times even admires me, but she thinks I'm a funny if talented little boy.*
>
> *She's witty and is at least as hot-tempered as I am. But when she drinks you in with her soft, warm blue eyes, you want to sleep in her arms while she croons lullabies to you for the rest of your life. She has an almost grim hunger for life, a passion for knowledge and experience and even power. An incredible will to live, given all that has happened to her. Yet she seems to think that she's already condemned, already maybe even among the dead. She preaches God's love to me, passionately, I would say, but doesn't think God loves her.*
>
> *Any God that doesn't love her is out of His mind.*

If you produce a creature like Andrea King and don't fall totally in love with her, you don't have much taste.

Is that a prayer? My night prayers for this twenty-second day of July in the year of Our Lord, whoever He may be, nineteen hundred and forty-six?

I don't know but it will have to do for night prayers. I love her as I have never loved anyone else. I've only known her for seventeen hours. If You who have known her all her life, indeed all eternity if my teachers are to be believed, are not prepared to take care of her and protect her, then screw you. Or screw You, if You prefer.

An incomplete but not inaccurate description, even from the perspective of forty years.

There is, as must be obvious, one important point that escaped me completely. Partly because I had no real experience of women yet and partly because I did not comprehend the nature of my impact on others, particularly women, it did not occur to me that I might have touched something deep and passionate within her soul.

Deep and passionate and quite possibly dangerous.

Only as I was falling into a happy, if slightly inebriated sleep, did I wonder who she thought had sent her into my life. If not God, then who else?

Then came the dreams, not of my lovely Andrea, but of the men I had killed about whom I would never tell her. My own men.

CHAPTER 7

I WOKE UP WITH A HEADACHE AND A CHILL, THE FORMER from too much cognac and too many nightmares—and maybe from a little sexual frustration—and the latter from the air conditioner.

"Pilots, man your planes," I ordered myself, pulled on swimming trunks, grabbed a towel and stumbled down the corridor to the swimming pool.

It was already hot and my friend was already in the pool, as grim-faced as I felt.

"Good morning," I tried.

"Prove it," she said, ducking her head back under water.

"Did you sleep well?" I tested the pool with my foot. It seemed too cold despite the hot tiles of the pool patio.

"No. Did you?"

"No."

She stopped swimming and clung to the side of the pool, watching me anxiously. "Was it my fault?"

"No," I answered, honestly enough. "Disappointed?"

She swam away in a huff, beating the water angrily. Ah, I thought, it's going to be one of those days.

I picked up her towel, so as to be ready with it when she decided that she had had enough swimming. A book fell out. *Crime and Punishment.* On my list to read someday. She was already seventy-five pages into it. Her night must have been as restless as mine.

She rose from the pool, an adequately clad and still angry Venus.

Like the dutiful servant I was, I wrapped the towel around her lovely shoulders and resisted, with considerable effort, the impulse to kiss the back of her lovely neck.

I presented her with Fyodor Mikhailovich Dostoyevsky. Accompanied by the usual deep bow I reserve for grand duchesses.

"Don't get it wet," she snapped.

"Yes, my lady Grand Duchess," I said with an even deeper bow.

She glared at me as she stomped off, but I think there was a twinkle in her eye.

I sighed with admiration for my virtue as I dived into the

water, regretting that she had not seen my nearly perfect swan dive.

One of the characters in back of my head rejoiced that I would be rid of the Grand Duchess by nightfall and another rejoiced that I would have her with me for the rest of my life.

I was quite abjectly in love, in other words, though perhaps not willing to admit it to myself yet.

Three-quarters of an hour later I joined her at the breakfast table, where she was eating corn flakes, raspberries and cream, and reading Fyodor.

"My, we look crisp and fresh in our white shirt and shorts," I said as I sat down.

She glared at me above her book. Maybe a little of the twinkle remained.

"You wind up early in the morning, don't you, Commander?"

"Always a bearer of good cheer and enthusiasm." I signaled the waiter. "Exactly what my daughter has, and some wheat cakes."

"She has eaten the wheat cakes already, sir," he said with a conspiratorial grin, as he poured a cup of coffee for me.

Daughter, hah.

Little do you know, buster.

She closed her book and essayed a tight little grin. "Two helpings of pancakes, actually."

It was my turn to be childish. I opened my guidebook, spread out my map and, coffee cup in hand, began to plan the strategy for today's mission.

With an audible sniff she returned to Raskolnikov and Sonia, as I had gathered were the names of the characters in *Crime and Punishment* when I peeked at her book.

I was only pretending to be mapping out the mission. In fact, I was worrying about Andrea. I wondered if I had offended her the night before. Perhaps she had expected me to make love to her. She was, after all, sexually experienced. I had treated her like a seventeen-year-old virgin on a prom date. Perhaps she was disappointed and frustrated.

Still, she had acted like a seventeen-year-old virgin on a prom date, hadn't she?

She had given no sign that she wanted me in bed with her, had she?

How would I know what the signs were like?

And pushed by the demons of curiosity that had almost landed me in naval intelligence instead of in the cockpit of an F6F, I had made my cursed phone call to the manager of the Del Coronado before I came to breakfast.

"No, Commander, we have not employed a woman named Andrea King since we reopened. No Andreas and no Kings. Not at all, Commander, glad to help."

Right.

"What's on the tour agenda for today?"

I looked up. Dostoyevksy had vanished. I figured it would not be too wise for me to comment on that fact.

"Drop you off at the Arizona Biltmore—built in 1929, designed by Frank Lloyd Wright, and looks a little like the Imperial Hotel in Tokyo. Wright was the architect—"

"I know who he is—"

"Then I tackle the Superstition Mountains."

"Why do they have such a terrible name?"

"Maybe because they look so strange; there are lots of legends about ghosts and Apache Thunder gods." I picked up the guidebook next to me and opened to the page where there was a picture of the Superstition Range—stern, foreboding fortress of volcanic tufa that seemed to warn you to stay away. "They are a bit intimidating, aren't they?"

She opened her eyes, looked at them, and shuddered. "How terrible."

"Just dactite rock."

She crossed her arms in front of her breasts, huddling from the cold that the mountains seemed to radiate for her. "That's where your Dutchman is?"

"And your Dutchman wanders around on a ship, wandering around singing melancholy Wagnerian songs!" I touched her arm in cautious reassurance. "Weird people, the Germans!"

Her face relaxed in that wonderful smile, as though I had pushed a button. "Aren't we Irish terrible bigots?"

I gulped and leaned back against a seat. "Has anyone ever told you about your smile?"

"No." She was watching me suspiciously. "What's wrong with it?"

"It turns out all the other lights."

"The Irish are terrible indeed." And she smiled again. I was captured. Years of celibacy, partly voluntary, partly involuntary, vanished in the mists. I wanted her.

"Tell me more about your Dutchman." She turned, embarrassed by my desires which she seemed to absorb like everything else I thought or felt. Embarrassed, but not frightened or repelled.

I gave her my second lecture in American Folklore 101.

I told her about the pre-Christian Indian mines, and Coronado, and the early Spanish mines, and Peralta's Sombrero Mine in the shadow of Weaver's Needle, and the Apache massacre, and the survival of one Mexican woman who for a time was "married" to Jacob Walz—the Dutchman. Then I added the more recent parts of the story: Walz's murder of his Mexican workers and eventually of his friend Meisner, the earthquake that closed the door of the mine, the floods which the Thunder gods sent; rumors of Apache warriors still guarding the approaches to Weaver's Needle; the death of Walz and his legacy of a map to Clara Thomas, a Negro ice-cream-shop proprietor; the search for the mine by Thomas and her friends the Petrasch brothers; the discovery of bodies with arrows in the back, the death of the woman doctor Ruth just before the war; the persistent stories of Apache horsemen seen on the tops of mountains just at sunset or on nights with full moons—horsemen dressed in the old warrior garments of the best light cavalry that humankind has ever produced.

I'm sure the lecture ended with my eyes shining. Jerry Keenan as committed treasure hunter, the man who would resolve forever the Lost Dutchman legend.

"And you want to find that treasure!" She regarded me with a mixture of terror and disbelief. "How could you?"

"Not really." I removed the guidebook gently from her hand and closed it. "I don't need the money or want it. But since I was a kid and read *Treasure Island* I've been fascinated by buried treasure." I shrugged indifferently, not exactly having an explanation. "It's a great American legend, like Wyatt Earp. And I'm on a great American tour."

"I'll go with you," she said decisively. "I think it's horrible and I'll be scared every moment. But I can't let you go up into that terrible place"—she gestured toward the guidebook—"by yourself. You might get hurt."

"And what would you do then?"

"Well . . ." She actually grinned. "I could drive for help."

"Can you drive?"

"No . . . But please let me come. I promise not to smile too much."

And she smiled again and I couldn't say no. I touched her red hair, glinting in the morning sunlight, and said, "Delighted to have you."

It sounds like the beginning of a romantic adventure story, which is just what I was looking for at that troubled time in my life. But even then it did not quite ring true. I had not forgotten the manager of the Del Coronado. And I had not shaken my strong instinct that this pale, pretty young woman was not quite alive, not the way the cashier at the Arizona Inn and I were alive. She was some sort of in-between creature, a red-haired Irish Flying Dutchman. Or Lost Dutchman. Or lost Irishwoman. Or whatever. Wandering for a time between life and death and seeking my help, even though she knew that I could not help.

It's been forty years, yet I don't think I embellish my memory of that feeling. Why did I not drive her to Phoenix and get rid of her?

Because she was young and beautiful and she needed help and because I was young and I wanted her?

And also because I didn't seem to have much choice. We

were both, I thought as I gathered up my maps at the end of breakfast, fated, and that was that.

"Be ready in forty-five minutes?" I asked.

She drained her coffee cup. "Half hour."

"Andrea King." I tilted her chin up, so I could look into her eyes.

"Yes," she said as she closed her eyes so I couldn't see them.

"Even in a bad breakfast mood, you are still one of the two or three most exquisite women in the world."

"Really?" A wonderful tint spread across her face.

"Really."

"*Queen Mary* type?"

"Not good enough for you."

"Give me a half hour"—she still wouldn't look at me—"and don't worry, please; you haven't done anything wrong. It's all inside of me."

I wasn't so sure, but I realized that it was not the time to argue. I packed my bag, loaded it in the tiny trunk of the Chevy, and went back to the dining room to collect the lunches that we had ordered.

"Sorry we're not going to have the lovely young lady around a little longer," said the hostess, who fetched the two neatly packed lunch boxes and the bottle of Cabernet I had ordered. "She brightens up the whole inn."

"Doesn't she?"

"Bring her back."

"You bet."

A promise I never kept.

I put the lunch boxes and the wine in the backseat under the blanket I kept there in case I should want to curl up in the car and spend the night with my Roxinante ("named after Don Quixote's horse?" she had demanded). Then I went back into the inn to pay the bill.

I gave the cashier one of my hundred-dollar bills and waited for the change.

"Very lovely young woman, sir." He had a leathery cowpoke's face. "Terribly pale, isn't she?"

"Pigmentation," I murmured.

"When she talks and smiles you don't notice, but before that you wonder if she's stepped out of a coffin."

I checked the remaining bills. Nine of them all right. "Doctor says she has very sensitive skin. Should stay out of the sun."

Already lying to protect her. Andrea King, or whoever she might be, was lonely and alone. She needed my protection. Everything else would take care of itself.

She looked as if she needed my help, if not my protection, when she carried her luggage out to the car, exactly a half hour after we'd left the breakfast room. I jumped out of the car to take it from her and encountered no protests. There was certainly an iron in the bag I hefted into the backseat of the Chevy.

She waited for me to open the door.

"Thank you."

"You're welcome." I closed the door and considered her charming legs.

"Something wrong, Commander?"

"Your legs."

"Last night they seemed to rate at least a C plus."

"Much higher marks than that, but I don't want them to get cut up and maybe infected by cactus. Do you have any slacks inside that boxcar you're lugging around?"

"Wool." She frowned miserably. "Should I go back and change?"

"That might be worse; the high today is supposed to be a hundred and eighteen."

She was not wearing her thin wedding band. What did that mean?

I was not sure I wanted to think about that subject.

"What should I do?"

I walked around to the driver's seat. "We are going to stop at Steinfeld's and buy you some new summer slacks, of the kind you lusted for when we walked by their window display yesterday."

"I can't afford . . . I don't have . . ."

"I said 'we'."

"No."

"Yes."

"You can't make me."

"Yes, I can. I'm bigger and stronger and smarter."

"You are not smarter."

"Anyone who wants to go up into those mountains on a day like this in shorts or wool slacks is stupid."

"And you're stupid if you think I intend to heal you of your virginity for some cheap clothes."

Nasty, huh? Very nasty. And strike right for the jugular.

"Expensive clothes?"

No response.

"Okay, what price?" We turned on Campbell so I could show her the university.

Again no response.

"That's the university over there." I turned onto Speedway Boulevard, which was later rated by *Life*, not without reason, as the ugliest street in America.

Dead silence.

I then pointed out the Hotel Geronimo, near the university, a red-and-green resort, not as elegant as the inn, but still attractive in a mixture of Miami and Mission architecture.

"Cute, if you like that sort of thing."

And that was that.

It was already blisteringly hot, worse than any day I could remember in the tropics. Can't beat the good old US of A for bad weather. Maybe everything that happened that day can be blamed on the heat. If it happened.

We turned left at Sixth and then right at Congress. I parked in front of Steinfeld's. Yes, Virginia, in those days you could park right in front of a department store.

I extended three ten-dollar bills in her direction. She wouldn't take them.

"Young woman, you will go in there and buy yourself some slacks, another shirt, and whatever else you need for a walk in the desert—underwear included. And you will do so this minute."

"I won't."

"Look"—I confess I was shouting—"either you buy those clothes or you get out right here and walk to Phoenix."

I can talk like that when I'm angry. Ask my wife and kids. I make a fool out of myself when I do but it's not ineffective.

I dropped the bills on the seat next to her.

She got out of the car and slammed the door shut.

For a moment I thought I had lost her.

Then she reached in the window and snapped up the thirty dollars. Her face would have done an Apache Thunder god proud.

"What color?"

"Huh?"

"You're paying for the slacks, you should choose the color."

"Blue to match your eyes. Thunderhead blue."

"There isn't any such color." She stalked away.

God, how much I loved her at that moment.

"Andrea King."

"Yes." She turned around.

"Mind you, no corsets! And if you need more money . . ."

She spun on her heel and stormed into the store, reminding me of one of the jets I had flown in Hawaii before I decided that I didn't want a career in the Navy.

Her shopping expedition didn't take very long. In less than half an hour she reappeared, head bowed, stride diffident, carrying several packages. She was wearing blue slacks that matched her eyes—not skin-tight like jeans today, but tightly fitting for the times—a thin white blouse, and solid, comfortable-looking black shoes.

And, I suspected, only the minimal necessities—as judged in those days—underneath.

God forgive me for it, but I whistled at her. She turned the deepest crimson yet but changed neither her stride nor her guilty expression.

"Here's your newspaper," she said timidly, passing the *Arizona Daily Star* and two one-dollar bills through the window. "And your change. Peace offering?"

I got out of the car, took the packages from her, put them

next to her luggage in the rear seat, and conducted her to the door on the other side.

"I'm glad to see that you went on a proper shopping expedition."

"I do what I'm told eventually, particularly when someone shouts at me."

I took both her hands and extended them at an angle from her body. "Inspection," I murmured.

"Do I pass muster, Commander?" She flushed but did not avert her eyes.

"No girdle?" I touched her delightful rear end respectfully.

"Certainly not!" Her blush deepened, but she grinned. "You're embarrassing me."

"You seem to enjoy it."

"Regardless." She slipped out of my grip and into the passenger's seat. "I seem to like being a kept woman."

"Prettiest woman I've ever kept."

Back in the driver's seat I glanced at the sports section. Cubs had lost a doubleheader.

I was about to flip quickly through the comics when I heard soft crying next to me. I abandoned Terry to the pirates and folded my poor little waif into my arms.

"I'm not like that at all. I've never acted that way in my life. I was horrible. You really should make me walk to Phoenix."

I let her cry her heart out.

"It's okay, Andrea. This hot weather is hard on the old temper for everyone."

"I've only known you for twenty-four—well, twenty-six —hours and I've lost my temper with you more than with anyone else in all my life. Even the nuns at school."

"Maybe I deserve it."

"No, you don't." She shook her head fiercely. "You're wonderful. I . . . I'm such a turd."

"Andrea!"

"Well, I am. I never used that word before, but that's what I am."

"Maybe it's a compliment to my limited, but very real trustworthiness that you feel free to lose your temper with me."

She blew her nose with a tiny handkerchief she had pulled from her purse and considered that possibility. "Maybe that's right. You certainly are patient. . . ."

"Look, Andrea," I said as I rearranged her in her seat, tossed the *Star* in the backseat, and turned on the ignition— so filled with trustworthy virtue was I—"we are a kind of strange pair, both with a lot on our minds and a lot of problems to solve. Let's say that no matter what happens, we're ready to forgive one another."

"You forgive me for the terrible things I said?"

I kissed her forehead, still the paladin of virtue. "I sure do, and I expect reciprocity when I say terrible things."

"Well . . ." She grinned and threw her arms around me for a brief hug. "I'll have to see how terrible they are."

"On to Phoenix?"

"On to the Dutchman and his mine!"

"And I meant every word of that whistle. You look wonderful!"

She poked my arm. "Pilot, man your plane. Let's get out of here."

"An F6F is kind of crowded with two people in it."

"Pilot"—she had to have the last word—"and Aircraft Commander."

So we drove down Oracle Road toward the Superstition Mountains, across Fort Lowell, and into the empty desert north of the Rilito River, in the foothills of the Catalinas.

Already Andrea's good humor seemed to have faded.

"Would you mind if we took the roundabout way and saw some mountains and copper mines?"

She hardly seemed to have heard me. "You're the tour guide."

"Okay."

"I'm sorry." She snapped herself back to attention. "I'd love to see some copper mines. Really."

With that decision, everything else that would happen was already determined.

CHAPTER

So we lurched toward our destiny across the desert under the scorching sun, sometimes in clouds of dust so thick they reminded me of the morning fog over the Sea of Japan.

In those days, US 89 was paved all the way from Tucson to Phoenix and Arizona 77 was blacktopped from Oracle Junction to the San Manuel Mine behind the Santa Catalina Mountains. But the rest of the picturesque trip through the Dripping Springs Mountains up to Superior and US 60 was on a "macadamized" road—an uneven mixture of treated gravel and dirt (the sort of highway in whose existence my children resolutely refuse to believe).

I was emotionally exhausted from my fight with Andrea King. I'd flown by the seat of my pants, the way I had often returned from combat missions in bad weather. My instincts had guided me pretty well in both sorts of bad weather, but Andrea could obviously turn into heavy weather without warning. Barbara would never have been so angry at me; but then she would never have delighted in my kisses the way Andrea had.

The Sonora Desert is a weird place—saguaro (giant cacti with arms raised to heaven in prayer), ocotillos (trees which produce leaves only after rain, but after every rain), palo verdes (trees with their chlorophyll in the bark), rattlers, sidewinders, scorpions, Gila monsters, tarantulas, an occasional herd of mountain sheep, and once in a great while (so my guidebook said) a solitary bobcat or mountain lion or perhaps even a very rare Mexican jaguar.

Andrea's moods changed as dramatically as did the scenery. In the barren desert north of Tucson she frowned with disapproval and informed me that she thought the yucca tree with its single skinny finger reaching skyward was "insane."

"Take that up with God. He made it."

"You don't believe in God."

"Thanks for reminding me. I forgot."

"Was it the second Navy Cross which kept you awake last night?"

"Not so much kept me awake. I had no trouble falling asleep. Indeed I had some pleasant memories of behavior just before I went to bed. To tell the truth I can't remember them. . . ."

Poke in the ribs, very gentle and affectionate poke.

"But then I woke up. Want to hear about it?"

"If you want to talk about it."

"I do, Andrea. I do."

But it wasn't my own men that I told her about.

We were still for a few moments as I looked for a way to begin.

"It was toward the end of the war . . . did you ever hear of the *Yamoto?*"

"Wasn't that the Japanese admiral who planned the raid on Pearl?"

"That was Yamamoto. We killed him in the islands. Someone broke the Japanese code, so we knew he was coming. The Army had P-38s waiting for him. So Pearl was avenged, for whatever that was worth. Poor bastard, he was against the war too."

"The *Yamoto* was a ship?"

"Biggest battleship in the world. Probably the biggest that will ever be. Sixty thousand tons, eighteen-inch guns. Pretty useless in a modern war, but awesome like a dinosaur. It also proved that the Japs could build better battlewagons than we could, not that it made any difference so long as we could build more carriers and train more air crews. We put its sister ship under the waves during the battle of the Philippine Sea. I wasn't there. Bill Halsey led us on a wild-goose chase up to the north. We sank four carriers, which were decoys because they didn't have any air crews to man them. Am I boring you with all this history?"

"Certainly not."

"In the last year of the war the Japs turned to suicide raids, kamikazes, or 'Divine Wind,' they called it. They crashed planes into a lot of our ships and we had a hard time figuring out how to stop them. It was hard for us even to understand them. They had lost the war, why kill yourself when it's not going to change anything? But then, why start a war with the United States anyway?

"So someone decided to send the *Yamoto* out on a Divine Wind raid. One morning our scout planes reported that it had sortied out into the Sea of Japan and was coming our way. There were no escorts, no air support because we had wiped all of that out. Just one big old battlewagon taking on the whole American Navy. Our group wasn't close enough to join the shoot-out the first day. But the boys who were put enough bombs and fish into it to stop it dead in the water. They had fired most of their ammunition too. We were supposed to finish it off. Proverbial duck in a shooting gallery."

"Poor men."

"Us or them?"

"Both."

"Yeah, I agree. Well, our task group put five hundred planes into the air—TBFs, F6Fs, SB2Ds—a cloudless run up to the Sea of Japan. My squadron was to fly top cover for the bombers, just in case the Japs found a few aircraft to put up against us. Nothing but a grandstand seat for killing. The CAG's plane experienced some mechanical problems. Then the second in command had to turn back. The word came from the admiral that the senior officer of our air group was to take charge. That would not ordinarily have been me, but the group commander had been grounded the day before with a sore throat. So it was my show."

"You were twenty-two then?" The compassion in her voice made my throat tighten.

"I think the admiral about died when he found out that he had a kid my age as CAG for five hundred planes. He couldn't complain because I didn't make any mistakes. I might just as well have been a quarterback against the Little Sisters of the Poor. Most of my classmates—the ones who were still alive—thought I was a lucky SOB to have the opportunity of a lifetime."

I pulled the car to the side of the road. "Do you mind if I stop until I finish? I can barely see the highway."

"I'd drive if I could."

"Someday soon I'll teach you how. So, I sat up there at ten thousand feet and directed in wave after wave of bombers. The Japs were still firing their eighteen-inch guns from the bow of the ship. It wasn't likely that they would hit anything, but I told the TBF groups to come in from the rear of the ship and then turn at the last minute. It was like gunnery practice. The CIC people claim we put eighteen fish into her. I thought she'd never sink.

"I had plenty of fuel because we were only a hundred miles away. The admiral, still not knowing he had a brat—"

"Spoiled River Forest brat . . ."

Perfect moment for comic relief. I squeezed her hand, which I discovered was holding mine.

"He told me to stay there and direct the next waves which were coming in. Finally—it seemed like it took forever—this big ship, the biggest one I'd ever seen, not counting the *Queen Mary*, started to heel over. Real slowly, the rust-colored underside began to appear. Then the strangest thing happened. . . ."

"Yes . . . ?"

"The crew swarmed up to the decks. They filled every inch topside. I circled down low so I could see what was happening. I told Air Control that I thought they were about to abandon ship. There was nothing much we could do about it. We didn't have any craft in the area. Then I saw that every one of them was wearing dress blue, like they were going to

the annual Christmas ball or whatever they had. I remember
shouting on my radio, 'They're all saluting.'

" 'Saluting?' the guy in Air Control said, like he thought
I'd lost my sanity. 'Who the fuck they saluting?'

" 'God, the emperor, how the fuck should I know?'

"Then the ship turned over and they began to fall off,
little navy dolls falling into the water off a toy ship. Most of
them managed to hang on till it slid under with a big whoosh
of water. I flew over the oil slick, maybe a hundred and fifty
feet over the water.

" 'CAG One to Air Control. CAG One to Air control.' "
I was back above the Sea of Japan, a football field over the
waves. " 'The *Yamoto* has just sunk with all hands. They went
down saluting.'

" 'Repeat, CAG One. Repeat. Do you read me? Please
repeat. Over.'

" 'Roger. This is CAG One. The *Yamoto* has sunk. I see
no survivors. Do you read me? Over.'

" 'Roger, CAG One. We read you. Did you say they went
down saluting? Over.'

" 'The whole crew. Topside. In dress blue. Recommend
recall of all our aircraft.'

"So they recalled all of us. I was the last one to leave, as
a CAG should be. I overflew the oil slick—it was getting bigger
by the minute, a rotten egg spreading on the blue ocean—
several more times. I don't know why. Even if I saw one of
those navy-blue dolls, I couldn't have been any help to him."

"And he wouldn't have wanted help."

"Wouldn't he? Maybe not. Who can say? Anyway, the
admiral shook my hand, took the Navy Cross ribbon off his
own uniform and pinned it on mine, told me I was a fine,
brave young man. I said it was like hunting bison with Buffalo
Bill. His frosty eyes glinted like maybe he understood. He
asked me about the salute and the dress blues. I confirmed it.
'Strangest thing ever,' he said. I agreed. They had pictures from
our observation planes developed in a couple of hours, so they
knew I wasn't around the bend."

The *Yamoto* business was so surrealistic in its horror that I could hardly believe it had actually happened. My voice was dry and cold.

"You stack the deck against yourself." Could she possibly be kissing my fingers? "You know that, don't you? You excuse the Japanese because their culture encourages them to kill prisoners, but you don't excuse yourself when their culture encourages them to think mass suicide is something beautiful."

"It was beautiful, Andrea. That's the weird part of it. It was beautiful. A terrible beauty."

"I think a poet named Yeats wrote that about Ireland. One of their crazy revolutions. But don't you see, you're tormenting yourself for other people's decisions?"

"That's what my head tells me. That's what the chaplain on the *Big E* told me. He said maybe I was too sensitive to be an air-crew commander. I don't think he understood me. I was a good commander. Do you know what I mean?"

"Yes, I think so, poor dear man."

"What? I'm not sure myself."

Now I was kissing her hand. The desert oven in which we both were steaming was becoming hotter. The sun devils were spinning all around us. There was no sound but that of our voices. I had the feeling, to be repeated many times in the next two days, that we were the only humans left in the world. The surrealism of the Sea of Japan merged with the surrealism of the Sonora Desert.

"You love people so much you don't want to see them hurt, even when they're hurting themselves. You want to stop all the hurts. You're not strong enough to do that, though you are strong. And sweet besides"—she patted my cheek—"and you're angry at God because He is strong enough and He doesn't stop the hurt."

I watched a sun devil leap up on the other side of the road. It might take a lifetime to ponder the wisdom in those sentences. The wisdom and the devastating criticism.

"That's an A plus."

"And you haven't figured out that it must hurt God even more than it hurts you."

"Where did you get that theology?"

"I don't know." She laughed lightly. "I just thought it up, but it seems reasonable, doesn't it?"

"Are you willing to apply it to yourself?"

She frowned. "I don't want to, but unless I'm a hypocrite I'll have to, won't I?"

I released her hand and started the car, now entirely drained.

"You're a good listener, Andrea King, a great listener."

"You've only made a beginning, Jerry Keenan."

"Grade on my beginning, please."

"Serious response, for a change. B plus."

"I'll take it."

We both laughed uneasily and I pushed my patient Roxy back on Arizona 77.

With the impressive wisdom of hindsight, I see now that the two of us were basket cases. Vulnerable, sensitive kids whom chance and circumstance had pushed to the breaking point and a little bit beyond.

It was not merely that we felt love, love driven by the fierce engine of sexual attraction. Not merely that we were obsessed with one another, although we surely were obsessed that morning long ago in the Sonora Desert. We both had been seized by titanic compulsions that, even if they were mostly within us, had become imprinted on the wild, barren, deadly environment around us.

We'd known each other for a day, an intense, roller-coaster day. But we'd linked our psyches with potent forces that were independent and automatic—energies, currents, chemistries. I was an open book to her. Her moods caused instant resonance in me.

The desert depressed and frightened my pretty, and now suitably attired, waif. She hardly listened to my lectures, but rather sat, schoolgirl-straight, next to me and tried to be polite while her daydreams wandered thousands of miles away.

But in the mountains she twisted in every direction to marvel at the spiral peaks, the occasional Mormon irrigated farm ("like a beautiful green carpet"), and the indifferent cattle grazing near a wash that provided enough moisture for grass and a stand of cottonwood or oak. ("Aren't they cute?")

I played the tour-guide role, explaining the formation of the mountains, the history of the Mormons, the reasons that the desert and the grass country often existed side by side, the terrible conflicts between the Wobblies (Industrial Workers of the World) and the copper-mining companies.

"You know everything." It was a statement of fact, neither criticism nor compliment.

"You know more about literature and music."

"Much good that does."

Then in the hills between Oracle and Mammoth, beyond the San Manuel Mine, Roxy became contentious. First she sputtered and coughed, then she heaved and wheezed, next she kind of buckled and slowed down. Finally she quit completely.

"Roxinante stopped."

"No kidding."

"She's tired. Not enough sleep last night. Too many dreams."

"You think it's funny?"

"No, Commander, it's not funny. But you are. Wonderful, but still funny."

"Do you want to roast inside," I said as I opened the door and climbed into the furnace, "or bake outside?"

"I think I'll stretch my pretty legs while you're playing with Roxy."

"Pretty?"

"I anticipate your flattery."

She kissed me.

"Is that a reward for losing our mount here in the desert hills?"

"A reward for being you. Now fix the car, please. And let the Grand Duchess know when you're done."

"Why don't you take your Russian buddy and the blanket in the backseat and go sit under one of the oak trees over by that wash."

"That what?"

"Wash."

"You talk funny. It's a wash, not a 'warsh'."

"You'll have to get used to the way we Chicagoans talk." I propped up Roxy's hood. "Now get out of my hair."

She climbed into the backseat, unstrapped her suitcase, added the packages from Steinfeld's to its neatly organized piles, removed her novel, and reached for the blanket.

"Be careful of the wine bottle."

She already had it in her hand. "Wine for lunch?"

"And thou under the bough."

She sniffed disdainfully as a Grand Duchess should and strolled down to the stand of oak trees. Meanwhile I turned my attention to Roxy.

There was a time, children, when cars did not have automatic chokes. The manual choke was not merely an aberration of the early VWs. Roxy's problems seemed to involve her choke. I would wait till I was sure the carburetor was no longer flooded, open the choke, step on the pedal, close the choke quickly, pump the pedal again, and pray that my mount would cooperate. She would sputter into life, hesitate as though considering the possibilities, and then die.

I worked on her for at least an hour and abused her with the best navy swear words I knew. All wasted.

And not a single car came from either direction. I might be marooned permanently in the steaming desert with two box lunches, a jug of wine, and a ghost girl under the bough.

Why did I think "ghost girl"?

She was sweet and appealing and lovable, but still uncanny, still not quite a creature of my world.

At that point even, halfway through a fateful day, I had some grip on my sanity.

Then she scared the living daylights out of me.

"Can't start the car?"

I didn't turn around. "Brilliant observation. Go back to your Russian."

"I fell asleep."

I looked up at her. The bookmark was halfway through *Crime and Punishment*. She read quickly. "Did you sleep at all last night?"

"Not much. Same for you?"

I nodded. "Bad influence on each other."

"Maybe . . . Do you know that you look funny with grease on your face?"

Wrench in hand, I advanced on her. "You're risking your life, woman."

"Get away." She backed off, taunting me. "I don't want any grease on my expensive new clothes. I'll have to pay enough for them."

"This car is not a laughing matter."

She ducked around my make-believe swing and peered into the Chevy's innards. "Mysterious."

"Not if you know anything about cars. Do you?"

"Certainly not. But it's that funny little black part that isn't working."

"What funny little black part?" I bent over next to her, my "uncanny" gauge shooting up.

"That one there. It needs cleaning." ·

"The distributor."

"I don't know what silly name you call it. But it does need cleaning."

I removed the distributor cap and, sure enough, it did need cleaning. My fingers trembling, I scrubbed it out with an old rag. "I'll probably have to buy a new filter when we get to Superior."

"Long way to Phoenix."

"In a hurry?"

"No, but I might fire the tour guide and mechanic for inefficiency."

I mounted the driver's seat of Roxy, went through the starting ritual, and—naturally—she started promptly and complacently.

"See. It was that funny little black part."

"Get in the car."

She deposited the blanket and her book in the backseat and climbed in next to me.

"Aren't we going on?"

"How did you know it was the funny little black part? And I'm serious; none of this 'I'm-a-good-guesser' stuff."

"Don't be angry at me," she pleaded.

"Did you know when we stopped?"

"I was afraid if I told you, you'd be mad. And I was right. When I did tell you, you were mad."

"You let me work for an hour?" I was fuming. Pretty rear end in tight-fitting blue slacks or not, she was an infuriating—and scary—wench.

"I don't know how I know." She was close to tears for the second time in this crazy day. "I just know, that's all. Please don't be angry at me. Don't be like the others."

"Did your uncle beat you?" I had made a quick guess.

"He thought I was a witch. I don't know"—tears appeared on her smooth skin—"maybe I am."

"A good witch."

"No, if I'm a witch, I'm a bad witch."

I eased Roxy back on the road. "I'm impressed, not angry."

"You're a good guesser too. About my uncle, I mean. . . ."

So indeed I was. Instincts, my group commander had once remarked. Sound instincts.

"I'll make a deal with you, lovely Witch of the East. I promise that I won't ever, for the rest of our lives, be angry at you like the others, and I'll never, never hit you. Never, never, never. You, on the other hand, promise that you will never, never withhold information from your guesses about mechanical malfunctions of this or any other automobile. Deal?"

"Deal." She shook my hand and dried her tears.

"Fine." I relaxed.

Only for a few seconds.

"Well." I heard a sharp intake of breath. "If I'm going to hold up my end of the deal, I think I better tell you that I guess all day long we will have a lot of trouble with that silly little part. You'll probably have to buy a new one."

"Where am I going to do that?" I demanded irritably.

"That's not part of the deal."

Deal or no deal, desert furnace or no desert furnace, I felt a cold chill creep up my back.

A witch at least.

CHAPTER 9

"DOES WINE SPOIL IN HEAT?"

We were slipping down into a valley from which we would soon ascend again into the Dripping Spring Mountains, a drive which the guidebook promised would be spectacular. With a problematic distributor, that prospect lost much of its appeal. On the other hand, Roxy was purring along smoothly. Maybe my resident witch was not right a hundred percent of the time.

"After several days. Why, are you thirsty?"

"And hungry."

"You ate two breakfasts."

"I know." She sounded sheepish.

"Was last night the first time you drank wine?"

"Was it that obvious?"

"You seemed to enjoy it."

"On my way to being a wino. Can we stop for lunch, please?"

"Sure, this is a town called Winkelman, a Mormon place, they're really good at bringing life out of the desert. Whenever you see an irrigation setup like those fields over there, you can be pretty sure that it's their work. The Mormons, you know, were founded by Joseph Smith—"

"Lunch now. Tour lecture later."

"All right!"

We found an oak tree near a large cotton field, spread our blanket and watched a bearded farmer drive a tilling machine as we disposed of our picnic. She ate both of her sandwiches and one of mine and my banana as well as her banana and orange. And all of our cookies. It was hard to measure our relative consumption of the Cabernet because we passed the bottle back and forth, but I'm sure she drank more than I did.

Ghosts don't have that kind of appetite.

"Lemonade?"

"Thank you, Andrea King. You're a useful little servant girl, all things considered. Once you learn proper manners."

"Huh. Do you realize you've been yawning all during lunch?"

"So have you."

"But I don't have to drive in the mountains."

Maybe, I thought, too late, I should have gone easy on the wine.

"I never had an accident in four years of carrier flying—except that one day on Lake Michigan."

"And you drank a half bottle of wine before each flight."

"Less than half."

"Regardless. And it wasn't the *Yamoto* that kept you awake last night, was it? That was terrible, but something else was more terrible."

"My dreams are not part of our deal." I stood up, brushed the crumbs off my trousers and stared up at the mountains. "They're none of your business."

"I never said they were."

I sat down again and picked up her inert hand.

"You want to know everything about me, don't you, Andrea King?"

"Only if it will help." She watched me solemnly, an acolyte trying to guess what the Monsignor would do next.

I hesitated, fully aware that I had sworn the day before never to tell her. I was trapped, however, in the pathos of her concern for me. It would not hurt to talk about Rusty and Hank, Tony and Marshal. I knew that I would have to start to talk about them someday.

"I was given my own squadron in December of 1944, VF29, fifteen planes, twenty pilots. Remember that the war was almost over, the Japanese didn't have any air crews or carriers left and only a few land-based planes. There were big battles for Okinawa Jima, and kamikaze attacks, but nothing like what had happened before. I suppose I should have expected I'd have trouble with casualties. I knew how hard I was hit by the death of buddies; if I'd had any sense I would have known that the death of my own men, men for whom I was responsible, would be much rougher. They offered me a desk job in Pearl, which I suppose I should have taken."

Her dagger eyes probed at the core of my soul, gently, kindly, and with reassuring concern.

"Ten of those men are dead, Andrea. Two in accidental crashes, one in an auto collision in Japan after the war, another disappeared in a storm, two of them were shot down by our own antiaircraft fire—trigger-happy idiots mistaking them for kamikazes."

She wrapped both her hands around one of mine. "You don't have to . . ."

"The other four I killed. Rusty, Tony, and I were strafing a Japanese position on Okinawa—marine work but there were not enough marine pilots. I directed them to follow on my left as I led the way down to the deck. It could just as well have been on the right. But I was the boss and I made the decisions. I chose them for the run—no particular reason other than that they were the best flyers in the squadron. We knew that it was a little risky. The Japs were sending up some pretty heavy automatic-weapon fire from the ground. But I was the CO, they trusted me; if I gave the order they obeyed, and that was that."

"You went first."

"Sure, I went first, giving the Jap gunners a chance to get ready."

"You thought of that?"

"No, but I should have. Anyway, I didn't see it because I was ahead of them. I heard an explosion as I pulled up from my run, looked behind me and saw nothing but a cloud of smoke and a fire on the ground. I later found out that Tony took some ordnance in his engine, lucky hit, I suppose; he veered to the right and crashed into Rusty, who was behind him. In a couple of seconds they both had been blown into little pieces." I felt the sting of tears in my eyes, but expelled them as unwanted intruders. "Two kids, both just twenty, Rusty with a wife and a little boy he'd never seen, dead because of my incompetence."

She continued to explore my soul with her devastating eyes.

"You think I'm too hard on myself?"

"Of course, but what I think doesn't matter."

"Another day we were flying cover on a run up to Osaka. A couple of Zeros—they had only a handful left—got behind Hank and me. I told him to dive and I began to climb. The Japs usually left the wing man alone, especially on a dive because the F6Fs were faster on a dive and the Zeros climbed quicker than we did. So they went after him instead and splashed him. I went down to see if there was a life raft and another Zero appeared behind me; Marshal dove after him to give me support. I evaded the Jap easily, probably a poor kid without any flight training, and Marshal never came out of his dive. He plunged into the ocean like a falling rock. Hydraulic failure, probably. They both were married, too."

In the distance, somewhere in the thick haze of humidity, the Mormon farmer's tractor motor was clunking away. A sound not like an F6F warming up. "Pilots, man your planes." A few lazy flies made desultory passes around my head, no kamikazes they. In addition to Andrea's sweet fragrance—she must have purchased perfume, which was not strictly within my rubrics—I smelled not high-octane aviation fuel but new-mown hay: a prudent Mormon preparing for winter.

"Each of those ten men had more reason to live than I did. If I had made different decisions, they would be alive still."

She moved my fingers up and down, as if experimenting with them to make sure they were still working. "Maybe you should have been the priest in the family."

"Instead of Packy? Funny, but I thought about it for a couple of years. The family expected me to join the firm, just as Dad did when he came home from the last war. Packy is certainly more at ease with girls than I am. . . ."

"I don't believe it." Her brilliant smile tore at my thumping heart. Did she love me? I wondered. Foolishly, so foolishly.

"They all trusted me, Andrea. I let them down. Why am I still alive?"

"Perhaps to do some great things that the rest of us desperately need."

"That's not very likely. In a well-run universe, I would be the one whose body is rotting at the bottom of the Sea of Japan."

"Who would be driving me to Phoenix?"

"You're not going to argue with me?'

"About God, sure; not about your men. You know all the arguments. I can't possibly know your feelings. I do respect them and love you."

She did say it. And I let it slip by.

Why?

Isn't it obvious? I was afraid of her. She knew too much. She was too much.

I rose from the blanket, my heart throbbing, my eyes watery, my legs weak. "Thanks for listening."

"I wish I could make the pain go away. Time . . ."

"I know. I just have to live with it."

"I wasn't going to say that."

But I did not want to talk anymore. We gathered up the remnants of our lunch and, like good environmentalists long before our time, packed them neatly in the boxes provided by the Arizona Inn.

"On to Globe," she said, trying to sound cheerful.

"Roxy willing, on to Globe."

Outside of Winkelman the road rises quickly on the way to Hayden and the Ray Mine.

"Who are you really, Andrea King?" I asked once I had regained some of my composure.

"What do you mean?" She stirred uneasily next to me.

"Sometimes you're a child, occasionally an imp child, yet other times you're a grand duchess; you have been known to be a raging fury. . . ."

"Threatened with dire punishment."

"That's the imp. . . . Then you're in rapid disorder a mind reader, a haunt, a chaplain, a mother, a sister, a daughter, a lover with wonderfully inviting lips, a wise old woman again, and now one who heals pain. . . . You delight me, confuse me, intrigue me, scare me. Who are you? What are you? Why are you?"

Rather heavy-handed and roundabout for a response to a declaration of love, don't you think?

"I can't answer any of those questions, Jerry; sometimes I think that I don't really exist at all, that maybe I'm a creature in someone else's dream. Your dreams maybe? Or in God's dreams? Perhaps we're both characters in a story someone else is telling or figures in some lesser God's dreams. The Indians, I mean the ones in India, think we are all products of the dreams of the gods. I don't think that is so unreasonable, not for me, anyway."

"Huh?" I had no idea what to say in response to that outburst.

"Since my husband died and my daughter, I'm often not sure whether I'm still alive. My existence is so . . . so transparent, like it really isn't there at all. Do you understand?" She didn't give me time to answer, but raced on, as though determined to reach the finish line of improbabilities. "For days I live a kind of shadow existence, then, when I come out of the mists, I'm often not sure who I am or where I am. I wonder if I'm really alive at all and whether other people can see me. Yesterday in the station in Tucson I wondered whether the waitress saw me. At first I thought I might not be there at all. Then I saw this big, handsome, officer-type person across from me and said to myself that I must be invisible to him too. Only I wasn't. So as long as he sees me, I'm alive, suspended between earth and hell."

"I still think you're an imp/grand duchess with wonderful lips."

"Silly," she said as she laughed and poked at my ribs, notably impeding my cautious assent up the Dripping Springs Mountains.

I've learned enough psychology in the days since July 1946 to know that such dissociation from self is the first step to a severe psychotic interlude. Even then, psychological naif that I was, I knew that there was something pretty crazy about what she was saying.

Or pretty scary.

Yet I was not prepared to take what she was saying as literally true.

She gave me fair warning.

"The kissing is so good that I think I might keep you alive for a long time."

"I thought you'd finished that last night." We were both laughing happily—young lovers at play.

"Just beginning."

As I urged Roxinante up the Dripping Springs Mountains, with the dried-up Gila River, looking like the biggest wash in all the world, beneath us on the left, I thought that so far today could easily be a day in one of my dreams, a continuation of last night's terrors.

Roxy expired twice more on the way to Superior and a blessed paved road. The second time I had to clean out the distributor on a hairpin turn at least a thousand feet above a canyon. If a car had come from the other direction, I might have gone over the side in panic.

"Do you want me to do it?" my dream woman asked helpfully.

"Stay in the car and shut up," I snarled.

"Yes, sir, Commander, sir."

At the lookout point above the vast Ray Mine between Hayden and Superior, we stared in silence at the rusty, tarnished, man-made grand canyon, stretching for miles in either direction.

I managed to take some reasonably good pictures of the Ray Mine. It was mostly luck; the sun was behind my left shoulder at just the right angle to bathe the terraced soft-brown hills in golden light. Only one picture didn't turn out: a shot of Andrea on the farthest reach of the lookout point, her hair a glowing ruby against the blue sky and copper hills. The slide came back a clear transparency, as though nothing had recorded on the film.

"Do you like it?" I asked after I surreptitiously snapped the picture.

"Strange but beautiful," she said, not having heard the loud click of the shutter release on my Kodak. "And scary too."

Still a child on a tour, curiosity and wonder not yet dead.

I put my arm around her and led her unprotestingly back to the car.

"People died here." She shuddered.

"It has always been violent in copper mining. Do you know the song about Joe Hill? His real name was Joe Hilstrom; he was a Swedish immigrant and he was shot for attempting to organize a union. What we now consider a fundamental human right, despite Senator Taft."

"I don't think I ever heard it. My uncle is against the unions. So was And—my husband. And the nuns at school."

So in my best whisky baritone, I sang,

I dreamed I saw Joe Hill last night, alive as you or me.
Says I, "But Joe, you're ten years dead."
"I never died," said he.

"The copper bosses killed you, Joe, they shot you, Joe," says I.
"Takes more than guns to kill a man," says Joe, "I didn't
*   die,"*
Says Joe, "I didn't die."

And standing there as big as life and smiling with his eyes.

Says Joe, "What they can never kill went on to organize,
Went on to organize."

From San Diego up to Maine, in every mine and mill
Where working men defend their rights, it's there you'll find
  Joe Hill.
It's there you'll find Joe Hill.

To tell the truth, I didn't sound much like Paul Robeson.

"That's a powerful song." She was still sagging against my shoulder. "And you sing it very well. . . . Are you in favor of the unions?"

"I sure am. So is the Church. Some of my father's clients are unions. You may as well know the awful truth, Andrea King; we may live in River Forest and we may sail on the *Queen Mary*, but we Keenans are Roosevelt Democrats."

"Really?" She seemed surprised, but hardly concerned.

"It's hard to know the history of copper mining and not be. Before the war, the copper companies used to load striking workers into boxcars and, helped by the National Guard bayonets and with the approval of the Republican governor, tow the cars far out into the desert. Then they would throw the workers off and maroon them in the desert. A thirty mile walk through the desert without any water cured the survivors of unionism pretty effectively. The unions haven't won yet. The Mine, Mill and Smelter Union is Communist. I can't blame them for being radical. . . ."

"Hold me, please," she said, pressing against me, trembling violently.

Normally I would have relished the opportunity to embrace again this attractive young woman. But there was too much terror in that slim frame for me to permit any erotic feelings. Anyway, I reassured myself, the heat and the trance we're both in has pretty well stifled sex.

"What should I do?"

"Get me out of here. Quickly."

So I led her to the car, closed the door after she had collapsed into the passenger's seat, and sauntered confidently around to the driver's seat.

Inside the car, the pathos of her fragility changed my perspective completely. I still loved her. I still wanted her.

"Do you know what, Andrea King?"

"You're not finished kissing me?" Her smile was wan, but still sufficient to drag a temporary curtain across the blazing sun.

"You got it."

I tried to be even more tender and soothing than I'd been the night before. She responded with a total gift of her self. Kiss me as long as you want, her meek surrender said, anyway you want. I belong to you.

It was frightening, but I enjoyed what I was doing too much to notice my fears.

I eased her back against the car seat, leaned over her like, I hope, a good genie, unbuttoned her blouse, moved it off her upper arms, and kissed and caressed her shoulders, her chest, her belly, her breasts. I salved what little conscience my hormones left me by leaving her bra undisturbed. Also, although it was a much lighter and less complicated variety than the one with which I had briefly dealt the day before, I still was not sure that I could sort out its mysteries.

At last she sighed deeply and eased me away.

She sat up, shook her hair back into place and stretched sensuously, her blouse still hanging on her arms.

"You're trustworthy, Commander," she laughed enthusiastically. "Barely trustworthy."

I almost told her I loved her. Instead I said, "You're the most perfect woman I've ever met."

"You *are* wonderful, Jeremiah Thomas Keenan, even when you're fibbing."

"Do you expect to arrive at the Arizona Biltmore tonight sound of life and limb, young woman?"

"Well." She stretched again. "Roxy may have trouble with that stupid distribution thing, but we're almost over the mountains, aren't we?"

"If you plan to survive, you'd better button up your blouse. Otherwise I won't be able to keep my eyes on the road."

"No." She twisted giddily away from me. "I like me this way."

"So do I." I pinned her with one arm and set about the task of rearranging her blouse with the other. "But not a thousand feet above a canyon floor."

She resisted my efforts just enough to make the task enchantingly difficult.

"Finished? Am I properly modest?" She sighed. "Now, if you don't mind, I think I'll curl up and take a nice little nap so I'll be prepared for whatever wonderful wine you're going to weaken my virtue with at supper tonight. Don't drive off the side of any mountains while I'm asleep."

"Pleasant dreams."

But she was already asleep.

I was too happy with my performance to pay any attention to the questions of my intelligence officer—like how had she known that my middle name was Thomas?

Roxy conked out at the worst hairpin curve, as I thought then, in all the world. Carefully I climbed out, clung to the hood as I eased around to the front and pried it open.

"Don't fall," she murmured in her sleep, and twisted for a more comfortable position.

"Shut up," I said as I polished the silly little cap thing.

While I made plans for what I was now convinced would be our long life together, we chugged up the mountains, across the sweeping curves and down toward Superior, driving slowly not only because of the dirt road, but because, inexperienced mountain driver that I was, I was scared stiff of the steep canyons that yawned only a few feet off the road.

Roxy limped wearily into Superior, a town two-thirds of the way down Queen Creek Canyon from Phoenix to Globe on US 80. The copper area on the upper end of the canyon, I announced to my sleeping beauty—Superior, Miami, Globe—had produced more wealth than all the gold and silver mines in the state. It was twenty miles to Globe and forty miles to Phoenix on 80, either way on paved road. If I drove around the back of the Superstition chain, it was eighty-one miles, half of it on a dirt road that skirted the mountain wall—not something to try at dusk, especially since I was still far more frightened of such roads than I had ever been of Zeros.

Why not drive her up to Phoenix, turn Andrea over to the Arizona Biltmore, stay the night there myself perhaps, and then continue on my tour? Once I was settled back home, I could cart her back to Chicago, if not for the Harvest Festival at Butterfield, then at least for the Christmas Ball.

It all seemed perfectly reasonable.

"Were you afraid you'd have to make love to that dreadful woman if you didn't get rid of her?" my wife asked me when I told her about my thoughts on this part of the trip many years later.

"Yes, though I wouldn't have admitted it quite that bluntly then."

"Why were you afraid?"

"Because I knew she'd be good and I wasn't sure whether I would be."

"Reasonable grounds for fear," my wife admitted.

Roxy settled the issue for us. She died, quite definitively, in the service station into which I'd driven at the corner of 177 and 80. Superior, at that time mostly a depressing collection of wood and corrugated-iron shanties clinging to the side of the hills, was evidence, if I needed any, of the failure of the copper-mining companies to share much of their wealth with the miners. Small wonder that communism was strong in Superior, Arizona.

The rawboned youth who was working the gas pumps ambled over to my car. "Sounds like you have some trouble."

"Distributor, among other things."

"You come over the mountains in this?" He poked around under the hood.

"From Tucson."

"Land sakes. . . . Little lady sound asleep, is she?"

"Marvelous sleeper."

"Pretty, too."

He then noticed my "Naval Air Station" parking sticker. "Fly-boy?"

"*Enterprise.*"

"Land sakes. I was in subs myself."

"A lot worse."

"You know it. Ensign?"

"Thanks for the compliment. Two-and-a-half striper."

"Land sakes, you must have done some damn-fool things."

"Nothing like going down in one of those sardine cans."

He leaned back on his heels and rocked with laughter.

"On your honeymoon?"

"What do you think?" I tried to grin like a brand-new husband.

"Can't beat it for fun." He laughed with me.

An iron law I have propounded to my children whenever the occasion permits is that if you find a potential mechanic who is sympathetically disposed in some wilderness or quasi-wilderness area, you do all you can to maintain that sympathy, even to the extent of modifying the truth a bit.

"Tell you what, Commander. . . ." He cocked his head. "You heading for Phoenix?"

"I thought we might."

He shook his head sadly. "You'll never make it tonight. Needs a heap of work. Can you stay around till tomorrow afternoon?"

I felt my stomach tighten, for reasons I did not want to ask.

"If we have to."

"You'll never make it in this heap tonight. You don't want to break down on the road at night, not with that pretty little lady in the car with you. Tell you what: There's a hotel down the road a half-mile. Picketpost House, after the mountain. Right above the arboretum. Good food. No fancy air-conditioning. But big windows and powerful fans, and it cools off here at night anyway. Thirty-five hundred feet above sea level. You leave the car here. I'll drive you up there and have the car ready by five-thirty tomorrow afternoon. You can get a good night's sleep and maybe look at the arboretum in the morning. Fair enough?"

"Carry on, Chief." I grinned and stuck out my hand, guessing at his rank.

"Yes, *sir*."

We shifted the baggage, including my mumbling sleeping beauty, to his pickup, which had probably been old in 1935, and rode up to Picketpost House, an appealing-looking inn on the edge of a cliff. High-arched windows and long balconies suggested that it had once been a home for a very baronial copper baron.

They were only operating a few rooms, the handsome middle-aged woman at the desk told me, since it was summer. But there was a honeymoon suite on the top floor, with big windows and a balcony. I gulped and registered Mr. and Mrs. Keenan. The distaff side of this hastily assembled team was drooping over her suitcase, looking much like a two-year-old who had been unceremoniously awakened from a nap.

"She's a lovely little thing, Commander." The woman had been filled in on my record by my admiring CPO from the service station. "You're a lucky man."

"Don't I know it."

We were conducted to our suite—two vast rooms with Western-style furniture, probably authentic, and Navaho blankets, certainly authentic, on the walls. My "bride" slumped into a deep chair and curled up, fully prepared to go back to sleep.

"Tell me again."

"We are in a suite in a hotel called the Picketpost House, after the mountain behind us. Roxy will be out of action till tomorrow. We'll have to stay here tonight. You take the bedroom. I'll sleep here in the parlor. I realize this is a cliché from any number of romantic comedies, but . . . ."

"For heaven's sake, Jerry. I told you that you were trustworthy."

"Barely."

"I'll settle for that. Now let me go back to sleep."

"You take the first shower."

"Don't order me around, Commander." She snuggled more deeply into the chair.

"Then we'll eat supper."

"Why didn't you say so in the first place." She bounded out of the chair. "Oh, what a lovely place. Where's the shower? What kind of a suite is this?"

"They call it the honeymoon suite."

As she sauntered into the bath that connected the two rooms, she laughed as if she thought that was hilariously funny.

Like Queen Victoria, I was not amused.

CHAPTER

SHE WORE A LOOSELY FITTING PRINT SUNDRESS, WITH THIN straps, mostly blue in color, at dinner. It was appropriate garb for the high-ceilinged dining room with a light breeze that was whipped into a pleasant minor tornado by the giant fans above us. She seemed to have recovered all of her vitality.

"You're staring at me, Commander."

"Yes, ma'am. I've been staring since the railroad station in Tucson. Women are meant to be stared at by men. Especially when they are as pretty as you are."

"I don't object, exactly, but people will think . . ."

"That we're on a honeymoon. They think that already. That's why we're in the bridal suite. I wish I were that lucky."

Darker flush.

"I'm sure no one thinks that."

"Want to bet?"

"How long did I sleep?" She changed the subject, ignoring what was, for all practical purposes, a proposal. It was a light-hearted one indeed, and I would have been scared stiff if she had responded positively to it. "What did I miss?"

"I think you were asleep for more than an hour and probably because you consumed more of that Cabernet than I did, just as you are well on your way to drinking more than your half of this Medoc. And I don't think it's crazy to imagine you as my wife."

"It is, Jerry." She was instantly serious. "It really is, but it's nice of you to pretend that it isn't. Did I dream that you kissed me up there by some horrible copper mine?"

"Do I strike you as the kind of pilot who would run a risk like that on a dangerous mission through those mountains?"

"Certainly not."

"So it must have been a dream. Was it a nice one?"

"Very," she said as she flushed brightly, "but you shouldn't pry into my dreams."

"I won't."

She considered me thoughtfully. "Are you telling me the truth?"

"About what?"

"About my dream?"

"No."

"You *did* kiss me." She clutched her throat.

"Repeatedly and avariciously. You enjoyed it. Not as much as you seem to be enjoying that steak."

Absently she played with a large bit of meat, already impaled on her fast-working fork.

"I was drunk."

"There was a taste of the creature on your breath. You smelled nice, however. Must have been the perfume you bought at Steinfeld's."

She put down the fork, closed her eyes, and turned purple. "Why did you let me drink so much?"

"I think it was as much horror at the stories I told you about the copper mines. I wouldn't have kissed you unless I thought you wanted me to."

"I'm sure"—her eyes opened—"I wanted you to. I don't want to be shameless. I'm really not."

"You really weren't."

"Sure? I don't always trust myself."

I finally realized that this was not a joke. "Andrea King," I said as I touched her fingertips, "stop worrying. You were both very generous and very modest. Now eat your steak before it gets cold and drink your wine and remember your pleasant dream with a clear conscience."

She picked up her fork. "Do you feel sometimes that these last two days have all been a dream—that the dreamworld and the other world . . . I mean . . ."

"That maybe the boundaries have slipped somewhere? You raised that question in the mountains too. Maybe, as far as I'm concerned, it has been a wonderful dream."

"So far." She was suddenly terrified. "Please, don't let it become a nightmare."

"It won't." I touched her fingertips. "Don't worry." Then stupidly I added, "I'll probably be able to get you to Phoenix tomorrow afternoon. It's only forty miles from here."

"But what about your Superstitious Mountains?"

"Superstition. I'll do that by myself."

"No, you won't." She waved her fork imperiously. "I thought I made that clear."

"Yes, ma'am."

"Carry on, Commander. . . . Now . . ." She paused as she wolfed in a large bite of steak and washed it down with a big gulp of Medoc. "Uhm . . . good . . . what was I saying? Oh, yes, when I was drunk on your wine up there and scared by your stories, did I persuade you to believe in God?"

"Not really."

"Not even when I was kissing you?"

"Mostly I was kissing you. . . ." I hesitated. An interesting answer was forming on my lips. I would not speak it.

"And if heaven will be like that"—I did say it—"I might sign on."

She didn't laugh. Rather, tears welled up in her vast blue eyes.

"That's very sweet, Jerry. Heaven should be much better."

Heaven—my lips against her lips, her throat, her breasts,

her belly for all eternity. An Islamic paradise, but none of your houris would be as contentious and combative as my Andrea. An interesting possibility.

A God who would be responsible for that sort of happiness—including especially a challenging and combative foil with whom both to love and fight—might be a God who, as my brother Packy says, would wipe away all our tears.

"Suddenly very quiet? Have I made progress in my debate with you?"

"Maybe a little. I was thinking about my lips against your breasts for all eternity."

She flushed again. "It would soon be a bore. . . . I didn't take off my new bra, did I?" Her hand fluttered protectively at her breasts.

"Nope. Not that I would have minded."

"Let's change the subject. I'm confused."

"So am I." My face felt as red as hers looked. "Let me tell you more about how they mine copper. Did you notice the tall smokestacks and the dirty ponds around all the mines? That's because they do the smelting right here. It's a lot easier to ship copper after it's been through the smelter."

"Can I have ice cream *and* that nice cognac drink?"

"As much as you want. We can sleep late tomorrow morning."

Do I have to say I was dizzy with affection and desire? But resolute in my intentions. CAG One does not falter. A Scout is trustworthy. Was that part of my Scout oath? I can't quite remember. I don't know whether I remembered then either.

I arranged to have the coffee, iced tea, and a bottle of Courvoisier delivered to our balcony. Pleasantly warm now, we watched the moon come up and once again bathe the desert mountains, more rugged here than in Tucson, in white forgiveness. For a few precious moments we were enveloped in the peace of the moon-washed peaks.

"This isn't the same as last night." She sniffed at her brandy goblet.

"That was Napoleon we had at the Arizona Inn. We're

lucky to get Courvoisier up here. It's high quality, or I would not dare offer it to you."

"I wasn't complaining. . . ." She stood up and walked to the rail of the balcony and gazed at the serried rows of mountains all around us, like giant protective picket fences. "It's all so lovely."

"It sure is."

"This really isn't the honeymoon suite?"

"All we could get, honest."

"My real honeymoon was in a bus riding from . . . from the East to San Diego."

What do you say to that?

She stepped back to her chair. "Poor boy. He meant no harm. He was smart but he wasn't too quick. I don't think he ever quite figured out what happened. A few drinks, some not very satisfying sex, and a few months later his whole life changed."

"For the better, I should think."

"Oh, no." She slipped gracefully back into her chair. "He didn't think so. He did his duty, however." Her voice trailed off. "We were happy for a few months, very happy. I think . . . it might have been all right if . . ."

"Any man who would not be happy with you," I said thickly, "would have been less than human."

"I tried hard, very hard, to make up to him for all the humiliation. He tried hard, too. It was just . . ." Again her voice faded on the night air.

She was being remarkably objective about her late husband, I thought. Almost clinically detached.

"He was a good boy, really, a nice, quiet, ambitious young man. I know you think he wanted only to go back to camp and tell the others he wasn't a virgin anymore."

"Kids that haven't had any sex are a target for crude humor in the barracks." I thought about my own case. No one had ever guessed the truth about me. "Unless they're sophisticated enough to fake it."

"But you're not being fair to him." Her voice was rising. "He wouldn't have . . . unless he thought I wanted . . ."

"Sure, you wanted affection, Andrea, we all do."

"The night's so beautiful that you won't even argue with me . . . Yes, I wanted affection desperately. That doesn't justify . . ."

"This God you want me to believe in, does He demand justification for everything?"

"If I had been a little stronger that night"—her voice was bitter—"he would still be alive, with all his life ahead of him."

"How do you figure that?" I demanded. "How were you responsible for him being on the *Indianapolis?* You're worse than I am."

"But I—" She stopped short, a revelation cut off. A damning revelation?

She swallowed a big gulp of cognac. "I could become an alcoholic very easily."

"I don't think so."

"Not with this stuff, it's too expensive. Cheap wine, maybe."

"Your tastes are too good for cheap wine."

She stumbled from her chair again.

"You think I'm dramatizing myself again?"

"Now you are *not* reading my mind!"

"I think I'd better go to bed now." She yawned. "You made me drink too much and now you're confusing me." She walked toward the French door and the balcony. "It's pretty out here, like the whole sky is on fire with love."

"Be sure you shake out your shoes in the morning. Scorpions can get in them at night. I don't want to have to bring you to a hospital on the way to Phoenix."

"Scorpions!"

"Little brown bugs with claws and poisonous stings in their tail. The venom won't kill you, but it will make you real sick."

"I don't care." She swayed at the French door. "Good night, Commander."

She strolled uncertainly toward the bathroom.

Now what was all that about? I wondered as I pondered

the silence of the desert night. There's a lot she isn't telling me.

I should phone home and do my journal. And get some sleep. I was drowsy, it had been a long day—heat, high emotions, a hard drive, too much to drink. And I didn't have a nap either.

Well, at least the sexual challenge had been surmounted. No lovemaking tonight.

Wearily I walked into the parlor and asked the hotel operator to put through a call to Chicago.

Only Packy was at home.

"Mom said you were going to bring a gorgeous babe home from Arizona for the Harvest Festival," he began with characteristic verve. "That I gotta see."

"What she probably said was that if I found one, I would try to bring her home."

"Yeah. Probably. I like my version better. Well?"

"Well what?"

"Have you found one?"

"How can you be a seminarian and have women on your mind so much?"

"That has nothing to do with it. So you have found her?"

"Why should I bother looking? Mother and Joanne have a whole list of names prepared for me."

"All with down payments made on furniture. That what you want?"

"You know better than that."

"This dream woman a blonde?"

"Redhead. Dark red, like a crisp halo."

"No kidding . . . am I gonna meet her?"

"It doesn't have any future, Packy."

"That's what they all say. Tell her that she will marry into a family with a superb clerical brother-in-law."

"I'm sure she'll fall in love instantly with my description of you."

"I bet."

When I hung up, I marveled at Packy's ability to worm

any secret out of me. You'll note he didn't ask whether I'd taken her to bed yet. That was not discretion on his part—Packy in those days was unaware of both the word "discretion" and the reality behind it.

Later, when the lines between dream and reality, between sanity and insanity had blurred, I could have asked Packy about the call. It might have established a bench mark. At that point, eleven o'clock Chicago time, July 23, 1946, did Jeremiah Thomas Keenan, late of the United States Navy, sometime commander of VF 39, sound reasonably sane and in as close touch with the hard edge of reality as he ever did.

But I forgot about the phone call until I read through my journal months later.

I turned on the reading lamp next to my chair, picked up the looseleaf notebook that served as my journal, and began to write.

I heard a terrible scream from the bathroom. Scorpion?

I rushed across the room, crashed through the door, and discovered my crisp-haloed redhead, modestly wrapped in a huge white towel, standing on the scale and pointing in terrified horror.

"A scorpion?"

"Five pounds! That terrible thing says I've gained five pounds. It's lying, isn't it?"

Bare feet, skin and hair wet from the shower, no makeup—she looked ten years old.

"You scared me," I said reproachfully.

"That scares me."

"You've been eating and drinking a lot these last two days."

"Five pounds!"

How delightfully an adolescent girl. What was this nonsense about her being dead? She was as alive as I was.

"You've just had dinner. By tomorrow morning, three of those pounds will be gone. And you can lose another by taking off that towel."

Automatically her fingers went to the top of the towel. Then she comprehended. "I will *not!*"

"It would have assured pleasant dreams for me, but let me show you." I dragged her off the scale and stepped on it myself. "See, a hundred and ninety-eight in my stocking feet. Right?"

She nodded dubiously, her hands clutching the top of her impromptu sarong. Come to think of it, she looked a little older than ten.

"Now, since you are not about to lend me that towel you are clinging to like you are Dorothy Lamour, I'll borrow this other one—which I note you have already soaked—wrap it around my admittedly less attractive frame and prove that it adds a pound to my weight. A hundred and ninety-nine, right?"

She peered at the scale. "Right, but you're heavier than I am, so it counts for more for me. . . ."

"When the scale hits a hundred and twelve, we'll begin to consider a starvation diet."

"You're making fun of me."

"Who, me?" I propelled her toward the door on her side of the bathroom. "Now go to bed."

"Yes, Commander." She yawned.

Reassured that the child was completely human, I returned to my journal. Carefully I detailed the adventures and emotions of the day, my account slanted in the direction of making everything seem rational, ordinary, unexciting.

I suppose I was whistling in the dark.

However, the last paragraph I wrote that night is not one of which I am proud.

The girl is perfectly ordinary. My romantic imagination tries periodically to cover her with a sheen of mystery. She eats too much and drinks too much and will probably be quite disgustingly fat by the time she's twenty-five. Her temperament is volatile, her mood erratic, her decisions impulsive. She is not without some native shrewdness and her tastes in literature are surprisingly good, though I'm not sure she understands what she reads. But she is uneducated and doubtless will remain so. She's a mildly diverting companion for a ride through the desert on a hot day, but I will be happy to deliver her to the Arizona Biltmore tomorrow afternoon. If necessary, I will tell her that I have changed my plans and instead of the Superstitious Mountains, as she persists on calling them, I am headed for the Grand Canyon—which, come to think of it, is not a bad idea. In any event, she will be out of my life by supper tomorrow night. What a relief that will be.

Afraid that I would have to make love with her?

Hell, yes. But I had passed that test by then, had I not? She was in bed and asleep, as I would be in a few minutes, after my shower.

When I showed that passage to my wife, she shrugged her shoulders. "You're being tough on yourself again. How do you distinguish between fear and natural delicacy. You are a very delicate man, can't help it. That's not bad.

"That poor little child was lonely," she continued. "She was trying to seduce you, and you were a prime target for seduction. What else did you think was going to happen?"

What indeed?

In the bathroom, I noted a pair of nylon stockings, two net panties, a garter belt and a bra hanging neatly—as neatly as such garments can—on a towel bar. The provident woman prepares for the morrow.

So she had not worn a bra at supper. And I had been too unperceptive to notice.

No, I was not much of a threat.

Packy would believe none of this should I ever tell him. But he would find it harder to believe that I got myself into this situation in the first place, than he would that I had ignored the possibilities and opportunities inherent in the situation.

Who cared what a younger brother thought?

I turned off the shower, wrapped the less-wet of the two bath towels around my waist, and turned off the light. There was no bar of light on the bathroom floor from her room.

Lights off and presumably asleep.

So, quite satisfied with myself, I dropped off to what started as a night of peaceful dreams.

CHAPTER 11

LIGHTNING CUT A SHARP GASH ACROSS THE SKY, ILLUMIN-
ing Rusty's face and at the same time slicing it as in a swipe
of a mighty saber. Then the darkness returned; another roar
of thunder hit my ears. Lightning crackled again, followed by
an instant roar of thunder—getting close, another typhoon
maybe. I was shivering from cold, biting rain. More lightning,
Rusty's face was now permanently etched on the pale sky,
blood oozing from the jagged cut that ran from his left temple
down to his right jaw. Despite his pain he was laughing at
me, delighting in my damnation.

I knew I was asleep, that this was another dream, but
some of it wasn't a dream. I strove desperately to fight my
way out of the swamp of nightmare. Lightning sizzled again,
thunder exploded simultaneously, I was drenched in icy water,
the kamikaze plowed into our ship, it exploded in a mushroom
ball, I jumped into the ocean, felt myself being dragged re-
morselessly toward the ocean floor and crashed into an honor
guard from the *Yamoto* in their dress blues, ceremonial swords
poised to strike me.

As I tried to scramble to my feet and run from them, they
plunged their weapons into me. I watched in horror as my
blood turned the water purple.

Then I woke up, naked, drenched, shivering, exhausted,
on my bed. Where was I? What had happened?

I reached for the blanket and pulled it up over me. Why
was I sleeping without any clothes or bed cover in the middle
of winter?

Where were we? Headed for Hong Kong? That's where
the other typhoon hit us.

Slowly I calmed down, took stock of the room: the French
windows with their thin draperies flapping in the breeze, the
shape of my foldaway bed, the full moon in the western sky,

ducking behind clouds, the thick, rich smell of soil after a heavy rain.

I was in Arizona; Superior, Arizona. In the Picketpost House. It had been hot when I went to bed, so I'd left the windows open, the ceiling fans on, and my shorts off. I must have kicked away the sheets when I was asleep. So the rainstorm, later today than usual, had caught me by surprise, chilled and drenched me.

Nothing abnormal.

Andrea King?

I listened in the darkness. No sound from the other room in the suite. She must be sleeping.

I was conscious then of great sexual hunger.

So what else is new?

"Yes," said the intelligence officer, whose job was to provide situation evaluations and not moral opinions, "but have you ever been presented with such a golden opportunity?"

"Go away," I told him. "I'm trustworthy."

"Barely," he replied and went away as instructed.

I struggled out of bed, staggered to the windows, and closed them. Damn climate, too hot or too cold. The storm clouds were disappearing and the moon was reasserting its dominance; white light, allegedly representing forgiveness, was glistening in pools of water on our balcony.

Had Andrea closed her windows? Was she shivering too?

Well, I told myself as I crawled back under my sheet, that's her problem.

I settled down, commanded my muscles and nerves to relax, and hoped fervently—since I had eschewed praying for things—that I could fall back to sleep.

I had dozed off when I heard her scream.

It was not like the cry of protest over the insult from the bathroom scale, but a terrified wail, a woman being raped, tortured, murdered.

Scream after scream after scream, each more pitiable than its predecessor.

Pilots, man your planes!

I charged through the bathroom in one quick leap and banged open the door of the master bedroom.

Andrea sat, bolt upright, in the middle of the vast bridal bed, her eyes closed, her hands clasped on her chest, her eyes jammed shut, her face contorted in horror.

"No, Andrew," she shrieked. "Please, no!"

I glanced quickly around the room, illumined in the silver light of the moon. No one there. Only a nightmare.

Who the hell was Andrew?

I hesitated. Maybe I was dreaming. Or maybe I wanted to hear the screams. Was this not some sort of cliché? Let her scream herself into wakefulness.

Our suite was the only one open on the top floor. But her screams were loud enough to be heard throughout the hotel. They'd think I was murdering my bride.

"Dear God, Andrew, don't! I'm sorry! I tried my best! Don't!"

Who was Andrew? Her husband was John. Her father? Her uncle?

She screamed again, so pathetically this time, as if she were resigned to death, that I didn't care who he was. I loved her.

I vaulted onto the immense bed and gathered her into my arms. "It's all right, Andrea, it's all right. It's only a dream. Wake up, no one will hurt you. It's all right."

She was wearing an old-fashioned white nightgown, long and elaborately lacy, simultaneously chaste and inviting. A wedding nightgown? The only one she owned? A substitute for the white wedding dress she was probably denied?

She was sobbing hysterically now, still mostly asleep and clinging to me for dear life.

"It's all right, kid, only a bad dream. You're safe and sound with old trustworthy Jerry Keenan in Superior, Arizona. Nothing to worry about."

She saw me then for the first time and, despite her hysteria and the horror that had assaulted her, she managed a quick impish grin. "Barely."

Slowly the rigid little body in my arms relaxed and became limp in my protecting embrace. "Terrible silly dream."

"What was it about?"

"I don't remember. They were coming for me."

"Who?"

"I don't know." She snuggled closer. "The demons who are waiting for me, I suppose."

"*Who?*"

"The demons," she insisted, as though I were being dense. "You know, the ones who watch me till it's time. It will be soon now. They're becoming impatient."

"What are you talking about, Andrea?" I held her even closer. "No one is waiting for you. It's only me."

She shook her head as though clearing it of foolishness. "I'm sorry, Jerry, I guess I'm still half asleep."

"It's all right now. Nothing more to worry about."

"Nothing more to worry about." She laid her head on my shoulder. "The commander will take care of me. Forever and forever."

"Amen."

"Praying?"

" 'To whom it may concern.' Or maybe 'Occupant.' "

She laughed at me, tenderly, appealingly, lovingly.

I don't quite know when in those grotesque few minutes protectiveness turned into desire, indeed desire so implacable that there was no longer a possibility, no longer a thought of resisting it. But by the time she laughed, I had passed the point of no return. The CIC in my brain signed off with a message that sounded like, "You're on your own, buddy."

Indeed I was.

I began to kiss her.

"More kissing? Aren't you bored with it by now?" She shifted in my arms, preparing to absorb affection as well as protection. Her body gave no hint of either resistance or reluctance. "I can't be *that* interesting?"

"I haven't yet begun to kiss you, Andrea," I murmured into her hair. "There's so much more of you that I haven't touched yet."

"Hmm . . ." she murmured contentedly. "I hope I don't disappoint you."

"Fat chance."

"Don't say 'fat' after that mean old scale lying to me."

I slipped the gown off her right shoulder and down her arm, exposing at long last one of her breasts. As I had expected, it was perfect: high, firm, exquisitely shaped.

She swallowed hard, leaned her head against my side, but carefully, so as not to interfere with my work.

There was no hurry, we had all the hours of night and day ahead of us. She had just emerged from horror; the journey to pleasure must be infinitely soothing, smooth, tender. For the moment all that mattered was the proper treatment of this astonishing and delicate breast.

I caressed it, fondled it, kissed it, nibbled it. I brought its pale nipple to rigid fullness. I licked the nipple, took it between my teeth, drew on it as if I were a nursing babe. Then I repeated the whole charming process time after time, always with the utmost care that every touch be tender and light. Passionate violence would come later, far down the road.

She watched me intently. This was a deadly serious business for Andrea King. There was to be pleasure, yes, and laughter, yes; but I was also a neophyte to be studied, mastered, led, guided. Her concern about my proper initiation poured gasoline on the fires of my desire.

She sighed often, twisting her buried head against my chest and murmuring contentedly.

"You're wonderful," she said once.

"Raw novice."

"Gifted lover."

I straightened her up and moved her away for a moment. There was a faint smile on her flushed face, her jaw hung lazily, her eyes were wide and content. "Not bored yet?"

"Not even begun."

She shivered complacently. "Marvelous."

I thought how wise I had been not to begin with Barbara. Then I peeled the gown from her left shoulder and down to her waist. The top of the white linen and lace garment hung against her lower arms, which were clasped, protectively, at her belly.

"Oh my." She swallowed again. "The officer is serious."

I took possession of her other breast. "He sure is."

"Do you like me?"

"What do you think?"

"Well, you have good taste in wine. . . ."

"And"—I lifted my lips from the new breast—"and women."

"And loving."

I kept one nipple erect and teased the other into the same condition. Her hand glided down my chest, across my flank and to my loins.

"As soon as I saw you in the station," she whispered, "I knew I wanted you."

"And, since you read minds," I responded, now lightly pushing both breasts against her ribs, waiting for my brain to explode, "you knew I wanted you."

"In clinical detail." She threw her head back and then gasped. "Don't stop, that was approval, not protest. Yes, that's better. But I never thought I'd get you. I was astonished when I heard your voice asking about my husband."

"Now you think you have me?"

Her fingers tightened on my loins, I moved the gown to her hips.

"I think we both have what we wanted that morning, so long ago."

"Yesterday."

"As I said, long, long ago . . . do you always come into women's bedrooms stark-naked?"

"When I hear screams. And this is the first time I've been in a woman's bedroom, as you well know."

I removed the rest of her nightgown. The nude Andrea King was a greater wonder than I had expected in the continuous fantasies that had tormented my imagination since I had first seen her in the railroad station.

Her breasts were fuller than I had imagined them, her waist more slender, her thighs more deftly carved, the dense auburn underbrush between them more luxuriant. She was a miniature odalisque, both timid and determined, both embarrassed and eager, my slave and my master.

Then neither of us said anything for a long time. Love was not mentioned. It didn't just then seem to be an issue. I explored her body with by hands and my lips, discovering all its fascinating detail.

So I lost my virginity, which had become, in retrospect, an impossible burden, and lost it to a child more than five years younger than I was, a sweet, clever, ingenious, sympathetic child. She initiated me into the mysteries of sex in such a way that our coupling seemed a promise of a vast and exciting and memorable journey that would last the rest of my life. She gave me the kind of first step on that pilgrimage which she had been denied. And she gave it generously and lovingly, holding nothing back.

Does the first act of love shape all subsequent acts of love? My kids, speaking from professional expertise of one sort or another and careful to exclude reflections on their own experience, offer me the typical psychological conclusion: maybe. The first time can be terribly important, but need not be. You can overcome a bad beginning. You can destroy the positive effects of a good beginning. But for me, perhaps because the beginning had been so long delayed, it was decisive. Despite the horror that would assault and destroy our union in just a few hours, the first act itself will always be with me, a paradigm every time I approach the body of a woman.

Without saying a word, she taught me about love—how gentle it must be even when it is most violent. About women—how much they need sensitive affection. And about life—how we must seize its opportunities before they are lost.

We played, we laughed, we teased, we gently tormented, and finally we drove each other over the brink of passion in uninhabited free fall through space that seemed to last for eternity and longer.

Her pedagogy was carefully tuned to the possible vulnerability of my novice's male ego. She taught by sigh, by gesture, by gentle guidance, so that I felt not a fool, but like a pilot who has just soloed or perhaps just finished flight training. Not only was I initiated, so her response told me, now I was a pro.

Well, I wasn't a pro, but at least I had made a presentable beginning. And, with considerable satisfaction, I knew that I had.

The religion teachers in my high school and college classrooms would have said that, if the storm returned and lightning struck us on our vast honeymoon bed, we both would have been damned to hell for all eternity.

That's what the new pastor at our parish preaches, a man who believes that we've lost our sense of sin (sexual sin, he doesn't seem concerned about any other kind). If I am to take seriously the documents emanating from the Holy See, that's what the Vatican wants us all to think too.

The big difference between now and 1946 is that no one believes them anymore. In my Catholic days before the war, I half believed them; but my hesitancy to immerse myself in the love game was probably based in great part on other motives (not all of them unworthy, such as affectionate respect for women, which I had absorbed from my father).

What would the various members of my family, experts on ethics each in their own way, judge about our romp in Picketpost House, should I provide them with the details?

Packy would say pretty much what he said in 1946. Under the circumstances, the power of passion was so great that I don't see how the issue of serious sin could arise.

My daughter the clinician would say that it was a statistically probable event and, so long as no one was hurt, it might well have been beneficial for both. Still, there is always the risk in such hastily consummated liaisons of considerable dysfunction later on.

My son the young priest would perhaps find it hard to understand why the question would come up; we were on an exploration toward a sacramental union (for which we both hoped, despite our respective reservations and fears). In general, the more chaste such explorations are, the better for both parties. But who can say what is appropriate in an individual case? Finally it is between the couple and God.

"The same thing, I'm saying," Packy would insist. "Only the vocabulary has changed, not the pastoral insight."

His namesake would agree.

And my wife, listening to this imaginary seminar with twinkling eyes, would comment, terminating the discussion, "If he hadn't started then, I would have had to teach him a lot later on. That dreadful girl obviously had some skills at seduction."

None of this debate occurred to me as the two of us, spent but happy, napped for a little while in each other's arms. My complaisant woman seemed utterly blissful. And I reveled in that self-satisfied sense of conquest that rewards the male of the species after every reasonably successful exercise in love.

Barbara would never have been like that, I reasoned, nor any of the girls or women I knew. My sister and my mother would be shocked at the suggestion of abandonment so complete.

Looking back on it, I may have underestimated my mother. In fact, I'm sure I did. The nighttime sounds in the next room during the vacations my wife and I took with my parents in later years suggested to me what ought to have been obvious—wantonness comes in a wide variety of packages.

I think most adult men of my generation would be shocked by that discovery. After what happened to me that night of July 23, 1946, barely trustworthy Jerry was pretty hard to shock.

We made love again that night, our hormones keeping up (in my case with some help) with our imaginations and our desires. We frolicked and experimented, explored and trifled with each other, lost our minds with turbulent passion and caressed one another with sweet reassurance. She knew my every fantasy and cheerfully indulged them almost before I knew which one came next.

Early in the morning, when light was breaking in the sky, Andrea stood at the window, her gown clutched at her breasts.

I had slipped away when she was sleeping and brought the Kodak into our bedroom. I snapped the shot quickly and hid the camera.

I still have the picture, next to the Compaq as I type these words—head and shoulders, piquant thoughtful face, auburn halo in attractive disarray, lips slightly open, eyes staring into the far distance. A pretty child, chaste and yet, with her delicate and smooth bare shoulders, miraculously erotic.

For all her earthy charm, there is something ever so slightly wrong about the picture. She looks misty and ethereal in the dim dawn, almost ectoplasmic, as if her image had been imposed on the chemicals by a cosmic ray instead of by ordinary light. She's not quite there, you see.

Yet she was there that morning. As solid as the keyboard on which I'm typing. I slipped up behind her and pried the gown away and let it drop to the floor.

"People will see me naked," she protested, covering her breasts with her hands. I bent over her and kissed her.

"Who? The voyeur in Phoenix with a telescope?" I removed her hands and replaced them with my own. I kept my lips against hers.

Like a well-satisfied cat, she arched her back against me, stirring me to even greater arousal.

"I think there's a strong streak of exhibitionist in me."

"In everyone." I allowed one of my hands to wander down her body, tickling her on its way.

She giggled and squirmed. "Stop it."

I didn't stop it but drew her even closer as my hand continued its journey to the russet forest of her loins, where it amused itself for a time and then journeyed back to her breast.

"You're driving me out of my mind." She tried to talk even though her lips were as much my prisoners as her bosom.

I dragged her back to the bed. "That's the general idea."

"You never have enough, do you?" She allowed me to place her face down on the bed, her toes touching the floor. "Now you're going to try another fantasy, aren't you?"

I certainly was. "I'm running out of fantasies."

"That will be the day."

When I showed my wife the picture before we were married, she considered it thoughtfully.

"I can see why you were spooked. The poor little thing does look otherworldly."

The recklessness of the damned.

CHAPTER **12**

AT TEN O'CLOCK I ORDERED BREAKFAST SENT UP BECAUSE my bride insisted that there would be no more lovemaking until her other appetites were satisfied. She had convinced herself that I was correct in my analysis of the scale. Her net gain, minus the towel, which was no longer necessary, though it was wrapped around her waist some of the time as a token concession to modesty, was a pound and a half.

"I'm not planning to eat this way for the rest of my life. Besides, I was hungry."

"And thirsty."

"Can we have cognac for breakfast?"

"We certainly cannot. The people here probably think we're crazy anyway."

"It's a shame you needed it for lovemaking."

"I needed it? You were the only one who drank cognac since . . ."

"Since we began"—she tossed aside the towel and threw herself on top of me—"to play."

The bellman—a silent Indian who looked as if he might be an Apache or a Kiowa—brought our breakfast. I had to persuade my modest bride by brute force that she couldn't answer the door clad only in her towel.

As we ate breakfast, the folks who watched everything I

do from the various corners in the attic of my brain were busy worrying, which is what they're paid to do.

Not only was she impetuously wanton, she was also skill-fully wanton. Could she have learned that from the barracks braggart who had been her husband? I rather doubted it. But from whom then? And how come so quickly? How do you make in a little more than two years the transition from in-nocent Irish Catholic virgin in a Catholic high school in the "East" to a playful temptress in an inn in the West?

I had a good time, a wonderful time. But I also wondered.

I learned through the years that some people are spon-taneously good at sex, if given half a chance and half a dose of encouragement (and, heaven knows, I was given more than that in July of 1946). Others never learn, no matter how hard they work at it and how much experience they collect and how many techniques they master or think they master.

Respect and obsession, judiciously blended like vermouth and vodka; that's the secret.

"You know, it's funny," she mused as we were lying side by side, after breakfast, tranquilly holding hands, both of us too spent to act yet on her suggestion that we go down and look at that pretty arboretum place. "I am lying here won-dering if I was a good lover for you and you're lying next to me wondering how come I am so outrageously good."

"Doesn't mind reading become a burden after a while?"

She nodded vigorously. "Neither of us are asking about you. The commander takes it for granted that he was outstanding—which he was—and I practically pass out when I think of all the things you did to me. But we both worry about me."

"I don't know what to say."

"You're not to say anything." She slapped my arm in a symbolic reprimand. "You're supposed to listen."

"Yes, ma'am."

"So listen." Suddenly she was very stern. "You're my second man, Jerry, just as surely as I'm your first woman. Whatever happens, remember that."

"I will, but I wasn't doubting—"

"I *said*, you're supposed to listen. . . . I've never been that way before, not even in my imagination—well, not in imaginations that I would admit to, anyway. Something inside me cracked and came apart when I saw you, so strong and good-looking and kind, in the station. Maybe the nuns were right after all about my being an immoral hussy. John . . . well, I'm afraid the poor boy was a little . . . kind of a puritan, if you know what I mean. After we were married I had to take the lead and I did all right . . . I mean, he was certainly satisfied and so was I, more or less. It was"—she sighed complacently—"never like last night."

"We should get up now if we're going to visit the arboretum."

"Why get up?" She stretched luxuriously.

"So we can go back to bed."

"That's wonderful." She jumped out of bed. "I'll beat you to the shower."

In fact, it was a tie. Which was just fine.

The Boyce Thompson Arboretum had once been the personal garden of the copper tycoon who had lived in Picketpost House. Unhappy with the desert view in the little canyon beneath his front window—the place where I had taken my bootleg photo of my "bride"—he had imported trees and flowers from all over the world. His heirs had expanded it by adding many desert plants too. I gather that the University of Arizona has taken it over and that now it's quite a distinguished botanical garden. Even forty years ago it was a fascinating mixture of desert and the rest of the world.

My companion was enthusiastic. She bounded around from plant to plant and tree to tree like a little kid at the zoo or a rabbit in a lettuce garden. My reputation for omniscience was irrevocably lost.

"You mean you don't know how they make those prickly-pear trees?"

"I was in pre-law, not botany."

"But you know *everything*."

"Not about desert plants."

"Especially when you don't have a chance to read the guidebook the night before."

"I was busy last night."

"I noticed."

"A woman in my suite, I don't know how she got in, was screaming. I had to calm her down."

"Were you successful?"

"No."

She laughed and gamboled over to an Australian pine tree. It didn't look any different from a Wisconsin pine tree to me.

She stopped abruptly, hesitated, and then walked back to me diffidently.

"Was that how it started? Did I really wake you up screaming?"

"That's why I came into the bedroom in the first place. Other processes started after I wakened you and told you that you were having bad dreams. Don't you remember?"

"I'm not sure. I remember being frightened and then you kissing me. Why was I frightened?"

" 'Hysterical' would be a better word. I think someone was trying to kill you or punish you horribly. Someone named Andrew. I kind of figured it was your uncle."

She was chalk-white, terrified again.

"No, not my uncle," she replied automatically. ". . . Are you sure?"

"I'm sure that was the name and that you thought you were in some terrible danger. You were sitting straight up, rigid, your eyes glued shut, and screaming your lungs out."

She nodded thoughtfully. "I don't remember my dreams usually. A lot of times when I wake up I feel like someone has tried to kill me."

"Has anyone ever tried to kill you?"

She looked at me with an expression of great misery. "Not exactly. My uncle beat me a lot, especially when I was a little girl. He stopped a couple of years ago—then began again after . . . after he found out I was pregnant."

"Why did he stop?"

"I told him I'd cut his throat with a butcher knife if he touched me again. . . . I think there was something sexual about the way he beat me. He enjoyed it too much."

"You threatened to cut his throat . . . did you mean it?"

"Course not, but he wasn't sure."

"I don't think I want to have you angry at me." We started to walk through the arboretum again.

"I'll never be that angry at you. And it was more fear than anger. I didn't know what else to do."

Silence for a few moments. Harsh memories had taken the spring out of her step.

Wonderful.

"Let's go back," she demanded abruptly.

"Why?"

"You know why. I'm hungry."

"For what?"

"Food. First, anyway."

Lunch was charcoal roast beef sandwiches with fresh tomatoes, chocolate ice cream, and a bottle of red wine.

Naturally.

Her radiant glow seemed to attract everyone—waiters, waitresses, the manager and his wife, the handful of other guests, to our table.

"See what a little sex does for you," I whispered.

"Be quiet. And pour me some more wine."

"All right." I emptied the bottle in her glass, all but the dregs. I had explained to her the previous night why you didn't consume the dregs. "Are you interested in the agenda for the rest of the day?"

"You mean after our nap? Sure."

"After our nap, my friend Chief Arnold at the service station will have Roxy ready at five-thirty. Then I'll drive you to the Biltmore, drop you off with whoever your friends are there, check in myself, spend a restful night, hopefully with you, leave Roxy in your charge, and catch a plane back to Chicago. It will take me a few weeks to get life organized there and then I'll come back for you. We can plan our future then."

Holes in it? Sure. I wanted to make up my mind about Andrea King without her physical presence to distract me. I should have said that we would both catch a plane to Chicago.

I wonder what my life would have been like if I had said those words.

Well, I didn't and that's that.

"No," she said flatly. "I don't believe you."

"I'm not lying, Andrea; I will come back for you."

"I'm not worried about that. I'm worried that you will sneak back into those terrible mountains by yourself. I won't let you."

"You're right, lovely mind reader, that's what I intended to do."

"Well," she said, grimly determined. "I won't let you."

I was learning that it was pointless to argue with my bride when she made up her mind.

Dear God in heaven, *she* wanted to protect *me*.

"All right," I said slowly, feeling somehow trapped, "we'll drive on to Globe, spend the night, and do the Apache Trail tomorrow."

"That's settled then. Now may I have just one more scoop of ice cream, please."

Outside of the dining room there was a small gift shop with souvenirs, mostly presentable handicraft and some clothes. I bought bolo ties for Dad and Packy and silver Apache jewelry for Mom and Joanne and another gift or two.

"Andrea King, see that red nightgown? It matches your hair. Buy it."

She gasped in horror. "That terrible, indecent thing? I will not. A person could see right through it."

Fairly close to being transparent, it was indecent for the time—long before Frederick's of Hollywood and the era when prostitute clothes of former ages became standard issue for suburban housewives.

"I believe that's the general idea."

"I will absolutely never buy it." Her hand reached out for the money I was offering her. "Never."

"I understand."

"What's more," she said as she held it briefly in front of her to make sure it would fit and then quickly pulled it away, "I certainly will not put it on the minute we go back to our silly old bridal suite."

"I understand."

I was banished from the store and forced to wait for my "bride"—as I was now routinely thinking of her despite my hesitations and reservations—in the lobby. She emerged from the store, flushed and pleased with herself, the gown in a small package hidden behind her back.

"The woman thought you would look gorgeous in it," I suggested with, I'm afraid, a lewd grin.

As I followed her up the steps, unable to match the speed of her happy bounce, and ogled her trim hips, for which I had scandalous plans, I realized how much I loved this strange, bewitching, rather frightening child/woman. I was not yet ready, however, to tell her that I loved her. Nor had I forgotten her uncle and the carving knife.

She let me open the door to our suite, leapt into the room, and closed the door in my face. I had to make a number of virtuous promises that I did not intend to keep before, with a great pretense of reluctance, she let me in.

I promptly took her in my arms, broke all my promises, and crushed her with my kisses.

"Stop that." She shoved against me unpersuasively. "You promised."

"You're a provoking woman. I hereby withdraw my promise not to spank you."

"You wouldn't dare."

"Go put on that nightgown."

"I won't."

"Then I'll tickle you all afternoon."

"Stop it! You're a brute and a beast! A . . . a Capone stooge!"

"Because I'm from Chicago?"

"Stop!" She was giggling, squirming to avoid my fingers, and provoking me all the more. "All Chicagoans are mobsters! Please stop!"

"Will you put on this expensive gown?"

"It's rayon and it shrinks and spots and tears easily. Just remember that when you try to take it off me."

"Am I supposed to do that?"

"*Well*"—she flounced toward the bathroom—"I certainly don't intend to. That would be what the nuns"—a final laugh before she slammed the door—"called immodest."

Poor little kid. Today was an oasis of laughter in the gloomy desert of her life. I would have to change all that.

I drew the draperies on the sky, which was now a thick roll of cotton—bunched-up white clouds with occasional dark and dirty patches—stretched from one far horizon to the other. Our bedroom was hot and in the twilight of the drawn draperies seemed to invite swampy, earthy licentiousness, which suited me fine. It was a time to be dissolute, orgiastic.

Orgies are an excellent idea; the mix of behavior changes with the years, but the pleasure, if anything, improves. I have never been able to understand why we humans don't arrange for more of them. Afraid of them, perhaps.

My wife has promised me a spectacular orgy if I ever finish this manuscript, the best ever she claims. We'll see.

I took off my clothes and hung them up carefully, lest my fastidious bride be offended. Then I opened the bottle of cognac I had smuggled into the room, filled two large glasses with ice and poured the liquor into them, up to the brim.

"Have you disappeared on me?" I yelled.

"I want to be perfect." The joking was over and we were now settling down to the serious business of orgy.

Then the door opened, slowly, hesitantly. "I'm embarrassed."

"And I'm sure radiant."

"I don't know." She peeked out the door. "Look at you, no clothes on at all." Her face softened. "Oh, Jerry, you're the one who's radiant. Why did the nuns tell us that women don't admire the bodies of men?"

"Maybe they didn't. . . . Come on out, woman, or I'll come and get you."

"And you're not embarrassed at all. If I were as beautiful as you . . ."

"Who said I wasn't embarrassed?" I was, to tell the truth, and also pleased and self-satisfied.

Finally, with the same modesty with which the sun rises, hesitant but still utterly self-confident, she joined me in our bedroom, head down, hands behind her back, face, neck and slim shoulders crimson and alluring.

I'll never forget that picture. Andrea King, as she claimed to be then, was all the beauty in the universe combined into one womanly body—and mine for the taking, the using, the enjoying. She wanted to be perfect for me. And she was. However I wanted and as long as I wanted.

She had carefully applied makeup and liberally doused herself in perfume. Every lovely portion of her lovely self was an invitation and a present.

"Stop looking at me that way," she murmured.

"How do you know how I'm looking at you," I laughed, "when you're not looking at me?"

"I can tell. Anyway, you know all my secrets. What's left to surprise you?"

"I know only a little bit." I pried one of her hands from behind her back and drew her to our bed. "About some of your secrets. It would take several lifetimes, at least, to be cured of surprise."

We sat on the bed, in no rush. I imprisoned the hand I had captured on my thigh, although it showed no disposition to attempt escape. Her other hand still hid behind her back, not yet ready for complete capitulation.

"What do you think of me, Jerry Keenan?"

"I adore you, isn't that obvious?"

"No, I mean, am I at all attractive?"

Later in life I would learn that women require constant assurance on that subject. And you can't provide too much. Maybe men require it, too.

"You're a magnificent woman, a grand duchess, like I've been saying."

Her other hand finally deserted its hideaway and rested comfortably on my thigh near its mate. "I'm not a woman, I'm only a girl, just a few years away from dolls. Almost any body my age is useful for screwing."

"Such terrible language from a sisters' school student."

"Regardless . . ."

I remembered something my father had once said about a pretty and promising fifteen-year-old on our pier at Lake Geneva.

"Give yourself a few more years, Andrea. Wait till you're twenty-four or twenty-five. Put on most of those ten pounds of which you're afraid. Enjoy a lot of loving. Experience more of life. Bear a child or two. Read a lot more of those heavy Russian novels. When all that's been done, you'll find one day that you've rounded, in a number of different senses of that word"—I smiled and began to explore some of her present roundness—"into a wonderfully mature woman at whom both men and women will stare in astonishment for at least a half century."

The other possibility, my father had observed, is that such a one can wither before she's twenty-one if the graces—his word—don't all fall into place.

"I won't live to be twenty-five," she said as though it were a settled matter. "Probably not even to be twenty."

My fingers ceased abruptly their stealthy journey toward the dense jungle of her loins. "Don't be ridiculous, my darling." I kissed her softly. "Of course you will. What makes you think you won't?"

"I won't, that's all. Maybe already . . ."

"Maybe already what?"

"Nothing."

"That's not an answer, my darling."

"It should be clear by now, Commander"—her eyes flared with quick anger—"that there are some questions I don't answer. Love me, please." The anger died, she bowed her head and pressed her lips to my loins. "Don't cross-examine me."

"I hate to disturb you, but perhaps I should remove this precious gown, lest we spoil it during our game."

"I'll take if off." She stripped off the gown in a single quick and breathtaking movement. "I don't know what's the point in dressing up like this, only to undress."

"To delight me as you walk to my bed. A place where we tolerate no nightgowns."

"Tell that to your other women."

"There are no other women, Andrea." I pulled her down on the bed next to me. "There never will be."

We rested contentedly next to each other. Then I remembered the cognac.

"Your health, Andrea." I gave her one of the glasses and toasted her with the other.

"And yours . . . Oh, my, this is good with ice. Why didn't you tell me about drinking it with ice before? You know that I'm a hedonist, like the nuns said."

"A strange time to be thinking about the nuns." I sipped some of my drink and with the other hand began to caress her again.

"I think about them all the time. Hmm . . . this is almost as good as you are."

"There's nothing wrong with being a hedonist." I put my glass aside. "Right now I'm about to become an unrestrained hedonist. No, not quite yet. Stand up, please. And close your eyes."

"A new part of the game?"

"Kind of. Eyes shut tight? Put your hands over them."

"Yes, Commander, sir."

"It's not proper for a woman to be totally naked when she's making love, so I have a present that will protect your modesty even when you've shed that delightful gown." I lowered the silver-and-jade Apache pendant over her head.

"Feels like something very seductive," she said softly. "Can I open my eyes and look?"

"Not too long, because I still have my hedonism to pursue."

She opened her eyes and burst into tears. "It's too nice, Jerry. You shouldn't have wasted your money."

Why a pendant instead of a ring? I'd almost purchased the ring and then lost my nerve.

"I'll take it back." I put my fingers over hers on the pendant.

"Don't you dare."

"Then let's drink a toast to the future."

"To the present."

"All right, to the present."

Naked in the dim light of our room, we solemnly drank to whatever the gift of the Apache jewelry meant.

"Now comes the hedonism." I suited my actions to my words, taking complete possession of her. I dragged her into the bed and promptly began to cover her smooth, soft body with kisses and nibbles.

"Oh, Jerry, I love you so much." Her capitulation was rapid and impetuous.

I don't know whether she expected a reply. I couldn't find the words for it.

Then, lying first side by side, then entwined with one another, and driven by our youthful hungers and desires and needs to the farthest extremes of rapture, we forgot about everything but our passion. I discovered in those moments what oblivion in sex really means.

Yet while I was on top of her and inside of her and she spread-eagled and helpless under me, long after I thought words were possible, she whispered, "Whatever happens, Jerry, always remember these few days were the happiest of my life."

Finally consumed by our game, we napped for a time in one another's arms.

Her words still echoed in my head when I awoke. What could I say? I had promised to take her home to Chicago and care for her through the rest of our lives. She didn't reject the offer; rather she treated it as thought it were nice but irrelevant.

She had awakened before me and, towel at her hips, was watching the big sky, which had turned from cotton white to somber gray while we had played and slept.

I slipped from the bed, put my arms around her as I had done the night before, and imprisoned her warm and sweat-covered breasts. It was again like holding the cosmos in my hands. She did not respond. Was the bloom wearing off?

"Something wrong?"

"No."

"Did I hurt you?"

Faint smile. "You'd never hurt anyone . . . your father must be terribly good to your mother and sister."

A fair enough Freudian observation long before we all became Freudians. The old man, as my wife would observe at his wake many years later, had treated every woman as if she were a queen. Old-fashioned, she continued, but marvelously effective.

"Sure there's nothing wrong?"

"No." Another faint grin.

I flicked away the towel. She drew a very deep breath, partly, it seemed, of dismay and disapproval. I moved my fingers back and forth across the fertile plains of her small, flat belly, brushing the forest regions beyond. "You're sure?"

"Uhm-hum."

If I'd been more experienced then, I would have known that a man never loses when he errs on the side of consideration for apparent reluctance. If the reluctance is real, he receives many points for his kindness and is rewarded later. If, on the other hand, it is merely temporary indecision, his consideration loads the scales in favor of a vehemently positive response to his advance.

Once my marriage was in the bottom of a deep trough. My wife and I had been fighting for months. We had not spoken to each other for a week. Nonetheless I accompanied her to another city, where she was to make a presentation at a professional meeting. She was brilliant, as always, and my hardened heart was filled with pride, then longing, and finally need, which I had thought would never return. Back in our hotel room I began the preliminaries of lovemaking. She responded with what I would describe as a patient submissiveness that only heightened my desires. I had her half undressed, more or less, when I realized that she was dubious about the whole enterprise, ready to do her wifely duty, but not ready to enjoy it, much less to use this potentially romantic situation—alone together in a hotel in a distant city—as an occasion to turn our wobbly marriage around.

So I stopped. "I haven't forced you and I never will."

"Damn it!" She turned furiously away from me. "I hate you. And the reason I hate you the most"—she turned back to me, her face softened, her body complaisant—"is that you are so wonderful that I can't hate you for more than five minutes at a time."

Then she threw herself on me and pinned me to the bed. "All the time I was talking," she said as I was being swept by a thunder squall of kisses, "I watched you beaming proudly, and I prayed to God that you'd want to make love. Then, when you did, I acted like a bitch."

"Only at first," I managed to say.

So we had our orgy and our turning point. There were other troughs, but none so deep.

So a man never loses if he's considerate. Which is not the same as being timid. My wife says that timidity is rarely my problem.

I don't suppose it would have made any difference in what happened later, but I did not have sense enough to use the same strategy that afternoon in Superior during July in 1946.

So my hands explored once again the dense copse at her thighs and then, as she was gasping with arousal, I bore her back to our bed and repeated the scenario of the previous night.

I certainly enjoyed it, but it was not a repeat venture into oblivion. She displayed all the movements and made all the noises of satisfaction too, and I'm sure she was not faking it, but it was not ecstasy for her either.

We had reached our turning point. The great dream had ended in less than twenty-four hours.

CHAPTER 13

"THE TOWN WAS CALLED GLOBE BECAUSE THE FOUNDERS discovered a perfectly round ball of silver nine inches in diameter, ninety-nine percent pure silver, valued at twelve thousand dollars. In those days that was a lot of money."

"Hmn . . ."

"Well, I should receive some credit for catching up on the guidebook, despite my other activities."

No response. Yes, the bloom was off. How short its time.

"The silver ore quickly ran out, so copper became the principal industry."

"Do you believe that?"

"About the copper?"

"No." She was impatient. "About the silver globe."

"Does it have to be true? It's folklore, not history. Can't we enjoy it as a good story without it having to be true?"

"Maybe you should be a folklorist instead of a lawyer."

"Can't I be both?"

"If you have enough money. And I guess you do."

End of conversation.

The big sky above Queen Creek Canyon had turned from somber gray to angry black, the kind of dark sky you never saw in the Western movies in those days and only occasionally even now, as, for example, when the mayor of Carmel drifts in from the high plains.

Chief Arnold assured me, when he delivered Roxinante back to us, that they were ". . . land sakes, only high clouds, not much moisture in them," and that they did not mean a three-day deluge, as a similar dark sky would promise in the Middle West. Nor did they mean much abatement in the steamy desert heat.

However, the somber gloom of the high clouds fit the change in my companion's mood. And her moods were clearly

defined as one of those subjects about which we did not talk
and concerning which I did not ask questions.

Tristis post coitus! Well, I thought, maybe. But I don't
feel sad at all. In fact, I'm proud of myself and delighted in
her. And it's just the beginning. However, if she wants to be
sad, that's her business. I'll be reassuring and patient.

"How do you go about doing that?" the intelligence officer, back in my brain again, demanded. "You know nothing
about the moods of the opposite sex or about how to respond
to them. You think that because you screwed her a few times
and she seemed to like it, that you've become an expert on
women?"

A fair point.

Our farewells at the Picketpost were comprehensive and
cheerful. The staff obviously felt they had been present at and
contributed to the turning point in a honeymoon—which they
had. They also adored the sparkling "bride," who had been
properly bedded, as they thought, again not without reason,
in their hotel. She, in her turn, proved to me, as if I needed
any proof, that she could be gracious and charming even when
her soul was rushing pell-mell for the nearest melancholy
cloud.

I turned in my second crisp hundred-dollar bill. There
were eight left, and enough change to cover us that night at
the Dominion in Globe, for which a phone call had already
arranged a reservation.

After promising our frequent return, we climbed back in
the refurbished Roxinante for the short ride up Queen Creek
Canyon to Globe—I wanted an early-morning start for the
Superstitions and Phoenix.

Her disposition promptly turned doleful. "I'm just a little
tired, Jerry," she pleaded. "Nothing to worry about, please."

Which meant, "please leave me alone."

A request I had sense enough to honor.

The gold-and-bronze peaks of the Upper Canyon stirred
her temporarily out of her depression.

"This is the most beautiful place I've ever been," she
exclaimed.

"Please sit still. I'm not used to driving on mountains. And stop laughing at me."

"How do you know I'm laughing when you don't even take your eyes off the road to look at me?"

"Shut up."

"Yes, Commander. But I won't stop laughing at the way CAG One drives in the mountains."

"I'm glad I amuse you."

The laughter stopped when we reached Miami and the vast stripped copper hills, raw and unnatural without their ground cover, above the highway.

"I don't like those dirty brown ponds. What are they for?"

"They hold waste products."

"And I don't like the smokestacks. They're ugly. And they smell."

"We'll try to find ways to refine copper without smokestacks and waste, ma'am."

"Do that."

Between Miami and Globe, above Pinal Creek Canyon where Arizona 88 turns off for the ride down to Theodore Roosevelt Lake, you can look back at the far eastern end of the Superstition Range (distinct from but a continuation of Superstition Mountain itself) and see Sleeping Beauty Mountain, a lovely young woman sound asleep on the top of the mountain peaks.

"Why are we stopping?" my lovely young woman demanded irritably. "Is *this* your ball-of-silver town?"

"We're looking for Sleeping Beauty Mountain. The guidebook says that there is a mountain which, from this point, looks like a sleeping young woman."

I couldn't find her.

"There she is," said my companion, who wasn't looking for the mountain, mind you. "My, she is lovely."

I followed her finger. Sure enough, she was a sleeping beauty.

"Reminds me of you when you are asleep."

"She has prettier breasts."

"That is decidedly not true, and I have some expert knowledge on the subject."

"Do you?"

We drove on in the fading light to the center of Globe, a more prosperous town than Miami or Superior, but in the dusk and under the dark clouds in the gloom of Andrea's mood it seemed a foreboding place, an outpost constructed perhaps on the foothills of purgatory. Its main street was County Seat USA—courthouse, bank, department store, train station, churches, with touches of the frontier still to be seen—a couple of horses and buggies, men in cowboy boots and hats— and the copper mountains all around us.

I checked us in at the Dominion, a fading relic of post-World-War-I elegance. Mr. and Mrs. J. T. Keenan. I felt a thrill of hope as I signed the register. She was my fair bride, was she not? My first woman, and if all went according to plan, my last? Who could want—or cope with—more than her?

I will admit that my conscience had returned to his locale in my brain, adjoining that of my intelligence officer. I felt no guilt, not yet, anyway, about our lovemaking. But I wondered whether I had not succumbed to the temptation that I had bitterly denounced (mostly in my head) when I'd seen it in others: to exploit war and its attendant dislocations, dangers, excitements, and opportunities to seduce women into risks that they otherwise would not and should not take.

A lot of women were badly used during the war. The excuse "I'm going away and I don't know whether I'll ever be back"—true in only a limited number of cases—had remarkable power to overcome a woman's resistance. Not that all of them wanted to resist anyway. War is a powerful aphrodisiac. Andrea King was not the only victim.

And was she now a victim again? Lonely, broke, frightened, had I not used her to cure my virginity?

As we were conducted up a dubious cage elevator to our room, I worried more about this possibility. Certainly I had promised, more or less and maybe more less than more, to take care of her, to bring her back to River Forest and Butterfield Country Club, and to cherish her for the rest of my life.

Did I really mean to honor that promise? If I did, why did I not try to make plane reservations from Phoenix to Chicago for tomorrow? Why did I buy her a pendant instead of a ring? Why was I hesitating?

Would I drop her at Frank Lloyd Wright's Arizona Biltmore tomorrow night and let her gradually slip out of my life, in the way a lot of my friends and comrades had done to other women during the war? If I did, was I any different from them?

And, perhaps most important of all, what was the mystery about her? All the areas of questioning that were off limits? If there were answers for them, would I have bought an Apache good-luck ring and forced it on the third finger of her left hand?

Maybe.

Our room was not air-conditioned—such amenities did not exist in Globe in 1946—and it was hardly the bridal suite. It was musty and faded, an opulent room of a quarter century before, which had never been refurnished or redecorated. For ventilation we had an open window, for bathing a rusty tub, and our marital bed, if that's what it was, was a narrow double bed with a dangerously sagging center.

Andrea did not complain, indeed hardly seemed to notice.

"Early supper and long sleep?" I asked as she briskly unpacked her huge and dilapidated suitcase.

"Definitely."

She dressed for supper as I watched, entertained and fascinated.

"Do you always stare at women dressing?"

"Never had the opportunity before."

"But you find it entertaining?"

"Immensely."

"I'm glad I amuse you." She pulled the strap of the sundress over her shoulder.

"Mind you, someone with less natural beauty and grace might not be nearly so diverting."

She permitted herself a bare hint of her smile, still enough to illumine the dank, dark room. "You're irresistibly cute, Jerry. I really am glad you like to watch me."

She fussed for a few moments with her hair and then we

went off to supper, arm in arm. Still pretending to be the happy honeymoon couple.

The dining room at the Dominion was similar to that at the Pioneer in Tucson—patterned carpets, mirrors, snowy white tablecloths. But the carpet was worn, the mirrors were tarnished, and the tablecloths, clean and white indeed, were frayed at the edges. Like the rest of the hotel, the dining room was trying to keep up appearances and hoping that there would eventually be enough money for a "postwar" remodeling. However, the food (roast beef and cottage fries tonight) was excellent and the service quick and polite. Everyone doted on my edgy and silent bride—who returned their smiles with smiles of her own, smiles that were never aimed at me.

She declined wine and played with her meat and potatoes, till I said something about starving children in China. I must have rung a bell of some sort, because, like Pavlov's dog, she gobbled down the rest of her meal, leaving the plate spanking clean.

I did not appreciate the thought that I had quoted her aunt.

We talked about families, mostly mine. And mostly because I could think of nothing else to talk about. And mostly about my family because she was not inclined to share much information about hers.

"Jeremiah Keenan, my grandfather, was drafted for the Civil War almost as soon as he got off the boat. Well, he wasn't drafted. He was purchased as a substitution for some rich man who had been drafted. That was the way it was done in those days. You could buy your way out of the military and pay a replacement to die for you. He used the money to bring Maggie, his bride-to-be, over from Ireland. Neither of them could read or write. They were married before the First Illinois left for Vicksburg, where it was wiped out a couple of times over. He didn't die, much to the surprise, I suppose, of the man whose place he took. He was mustered out in Washington as a captain, walked home from there to Chicago, found the major who had commanded his battalion and had been elected alderman. Somewhere he learned to read and write and pass the bar exam; maybe—no, probably—by bribing someone. Both he and my grandmother were Irish-speaking, though you'd never persuade them to talk it. The kids had to speak English.

"He made himself a fortune and lost it a couple of times over, not in ways that were always honest. They produced eight kids, of whom four lived. My father was the youngest, born in 1892, when both of them were in their forties. He was the smartest of the lot and was destined for St. Ignatius College (which eventually became Loyola University) and law school from the very beginning. When the First World War began, he enlisted in the First Illinois, 131st Infantry, as it had become, and saw a little bit of combat in France. . . ."

"And you had to break the family tradition and become a sailor and a flyer . . . showing your independence, I suppose."

"That's what Dad said too. He was the only respectable one of the family, I think. Old Granddad Keenan was a hard drinker and I guess my grandmother was too. Piety and respectability never quite got to the Irish-speaking sections of the Old Country till about 1880. Mom's family—the Slatterys—had less money but more respectability. Her father was a head clerk for the Pullman Company and she's proud that she graduated from Saint Mary's High School. Most of her generation only went to high school for two years."

"What are their names?"

"Is this a catechism class?"

She frowned, not amused. "It's a civil question. Can't you give a civil answer?"

"Sorry. He is Thomas Patrick Keenan, and she is Mary Anne Catherine Slattery. Do you want to know their height and weight and other crucial measurements?"

"Your father's fifty-four." She was still not amused. "How old is your mother?"

"Forty-six, a lot younger. Dad chose to organize his life pretty well before he married. He was thirty, she was only twenty-two."

"A kid." Was that a smile?

"She was a knockout as a girl. Still is quite attractive. . . ."

"You look like her?" She raised a suspicious eyebrow.

"People say that I do."

"Then I believe she is very attractive."

"I think I've been complimented."

"You have. Don't let it go to your head."

"You did smile."

"No, I did *NOT*." And now she smiled again. "What do they think of you—your parents, I mean?"

"They worry. Everyone before me has had to struggle, you see. Dad less than his father, but still, there wasn't much family wealth left when he graduated from law school, only a big home in Austin—that's a Chicago neighborhood which used to be a separate town—and a family reputation for generosity. I grew up, like you did, in the Depression, but unlike most others my age, it never touched me. Both Dad and Mom wonder if I can make it in the tough world of work and competition. Servants, trips to Europe, summer home, everything I've always wanted."

"They've tried to give you everything they never had and are worried that it might spoil you?" She shoved aside her plate and was studying me intently, as though I were a complex algebra problem to be solved.

"Kind of contradictory, huh?" I wasn't sure I wanted to be considered that gravely.

"Can you be a success in the big world?"

"I suppose so. I did all right in the Navy. They wanted me to stay in and learn to fly the new jets. I almost went along. There won't be any more wars for a long time. I wouldn't have to worry about a job. On the other hand, I didn't go to Annapolis or even graduate from college. I'd never make admiral."

"And you wanted to?"

"Sure. They said they'd get me an Annapolis appointment. Can you imagine that? Demoted from a lieutenant commander to a midshipman."

"So you told them to forget it. And now you have to prove to yourself and your parents that you can succeed in law just like your father." She shook her head in response to the waiter's query about dessert.

"That's what they think."

"And what do you think when you're not worried about all those who died in the war?"

"You really want to know?" I touched her fingers. She did not pull them back, as I half expected she would.

"Yes." She was probing at my soul again with those damn all-seeing sapphire eyes. It was even more naked than my body had been earlier in the day.

"I think my parents need not worry. I can succeed as a political lawyer as easily as I did in the Navy. With a lot of energy and ambition left over. But that won't be enough to keep me happy."

"So instead of or in addition to that, you have to find something else?"

"Or someone else."

"And you're not sure that you can find either."

"I'm more certain now than I was two days ago."

She turned her head away at that observation, not liking its implications, though I had intended to flatter her.

The waiter interrupted to take our coffee orders. I wanted black coffee, she settled for iced tea. And no, she did not care for an after-dinner drink.

"Your family?"

She shrugged indifferently. "The opposite of yours, I'm afraid. While the Keenans were on the way up, the . . . we were on the way down. I don't know much about us. We were once very wealthy. One of my father's grandfathers organized the Catholics who protected the churches and the convents when the Know-Nothings tried to burn them down. . . ."

"More than a hundred years ago. So they came before most of the other Irish." She paused, pondering her family's story. "There was a lot of drinking through the years. And gambling. And lost opportunities. TB on my mother's side. Wasted money and opportunities. Early death. Both my mother and father were supposed to have great promise; shallow and empty, my aunt always said, handsome but without substance. My mother even went to finishing school before she got sick. The first time. I'm all that's left on either side. A story of failure to match your story of success."

She said the last words in a cool, matter-of-fact voice, neither bitter nor sad. She shrugged again and turned to her iced tea.

"No process which produced you, Andrea King, can be called a failure."

"That's sweet, Commander." She contemplated my face as though still searching for something. "It isn't really true, but it's nice of you to say it."

"It is true." I took her hand in mine.

She pulled it away. "It is *not*. I am a worthless little nothing. I have done nothing with my life except cause two persons I loved to die. And I don't have enough time left to do anything. It's too late. You want to romanticize me into someone special and great and wonderful. All I really am is your first woman. When you leave me tomorrow night, you will never want to see me again."

CHAPTER **14**

"DON'T YOU UNDERSTAND," SHE SAID, HER FACE CONtorted with icy fury as she struggled to free herself from my amorous grasp, "that we're finished making love? Your virginity is cured, isn't that enough? Can't you leave me alone? Haven't we committed enough sins already?"

So that was it. Sin. The nuns, damn them, were still with her.

After supper we had strolled aimlessly through Globe, both

of us reluctant to return to our hotel room. The moon hadn't risen yet and the murky streetlights didn't illumine much of the town. In fact, however, neither of us was interested in sightseeing. Rather, we were afraid of the intimacy of the room and the demands and the conflicts that had already become part of our intimacy. I would have the same experience, not too often, but often enough, in my marriage later on. In the rhythm of attraction and repulsion, communion fighting with individuation, bodily desire contesting with mental hurt, love struggling with resentment and anger, I would find myself drawn to my partner and repelled by her. And she would feel the same way.

But this was not my wife. This was my first love. I did not understand what she felt and I did not understand my reaction to her reaction. Hence I did not know what to do, but was pretty well convinced that whatever I would do, I would make a mess of it.

Safe prediction.

Globe was Camelot. I was Gawain or Lancelot or Galahad or maybe Prince Valiant (and I'd been so busy with other things that morning that I had missed both the comics and the Cub scores). She was Guinevere or Aletha or some other such desirable woman. (I didn't know the Parsifal version of the legend, much less the more memorable, it seems to me, Airt MacConn version, in which both grail and princess are firmly and indeed definitively captured by the quester.) And up there in the mountains, lurking as a dark wall in the distance, was the grail, or the pot of gold, either at the end of a rainbow or in the charge of some mean-spirited leprechaun.

It was an absurd fantasy. There was no Lost Dutchman Mine. I was interested in a grand old folktale, not a real lode. I didn't need or even want the gold. I had read the story during a bad (and lonely) night in the South China Sea and thought it might be fun to poke around the Superstition Range someday. Nothing more than that.

Well, if I did find buried treasure . . .

This was not, in fact, Camelot, only an aging copper town. There was no Grail, only a worn-out legend. She was not a magic princess, only a badly confused and uneducated, if very intelligent, child. And I was not Lancelot du Lac.

Or was I?

I might not love her, exactly, but at the moment I was certainly in her thrall. And it seemed that was where, among other locales, she didn't want me.

"We'd better get some sleep. Tomorrow is likely to be another long hot day."

She nodded reluctant agreement. "It's hot enough now, isn't it?"

So, with notable lack of enthusiasm, we dragged ourselves back to the Dominion and rode silently up the creaking cage elevator.

In the room we discovered that the fan worked only when we turned on the light. Hence the air in the room was stagnant and heavy, even though we had left the windows open when we went down for supper. As soon as I turned on the light— a single bulb in the center of the high ceiling—a myriad of bugs began to pound against the screen.

"Can't you turn off the light?" she snapped. "The moon is up now."

"So it is."

I stood on a chair, and by extending my six-foot-one frame to its maximum, barely managed to twist the light bulb sufficiently loose so it went off and the fan continued its noisy rotation.

"Be sure to put it back in the morning."

"Yes, ma'am."

She turned her back on me and with the quick, sure motion with which women remove dresses (a motion I've come to love) slipped out of her sundress. The grace of her movement and the even greater grace of her body so delicately revealed deprived me of what little reason I had left.

I grabbed her, swung her around, pulled her against my chest and began to kiss her. She struggled to escape; so aroused was I that I hardly noticed. Then her resistance aroused me all the more. We wrestled wordlessly (she was a fierce little warrior). I sensed that she was about to quit, to let me have my hollow victory. Then came her barrage about sin. I gave up, not a minute too soon for either of us.

"I don't think we're sinning," I pleaded. Hurt, rejection, humiliation quickly replaced my clumsy passion.

"Then what would you call it?" Her lips were drawn in a tight, bitter line. She faced me, clad in her girdle and stockings, hands on hips, a furious little Amazon with wildly heaving breasts and thin, bitter lips. " 'Fornication' is the usual name, isn't it?"

If there was sin involved, it was in my failure to tell her I loved her, my hesitancy in making that plane reservation for Chicago, and my pusillanimity in substituting an Apache pendant for the ring I ought to have given her.

"Well, at least you didn't come after me with a carving knife." I slumped into the only chair in the room.

"Not yet," she snapped.

"I didn't think it was sinful," I said slowly. "I won't force you, now or ever; but I do feel a little rejected."

"Whether you think it's sinful or not"—she would have made a fine mother superior at the moment, with more clothes on—"God thinks it's sinful."

"I don't believe in God."

"That doesn't matter." She snatched open her case, plucked out a pitiably tattered beige velvet robe and threw it around herself. "God will still punish you."

"Wait a minute." I searched for an answer in the depths of my memory, convinced that I had the textbook on my side. "I've had college religion courses, we called them 'theology' at Notre Dame. And we learned that you can't sin unless you know that what you're doing is sinful. And"—I was warming to my task of specious casuistry—"since sin is an offense against God and since I don't believe that there is any such, I didn't sin. In fact"—I was now addressing the jury—"I am incapable of sin."

Quad erat demonstrandum.

She frowned, trying to find the holes in my reasoning.

"Very nice appeal, Counselor. The women in the jury are doubtless swayed by your good looks, but the Judge is skeptical."

"You or God?"

"But if there is a God, won't He hold it against you?"

"Not if I'm sincere and in good faith and invincibly ignorant."

"What does that mean?" She folded her arms across her tightly bound robe.

"It's not my fault that I'm wrong about God—assuming, for the sake of the argument, that I'm wrong, which I doubt."

"You're too well-educated for me."

"That's a cop-out, but it doesn't matter." I was quickly losing interest in the argument and, to tell the truth, in lovemaking. "Anyway, it doesn't matter. I certainly will not force you to commit sin."

"It doesn't make any difference for me," she said automatically, sagging to the edge of the bed. "I'm damned anyway."

"I won't argue with that absurd notion." I sighed, opened my suitcase and rummaged through it for my loose leaf journal. "And we were told in theology class that it does too make a difference. More sin simply puts you deeper in hell."

"Hell," she stated as she rose from the bed, "is hell. I assure you of that. What are you doing?"

"Digging out my journal. I learned during the war that if you don't make an entry at the end of every day, you soon give it up."

"That would be bad?"

"I like to write."

"I see."

I still keep the journal, it's been useful for this book, but for many other tasks too. Now I mostly dictate it to a tape recorder—you don't have to scribble away on a hard windowsill by indistinct daylight when you have a tiny Sony that fits into your coat pocket. Sometimes I dictate into our JVC video camera, which amuses my wife greatly. She thinks it a hilarious vanity in a man who, if she is to be believed, is normally not vain enough. Moreover, she finds my obsession with Japanese gadgets bizarre in a man who fought the Japanese for three years.

To which I reply that there is no point in holding a grudge.

But I held a grudge that night.

"Why don't you dig a modest nightdress out of that huge bag of yours, go into the bathroom and put it on while I finish this task. It's important to me even if you find it childish."

"I didn't say it was childish." She opened her bag, adroitly rearranged its contents to eliminate the disorder created by her hasty search for a robe, pulled out the same old-fashioned gown she had worn last night, shook it, and carried it toward the bathroom.

"You'll be terribly hot in that."

"I am not unaware of the fact."

I turned to my notebook.

She paused at the bathroom door. "I'm sorry, terribly sorry. I was worried about your soul, not mine."

"I see."

"I didn't meant to hurt or humiliate you."

"You didn't," I said, resolutely not looking up from my notes, "hurt or humiliate me."

She closed the door softly. I was both hurt and humiliated and now disgusted. And there was no point in lying to her because she could read my mind anyway.

"By tomorrow night," I scrawled the words in angry shorthand, "I would be rid of her."

The sentence tore at my soul. Nonetheless, I added, "good riddance."

"Will you be angry if I ask you why you're writing that?"

"I like to write." I looked up. She was sitting in the bed, huddled under the sheet, arms across her knees. "I didn't hear you coming out of the bathroom."

"Who will read it?"

"I can't imagine that anyone else would be interested. I write the personal stuff in shorthand anyway. So don't try to peek when I'm in the bathroom."

"I wouldn't do that." She sounded sad, beaten.

Let up on her, you idiot. It's not her fault. She's had a harsh life.

"We have a family tradition of keeping diaries while we're in the service. Grandpa Keenan's is fascinating. I hope to get it published someday. My father hasn't shown me his yet. But when I went into the Navy he suggested I keep the tradition alive."

"You're out of the Navy now."

"That's right, I am." Then I tried to soften the anger in my wounded male pride. "Maybe if decide to be a writer someday, I'll find it useful."

"Do you want to be a writer?" There was so much reverence in her voice that I had to look up at her. Across the room in the moonlight there was an awed little girl watching me.

"Not like Robert Penn Warren or Fyodor Mikhailovich Dostoyevksy. I don't have that kind of talent. Maybe just little books for my kids and grandkids, if I ever have any."

"How do you know you don't have the talent?"

"Do I look like a writer? Or act like one?"

"What does a writer look like and act like?"

I paused in my scribbling. She was reading my mind again. So she knew about that dream, too.

"Maybe someday I'll know, if everything works out. Go to sleep now, Andrea; we have a hard day ahead of us tomorrow."

"Yes, sir, Commander, sir." She stretched out on the bed, turned her head against the wall, and feigned sleep. "Good night."

"Good night, Andrea."

I thought about another "Good riddance" on the page and thought better of it.

Instead I wrote these fateful words: "These last twenty-four hours have been the most remarkable day in my life. I am confused, uncertain, and terribly apprehensive about our trip tomorrow. I would get out of it if I could. She taught me how to love a woman physically and I'll never be able to thank her enough for that grace. . . ." I hesitated, my pencil above the almost invisible page. Yes, she was wrong. It was grace, not sin. "She also is nun-ridden, erratic, unpredictable, and possibly a little crazy. She thinks she will die soon and be damned to hell forever. Crazy, but, darn it, I still love her."

I finished my notes, closed the journal book, and laid it on the dresser. Somewhere in my duffel bag there were some navy-issue pajamas. I pulled them out in the dark, took off my clothes, tossed them on the floor and pulled on the pajama bottom. I'd be damned if I'd wear the top too. I wasn't going to suffocate because of her change of heart.

Then I remembered to pick up my clothes and put them on hangers. There was no point in having another fight with my traveling companion.

I drew the shades, turning off the moonlight. The old fan continued to rumble uncertainly above our heads. It sounded a little like Roxinante in extremis.

Then I slipped quietly into bed next to my Dulcinea, maintaining the fiction that she was already asleep.

The Superstition Range was out there, stretching off toward Phoenix and the Sky Harbor airport. Tomorrow night the two of us could be on a DC-4 for Chicago. And Butterfield.

When I had pulled down the shades I'd caught a brief glimpse of the Sleeping Beauty Mountain in the moonlight. It had somehow looked sinister. My imagination, probably.

Without any conscious decision, I searched for her hand. It was easy enough to find. Our fingers closed on each other.

And I made the remarkable discovery that there are some activities that are, in their own way, more pleasurable than orgasm.

Such as a slight sign of reconciliation.

I almost told her then that I loved her. But I fell asleep before the words came out of my mouth.

I woke up sometime before morning—it was still dark—to hear the woman next to me in bed softly sobbing. Who was she?

Then I remembered. I wrapped my arms protectively around her. "Go back to sleep, Andrea, I'll take care of you. Always."

The tears stopped. She sighed peacefully. In a few moments she was asleep again in my arms. I fell asleep too, silently repeating my promise.

But "always" turned out to be substantially less than a day.

CHAPTER **15**

WHEN I WOKE EARLY THE FOLLOWING MORNING, THE NAKED blue sky was already threatening a day without pity. The high clouds were gone, the sun was a sizzling orange in the east, the air heavy with the smell of nauseous heat.

My charge was peacefully asleep in my arms. I had slept peacefully too, come to think of it—the first night of serenity in months. Perhaps we were both exhausted from our exertions on the bridal bed in Superior.

At rest she was even more the small, innocent girl child. I eased away from her and out of the bed so as not to awaken her, shaved, dressed, and packed my duffel.

The room clerk had said that a store down the street opened early for the fishermen trade—Lake Roosevelt, over in the next canyon (the Salt River) was a mecca, he said, for fishermen. So I tore a blank page out of my journal and wrote a note to Andrea: "Gone shopping. If you wake before I come back, I'll see you at breakfast."

I almost added "Love," but again the word would not come. So I left the note on the mirror in the bathroom, kissed her on the forehead, and, carrying my duffel, stole silently out of the acrid, musty room. Not much of a place for lovemaking anyway. I asked the night clerk, who was still in charge, directions to the store and emerged into the early-morning unease of Globe, Arizona. Like the Dominion Hotel, Globe was careworn. It had known better days and did not expect to see their likes again. Yet somehow it was more charming than Miami or Superior. Maybe it was the bustle of a county seat or the feeling that one was on the top of very high hills or the faint afterbreath of a Western boom town in which the old buildings were so steeped that they would never lose a touch of their allure.

I decided that I would not want to live in a place like Globe. Worse than the pall of poverty that seemed to hang over the whole Queen Creek area was the atmosphere of discouragement—too many men, some of them still young, walking the streets in the light of early morning with heads bowed in defeat.

(Mining towns always look poor, even when they are prospering. I saw Globe on TV during a recent strike. I was struck by how little the feeling of poverty had changed.)

I purchased bread and cheese and oranges and several thermos bottles for water and a couple of bags of chocolate-chip cookies. I hesitated about a bottle of wine and then decided that I wouldn't drink much of it anyway, so it would not interfere with the curves and the hairpin turns on the Apache Trail. I packed my supplies, except for the thermos jugs, in the trunk of the car next to my duffel.

Andrea was waiting for me in the dining room, which early in the morning smelled of unwashed laundry. She was wearing "my" blue slacks and white blouse and looked even paler than usual and unbearably weary. The top button of her blouse was open.

"Good morning." She did not sound as if she thought there was anything good about it.

"I've been out buying provisions."

"What I like about this ship is that we have an effective commanding officer." Her smile was feeble, but it still made me forget about the sun. "We have not only a happy ship but a well-fed ship. What are the thermoses for? Aren't there lakes along the trail?"

I told the enduringly bored waitress that toast, bacon, and coffee would be fine for me.

"Sure, right along the trail, and sometimes a thousand feet down. They're man-made lakes, partially filled canyons. If you're thirsty and a mountain sheep, you don't need a thermos."

"The captain of this ship is not only effective, he is provident. He reads his guidebooks even if it means rising with the sun."

"He tries hard. Even though this is a cruise ship, he remembers his wartime experiences and superb training he had at Annapolis."

"And on the USS *Wolverine* on Lake Michigan."

"Don't mention that scow."

I was pretty sure I hadn't told her the name of the half-assed carrier on which we practiced landings on flights from Glenview. Moreover, I wasn't thinking about it then. She must have recorded it from an earlier examination of my memory. She had a good filing system. Still maybe I had mentioned it to her after all. Maybe it was merely a case of a better memory of what I had said than I had.

"Furthermore," she said as she stared at the piece of toast in her fingers, "the captain of his ship even holds bitchy, weepy women in his arms most of the night, even after they reject and hurt him."

"You seemed to sleep well in that location."

"Oh, yes." She glanced at me nervously and then returned to her toast. "It was a very restful position. I could use four or five more hours. . . . Are we reconciled?" I felt her fingers on mine. Her eyes filled with tears.

"I am. I was last night."

"If you are, I am . . . I . . ."

Instead of crying, she laughed at me.

And wiped her eyes with tissue.

After breakfast, we walked, at her suggestion, along Broad Street: past a two-story, brick Masonic temple down the street from the hotel; a depressing department store next to it; a stone county courthouse that you could have found in almost

any town west of the Alleghenies; an old Southern Pacific
station farther down.

"I could put you on the train to Phoenix. . . ."

"Certainly not," she snapped. Then she asked, "I should
wear slacks today instead of shorts? If feels like it will be the
hottest day yet."

"Might be a good idea. Rattlesnakes."

"On this tour?"

"Can't promise them, but we'll try. It will be hot all right,
but you'd better leave on the slacks, much as I like admiring
your legs when you wear shorts."

It was, after all, only a mildly suggestive comment. I was
not hoping for a response and I did not get one. Instead there
was a long period of silence as we stared thoughtfully at the
SP station. I tried to break it.

"It would be horrible to live in a place like this, wouldn't
it?"

"Do you really think so?" She wandered over to the schedule board on the station. "You couldn't put me on the train
to Phoenix because there isn't one. I could go to Bowie and
from there to El Paso."

"El Paso?"

"That's in Texas, isn't it?"

"West Texas, it's still a long way. Do you want to go
there?"

"No. I was trying to make an early-morning joke. I guess
it wasn't very funny."

Across from the station, at the top of high steps, was a
squat but quaintly attractive Romanesque church—Our Lady
of the Angels.

"Can we go in?" She nodded toward the church.

"Why not?"

"I haven't been to Mass since my husband's death."

"Really? You miss Mass on Sunday? God won't like that."

"God won't care if He never sees me again."

We hiked up the steep stairs, pushed open the heavy door
and entered the church. It was like entering a different world,
timeless, immutable, patient, confident—a world that would

vanish in the middle nineteen sixties, to be replaced by a more interesting but less reassuring Church.

An old priest was finishing Mass, polishing the chalice after Communion. There were twenty or thirty people scattered in the pews. The inside was modest but tasteful. Some of the names in the stained-glass windows suggested a Czech past, but the priest's Latin did not hide his Irish brogue.

I stood at the back while she kneeled in one of the pews and, as she had in the Saint Xavier Mission, bowed her head in what seemed to be desperate prayer.

"Were your prayers heard?" I asked as we walked back down the steps.

"No."

That was that.

The old priest was standing on the street corner in front of the tiny white rectory next to the church. He saw us and strolled over.

"Sure, if I knew we were going to be after having visitors, wouldn't I have started a few minutes later so you could have received Communion?"

"Would you have?" I said, playing the rules of answering a question by asking one.

"Would I not?"

He chatted pleasantly for a few minutes, asking where we were from and where we were going and, convinced that we were on our honeymoon, cheerfully wishing us a lifetime of blessings. "May God be with you on your way, and may you live to see your children's grandchildren."

"At least," said I.

"Wasn't I after meaning that?" said he with a wink. "And won't you be living at least that long with such a fine woman as herself here to take care of you?"

Andrea hung back from the conversation, apparently afraid of the kindly old man.

"Why didn't you talk to the poor man?" I asked as we walked back to the hotel.

"Where I grew up, priests never stand in front of the

church to talk to the people. The sisters said that Protestant ministers did that."

"Well, I guess that makes us Protestant in Chicago. Packy, my brother the seminarian, says all you have to do to be a good priest is preach a decent sermon, stand in front of the church and smile, and be nice to kids."

"Where I grew up, priests didn't do any of those things."

"You'll have to try Chicago Catholicism."

She ignored, rather pointedly, my suggestion.

"Why should a priest talk to someone who is already damned?"

"If I believed in God, I know He wouldn't damn you."

"I wish I could escape from believing in Him."

"The friars taught us in high school that no one is damned till the end of their life. You're still alive. So you're not damned."

"Oh?"

"Don't give me that elusive 'oh' of yours, Andrea King." I was suddenly furious at her. "I do have some rights with you now, you know." She opened her mouth and I put my hand over it. "Would you just shut up for a second, please? We'll leave the nature and extent of those rights for another discussion." I was warming up again for the jury. "I'm fed up with this divine-rejection theme of yours. You're not entitled to think that you're a great sinner or that you have somehow committed a sin against the Holy Spirit, whatever that is." Ah, her eyes bulged; I'd hit home.

She tried to free her mouth to speak. I clamped my hand on the back of her head, paying no heed to the possibility that the natives might think I was engaged in some odd form of sexual perversity.

"Shut up, would you ever, for a minute? Forget your Irish and listen till I'm finished." She stopped fighting. I searched for a summation. You must not keep a jury waiting. "If there is a God, He feels about you the same way I do. He adores you. He's crazy-mad in love with you. He can hardly wait to get your clothes off and get into bed with you. He wants to play with you, kiss you, bury himself inside of you." Not bad for a spur-of-the-moment argument, huh? "He'll put up with holding you in His arms if that's all He can get. And don't tell me that God isn't that way, because, whatever the nuns may have told you in that creepy place you were raised, that's what Jesus told us about God."

I removed my hand from her mouth, because I knew she'd listen now. I continued, however, to restrain the back of her red-haloed head because that was fun.

"I don't doubt God's love. I doubt his power. What's the point in having a God if He can't prevent the bad things from happening? But I'd never for a moment doubt that He wants to prevent them. The God in whom you believe is a terrible God. He doesn't love you, which is bad taste, since He made you so lovable. The God who may exist for me is a sweet, nice old God who means well and thinks you're irresistible. Now, Andrea King, you go back to our chaste bedroom in the Dominion Hotel and take out the Gideon Bible in the drawer of the dresser—if you're damned anyway, you won't go much deeper into hell for reading a Protestant Bible—and ask which God is the one Jesus talks about in the Gospels: your powerful God who hates or my sometimes weak God who loves."

Now very angry at her, I grasped her thin shoulders and began to shake her.

"If God has anything to say about the rest of your life, it will be happy . . ."

"You're hurting me!"

"I am *not* hurting you," I shouted. "I am shaking you. There's a big difference. And I'm shaking you because God, if He exists, wants to shake you too, you stupid, damn-fool little bitch. Then He wants to absorb you in his love just like I do. You're an idiot for believing anything else."

Not a bad final argument, huh? For the spur of the moment? So good I had begun to persuade myself. I guess I started to believe again at that moment on Broad Street in Globe, Arizona, on July 26, 1946. Tentatively. Or maybe to realize that I had never stopped, could never stop believing.

"What's God like? He's like me, you gorgeous little nitwit—loving, inept, and dumb. Run from that if you want, but don't make up an imaginary hanging judge who won't give you a second chance."

Loving, inept, and dumb—that was the God into a belief in whose existence I had talked myself. Tentatively. When I read over my journal, written up several days later, and see that line, I have this hilarious and not altogether irreverent image of a deep basso voice from heaven saying, "Dumb I may be, buster, but not as dumb as you."

If You're thinking that, touché.

"If only I could . . ." she began.

"If only you *would*. Just keep this in your thick little skull: the God Jesus talked about is not interested in damning you. He's like me—say that over and over—and right now He wants to do the divine equivalent of finding a quiet corner somewhere, taking off your clothes and making love to you all day long. And into the night. Any other God is a faker."

"If He feels that way about me, why did He let my daughter die?" She clenched her fists, angry at the traitor God.

"Hey, I don't believe in Him."

"You're talking yourself into it."

Dear God, if you are there at all, do you look at me with a similar magic smile?

"All I can say is that He has to have loved your daughter too, and that, as best He can—inept, dumb, and loving, maybe—He'll take care of her too." Then I remembered a sermon I'd heard at Easter from a young chaplain. "As best He can, He wants to wipe away all our tears so that we will all be young again and all laugh again."

"You *should* be a priest."

"I doubt it. Have I convinced you that whatever you've done wrong or think you've done wrong, you have a second chance?"

She tilted her jaw stubbornly up. "Some people don't deserve second chances."

"No one deserves a second chance." I grabbed her shoulders and shook her again. " 'Deserve' isn't the point. Lovers give second and third and fourth chances because they can't help themselves."

Now that's a theological observation of which I'm proud even today.

"You've given me a lot to think about." She was both agitated and miserable, her eyes darting back and forth, her fingers jerking anxiously. "If you're right . . . If only . . . I don't know, Jerry. It would be wonderful if you're right."

"I'm rarely wrong. Come on, pretty lady, let's get this Apache Trail out of the way."

The argument—no, my sermon—was over. I had accomplished two things for myself. I had veered back toward God —on my terms but in my hypothesis that was all right. Lovers don't give a damn about terms. And I had told my "bride" of the day before that I loved her. Obscurely and indirectly, but she was too smart to have missed it.

Was she happy to hear it? Hard to tell.

But we did walk back down Broad Street to the Dominion hand in hand.

"Are you packed, Dulci?" I asked her when we came up to the faithfully waiting Roxinante.

"Ready to go."

"I'll bring down your luggage and you see the folks in the kitchen about water and ice for these thermoses."

"Yes sir, Commander, sir."

"I thought I was a captain?"

"Only on board ship."

Our room was already stifling. Better face the heat in the great outdoors than in this place.

Her bag was packed and on the bed. The room was as neat as it could be. Her compulsion for order was impressive.

Then I saw my journal on the dresser top where I had left it the night before. Dumb.

I'd lost portions of it before and had to do all the work of filling it out again. Talk about compulsions. This notebook had only a couple of weeks of my raw memories. But they were interesting memories and it would not do to lose them.

I opened the journal and glanced at the last page. There was an entry in someone else's handwriting, neat Catholic-school Palmer Method:

"I haven't looked at any of the other pages. I hate you, Jerry Keenan. I had given up all hope and you've driven me to hope for hope. I had believed that love was impossible and you've made me want to love again."

That's all.

That short paragraph is in front of me now, on my Wilson Jones copyholder, mute testimony that at least some of my Quixotic and bumbling search for the grail forty years ago was not just a dream.

I paid our bill with the remnants of the two one hundred dollar bills that I had broken in Tucson and Superior. I had a $1.40 and eight new hundreds.

Three nights for two people, two of the nights in excellent hotels, for less than two hundred dollars. My children and grandchildren will no more believe that than they will believe that I purchased poor old Roxy for a hundred and twenty-five dollars and that brand-new the Chevy had cost $699 FOB Detroit.

I put Andrea's trunk and my journal in the backseat, climbed into the driver's seat of Roxy and reached for the manual clutch. I wanted to say something about her entry in my diary, but my muse had overworked in front of Our Lady of the Angels and was now sleeping somewhere in the inner recesses of my brain.

I did notice that another button was open on her blouse, a signal surely. As my wife later remarked apropos of another woman, rarely does something come unbuttoned by chance. There's usually a message, only the message changes, even with the same person.

So I said nothing about my journal and her button, and she asked nothing about the journal. I started the car, backed up, turned around, and started down the road to Miami, the Superstitions, and Phoenix. Just short of the town, we turned off US 60 and down the unpaved tracks of Arizona 88 toward Roosevelt Lake and the "back door" to the Superstition Range.

"More dirt roads?"

"That's all there is up here."

"If I had not packed my rosary, I'd say it."

"Not much confidence in the captain. Count it on your fingers. Quietly. I may need prayers, but I don't need distractions."

In response she kissed my cheek. Lightly, but that was enough. Even forty years later that kiss still stands out as the happiest moment in the trip.

CHAPTER **16**

"If I weren't traveling with such a literate woman, I'd say that the ride from Globe down Pinal Creek Canyon was like jumping from the frying pan into the fire. But with you I'll say it's like descending from the hills of purgatory to the valleys of hell."

"If you believe Dante, the bottom of hell is ice."

"You've read the *Divine Comedy*?"

"Certainly, although my nuns thought part of it was risqué. Actually Dante called it simply *La Commedia* in Italian. Someone else added the 'divine' later on. Haven't you read it yet?"

"No ... It's ..."

"On your list."

"Right."

Was she making fun of me? Probably. The light kiss had somehow rearranged our relationship, making it both more personal and less volatile. Now we could laugh at each other, complain, bicker, even argue without fear that something vital would be hurt.

Such is the power of the right kiss at the right time.

"If you intend to be a writer you'll have to catch up with those books."

"It's unnatural how many books you've read. Here, tackle this one." I tossed her Barry Storm's *Thunder God's Gold.* "It will save me the obligation to lecture you.

"After Roosevelt Lake," I continued, violating my promise not to lecture, "we will enter what is properly called the Apache Trail, named after the Apaches who built Roosevelt Dam at the turn of the century, the first big reclamation project in this country. It was not an original trail used by the Apaches when this was their territory, though they probably did wend their way through the maze of creek and river canyon and washes which crisscross these hills. It is a perfect hideout for light cavalry, as you might imagine."

"Yes, Professor."

Since the road down to Pinal Creek Canyon is relatively straight, I took my eyes off it for an instant to determine whether she was laughing at me or reading her assignment.

She was doing both.

"If you don't like the tour, you can get off and take the stage."

"Stage? You mean one of those horse-drawn things? That would be even worse than your driving."

She was still laughing. Damned but capable of being amused by a foolish male boy child.

"They don't use horses anymore. The picture in the hotel suggests a very old motor bus. Before the war it went through to Roosevelt from Phoenix. Now it stops at Tortilla Flat."

"What?"

"Not the place in the novel."

"I'm glad. How far is it to this stage stop?"

"Maybe fifty miles. It's only a few miles beyond Fish Creek, where Clinton is. That's our ghost town. In Lost Dutchman Canyon."

"So I have to stay with the tour till then, Commander?" Now she was chuckling loud enough for me to hear her.

I hunched the old car to the side of the road, turned off the ignition and took her into my arms. "We seem to have forgotten something last night."

She did not protest or resist, but permitted me to smother her with quick, delightful kisses. "The more you complain" —I paused for breath—"the more I kiss you."

"Maybe I'll complain all day. But then"—more laughter —"you won't be able to glue your eyes to the next curve, will you?"

"Just watch me."

I was quite sure that there would be no more kissing till Tortilla Flat. If then.

So I tried for a whole day's kissing. It was very modest kissing, like our affection in the corridor of the Arizona Inn. We both tried to pretend that nothing more explosive had happened in the interim. We were starting over with a clean slate.

"You still like to be kissed," I observed.

"Of course."

Reluctantly I released her, started the car and lurched back on the highway. The words "I love you" were on the tip of my tongue, but did not quite break free. Hadn't I said them already in front of Our Lady of the Angels?

We continued through the lush grass and oak country toward Roosevelt Dam.

"It's so much like in the movies," she said, again a little girl admiring the cattle standing patiently in the shade of the trees.

"You haven't seen anything yet . . . what do you think of Barry Storm?"

"It's lucky you told me it was folklore. I would hate to think you felt this stuff was history."

"The book ought to be taken seriously. The man did a lot of work. . . ."

"And forgot to offer any evidence."

Her judgment would prove later on to be solid. Storm's book was more fiction than fact, though it was closer to fact than the film allegedly based on it—*Lust for Gold*, with Glenn

Ford as Jacob Walz—that was made several years later. Can you imagine Glenn Ford as the Dutchman, a scruffy, mostly alcoholic ne'er-do-well? He is one of my favorite actors, but as Ben Hogan the golfer, not Jacob Walz the Dutchman.

Barry Storm was not the author's name, I would learn many years later, but the nom de plume of a man named John T. Clymenson. He borrowed the first of his plume names from his photographer, a young Phoenix department-store heir named Barry Goldwater.

I remember how happy I was when we defeated that "extremist" in the 1964 election. We all knew that he would involve us in a war somewhere. Lyndon Johnson would never do that. So instead of a reactionary with common sense, we elected a phony liberal whose first election to Congress was accomplished by vote theft and who would later prove to be a crook, arguably a murderer, and at the end of his term a lunatic.

How could anyone forget the lesson of Korea and involve us in another land war in Asia so soon?

I feel strongly because I lost one child in the Viet Nam fiasco and almost lost another.

"I take it," I observed on that July day in 1946 when my world was not so much complicated as mysterious, "that you are not fascinated by the hunt for buried treasure."

"I feel like Becky Thatcher chaperoning a boy who is a mixture of Tom Sawyer and Huck Finn . . . and don't even think of stopping the car to kiss me as reward for such a remarkably humorous comment. Keep your eyes on the road."

"Yes, ma'am. I'll catch up with the kissing later."

"I bet you will."

I wanted to be rid of her in Phoenix at the end of the day and I wanted her next to me in the car for the rest of my life. Huck Finn and Dante and I ought to be a writer.

"You might even make a good writer," she completed my thought. "You certainly seem to understand women better than most male writers."

At the Tonto National Monument, I halfheartedly suggested that we climb up to the ruins of the pueblos where the *salados* (the "salt people," after the Salt River along which they had lived) had moved when unfriendly tribes invaded the flood plain.

"Please," she said with a shudder, "no."

We did get out of the car at Roosevelt and admired the shimmering blue lake. "I could stay here forever," she said, and then sighed. We watched the fishermen and inspected the dam, mostly masonry, but impressive for the early part of the century.

Then we returned to the patiently waiting Roxinante and turned up 88 toward Fish Creek.

There were two mental and emotional processes going on in my soul: fascination and increasing desire for this marvelous little woman whom I had made my own and fear for the increasingly haunted (or so it seemed to me) mountain range.

In the tug-of-war between these two emotions my love for Andrea King was a temporary winner as we cautiously picked our way around the treacherous curves and climbed up over the dull-blue lakes that humans had carved out of the barren desert valleys. Above us the ruthless sun glared ominously. In the back of my head one of the various voices, perhaps CIC, warned me to turn back.

So bemused was I by the precious treasure next to me in the front seat of Roxy that I didn't even notice that my shirt was wet with perspiration—heat and fear working together on my pores.

"We'll probably encounter only one or two cars today," I commented, trying to sound like a briefing officer before a routine mission. "It's hot and we're coming from the opposite direction early in the morning, and it's midweek and it's not tourist season. But after noon tomorrow, Friday, there'll be a lot more fishermen."

"I'm reassured. But suppose that despite all your well-reasoned arguments, a Packard or a Cadillac or a truck appears from the other direction."

"Well, first of all, we'll both be moving at only ten or fifteen miles an hour and driving carefully, so there is no danger of a crash. Secondly, one of us would have to back up."

"Which one?"

"The one driving downhill . . . I think."

"Marvelous." My tourist with the sweet and willing, even eager lips, had turned sarcastic.

"Sorry."

"I wonder if I can make the Stations of the Cross on my fingers too."

"I'm keeping my eyes on the road."

"It's terribly hot, isn't it? Could we go down to one of those lakes and swim?"

"We'd have to unpack our swimsuits."

"Why?"

That was an interesting idea.

"If I swam with you in the nude, you'd end up being ravished."

"No flat place down there."

"That wouldn't stop me."

"Brave officer hero."

I stopped the car, regardless of the possibility of another car coming around the bend, and silenced her taunts with vehement kisses—lips, throat, neck, breasts.

"Oh, Jerry . . ." She closed her eyes and sighed. "I love you so much."

I almost pulled off the side of the road into the desert and carried her down to the sinister blue lake that seemed to be inviting us. I was within a hair's breadth of doing just that. Fear of the stark, grimly watching mountain peaks and the malevolent desert sky won out over desire.

My life might have been very different if I had not been so afraid.

Of what was I afraid?

I didn't know then, and even now I'm not sure. But the closer we came to Clinton, Arizona, the more the icy tentacles of fear clutched at my gut.

"You are going to get yourself savagely assaulted, young woman, when we finish this damn road."

"How wonderful!" she whispered.

While I would not dream of returning to the Tonto National Monument, one of my kids—the woman doctor who, before she married, used to travel with a sleeping bag in the trunk of *her* Chevy and has been known to spend the night in cemeteries—went to Arizona on her honeymoon. (She had married a man who had accepted her condition that, before she considered him, he would have to spend a night in a sleeping bag in a graveyard with her, separate bag too, but that's another story.) She reports that the upper half of the Apache trail has not changed. It's still a one lane dirt trail clinging dubiously to blood red, rust brown, and burnished gold cliffs with smooth blue lakes below and soaring mountains above. I was too busy watching the road to enjoy the scenery very much.

"Why are we going up here?" Andrea demanded impatiently. "I thought you were taking me to Phoenix."

"The Flying . . . I mean the Lost Dutchman Mine." I stole a glance at her. "Remember, we've talked about it?"

"You think you can find in a few hours what others have hunted for decades?" Her lips curled in withering contempt. "You're a bigger fool than I thought you were."

"I wanted to be able to tell my kids that I looked for it, if only for a few minutes. And saw Clinton, the Dutchman's ghost town."

She did not choose to respond to such foolishness but instead curled into a tight, hard knot, turned away from me, and ignored both the tour and the tour guide.

Fifteen minutes and three miles later, she uncurled.

"Who was that snippy little bitch that was in this car while I was away? Don't let her in the car again."

"I didn't get too close a look at her. I was watching the road."

"Well, don't let her back in, she's a pain."

"She comes and she goes."

I was rewarded with another kiss on my right ear.

"I'm jittery for some reason, Jerry. Forgive me. I guess it's the heat. And this place scares me. Now don't say I insisted on coming. I know I did."

"Yes, Miss Thatcher."

We drove on, her left hand now protectively on my arm.

I hoped the right was tolling the imaginary beads. I was not so far along in my reconversion that I believed God was capable of protecting us from the dangers of the Apache Trail. But I was sufficiently frightened by the narrow road and the hairpin turns to welcome prayers "to whom it may concern."

The Superstition Mountains earn their name. While the colors and the sweep of orderly ranks of mountain ridges are beautifully stunning, the general effect is still to create a feeling of the eerie—huge rocks poised over the dirt road as though they were ready to plunge down on you; steep, dark canyons; mad hairpin turns; brooding mountains that seemed ready on an instant's notice to become dangerous volcanoes again. The foothills of hell, perhaps. Any evil that could be, might be here.

We paused for a picnic lunch on the side of Apache Lake. And some mild necking and petting. It was too hot even to think of anything more affectionate.

I smothered her breasts with gentle kisses, affectionate and respectful, not demanding.

"I love you," I said when I knew it was time to stop and removed my hungry lips from her warm skin.

"I love you, Jerry," she said simply as she buttoned her blouse.

I kissed her lips. Then, as quiet as the watching mountains, we assembled our gear and scrambled up the canyon wall to my patiently waiting and overheated car.

In the distance, at the far end of the range, perhaps over Superstition Mountain itself, there appeared a coal-black thunderhead, a smudge on the hard-blue sky, no bigger, as the Bible says, than a man's hand, an apparent harbinger of a colossal storm.

Were the Thunder gods, fanatically puritanical like most Indian gods, angry that I had fondled a half-naked woman in their sacred domain?

CHAPTER 17

I INCHED PAST CASTLE MOUNTAIN, AWAY FROM THE LAKES and up the walls of Fish Creek Canyon. The eighteen-inch guns of the *Yamoto*, blazing away at us till the bitter end, were less dreadful than the steep drop of thousands of feet that seemed just a few inches outside the window.

The heat was insufferable, a blast-furnace door left open; water quenched our thirst for only a few minutes; we were enervated, exhausted, drained. The road was designed by the same architects who had worked on hell. Even on a cool day, driving it would have been a nerve-racking experience.

"That's Castle Mountain on the left, Andrea," I said through gritted teeth. "Doesn't it look like a blood-red medieval fortress with turrets and towers and battlements?"

"No."

"Well, what does it look like?"

"It looks like a mountain trying to look like a medieval castle with—watch out!"

I'll admit we skidded a little.

"Nothing to worry about." The sweat was pouring off my forehead as if the Thunder gods were emptying buckets of water on me. From not believing in any God I had quickly drifted to wondering whether the Thunder gods could be real and might punish me for violating their sexual rules.

That's ridiculous. Surely there had been other lovers along this mountain range. You're losing your nerve, that's the problem, not the Thunder gods. Cool Jerry Keenan, never frightened in combat. Right?

"Are you scared, Commander?" she asked as her fingers dug into my right arm.

"Sure am."

"Good." She sighed in mock relief. "Then I don't have to be."

The turns and curves became a little bit less spectacular as we drew near the side road up the side of Fish Creek Peak to Lost Dutchman Canyon.

And today's batch of ominous thunderheads were already building up—dark, fierce, angry.

I stopped the car in the area where there was supposed to be a road back to Clinton. Ought I to call the game on account of darkness? Did I want to drive down this mountain goat's trail in a storm? Or after it had turned into an instant river with treacherous waterfalls?

Take her on to Phoenix before dark. Be done with her. She's haunted. Bad news.

The F6F pilot with his Navy Cross and Star tucked away somewhere, not quite sure where—would he lose his nerve and turn back?

I would, instead, compromise.

"We'll look at the ghost town for a few minutes and then come back. It's maybe a half-mile up from here," I said to my reluctant tourist. "It's called Clinton; most ghost towns have Anglo-Saxon rather than Spanish—"

Her mood changed instantly. She was no longer a scared but witty companion on an unnerving auto ride, rather like the girls who used to ride with me on the bobs at Riverview Amusement park. Now she was crazy. "Ghost town!" she screamed hysterically.

She curled up into her familiar knot against the car door.

"Relax, Andrea," I said, firmly gripping her shoulder, "ghost towns don't have ghosts. They're just old abandoned mining towns. Relics of the past."

She changed again. Instead of the hard knot at the far end of the front seat, she became a soft little girl clinging to my arm, as she had at the worst of the hair turns.

"Sorry." She struggled upright in the car seat. "It's that little bitch again. She sneaks into your car when I'm gone. You really shouldn't tolerate her. Send her home."

"I'll keep that recommendation in mind."

"I'd never act that way."

"What I like is a satisfied tourist."

She laughed and I laughed too. Contagious enthusiasm.

I started the car again and crept along the road, map in one hand, searching for the Clinton turnoff. I finally found it and wished that I had not.

One glance at the real-world counterpart of the "road" marked on my map, jutting off at right angles from Arizona 88, told me that we could not drive it. I parked the car close to the wall of the mountain, turned to her, and tilted her chin up. "I'm afraid we'll have to walk. Do you want to wait? I'll be back in an hour."

"I'll come with you, Commander. That's why I'm here."

The two of us climbed out of Roxinante, she with more vigor than I.

"Are you sure?"

"Pilots, man your planes," she said gamely.

"Make love first," my CIC insisted; "screw her real good and tell her irrevocably that you love her. Wrap it all up before you go up that road."

"You've never recommended anything that impulsive before."

"We've never been in a situation like this before. Have I ever been wrong?"

I turned him off, put my arm around Andrea and led her up the trail toward Clinton, Arizona.

"Lost Dutchman's Canyon," I told her as we trudged up the tilting path, "is a long way from Weaver's Needle, where the mine is supposed to be. But a substantial lode of gold was discovered up here a few years after the Dutchman died. Clinton was founded to extract the gold, and later on, after it closed down, the name of the Dutchman was given to the canyon."

"Oh." She accepted my helping hand and held on to it. "Why did it close down?"

"Various reasons. Earthquakes. Rainstorms' which flooded the mines, revenge of the Thunder gods, if you believe the legends."

"There's still gold?"

"Probably not. The veins were running out anyway."

"Can't blame the Thunder gods for that, can you?"

"I don't think the Thunder gods"—I tightened my arm around her—"would approve of the way I feel about you. They were puritans."

"Well"—she snuggled closer to me—"the God you claim you might believe in again is not a puritan, is He? Not according to what you said this morning."

"She's as eager to be laid as you are to lay her." CIC was back, using uncharacteristic language. "Take her back to the car, fuck, and wind up this mission. Who needs a ghost town?"

I ordered him to the brig and continued climbing up the dusty, cactus-strewn trail. We finally arrived at the top and beheld the shabby relics of Clinton, Arizona. Drenched in sweat, as wet as if I'd stood fully dressed under a shower, all I wanted to do was collapse and sleep for an hour or two.

Andrea, calm now and self-possessed, stood next to me examining the town curiously. "I don't think it looks scary at all. Run-down and kind of cute."

"No reason why it should be scary." I was struggling to remember how to breathe. "As I said before, ghost towns don't have ghosts."

Ghost towns don't have ghosts, right? I imagine that you can buy a book even today in any Tucson or Phoenix bookstore and read all about the ghost towns and never read a word about haunting. Ghost towns are so called because they are dead towns, not because they have the spirits of dead people.

Keep that in mind.

If you've ever visited an Arizona ghost town, your first reaction, very likely, was disappointment. Just a few old buildings without any roofs or windowpanes, vegetation growing through the floorboards, an occasional sign tilting at a crazy angle, wind maybe rustling loose clapboard, an infrequent small creature darting away in righteous surprise that its haven has been invaded, broken pieces of what might have been furniture littering the land between the buildings.

Not much.

You think to yourself that it's hard to imagine that anyone ever lived here and that Hollywood could build better ghost towns than Arizona has.

Clinton produced exactly that reaction after our exhausting pull up the trail. It was nothing more than the remains of a mill with a few bricks of the smokestack; some crumbling stone walls; a dilapidated two-story clapboard building on a stone foundation, with a sagging front porch on the first floor and the remains of a balcony on the second—the mine office.

A couple of posts tilting crazily behind the town hall were all that remained of the water tower, which in one of the pictures had "Clinton A.T." proudly painted on it a half century before.

At some distance, closer to the canyon, there were four more broken-down buildings: three small A-frames and another larger one—town hall, tavern, and hotel all rolled into one, according to my guidebook.

"No, it doesn't look very scary at all." She released my arm, but still snuggled close to me as we stood at the top of the ridge looking at the remains of Clinton.

"It isn't. Do you want to stay here or explore with me?"

She looked up at the sky, now a threatening gray. "I want to stay with you."

"Be very careful where you walk. This area is pockmarked with shafts sunk into the ground. They were boarded up years ago, but the wood is probably rotten by now."

"Yes, Commander Guidebook, sir; I'll be very careful, sir!"

Tentatively I extended again an arm around her shoulders. Her poor little heart was pounding wildly. She cuddled close to me.

Oh, no, Clinton wasn't scaring her.

And I owned her now. She was my Lost Dutchman lode, more precious than any gold vein in these mountains.

"Clinton, Arizona, or Arizona Territory, to be precise. That canyon was a stream—or a creek, as they call them out here—fifty years ago." I pointed to a deep gorge behind the pathetic row of fading shacks. "Lost Dutchman Canyon. It's still a drainage wash that fills up in a hurry when the Thunder gods go on a rampage.

"They came up the mountains on the same road we did, then down the side of that mountain and pitched their tents and put up these buildings here. They prospected in the stream and in the caves on the side of the canyon. They found a vein of gold and others poured in. They sank mine shafts all over the place. There is a tunnel somewhere back in the hills, but most of the mines are merely holes in the ground. They're not like the coal mines back in the East. Nor the one in the Museum of Science and Industry—"

"What?"

"I'm sorry. You're not from Chicago. I keep forgetting. Where did you say you were from?"

"I didn't."

We walked toward the pathetic little street. It must have looked pathetic to them too, but they didn't mind how primitive and uncomfortable were the circumstances of their lives. They had a bright dream of an earthly paradise. Gold! The Dutchman was not a romantic figure at all, but a poor, illiterate kid who left his home in Germany with a dream of a better life. Before Grandpa Keenan, but with the same dream. He never found his stake, though he searched for it till he was an impoverished and crippled old man, living in a hut near where Sky Harbor Airport was now, cared for by a kindly Negro ice-cream-shop proprietor, whom he infected with gold fever.

The Dutchman was famous in legend, but in real life he was a failure. He never found even a Maggie Keenan for whom to risk his life and with whom to live to a roistering, difficult, happy old age.

The ground caved in beneath me with an explosive crack. I was falling, as if the engine had conked out at eight thousand feet. I grabbed desperately for something, anything, and found only a shaky timber

And a very determined human hand.

"Don't you dare let go," she ordered me.

"I'll pull you down." My throat was tight with desperation. Now I had time to be terrified.

"No, you won't. I'm on a little rise or something."

My feet were kicking over what seemed like miles of nothingness. The timber began to crack.

"It's breaking, Andrea, I don't think I can make it."

"Sure you can. Put your other hand up on the ground, it's just above your head."

Sure enough, it was. I could pull myself up easily. A stupid, unnecessary panic.

"Hang on for another second, I'll heave myself out of here."

"I have no intention of letting go."

"Ready?"

"Ready."

"One . . ."

"Two . . ."

"Three . . ."

And together we shouted, "Heave!"

I flew out of the mine shaft as if I had been catapulted off the stern of a cruiser and landed on top of her.

She laughed loudly. "Be careful of the shafts, Andrea, a dumb little girl kid like you could get hurt if she's not careful."

"Shut up," I said irritably.

"Yes, sir."

It was quite pleasant on top of her, even if I was quivering like a frightened autumn leaf. Why not stay here for a while?

"You saved my life, dumb little girl kid. If it wasn't for you, I'd be in the water at the bottom of that shaft now, probably unconscious with a couple of broken legs."

Her stunning body shivered beneath me. "You would have pulled yourself out anyway."

"Maybe yes, maybe no. I'm glad you came." I brushed my lips against hers. "I did need my own personal Becky Thatcher."

I stood up, my knees weak, my leg muscles shuddering uncontrollably. I helped her up and kissed her again. To hell with what the Thunder gods thought.

"I like being Becky Thatcher, but do be careful, Tom. I don't want to dig you out of another one of your holes."

"I'm sorry I messed up your blouse and slacks. I'll buy you new ones." I was brushing the desert dirt off her slacks, necessitating delightful contact with her delightful rear. "A whole new wardrobe. At least."

"I won't fight you this time." She continued to laugh at me, affectionately like a mother with a foolish little boy child.

"Well." I ignored her laughter. For someone who thought she was damned, she could certainly laugh at me. "To return to my lecture, they exhausted the vein pretty quickly and then everyone left." My voice was still unsteady. "Whether this was the Dutchman's lode or not depends on which legend you believe."

"How much time did you spend with the guidebook"— her eyes glinted briefly with amusement—"before you left San Diego?"

"Two weeks." Damn it, she had made me blush again. "I like to be prepared. . . ."

"And you didn't know you'd have a worshiping audience to hang on your every word."

I was still badly shaken by my narrow escape—more narrow, to tell the truth, than any in the war. But I could not help joining in her laughter.

"A gorgeous audience at that." I patted her cheek. "Attentive and respectful and docile."

It's important to remember this conversation when you try to make sense out of what I'm going to describe shortly. The volatile dream in which I had lived with Andrea King since we'd left Tucson was fading in Clinton. We were both returning to the real world. Sky Harbor Airport was almost around the corner. We were laughing at each other like two utterly human young lovers. Neither of us had any sense of the uncanny or any premonitions of the mysterious. At least I didn't, and as best as I can recollect Andrea's behavior from the notes I frantically scrawled the next day, neither did she.

I was now assuming, without quite admitting it explicitly to myself, that tomorrow night she would be safely ensconced in the guest room in the back of our River Forest home.

"Anyway," I continued to lecture, "right along here, on

this rise at the end of the main street, and the only street of the town, they dug a tunnel. According to some of the stories, deep inside the mountain, beneath here, actually, the tunnel splits into two passages— Hey, Andrea, here it is—right behind this saguaro! The entrance to the tunnel!"

It was not a big, dramatic entrance as you see in the various film versions of King Solomon's Mines (of which my favorite is the Deborah Kerr one, for reasons so obvious that I need not dwell on them). Rather, it was a narrow opening in the wall of the mountain, with the remnants of a beam at the top, hardly wide enough for one person to slip into.

"If you go in there," my dogged companion notified me, "I'm coming with you."

She meant it. I deferred the decision.

"The tunnel splits into two deep down inside; according to one story, they took a little bit of gold out of one of the tunnels, but had a lot of trouble with the other. Cave-ins, wooden supports collapsing, flooding after storms."

"And, I bet I can guess, beyond that, according to the rumors, someone found the beginning of the Dutchman's treasure."

"Right. Everyone who got back that far died mysteriously. Or so the legend says."

"And you're going to be the first one not to die?"

"Don't be ridiculous." I took her arm and steered her away from the tunnel mouth. "I've already found my Arizona treasure."

"I'm glad." She huddled close to me.

"They had a lot of sickness too. Something like typhoid fever, though a little different. The canyon was supposed to be an ancient Apache sacred place. Couldn't have been too ancient, because the Apache only came here in the seventeen hundreds, after the Cherokee chased them out of Texas and Oklahoma, where they were herdsmen rather than rustlers. Anyway, one story says that before each new outbreak of the disease, a huge black cloud came to the town at night. Not much regret when Clinton closed down."

"Poor people."

"Any poorer than us?"

"A lot."

"I suppose."

We walked along the creaking remnants of a porch on the front of the main building. She stumbled on a loose board and I held her close.

"Water was not a problem here, as it might be in other places in the Superstitions. Even when it isn't the rainy season, there is a spring back there up in the hills which is now called Lost Dutchman Spring. In a way they had too much water. Every time it rained, the mine shafts and the tunnels flooded. Too much water in the middle of the desert, a paradox, but one that is crucial for the mining industry."

"What is the odd smell? Not dead people, I hope."

"You mean like sawdust? Dried-out wood."

She turned and looked up the street toward the mine offices. "Kind of disappointing, isn't it?"

"You're right. Hollywood could do it better."

I kicked open the loosely hanging door of the main building. A mouse or some other small creature darted nervously across the floor, stirring up a cloud of smoke behind him.

"Dust," she said, "decades of dust. There must be an inch of it on the floor."

"In the desert, that could be only a year's collection."

"Do you want to go in?" she asked respectfully.

"The commander does not want to go in." I hugged her shoulders. "Not at all, thank you very much."

A bolt of lightning leapt from one of the immense mountains behind us, jumped across the sky and buried itself in another mountain. Distant thunder rolled grimly. Andrea threw her arms around me in abject terror.

"Don't worry, Andrea King," I said, trying to sound like the squadron leader of VF 39. "I'll take care of you. Always. If you give me a chance."

I touched her face. It was cold, cold as death, I thought, even though the gray sky and the occasional raindrops had not cooled the air.

"If only you could . . ."

Protectiveness turned without warning to passion. My lips sought hers again, much more violently than earlier in the day, my fingers searched for her breasts, our bodies pushed together. She was mine for the taking. I pushed the blouse off her shoulders.

She pulled away from me.

I stopped. Not this way. Not here.

"Sorry," I said. "I didn't mean to . . ."

"My fault," she replied miserably. "But it doesn't mean that I still think we were sinning . . . it was the little bitch who said that."

"My fault . . ." I insisted. Then we both laughed and relaxed. "I do love you."

"Don't say it." She laid her fingers on my lips. "Not yet. Not ever."

"Let's get out of here." I readjusted her blouse and fastened the buttons again.

"Thank you, Commander." Her marvelous blue eyes danced with mischief.

It was indeed all settled at that instant. We were more than just casual bedmates. We were to be lifelong lovers.

Later in the night, in the midst of the horror, I had the strange feeling that none of it would have happened if I had made love to her at that moment—not in the first wild rush of passion, but in the magic of our eyes dancing happily with one another. Or maybe it was the other way around. Maybe if I had not stirred up our passions as the storm closed in on us, the Thunder gods would not have been angry.

Because I didn't believe in God quite yet, it did not follow that I did not believe in the Thunder gods. The existence of good spirits may be problematic. The reality of evil spirits is certain.

"I *will* take care of you, Andrea." I touched her face gently with my fingers. "Please believe that, at least."

We strolled, arm-in-arm, back to the Chevy—two strong, happy young people rejoicing in the prospects of life ahead of them, hardly aware of the half-mile of rough mountain trail down which they were stumbling.

I must insist on that point. Whatever sense of doom she had felt since Bing Crosby and the train station and I had felt driving up the far side of the Superstition Mountains, had vanished. Neither of us sensed evil closing in.

I opened the door of the Chevy for her.

"Thank you, Commander, sir. . . . No, wait a minute, please, Jerry. Let me apologize for having been so boorish. You're a good and kind and wonderful man. You should never have adopted me. I should never have come along. Regardless of that, I'm not as bad as I've behaved some of the time."

"So long as you continue to be as good as you were the rest of the trip." I kissed her gently.

For the last time.

I went around to the other side, noticing that the first torrent of rain was racing along the gorge toward us.

I turned the ignition key over. Nothing happened. The Chevy had its temperament, but it always started. I pulled out the choke, cranked the gas pedal once, and flipped the key again.

"That's funny," I said. "It has always started since Chief Arnold fixed it."

The rain was on us, plunging the inside of the car into midnight darkness.

"It's coming for us," she said calmly. "Don't worry, Jerry, I'll take care of you."

CHAPTER **18**

THE ONLY NAME FOR IT IS HORROR.

The doors of the Chevy swung open as though a giant had flipped them open as he raced by us. Wind, I told myself.

It wasn't ordinary wind, however, which grabbed the two of us and hurled us out of the car. I tried to stand up and fight back, flaying uselessly against the furiously rushing air currents. I grabbed Andrea, pulled her against my chest and clung to her. Not all the Thunder gods in hell would take her from me. Lightning struck next to us, thunder rolled down the canyon walls like charging troops of cavalry. Again lightning sizzled all around us, spawning a thick, nauseous sulfur odor.

The Thunder gods wrestled with me for only a few seconds before they tore my love out of my arms and hurled her up the trail like a fragile cloth doll, tumbling head over heels in the air currents.

Then they swept me off the ground and pitched me up the mountainside after her. The maniac howling wind carried us through the air, like parachutists in free-fall back up the half-mile of steep trail, as the thunder boomed and the lightning crackled, and toward the main building and through the door, which opened just before we slammed into it.

A tornado?

They don't have tornadoes in Arizona.

An especially severe thunderstorm at a high altitude? Were we not almost five thousand feet above sea level?

All right. Arizona thunderstorms can develop sudden and furious gusts of high-speed wind. But not strong enough to carry someone up a half-mile of mountain trail.

Might not the wind have slammed me into the Chevy and knocked me out? Might not everything else be the product of unconscious fantasies boiling up from the last several hectic days?

Possibly. I don't think so. Not the events at the beginning of the horror anyway. The thunderstorm really happened.

Anyway, we were swept into the main building of the ghost town of Clinton and our hell began.

The thick black cloud was there already, licking its chops in anticipation. We were both slammed against the wall across the room and pinned against it, a couple of feet off the floor. Instantly the place was suffused with a terrible stench, a combination of all the outdoor latrines in the Philippines and the burning flesh and aviation fuel after a kamikaze hit the carrier next to us at Okinawa Jima. I thought I would suffocate with the stench. Before they were finished with us, I would wish that death might be that easy.

Invisible hands jabbed and poked at us, the way Indians were said to torture their victims before killing them. For a few moments I saw Andrea twisting and turning against the wall. Her clothes were ripped away. She was spun around and around as though she were being beaten by invisible whips. Then she disappeared in the inky darkness. Her screams continued for a long time, shrieks more terrible than those that had awakened me during our night in Globe; the anguished agony of a woman being raped, mutilated, murdered; the cries of a damned child pleading for the end of her suffering. Then they stopped.

What happened next seemed like the whole of eternity. In fact, it lasted at the most only a few hours, and maybe only a few minutes. It was like being tumbled down the side of a mountain in a landslide of nightmares.

My nightmares and Andrea's fused and consumed us both. I was being destroyed by these combined nightmares and, even if I could no longer hear her screams, she was being destroyed with me.

My first accusers were the men I'd lost in VF 39—Rusty, Hank, Tony, Marshal, all the others. They circled around me, their dead distorted faces and empty eyes fading in and out in the blackness, screaming curses and accusations. I had cut short their lives, stolen them from their wives and sweethearts and from the children they never knew. I had sent them all to hell.

I shouted my innocence. I had tried to protect all my men, war was hell, casualties were inevitable. I had done my best. . . .

Either they did not hear or they did not care. They were dead and in hell and I was still alive.

And the heat of the wall to which I was pinned became with each accusation more like a frying pan.

Rusty turned into a tiny baby, gurgling helplessly as it

was held under water; Tony changed into a sailor half of whose head had been bashed in. They too accused me of cutting short their lives.

"I didn't kill you," I shrieked. "She did!"

So much for taking care of Andrea.

My betrayal did not save me, the screams of outrage continued. My frying pan was now white-hot, my clothes were ripped off, the invisible hands tormenting me became more insistent and determined. I too was spun around to be tortured by the steel-tip whips, which tore off my flesh in great bleeding hunks. I was to be flayed alive and not permitted to die.

Then the new dead were replaced by the old dead—brown-skinned, primitive people from long ago; the timid, diffident *Salados* from their pueblos high above the river valley; Spaniards; Apaches; other Indians; Americans; my grandparents from Ireland, Jeremiah and Maggie Keenan, both drunk; men and women whom I did not recognize, from her past, not mine.

The Dutchman was there, a horrible grin on his ancient bearded face. And Peralta and Meisner and the Mexicans the Dutchman had killed. And the victims of the Apache massacre. And Clara Thomas—all the people in the legend, all come back to judge me guilty of their deaths.

They all died horribly: tortured, scalped, raped, butchered, ravaged by disease; men burned at the stake; women cut into tiny pieces that were then roasted over campfires; children whose heads were smashed against the rock walls of the canyon.

They all accused me; I was the master murderer, the true Hitler of all history. I was the death that had slain them all.

"No! No!" I screamed. "I didn't do it! She did! She is death, not I!"

Even then the one or two sane cells that still were working in my brain wondered when the Japanese whom I had undoubtedly really killed in aerial combat would come to accuse me of their murder.

They never showed up.

The dead and the dying faded into the blackness and the

blackness itself slowly lifted, to hover like the threat of pestilence beneath the ceiling. Then the dead returned to dance.

They whirled and spun, leapt and cavorted, jumped and gamboled as if they were celebrating a graveyard Mardi Gras, all the time performing unspeakably lascivious acts on each other. I was pulled off the wall, like a prize trophy, and made to dance with them. Why not? I would soon join them, if I had not done so already.

It was as real as the Compaq 286 on which I am setting down the story of Andrea King.

Maybe the horror was on a different plane of reality (whatever that means) than my micro, but it was still real. More real.

Why am I alive then? Why did I receive a several-decade—still indeterminate—stay of execution?

I don't know. Not for sure. Anyway, they didn't get me that night in the Superstition Mountains. Or, obviously, I wouldn't be writing this story.

The dead left me, with a strong promise that they would be back in a little while. I was still pinned against the wall in total blackness. I shouted for Andrea, but she did not or could not reply.

Then I heard a clink beneath my feet, coins falling on the floor. Despite the darkness I could see the glint of gold. Hundreds, then thousands of gold coins piled up beneath me, around me, rising rapidly to my throat. I was being buried in gold.

I pleaded with the horror to spare me. I had not come looking for gold.

But you did, the darkness screamed, *you wanted to search for the mine of the Dutchman.*

Only as a joke.

The clinking stopped.

Then the Dutchman again. Not the Flying Dutchman. The Lost Dutchman, though he did not think he was lost. And he wasn't lost. It was the mine that was lost.

Jacob Walz was only dead.

He was a tall, cadaverous old man with a bald head and a dirty white beard. He told me where his mine was. All the searchers are totally wrong about where it might be.

More gold than in South Africa and Russia put together. A mountain, quite literally, of gold. I know exactly where it is.

The Dutchman disappeared with his hoard of gold and the dead—the other dead—returned for more dancing. The men of VF 39 and Andrea's half-headed husband and drowned baby were with them.

They told me there was going to be a trial. I was guilty, no doubt about it, but I was going to be tried officially and formally before my sentence of eternal damnation was passed.

The charge? Violating the sanctity of these sacred mountains by fucking a cunt who had already been damned to hell.

Andrea's husband was the judge, her little girl the prosecutor, the dead from VF 39 were the jury. Maggie Keenan, my grandmother, of all people, was the defense attorney. And she was roaring drunk.

They turned on the light of the full moon. Andrea's body, flayed, but still breathing, a twisted, squirming mass of agony and disease, was staked out on the floor in front of me.

"Fuck my mommy now," the baby screamed. "Is she a good lay when she's rotting flesh?"

"No, no," I pleaded.

"Not till he's convicted," her grotesque, one-eyed father cautioned. "But let him know that he is already damned to screw a skinless corpse for all eternity."

The men of VF 39 cheered enthusiastically.

The trial was quick. Instant replays were flashed on the wall of the dance hall. My love was made to seem a hideous obscenity.

After each terrible scene, Andrea's husband chanted mechanically, "Your witness, defense counsel."

"Let's all drink a toast to the damned!" Grandma Keenan would shout.

Producing bottles of wine magically, they all drank, "To the damned, long live the damned!"

Andrea's baby summed up the evidence, "He fucked the cunt who murdered my father and me, her husband and her daughter."

"And violated our sacred hills because of his greed and lust," the thunder boomed out.

"How do you find, officers and gentlemen of the jury?" shrieked the hideous judge.

"Guilty!" my shipmates shouted gleefully.

"Hey, can't I defend myself?"

"Guilty!"

They began to dance again. I was dragged into the dance, forced to pair with Andrea's repulsive body. I searched for some sign in her eyes.

But there were no eyes, only empty sockets.

I knew I was going to die. The *danse macabre* was for me. I spun faster and faster as I was passed from one set of obscene hands to another. I teetered on the brink of an eternity of hell, where the torments of my dance of death would endure forever.

Then, from the depths of my being, so deep down that I doubted there could be any reality there, something powerful, indeed indomitable, began to struggle to break free. I lost it, groped for it, found it, lost it again, and then had it thrust unceremoniously into my hands. What was it? A magic sword? A massive pike? A deadly lance? An eighteen-inch gun from the *Yamoto?* An FH-1, the jet I had flown in Hawaii?

All of these and more.

Made bold by the surge of courage which that mighty weapon gave me, I informed my tormentors that they could jolly well fuck off.

Well, I was using the same language they used.

"What do you mean, you poor damned fool!" Andrea's little girl screamed at me. "You are going to hell for screwing my mommy, that goddamned cunt!"

I told the child and the rest of them I was very sorry, but I was not about to join them on their return trip to Hades. I didn't belong there. Purgatory maybe, but not hell. So the bus would have to leave without me.

They didn't like it. The violins screeched more wildly, the dancers whirled more insanely. Jeremiah Thomas Peter Keenan, USNR, dug in his heels. "No. And I mean no."

"All right, we'll take her." John King glared furiously at me from his single bloodstained eye.

"She's the one we want anyway," the men of VF 39 shouted barbarously. "You took our women, we have come to take your cunt to hell with us forever and ever. Amen."

Fine. You can have her. She belongs in hell.

They tossed me back to the wall and continued their feverish gavotte. Andrea's skinless, mutilated body was caught up in their dance. She shrieked in her terrible agony but danced with them, tossed from one to another, because this was an assigned part of her eternal torment.

"Yes, she is the one we want. We will come for him later."

"It's all right with me. I thought she looked like she was dead the first time I saw her. Take her and you're welcome."

Exhausted, burning with heat, terrified, ready to die if only to escape the madness, I thought about my decision.

The magic sword was still in my hands. "Coward. Use it for her."

"I don't want her. I never wanted her."

"Your life will be empty without her. You know it."

How did CIC get in this courthouse?

"Never mind, I'm correct as always. Take her away from them."

"Your name and rank and specialty, CIC."

"Michael, Seraph, wars in heaven. Now get her back, you stupid bastard. We've put a lot of work into her."

"Really?"

"You've known all along that she's special."

"I guess. Did you guys make her such a good lay?"

"Who else? Now stop this stupid discussion and get her back before you really upset us, you worthless, gutless, frigging son of a bitch."

"You betcha, sir. Right away, sir."

Never argue with a seraph.

"Wait a minute, guys; I'm the hero of this Western. I've

just made up my mind you can't have her either. Why not? Because she's mine, not yours, that's why not. I have staked my claim on her. The Dutchman can have his damn mine. I'll take her. The matter is not subject for discussion."

"Who says so?"

"CAG One says so! Pilots, man your planes!"

"You can't have her. She is already damned."

"Sorry, that judgment has been reversed on appeal."

"No one reverses our appeal." The Dutchman again.

"Someone does. And He's on my side."

"You don't believe in Him!"

"That's irrelevant. It has been ruled on appeal that she gets another chance."

"*Fuck him!* We've got her."

"*Fuck you!* I'm taking her back."

Many years later I wondered if what came next really was a war in heaven.

Leyte Gulf on a bigger scale. Between good and evil. Was she that important?

At that moment, despite my pain and fear and near madness, I had no doubt. No one was ever more important.

Whatever it was, the struggle for Andrea King—if that was her name—was titanic. Not a debate, not a trial, not an argument, but a furious tug of war, a war in heaven. I wanted her and they wanted her. I loved her and they hated her. We fought all night. Often I gave up and consigned her to their mercies for all eternity. Equally often I stopped them at the last moment and, with a mighty stroke of my magic sword or a burst of flame from my FH-1, I recovered her flayed body from them.

Or so it seemed.

Sometimes I thought I had won her. Other times I thought the black cloud had defeated me and carried her off. Sometimes I hated her. Sometimes I loved her. Sometimes I wanted to be rid of her permanently.

The last time, when I was finally willing to give her up and, out of weariness and discouragement and a desire to be done with all this foolishness, to consign her to hell for eternity, CIC appeared momentarily, or so I thought. He was a blond-winged giant in navy dress whites and the five stars of a fleet admiral. He carried a Browning automatic rifle under his arm.

"Where the fuck have you been?" I demanded.

"She will be part of your soul forever."

"If you say so. But let's get rid of these guys first."

I imagined I heard the BAR rumble.

Then someone turned off the light of the full moon. Darkness settled in on me, permanently, it seemed. I was not sure whether I had won or lost.

CHAPTER 19

THE DARKNESS SEEMED TO LAST FOREVER.

There were hints of a world beyond the darkness. A whiff of a woman's scent, alluring, inviting . . . and then fading away.

Next the sound of an aircraft engine. Two of them, plugging away through the sky. A C-47. Headed for Sky Harbor. Where was Sky Harbor? And who was I?

Then, higher in the sky, a whine. A jet? An F-80 or maybe one of the new Sabers.

What was a jet?

The final whine was of a pesky fly, circling around my head. It wanted to wake me. I wanted to sleep. For a long time. There was no reason to wake up, was there?

Consciousness slowly ebbed back into my organism. At first I thought I was in hell. Well, maybe purgatory. Wherever, I was on fire. I tried to open my eyes. The lids wouldn't move. I tried again, hard. Finally they flickered open. Before they closed I realized that I was neither in hell nor purgatory but under a blazing sun on the edge of a cliff. On Highway 88 on the far side of the Superstition Mountains.

What was I doing here?

Then I remembered the horror.

Andrea!

I struggled to my feet. The Chevy stood mutely next to me. I looked in the window. The key was still in the ignition. I opened the door and turned the key.

My faithful mount purred contentedly.

Where was Andrea?

No luggage in the backseat. No trace of her, not even of the remains of our picnic lunch.

I turned off the ignition and raced—well, hobbled—up the trail to the ridge. It took a couple of eternities to scramble to the top. Clinton, Arizona Territory, what was left of it, stood serenely at the edge of Lost Dutchman Canyon, as though nothing had happened there since the last miners left.

"Andrea!" I screamed. No response.

I rushed to the main building of the ghost town. She wasn't there.

I searched desperately in every corner of that shriveled old town. Not a trace.

I collapsed on the dilapidated steps of the main building. Panting for breath, I glanced at my watch—one fifteen in the afternoon. If she had started at, say, midnight, she would have had time to walk to Tortilla Flat, which was only a couple of miles away, and catch the morning "stage" to Apache Junction or even to Phoenix.

Walk down a mountain road with that big, heavy bag?

If she wanted to get away badly enough, perhaps she would have been able to lug it along.

Or she might have thumbed a ride in the opposite direction, back to Globe—if there were any cars on the precarious dirt road. Who would turn down a pretty girl lugging a heavy bag on a hot, dusty morning?

Improbable? Sure. It was all improbable. Maybe she had been carried off to hell, paperboard suitcase and all.

I stumbled back to the car and, ignoring the dangers, drove

as rapidly as I could down to the general store, which was about all there was to Tortilla Flat. Yes, the stage had left several hours ago. No, there had been no young woman with dark red hair on it.

I got much the same answer at Canyon Lake and in Apache Junction. No one could remember. "Well, there might have been a pretty girl, but, gosh, I can't recollect, young man. Sorry."

She might have jumped on a train in Apache Junction and gone back to Globe or to Phoenix or Bowie or El Paso or anywhere in the world.

Or nowhere in this world.

I raced recklessly back to Globe on US 60. No, the woman at the registration desk of the Dominion had not seen my wife. In fact, she did not remember either of us. She considered me suspiciously. "Is there something wrong? Maybe you ought to walk down to the courthouse and talk to the sheriff."

Back in the car, I realized that I was making a fool out of myself and taking a big chance. If the police became interested and asked for an explanation . . . what would I say?

They'd want to send me to an asylum, much to the horror of my poor parents.

What was there left to do?

I would drive as far as the Arizona Biltmore, on the chance I would see her. Then . . .

Then it didn't matter.

What had happened? Had she somehow become a magnet, drawing evil energies down to that sick old place?

Or was she really dead, as I thought the first moment I had seen her? A lost soul seeking her way to hell?

Was she being punished, perhaps, for having murdered her husband and child? Doomed to wander the earth like . . .

Like the Flying Dutchman!

Or had I imagined it all?

Halfway back to Apache Junction, the gray clouds were gathering again, the Thunder gods threatening once more, perhaps their final strike. I turned off the ignition and, as I would do when I was scanning the ocean and searching for life rafts before returning to the *Big E*, thought about the possibilities.

Had it all been a nightmare? My body was intact. I had not been whipped as I had imagined. I awoke not in the dance hall but next to the car. I had seen no traces of any of the events that I thought had occurred.

And the craziness at the end. Saint Michael appearing dressed as a fleet admiral and carrying a BAR? That was low comedy, not horror.

Yet there had been horror of some sort, had there not?

Perhaps the poor woman's nervous breakdown had somehow enveloped me. I was exhausted, tired, hungry, troubled by the war, haunted by my lost comrades, stimulated by sex. Perhaps . . . perhaps what?

Perhaps it was a kind of joint nervous breakdown. No wonder people are looking at me oddly—an unshaven man with wild eyes and wilder questions about a missing girl.

A little bit crazy?

I resolved to get control of myself, calm down, relax. There was just so much one person could do, as my father always insisted.

I'd try the Biltmore. If she wasn't there, I'd fly one more sweep over the ocean to make sure. Then I'd find somewhere to sleep and calculate my next move only after sleep and a meal and a shave.

How could I help someone who did not want my help?

And was I not, after all, well rid of her?

So I drove to Phoenix and found the Biltmore without any difficulty in that small city. It did indeed remind me of the Imperial in Tokyo, a little newer and a little bigger, but unmistakably Wright.

The hotel was being refurbished, as was everything else in America at the time; the manager responded to my Irish charm despite my bedraggled appearance. No, they had not hired any waitresses recently and they did not anticipate any hirings in the immediate future. When the reconstruction was finished. He shrugged. "We really do expect a boom this coming winter, sir. It looks like we may have prosperity before the Depression sets in again."

That seemed to be that. I could check other hotels in Phoenix, but . . . If she had lied to me about the hotel, what else might she not have lied about?

I walked around the grounds, thinking about what came next. It was a romantic place—palm trees, flowers, Frank Lloyd Wight building blocks, citrus smell, paths wandering through gardens. Very romantic, I thought. She'd like it, just as she had liked the Arizona Inn. Whoever or whatever she was, she could act as if she belonged in a classy environment.

I wandered into the gold-domed Aztec Lounge, thought about having a drink, and decided that I wasn't thirsty. She'd like it in here too, I thought.

Was she real? If I could imagine her in here, must she not be real?

Should I stay the night at the Biltmore? Get a good rest and search for her tomorrow?

No, I wanted to get away from Phoenix, as far away as I could. Tucson . . . back to the Arizona Inn and start over.

I called home from a public phone booth in the Biltmore. Joanne answered.

"I don't see why you pick the middle of the summer," she began with her usual whine, "to drive through the South. It must be terribly hot. We're having wonderful weather here in Chicago. Mom and Dad can hardly wait to see you. . . ."

"Tell them I'll be back in the Arizona Inn in Tucson," I cut through her sermon, "and will phone them tomorrow."

"What's this about a girl?" she continued accusingly, as if she had not heard what I said—Joanne never acknowledged any message given her. "You're not bringing some trollop home, are you?"

"Not if I can help it."

I ended the conversation as quickly as I could without being rude. Prudence dictated staying here. A good night's sleep, then make up my mind.

No, get the hell out of this part of the world.

One more flight over the ocean?

Why bother?

Because that's your own rule.

Doggedly I filled up the tank of my Chevy and, ignoring the rain that had started while I was in the Biltmore, drove back through Tempe (where there is now a big university replacing Tempe Teachers College) and toward Apache Junction.

At Apache Junction I noticed for the first time Superstition Mountain itself. I had driven by it twice before that crazy day, but had paid no attention to it.

It did indeed look like a vast fortress in which demons or Thunder gods might hole up for aeons. No wonder there were so many legends about it and the rest of the range.

A five-star angel with a BAR under his arm up there?

What decent, self-respecting seraph would bother with such a place?

Yet the image of the angel was as vivid as anything else in my crazy nightmare—for such was the label I was using for the experience. I did not want to let the words "nervous breakdown" into my mental vocabulary.

I was not—repeat, *not*—losing my mind.

It was dusk when I climbed the trail from the road up to Clinton for the last time. The rain had stopped. There was no wind. The smell of rain-soaked earth and waterlogged creosote was strong and somehow reassuring on the dark-purple mountain air, a slide shot that I might label "Twilight Peace in the Mountains."

Flashlight in hand, I strode bravely into the main building. Navy Cross hero at work.

The hero nearly jumped out of his shoes when the glare of his flashlight caused a stirring in one corner.

Only rats. Or some similar desert creatures.

After they had left, there was total silence.

Carefully I explored every corner, as though my precision would exorcise the demons. As the minutes slipped away, I realized that I was no longer afraid.

The full moon bathed the desert outside in quiet light. Inside, everything seemed peaceful. How could I ever have thought that the moon was sinister? I swept the ground in front of the "main street" with my light. No trace of the mine shaft into which I thought I had fallen.

Was that part of the nightmare too?

My light was getting weak. It would not be wise to try to walk back to the car—I no longer called it Roxinante—by the light of the silvery moon.

I began to hum the tune about the silvery moon.

Time to return to Tucson.

I went back to the main building—the dance hall of our *danse macabre*—and shone the light around it for the last time. Then I noticed that the dust had disappeared from the floor. Maybe I had only imagined that there was dust yesterday.

Or maybe the dust had been cleared out by a dance the night before.

Or maybe by a rainstorm.

And I saw in one corner of the room a bit of white cloth crumpled into a loose ball. I picked it up and rubbed it with my fingers. Cloth from her blouse?

Maybe.

It was my turn to shiver. I should call the state police. What could I tell them? A woman whose name I did not know had disappeared I knew not where, because demons out of hell had swept through a ghost town in the Superstition Mountains. What had happened to the demons? Oh, Saint Michael had shown up with a BAR and eliminated them.

Sure.

I'd be locked up for psychiatric observation. No one would search for her.

I tossed the cotton rag on the floor, limped back to the Chevy, backed it up, turned around and went down the mountains.

Ought I not return for one more search? Had I not discovered two rafts after the Mariannas Turkey Shoot and saved seven lives?

Yeah, and your tank had a thimbleful of gas when you landed on the *E*.

Fuel is not a problem in this mission.

She's not there. She's not anywhere.

In Apache Junction I passed a Catholic church. There's something that's ingrained in a Chicago Irish Catholic from birth, if not before: when you have a problem, go over to the Rectory. From term paper to terminal illness, as Packy says.

The light was on in the rectory. An old Irish priest answered the door when I rang the bell. He looked as if he might be a relative of the man in Globe. Or maybe all men in cassocks with brogues look alike.

He was dressed in a tattered old cassock, open to his waist. I'm sure it would have smelled of human sweat, but the aroma of whiskey was much stronger than that of sweat.

I poured out my story.

"Oh, those are terrible places up there altogether, young man," he wailed in a near-soprano voice. "You shouldn't go up in those mountains at night, not at all, at all. There are demons in them, if you take my meaning, terrible demons."

He seemed to have missed the point that I was searching for a lost young woman.

"I can't find the girl I was with, Father. I'm afraid she might be lost up there."

"Had you known her long, my son?"

"Only a few days, Father."

"Jesus, Mary, and Joseph, save and protect us," he said as he made the sign of the cross. "Isn't it just the way young people are these days? Isn't it what the terrible war has done to all sense of morality? Were you in the service now, young man?"

"I was, Father." I felt as if I were admitting a mortal sin.

"Ah, wasn't I after knowing it? Brigid, Patrick, and Columcille, hasn't all human decency vanished from the earth? Your war was nothing more than an excuse for immorality, isn't that the truth now?"

"There were real enemies out there, Father."

What was I doing in a debate about the war with a drunken old priest?

"Did you take indaycent liberties with the young woman?"

The question came at me like a sniper's shot.

In Chicago they trained you always to tell the priest the truth in confession. Somehow it seemed like I was in the confessional.

"Yes, Father."

"Up there in the mountains, was it?"

"Yes, Father."

"Did you violate the holy virtue completely?"

In those days the "holy" virtue, the only virtue, as a matter of fact, was purity.

"Not in the mountains."

"Don't try to trick me, young man, with your clever answers. Did you violate the holy virtue completely with her?"

"I did, Father."

"And how many times?"

Good question.

"I don't remember, Father. Often."

"Over what period of time?"

"A couple of days."

"Glory be to God, you're damned to hell, young man, don't you realize that? . . ." He rushed from the room and returned a few seconds later with a massive vessel of holy water and a huge aspergil. He sprinkled me with a tidal wave of holy water and waited to see what happened.

Nothing happened, to his considerable disappointment.

"Well, you're not a demon yourself, anyway. But the woman was, a succubus sent straight from hell to capture your soul. You must spend the rest of your life in a monastery doing penance or you'll be damned forever. She'll fight with God for you and she'll win. They're terrible demons, and them mountains up there are filled with them, they're getting stronger. If it wasn't for the power of the Blessed Mother, they'd come down and carry us all off to hell tomorrow. Do you understand?"

"Yes, Father." I rose to leave before he sprinkled me again.

"God have mercy on your soul, poor young man." He had

begun to weep. I suppose he needed a drink badly. Well, I'd give him something to think about.

"Something else I forgot to tell you, Father."

"What else, poor damned sinner?"

"I had an ally up there. Saint Michael. He was dressed like a fleet admiral in the United States Navy and was carrying an automatic rifle."

It was a nice note on which to leave.

I know that I probably would have been treated very differently in other rectories. The poor lonely old man was not typical. It was just my bad luck to encounter a loony when I needed help. As a lot of other Catholics have encountered loonies these last forty years when they needed help, a point I make, perhaps ad nauseam, to my brother and my son.

When, months later, I told Packy most of the story of the night at Lost Dutchman's Canyon, he said the part about Saint Michael was the only thing in the story he found reasonable.

So I drove on to Tucson. Arriving after midnight, I collapsed into bed in my old room at the Arizona Inn. The registration clerk had not asked about Andrea, thank God. None of the lies I had concocted on the way back from the Superstition Mountains would have been very persuasive. Nor did I have the courage to ask him whether he remembered her.

I slept till noon the next day. If I had any dreams, I don't remember them.

I woke up with a terrible headache, a thick tongue, a bad sunburn, and an acute fit of depression. Having demanded black coffee and orange juice from room service, I gave the depression my full attention.

Who was she? Or, better, what was she?

A lost soul doomed to wander the earth like the Flying Dutchman?

A demon sent to tempt me? God knows she'd been successful at that.

A creation of my disturbed imagination? So maybe I should see a therapist, as my father had suggested when I told him I wanted to tour the whole continent before coming home.

A ghost haunting navy flyers?

I would never know.

I soaked a washcloth, put it on my head, and pitched back into bed.

Only to be pulled out of it by room service. The *Arizona Star* headlined WALLACE PROPOSES TRUMAN APPEASE RUSSIA.

A secret letter had been released in which the former Vice President advocated that the United States destroy its atomic bombs because the Russians resented the American monopoly.

Most senators ridiculed the suggestion. Wallace might be a nut, I thought, but how many of those who ridiculed him had seen Nagasaki?

Halfway through my first cup of coffee I had an idea. My contact at the Bureau of Personnel quickly confirmed what I had suspected: a radar technician named John King had never served on the USS *Indianapolis*.

Who was I to think, I could hear my sister's voice, that I was someone special? The great war adventure, ugly but exhilarating, was over. There would be no more adventures, and I should accept that and settle down. Right?

Besides, this last great romantic adventure with the widow of a radar technician who had never lived, turned into a nightmare, a real-life nightmare, that made the kamikaze attacks seem boring.

Forget it, Keenan. Go back to River Forest and act like the ordinary human being that you are supposed to be. Marriage, family, career are enough for everyone else, why not for you? Why do you need some special purpose in life?

Your sister and your mother will find a nice Trinity-grad virgin who will be a good, unexciting, spouse.

In fact, get on with it. Since you're horny again, go home and inspect the girls they've lined up.

I drained the coffee cup and filled it again.

Abandon this quixotic jaunt across the continent and fly home tomorrow. Catch a plane in Phoenix. Who flies there? TWA? They must. What sense does it make to call yourself Transcontinental and Western if Western doesn't include

Phoenix? (In 1946 they had just become Transworld, but no one paid attention to that title yet.)

I had the money for a ticket, didn't I?

I stretched out on my bed, reached into the pocket of my soiled jacket and pulled out my wallet.

Sure enough, the thin stack of bills was still there. I counted them. Seven. Just as there should be.

I replaced the wallet and returned to my coffee.

Seven?

I reflected very carefully, while my heart pounded like a damaged engine on an F6F. I had ten of them when I drove into Tucson. I used one to pay the charges here the night before last. I broke the second at the Picketpost Hotel.

There should be eight.

I thought about that. Go on, dopey, count them again.

Fingers trembling, I recovered my wallet. I removed the bills gently and counted. My heart sank. There were indeed eight, just as there should be.

Try again.

This time there were seven.

You're losing control.

I spread the C-notes out on the bed in pairs.

Three pairs and one single. Three times two is six and one is seven.

I felt my painfully burned face cracking into a grin.

I replaced the wallet, set aside my coffee cup, and relaxed on the bed, hands behind my head in complacent satisfaction.

My grin widened as I reviewed the bidding. I whistled "Anchors Aweigh," extraordinarily pleased with myself.

A thief would have taken all eight.

A ghost would not have needed any.

So she was a human girl—lonely, frightened, perhaps in some crazy way possessed. Or maybe only working on a nervous breakdown to which she was entitled. Yet she was out there, still running. Still in the grip of her fierce desire to live.

She was mine. Had I not won her? Was she not the real buried treasure? The real lode of gold on which I had staked a claim?

Mine. And I was hers too. Fair enough.

Had she murdered her husband and child?

Had I murdered Rusty and Tony and Hank?

No.

If she was out there, I would find her. And drag her home by her thick red hair. With a stop here for purposes of love-making. Honeymoon. Second honeymoon. Whatever. We'd see about how hard indeed it was for a determined lover to remove a corsetlike wet swimsuit.

Not too hard, surely.

Then River Forest. It would never be the same.

I would hunt down my leprechaun girl with her pot of gold.

My own Holy Grail to pursue, to drink from, to keep, to treasure.

She was somewhere out there. Terrified. I would find her and save her from whatever was causing the terror.

No, with someone like Andrea King—if that was her name—you helped her to save herself from the terror. And then you protected her from more terror by loving her passionately and tenderly forever.

There was no room for doubt. I would indeed love her forever.

Pilots, man your planes!

CAG One called room service again and ordered pancakes. And steak.

PART TWO

Dulcinea

CHAPTER 20

IN THE SUMMER OF 1946 YOU COULD FIND IN THE WESTERN half of our republic an enormous number of young women slightly under medium height with generous curves, very generous, in fact, and auburn hair shaped like a crisp halo. I think I saw every one of them during the next two weeks. I frightened some of them, astonished others and, I think, intrigued still others.

Those whose dark-red halo I saw from the back I followed until I could catch up with them and get a good look at their faces. Those I approached from the front, I stared at with either flattering or frightening intensity, depending on the young woman's perspective.

Most of them, I think, concluded that I was a harmless nut. On a couple of occasions all my Irish charm was required to confirm the "harmless" part.

Maybe I was a bit of a nut. I had endured a traumatic emotional experience that night in Clinton. It would be years before those terrible images ceased to be the raw material of my dreams. Even now I wake occasionally to the Dutchman's laughter or to the rumble, as it seems, of Michael's automatic-weapon fire. My wife must, under such circumstances, hold me tight until my nerves relax and I realize that I am not in Clinton anymore—activity that both of us find comforting, I might add.

I was also in an almost constant state of sexual arousal. My romps with Andrea had only teased my appetite. I wanted more of her. In her absence I wanted more of someone, anyone. I didn't act on these fantasies because I was caught up in the fervor of my quest.

Quixote, desperately afraid of the return to La Mancha and first-year law school, had found a cause. He was convinced that Andrea King was not a haunt, but a real if deeply troubled woman and that he loved her. She needed his help and protection, whether she knew it or not.

And whether she wanted it or not.

Obviously she didn't want my help or she would not have slipped away from the site of our inconclusive battle with the forces of evil, my hundred-dollar bill in her purse. Just as obviously my chances of finding her in the train stations, bus depots, and hotels of cities from Santa Fe to Seattle were pretty slim.

Twice I thought I had found her—the same gait, a mixture of convent-school modesty and the slightest bit of provocation, the same thin, determined shoulders, even the same pale-blue eyes.

"Andrea"—I grabbed one such woman by the shoulders —"I've found you."

"I'm not Andrea." The kid—that's all she was—grinned at me. "And I'm not lost." She took me in at a glance. "But I'm willing to be found."

For a few seconds I thought she was lying. Then I realized that, although the young woman of whose shoulders I had taken possession was lovely indeed, her beauty was not the same as my Andrea's, not quite so fine-drawn and haunted.

"My mistake." I released her as though there were a live electric current in her trim young body. "I'm sorry."

"Lost your girl . . ."—she hesitated and then guessed accurately—"sailor? I must say she has bad taste."

I think we were on Fisherman's Wharf in San Francisco, though the memories of those frantic days are blurred now.

"I wonder if you've seen her," I pleaded. "She's about your

height and looks like you. She'd probably be wearing a brown suit or maybe blue slacks and a white shirt."

"I don't think so." The girl wrinkled her nose. "Where did you see her last?"

"In Tucson," I blurted the words without thinking.

"You have it bad, sailor." She shook her head sadly. "Were you on a sub?"

"Carrier. Her hair was shaped just like yours."

"Maybe, but I'm still not Andrea, worse luck for me perhaps. Air Crew?"

"Yeah, F6F. I'm sorry, miss. I think I've made a fool out of myself."

"I hope she's worth it." The girl's smile was warm and sympathetic, inviting friendship but without pushing me too hard.

"She is. If you'll excuse me . . . again, I'm terribly sorry."

"Good hunting." She looked a little wistful. "I hope you find her."

As I said, I can't remember the city, but I can remember the smile. And, naturally I suppose, the figure. I wonder what might have happened if Quixote had been able to slow down his mad dash for a few moments and offer the kid a drink, or possibly a Coke. It was an era of frantic search for domesticity. Everyone in our generation was desperately searching for a partner with whom to settle down to child-producing suburban prosperity. We weren't very subtle about it. My own goals were different. I wanted my permanent quest, but that didn't exclude a partner and child-producing. I was chasing a girl as well as a grail, after all.

In the final analysis, I have done well enough in the girl department and I would not, save in occasional moments of conflict, want to trade her in on might-have-beens. Still, it's pleasant on occasion to fantasize on our might-have-beens. The girl on Fisherman's Wharf was cute and smart. It was dumb of me not to get her name.

Even my wife agrees that it was dumb.

I was not without a strategy, though it was the sort that

would have flunked me out of preflight if I had turned in a paper describing it.

I hit all the West Coast cities—Seattle, Portland, San Francisco, Los Angeles; and then the inland cities—Santa Fe, Salt Lake, Denver; airline service wasn't what it is now, needless to say, but there were a lot of C-47s (DC-3s to you) left over from the war, and for the first time in our history you could be in a different city every day, if you moved quickly enough from the downtown hotels to the airports—all of which were erecting terminals that summer.

I raced about the western states in a twilight haze of not enough sleep, too much caffeine, dirty clothes, unshaved face and automatic responses. I was a "tough guy" detective, who was neither very tough nor much of a detective.

Many of the flights were on Western Airlines, which was boasting then that it was the oldest airline in America— twenty years old. The DC-3 was its big plane. I had two flights on a Boeing 247D, which was the first passenger airplane that looked like an airplane—a kind of sawed-off DC-3. And one on a Fokker F-10 trimotor, which was a newer aircraft in those days than the 747 is today.

The latter is almost as safe as the Ford and Fokker trimotors.

Like most pilots, I must go through the mental motions of flying every plane I'm on. None of the trimotors were easy to fly, even mentally. And they may have been the noisiest machines humans have ever invented. By the time we finally landed, in Spokane, I think it was, I was ready to trade it in on a trainer and try to land on the *Wolverine* again.

Flying was the easy part—the time to catch my breath, worry a little bit about my dirty clothes and whether there was a quick laundry service at my next hotel and maybe sleep. Once the plane landed, I had to return to the quest or the chase or whatever it was.

Besides stupid.

My technique was to visit the major hotels and inquire, with all my haut-bourgeois Irish charm working at full blast, whether they had hired any new waitresses lately. If Irish charm didn't work—and it usually did—and does, for that matter—I'd fall back on the Navy Cross with star. I became skillful at subtly raising the subject of my war record. I never told anyone that my Hellcat had never once encountered an enemy bullet.

Then I'd check out the bus terminal and the train station. I'd hang around until the cops began to look at me suspiciously, watching young women get on and off the buses or trains.

It was in a bus terminal in Salt Lake, just down the street from Temple Square, that I thought I had found her for sure. I won't go through the embarrassing details. (My wife rarely advises me while I'm writing, except to ask me where I am in a story. When I told her that I was describing my race around half a continent searching for my first love, she said, "Well, I hope you're not going to make yourself look ridiculous by writing about that foolish business in Salt Lake City when you were hunting for that dreadful girl.")

It suffices to say that the woman, unlike her look-alike in San Francisco, was definitely not amused.

And the Salt Lake police, presumably devout Mormons, were immune to Gaelic charm.

I finally escaped after showing them the documentation for both my navy crosses—the medals were not enough. Suspicious people.

In some terminals I would ask whether anyone had seen a young woman who fit Andrea's description. Everyone had, but none of the leads, which in Denver and Seattle sent me on a tour of inexpensive hotels and a hunt for taxi drivers, proved to be helpful.

Did I show them the picture of Andrea? That question dates the asker; as I've said before, only Kodak could develop Kodak films in those days (later the courts properly ruled that the practice was a restraint of trade). I wasn't in one place long enough to put my films in the mail and wait the week or so until they came back. I'm not sure the picture would have been that much help anyway. She looked charming in it, but a little too fey to be recognized on the street.

I called home almost every night. I had told the folks I had left my car in San Diego, and was seeing America by air. My father was convinced that I was suffering from "a minor case of shell shock, nothing serious," so the family humored me. I made the daily journal entries, which demonstrate a level of stupidity that I will not inflict on my readers.

My chances of finding her by these frantic perambulations were virtually nil. She could have chosen almost anywhere in America. And I had only her word that she worked as a waitress. Indeed both the hotels she had mentioned to me—the Del Coronado and the Arizona Biltmore—had never heard of her.

She could easily have been in any of those cities, perhaps only a few minutes' walk from the hotel in which I slept (if I didn't opt for a bench in the airport), and I would have missed her completely. I guess I knew that, but in my manic and lovelorn condition I had to do something.

And on the list of the things that might be done I had not placed "thinking."

My narrow escape from the law in Salt Lake slowed me down a bit. That night, in the DC-3 which picked a very careful way through the peaks of the Rockies on either side en route to Denver, I read over my journal and began to listen again to my resident intelligence officer, who was, incidentally, no longer seraphic.

"An F in strategy," he told me candidly.

"So what?"

"So even if you never find her . . ."

"I'll find her. I love her."

"Regardless. Even if you never find her, you could at least be intelligent about your search."

"What do you mean by that?"

"You might think about the clues she gave you."

"What clues?"

He had signed off, as he always does when I raise that kind of question.

So I pondered and agonized and finally, two weeks too late, began to think.

From the hotel in Denver I called home, even though it was midnight in Chicago. Fortunately Packy answered.

My brother, Patrick Joseph, now an outspoken Catholic priest (and monsignor), was just a little short of his nineteenth birthday. He had been an obnoxious little adolescent punk when I left for the service. In the years I was away he had grown into a tall, marvelously handsome, utterly self-possessed young man. I had been convinced that Quigley, the high school preparatory seminary, would inhibit maturity. Now I wondered if maybe I should have gone there instead of to Fenwick.

Did my brother threaten me just a little in those days? You'd better believe it.

"Still hunting for that luscious broad you met in Tucson?"

"How come a seminarian is always thinking about women?"

"All men of our age," he promptly replied, "think about women. All the time."

"When does that age end?"

"A hundred or so if you're unlucky."

"Packy." I had put all my clues together. "I need a big American city."

"Be glad to provide one for you. What are the characteristics?"

"Heavily Catholic, pretty conservative, standoff clergy, lots of Catholic schools, some parishes with a grammar school and high school, taught by nuns though the school is coed."

"Need more."

I pushed hard at my memory. "Churches burned in the eighteen thirties."

"Philly," he cut in sharply. "New York and Boston don't have the schools. What order?"

"Dominican."

"Call me tomorrow night and I'll have a list of schools. Any special neighborhood description?"

"Not a River Forest kind of place. Poor but hardworking."

"Like Saint Mel's. Okay. See what I can do."

He was almost too helpful. As a Sancho, my brother Packy

was, to use the modern term, dangerously overqualified. I, not Packy, was supposed to find the girl.

In my dream that night I was inside of Andrea at the height of passion when she turned into a madly screaming demon. It's a dream that still recurs. I woke up, not so much aroused as frightened and frustrated.

How much of my quest was sexual? A lot of it, obviously. As Packy said, I was at the age when men pursue women.

But not so sexual that any attractive woman would do. The girl in San Francisco would have been perfect if that were all I had in mind.

I'm not sure how important Andrea still was. After the snafu in Salt Lake, I realized that I couldn't remember precisely what she looked like. My sexual hunger was for the chase, an impossible chase, obviously, and I think that I knew that even when I woke up in Denver the next morning. But I still had to get it out of my system before I returned to River Forest and domesticity.

I went through the motions in Denver, even imagining I saw her board the Denver and Rio Grande. For a moment I was sure that it was Andrea. Then, fearful of making a fool out of myself again, I stopped chasing the train and returned disconsolately to the terminal.

I could have sworn it was Andrea. But that's what I had thought in Salt Lake too.

Packy had the information that night.

"Three parishes, Saint Dominic, Saint Pius, and Saint Malachy, all in South Philly. If they don't work out, call me. There's a couple of other places, but they don't seem to fit the description so well."

"You didn't ask me why I wanted to know about these parishes."

"I figure when you want to tell me, you will. Besides, I think I can guess."

"I very much doubt it."

United Airlines, I learned from a phone call, had a C-54 (DC-4 to you civilians) that flew from Denver to Philadelphia with a stop at Chicago, in the "mainliner time" of ten hours.

I slept soundly that night for the first time since I had left San Diego.

San Diego, you say, why didn't dummy go to San Diego, save to park his car, first thing after he left Tucson?

If you'd asked me that as July turned into August in 1946, I would have said because that's where she came from. Why should she go back there?

To which you might have replied, "But you don't know how long ago she left San Diego." Or, perhaps even more wisely, "Is not that the first place to look for a solution to the mystery of Andrea King, the city where she lived with the husband she might have murdered?"

If you asked me that question now, I'd say I was young and in love and the last possibility I wanted to consider seriously was that the woman I loved, the woman who was the object of my quest before I returned to La Mancha on the Des Plaines River, might actually be a murderer, perhaps a double murderer.

The ride from Denver to Chicago in the C-54 was rough. We found ourselves in a thunderstorm and rode it all the way into Midway Airport, which even in those days had become a typical Chicago airport—a mess. The DC-4, you may remember, was not pressurized (that came with the DC-6), so it couldn't go much above ten thousand feet at the most, which meant you either flew around thunderstorms or through them. We flew through as many as we could find.

I was woozy from motion sickness at Midway and wished I had my good old stable F6F with its reliable Pratt & Whitney instead of being forced to sit in what was merely an oversized four-engine DC-3.

Despite my reluctance to return home and face law school and domestic respectability, it seemed kind of nice to see Cicero Avenue again. When I was a kid and my mother and I would ride back from the Loop on the Lake Street El, Cicero Avenue was the first sign we were nearing home. After Laramie, the next stop, we'd descend to ground level and that was almost as good as being home.

I called the family but only Joanne was in the house.

"Where are you *NOW?*" I could tell she was pouting even over the phone.

"Denver," I lied.

"Aren't you going to be back for the Harvest Ball?"

"I don't think so."

"Mom will be so disappointed," she said triumphantly, another score against the despised older sibling.

Then I listened patiently to a list of who had received diamonds last week.

"If you don't hurry up and get one, Jo, you'll be an old maid for sure."

"I think you're horrible," she screamed.

"Horrible and with a plane to catch."

Mom and Dad would hear about how horrible I was for the next day and a half. Well, it was their fault for permitting the spoiled little brat to use the phone.

My ride from Chicago to Philadelphia was enlivened by a gorgeous stewardess who flirted with me from the first moment I reboarded the plane. I told her in elaborate detail how I had, with little help from Bill Halsey and Chet Nimitz, won the war single-handedly.

I'm sure she would have been happy to share a bed with me when we finally found the Philadelphia airport at ten o'-clock that night. She even asked at what hotel I was staying.

I didn't rise to the bait. But that I noticed the bait and considered it, however remotely, was evidence that I was returning to normal.

As I unpacked my duffel and sorted out the laundry—practically everything—I told myself that at last my brain was beginning to function again.

"About time," said the ship's intelligence officer.

"I want Mike back."

"Who's he?"

But the ride to Philly was the turning point in that phase of my quest. From then on my search was reasonably sure-footed.

Not that I would like what I found at the end of it.

CHAPTER 21

AT SAINT DOMINIC'S SCHOOL IN SOUTH PHILADELPHIA, east of the docks and above the Naval Yard, just off Oregon Street, I learned that it was not only the Mormons in Salt Lake who found my Irish charm resistible and my title "Commander" unimpressive. Sister Mary Regina (pronounced like the city in Canada) viewed me with the same fastidious dismay with which she would consider a fly in the convent butter supply. It was an attitude, I felt sure, she maintained toward anyone who was not a member of her order and probably anyone who was not a sister superior in the order.

"I'm sorry, uh, Commander Keenan," she said with a tone indicating her contempt for the title, "I really can't be of any help to you."

She was a tall, lean woman of indeterminate age, with thin lips, metal-rim glasses, and one of those handbells on which sisters superior used to ring for order. She fingered the bell lovingly, as if it were a fetish. I felt that she counted as wasted any moment in which she was not clanging away on the bell to exorcise disorder from the world over which she reigned.

"The young man who was in my command," I repeated my story, "may have graduated from your school, Sister. He was, I believe, very intelligent and very industrious. On his final leave it was necessary for him to marry a young woman who, it would seem, was a junior or possibly a senior in your school. She left school and went to San Diego with him."

"We had no such incident in our school, Commander, as I have already told you. We do not tolerate that sort of provocative behavior."

She spit out "provocative" as though it were a word that represented the summary and the quintessence of all evil. She sounded exactly like the kind of nun who had hounded my Andrea.

"But what if such behavior happened?"

"It does *not* happen here."

"It's very important that we find the family of either of these children," I continued with my story. "There are pension rights, military honors, and debts to be paid, all of great importance to many people."

"I'm sorry, uh, Commander, I have said for the last time that I can be of no assistance to you. Your persistence gives me no choice but to dismiss you."

I thought she was going to ring the bell. Instead she dipped a pen in an inkwell and began to write, in fine, nunnish script, on a sheet of snow white parchment paper, the only item other than a blotter on her black oak desk.

"Thank you just the same, Sister."

She did not bother to acknowledge my gratitude as I left her office.

I went silently into that good night, you say?

Not for want of appropriate curses for the old bitch. But I did not want to offend her because I might be able to obtain her help anyway.

My family was not without what we call in Chicago clout. Still has it, as a matter of fact, my wife especially. A call to my father would lead to a call to the Chicago Chancery, which in turn would produce a call at a sufficiently high level to the Chancery here in Philly that might make Sister Mary Regina a good deal more cooperative.

The rules to be remembered about clout, which is a relationship based on the exchange of favors, is that you never use it unless you have to, you never demand more of it than you have to, you never cause anyone to lose face unnecessarily, and you never call upon it until other means have been exhausted.

All these rules indicated that I leave Sister's office politely and check the other schools, even that I return and inquire politely again before I mobilized the Seventh Cavalry.

No one teaches you these rules. If you have to be taught

them you'll never learn them, much less understand the need for them. You just know them.

But I was convinced that here in Saint Dominic's would be my first lead in the hunt of Andrea King.

My confidence that I could beat Sister Mary Regina consoled me, although the first step in my "smart" quest had met a blank and very solid wall. I'd be back.

So I walked into the scorching street in front of the school—a shabby red brick building built before the First War (and shabby then doubtless) with the same sense of excitement and confidence that I felt the first moment I was airborne off the *Big E.*

The neighborhood matched the school, moldering row houses that had probably never been attractive places in which to live but which had become grimly depressing through the decades of their existence. Ready-made slums for the ethnic immigrants. Many years later the descendants of those immigrants would grimly resist the attempts of immigrants with different skin color to move into their row houses. If I didn't know how important a neighborhood is to those who live in it, I would not have been able to understand why those low-slung, ugly, morose rows of brick would be worth fighting about. Still later, the mayor and the police chief of Philadelphia would destroy part of a similar neighborhood by dropping an incendiary bomb on the roof of one of the homes in which a group of well-armed and crazy radicals had holed up.

It was, not to put too fine an edge on matters, a sad and sour place.

Enough to make any bright and vivacious young woman growing up in it feel depressed.

Saint Pius's was in a community on the southwest side of Philadelphia that was much less depressing: frame homes once occupied by the respectable Protestant middle class and now painted and maintained by the sober Irish Catholic middle class. It was a neighborhood in which even then the term "lace curtain" was not opprobrious.

Sister Mathilda was helpful.

"Such things do happen"—her gray eyes twinkled—

"Commander, don't they? And not always to the bad ones. We had a case here recently of a young woman whose parents were raised in our parish. Poor child, she was very unlucky in her timing. Well, the father and mother made such a fuss that I persuaded the pastor to look up the girl's birthdate and the parent's wedding date in the parish records. Would you believe, and I'm sure your laugh tells me that you will, that the daughter was born three months after their marriage? Decidedly premature, wouldn't you say, Commander?"

"The parents quieted down when you made that observation, S'ter?"

"Did they ever.... Well, now let me see, we had three cases during the war of such unfortunate young women. Two of them did involve young men who had graduated from here. War encourages these sorts of occurrences, doesn't it? Ah, here are the names. Marie O'Malley and Jane McDermott, both from large families. And the young men were Martin Finnegan, a terror, that one, and John Comaford. Marie and Martin live in the parish. They have two children now and are, I gather, expecting a third. Jane and John . . . hmn, I don't know where they are, though I believe there are cousins in the neighborhood. I would have heard if he had been killed. Here we are; this yearbook will have pictures."

Jane was a thin girl with dark hair who bore no resemblance to Andrea. Marie did look a little bit like her. But Sister was sure that mother and father and two and a half children were diligent and devout members of the parish.

Maybe if I continued to be drawn low cards I would come back and see them. I thanked Sister, found my hired cabby sound asleep in his car and directed him to Saint Malachy's parish and school on the northwest side, near the railroad tracks that gave the adjacent suburbs their name, the Main Line.

It was yet another step down the road which in a few years would lead the Irish to the suburbs—to catch up with those few who had gone there before the war, like my family: solid new homes and apartment buildings, Philly's equivalent of Chicago's bungalow belt, constructed during the nineteen twenties, before the Depression extinguished the building boom of that decade.

Sister Irene Marie listened sympathetically, told me that she was new in the school, called in another nun and told her my story.

The veteran nun was sure they had just the family I was looking for. The young man was a war hero, killed in Sicily, and the bride had come home to live with her parents and five sisters and raise her infant son. She would soon marry a young man of the parish who was doing very well at St. Joseph's and would enroll next year in Penn law school.

In her picture the kid was a cute, plump little blond who would doubtless keep the lawyer well fed and well tended even when he had made enough money to vote Republican.

But Andrea she was not and could not be.

Both the good ladies were quite disappointed when I left, so sure were they that I was making a mistake and missing an opportunity to end my search, an effort for which they praised me effusively.

"Back to Saint Dominic's," I told my cabby.

"Saint Dom's is a real hellhole," he said. "It's had a bad reputation since I was a kid. Nuns who enjoy being mean."

I admitted that I could believe it.

The school day was over by the time we returned to St. Dom's, though many sullen students, with the hangdog look of reform-school inmates in the Dead End Kids films, were busy sweeping corridors, erasing blackboards, and scribbling furiously at their desks.

My days of being kept after school were sufficiently close that I felt as guilty as they looked.

Sister Mary Regina was not in her office. But in the office next door I found Sister Marie Neri, a much younger woman, not any older than thirty, I suspected, though in those days the age of nuns was impossible to guess. Her refined courtesy ("How may I help you, young man?) and tony voice suggested Main Line: Irish aristocracy like us.

So my charm worked.

"Sister is the superior and I am the principal, Commander." She smiled graciously. "She is a bit more set in her ways. I will be happy to help if I can."

Fine, but you have that hair-shirt-wearing fanatic's glow in your eyes, Sister. In ten years you'll be worse than your patron.

I told her my story.

"We don't like to admit that such things happen at Saint Dominic's, Commander Keenan," she said with a sigh, "as I'm sure you understand. We have had a long tradition of high moral standards. But, as you realize, this dreadful war has had a terrible effect on morality. So, to be perfectly candid, yes, we did have a number of such cases."

"I'm sorry to hear that," I said with all the phony sympathy I could muster.

"From what you tell me, it sounds like the case of Andrew Koenig and—let me see—what was that little chit's name? Oh, yes. Margaret Mary Ward."

"Andrew Koenig?" I felt as if I had been hit with a two-by-four. Koenig meant King. And that was *his* name. "Yes, that does seem to be the name. He was called King when he was in our outfit."

"Here"—she offered me the yearbook—"is Miss Ward. I must say, Commander, she was an extremely provocative young lady."

Hands shaking, I hoped not visibly, I took the book from her and turned it around. On the page was a class picture of young women in drab serge uniform dresses that might have been appropriate for a prison.

"Third one from the left in the front row; she was on the short side," Sister remarked smoothly, "M. M. Ward."

"I see."

My fair bride? This innocent little girl with the pixie face, looking up at me somber and maybe a little frightened? Or angry?

I wasn't sure. Margaret?

"It seems to fit, Sister. May I ask a few questions about the case and the families?"

"Certainly, Commander. I'm afraid that the older sisters

are almost superstitious about it, and I don't accept the validity of such explanations. Yet they may have had a point when they said that Margaret Mary had bad blood."

Bingo!

"Bad blood?"

"Yes, poor Andrew John—his parents used both names— was a good boy, hardworking, studious, docile. He refused to be part of the wild bunch who used the war as an excuse for provoking behavior during the senior year. We thought he might very well consider college before he was called up or a college service program. His parents, however, hardworking immigrants who are the strength of this rather impoverished parish, thought otherwise. They felt that Andrew should learn a trade skill in the service. I remember his father saying to me that when the Depression returned, a tradesman—he himself was a mechanic—would never lack a job while many college graduates would be unemployed. It was, I assume you would agree, a realistic viewpoint?"

"The Depression hasn't returned yet, Sister."

"But it will." She withdrew a large watch from somewhere in her skirt and glanced at it with a disapproving frown. Time had dared to slip on without her permission. "He is dead, isn't he? Andrew, I mean. We had heard that, but we were never officially informed."

"Yes, Sister, he is. It might have been better advice to enroll in a V-12 program. He would have missed the war and would still be alive."

She missed my irony. "That will mean one more gold star for our flag." She made a note with the same sort of straight pen that Sister Mary Regina used. Apparently the order did not countenance fountain pens yet. "Most unfortunate."

"Especially for him. His parents no longer live in the community?"

"They took the scandal very hard, Commander." She laid the pen aside at a neat right angle to her inkwell. "Quite properly so. It was a disgrace even if it was not their fault. Shortly after the wedding they moved away, very quietly. I believe that no one in the neighborhood knows where they went. It's quite sad, really. He was their only son." She timed her pause carefully to indicate appropriate grief over the Koenigs' loss and still not waste any of the precious moments that were slipping by on her watch. "And all because of that foolish little girl." Sister's fine alabaster features contorted in a quick frown. "She was so . . ."

"Provoking?"

"Precisely. Bad blood, as the older sisters said. Her grandfather was an official of the city who was sent to prison for corruption. Her uncles were ne'er-do-wells, alcoholics and gamblers, you know. Her father, I am told, was a flashy young man, attractive and bright in a shallow way. He married a woman who was a model and a beauty queen: Mary Phalen was her name, as I remember. They were married with considerable ceremony just before the crash. I remember my parents saying—I was a little girl then—that no good would come of an alliance between Allen Ward and Mary Phalen. They were quite correct in their prediction, as it turned out. Mary Phalen may not have had bad blood, but she certainly had bad lungs. And Allen Ward did not have the courage to face life after his pretty little wife's death."

So far there was little difference, except in the names, between Sister's story and Andrea's. But I could not understand the animosity toward Andrea's—or should I say Margaret Mary's—parents. Whatever the reason for the animosity, little Margaret seemed to have inherited it.

"So the child was passed on to Mary Phalen's sister at the age of five. It was all in the papers." She frowned again, this time as if she had swallowed something distasteful. "Isobel Phalen was older than her sister and more sensible both in her personal life and in her choice of husband, Howard Quinn, a solid and respectable butcher. They had their hands full with that spoiled little girl, I can tell you."

Butcher? Andrea had corrected me when I said she went after her uncle with a carving knife. "Butcher knife." It all fit perfectly. And tragically.

"Mrs. Quinn had better fortune in her lungs too."

"Yes, indeed." My Irish charm was not wasted on this

youngish fanatic from the Main Line, but my Irish irony was still useless. "Actually, Sister Mary Regina, who was principal as well as superior then, did not want to accept the girl into school. The Monsignor, a little too much impressed with the power the Ward family had once enjoyed, insisted."

"She was troublesome from the beginning?"

"She was always most provoking." Sister laid the huge watch on the desk in front of her, at the opposite end of the blotter from her inkwell, an angel to monitor the time she would waste talking to me. "She pretended to be shy and studious, but she asked the most undocile questions in class and had a very bad habit of guessing what your thoughts were. She kept to herself, since the more respectable young women would not associate with her, though there was a small group totally lacking in docility of which she was the ringleader in high school."

"A constant disciplinary problem? I'm amazed that you kept her in the school."

Sister sighed patiently, hinting at the great forbearance of her order when confronted with undocile young women. "She was a very clever little miss. It was difficult to catch her in an actual disciplinary violation, until the end. Needless to say, we tried hard to find her in violations, but she usually eluded us. Poor Andrew John, he was an innocent victim, I am sure. Now, Commander," she said as she rose from her stern wooden chair and scooped up her watch, "I really must ask to be excused. I have a number of obligations to discharge before prayer."

She gave me the addresses of both families at the time of the great scandal. The Quinns had moved away too. Sister did not know where. Perhaps they would know at the rectory.

"Oh, yes, Commander." She stopped me at the door of her office. "Sister Patrice, our librarian, tried to help the girl when she was in high school. Sister is quite advanced in age now, but you might wish to talk to her. I don't believe that she has maintained contact with her, however."

"Thank you, Sister."

The "library" was a couple of dusty classrooms with

books on the walls and in dilapidated wooden shelves stretched across the rooms. There were no students in it and little sign that the dust had been disturbed very often. Pious and respectable students of Saint Dom's learn to read. They also learn not to read too much. For if you read too much, you may read the wrong kind of books.

Sister Patrice Marie was sitting in a corner at a small desk, sorting cards by the dim light of a single lamp. She was a cheerful, dotty nun who needed no explanation and no charm to tell me about Margaret Mary Ward.

"Maggie Ward, young man? Poor little tyke; *they* had it in for her from the first day she came here to school. Proper folk don't get their names in the paper, you see. And Maggie's family's name was in the paper all the time, fifteen or twenty years ago. Her mother was a great beauty, you remember. Maggie will be too, in a few years, poor thing. But if you're running a school for respectable young women, you don't want them contaminated by a child who might be a beauty and might get her name in the paper too, now do you?"

"No, S'ter," I said respectfully.

The old nun cackled. Clearly I understood.

"She was in here all the time. Read 'most every book I had. Got herself educated despite them. Course they held that against her too. A child that reads too much may get undocile thoughts, eh, young man?" She cackled again. "Become provocative. Even think for herself. Ask questions we aren't able to answer. Can't have that, can we, young man, eh? What'd you say your name was?"

"Jerry, S'ter. Jeremiah."

"Major prophet, huh? Do you know Maggie? Where is she?"

"I thought you'd be able to tell me."

" 'Fraid not. Got a card from her when the baby was born; lemme see, girl baby, I think. About a year ago. Just before the war ended. No return address, just a San Diego postcard."

So the child had not died in a miscarriage.

"They made her life miserable here, did they?"

"Terrible. Some women"—she winked—"need a child in

the school to hate, hold up as an example of evil to be avoided. Why, even though she had the prettiest voice in the school, they wouldn't let her sing in the choir or even try out for a part in the play. Fired her from the debate team because she won all the time. . . . Ever try to argue with her, young fella?"

"It didn't do much good."

"See? I told you. She would have been a state champion. Someday the order is going to have to pay for such cruelty."

Her merry eyes snapped with delight at the prospect of the order being punished. I too hoped that I would be around for the assignment to appropriate regions of hell of Sister Mary Regina and her stooges.

"You're hunting for Maggie?"

"In a way, S'ter."

"In love with her?"

"Not that way, S'ter," I lied.

"Hmmp." Clearly she didn't believe me. "Could turn out to be a fine woman if someone loved her properly. Wouldn't blame her at all if she killed that little brute who got her pregnant. Always thought he was a sneak."

"Andrew Koenig?"

"Andrew *John*," she said with a sneer. "One name for each cretin grandfather. Shifty-eyed little ape."

"Did you hear that she killed him?" I rose to leave. My friend at the Bureau of Personnel should be able to do something about the name Andrew Koenig.

"Little Maggie? She wouldn't hurt a fly. He died in the war, didn't he?"

"I believe so. Thank you very much, S'ter. You've been a big help."

"She was a funny little one, all the same." Sister's eyes were cloudy with memories. "Knew what people were thinking a lot of the time. You can imagine what that did to certain women who were already afraid she'd contaminate their precious little respectable school."

"And she did contaminate it in the end, didn't she, S'ter?"

"Young man, Jeremiah, major prophet." Sister shook an amused finger at me. "You and I both know there's a lot worse things in the world and in this school building than a pregnancy, don't we?"

"Yes, S'ter, we sure do."

CHAPTER **22**

"YOU KNOW HOW MANY NAMES WE HAVE IN THIS BUILDing?" my friend from the Bureau of Personnel demanded. "I'd probably have a hard time finding your records if you didn't have that medal. Give us a couple of years to get organized."

"You didn't have any trouble when I asked about the *Indianapolis*." I was sitting in my room at the Latham Hotel, at Seventeenth and Walnut streets, talking above the noise of the renovators who could be found in this first summer after the war in most older American hotels.

"That was different. If your Andrew John Koenig was on a major loss like that and you can tell me the ship, I won't have any trouble checking him out. Or if there's some sort of pension or insurance payment. Anything else will be pure luck."

"Well, check the *Indianapolis* again. And see if anyone is collecting insurance benefits. And try your luck on anything else. I'll call back tomorrow."

After I check out Maggie Ward's neighborhood and see if I can find out where her aunt and uncle live.

The fellow with the butcher knife.

Maggie Ward. Can you have a grail quest for someone with that kind of name? Andrea King has a hint of mystery and adventure. Maggie Ward, short for Margaret Mary Ward, is the name of the girl down the street.

And if perchance she should change it to Maggie Keenan,

it would bring memories of an earlier generation of madcap micks.

A "Maggie Ward" is the kind of a girl who wants to look at furniture on the second date. Not the kind with whom you encounter demons and perhaps a gun-toting angel in a ghost town in the Superstition Mountains.

In the dour, dry respectability of Saint Dominic's parish, Clinton, Arizona Territory, seemed quite improbable. So, too, did lustful romps in the Picketpost House bridal suite.

Nonetheless, any girl who could survive Saint Dom's with the capability for such a romp would be well worth hunting, the girl next door with a few extra added attractions, as they used to say in the film previews.

Only one tough little bitch would survive at all.

Maggie Ward Keenan, it had a certain promising rhythm, hinting at several pixie-faced, tough little girl children, with freckle cheeks and turned-up noses.

Among other things.

I phoned home. My parents had gone up to Lake Geneva for the weekend. Packy was about to leave to join them when I called.

"Find the girl yet, kid?"

"Your information was very useful," I said guardedly. "I'll tell you the whole story someday."

"To hell with the story. I want to meet the broad."

"I never said there was a broad."

"Yeah? Well, where to next?"

"Here, for another day, anyway. I'll stay in touch. Have a good time at the lake."

"I plan to. I'm going to try waterskiing."

"What's that?"

"Skiing on water, what else, genius? Behind a boat. They started it on the Riviera before the war. It looks like fun."

"It will never catch on here," I said. Another one of my prize-winning predictions. I thought it was definitely confirmed later when I read an article in *Life* that pointed out that it would cost thirty-five dollars to buy the seven-foot-long, seven-inch-wide skis!

Having discharged my obligation to phone my family, I turned to the twin responsibility of my journal, which in those early August days of 1946 was devoted almost entirely to the search for Andrea King, possibly née Margaret Mary (Maggie) Ward.

August 9th. The Philadelphia Inquirer *reports that they're still fighting at the Paris Peace Conference, there's a race riot in Athens, Georgia, it's the 100th anniversary of the Smithsonian Institution; and Ben Hogan has won the Canadian PGA. My family has departed for a long weekend at Lake Geneva, for which I find myself unaccountably longing, even if I would have to travel through La Mancha to get there.*

And I continue my search for Andrea, whose real name might be Maggie. I have confirmed today some elements in her story.

1) Her family was indeed fading well-to-do Irish: fashionable weddings, society pages in the papers, summer homes at Cape May and in the Poconos, all of this before she was born.

2) Her father did disappear shortly after her mother's death and she was raised by an aunt and uncle, the latter a man who would have a butcher knife readily available because he was a butcher. They were indeed strict, not to say cruel.

3) The nuns at her school did not like her, mostly because of her family background. Andrea did not mention the family resentment element in their dislike for her. Maybe she was unaware of it or did not understand it.

4) She was intelligent, shy, and mysterious, reading the minds of her teachers, asking "undocile" questions, and devouring serious books borrowed from the school library.

5) She was pregnant at the time of her marriage to an industrious only son of an immigrant family.

On the other hand, there are some parts of her story that are at odds with the history I gathered today:

1) She told me that she had lost a child through a miscarriage. It would appear, however, that she did have a live baby, possibly a girl, about a year ago. This would fix the time of her marriage in January or February of 1945, when she was a junior in high school, perhaps not yet seventeen. If her husband was on the Indianapolis, which I am not able to confirm, he would have died about the same time the baby was born. The nuns seem to agree that he died in the war, but there is some uncertainty about when and where and how. Indeed, the principal of St. Dom's only added him to her list of gold stars when I confirmed his death.

2) There is conflicting evidence about her husband. She admitted that he was dull and slow, but claimed to have loved him. The anti-Maggie nuns at St. Dom's are high in their praise for Andrew Koenig, but nonetheless he sounds in their description like the same young man Andrea portrayed for me. On the other hand, Sister Patrice Marie said he was a brute and she would not have blamed Maggie for killing him. She quickly added that Maggie wouldn't hurt anyone.

The picture in the 1944 yearbook when she was a sophomore is enough like the young woman I encountered in the station in Tucson almost three weeks ago to persuade me that they are the same person. She looks so young and frail. So, too, did Andrea.

So I have found my Andrea's neighborhood, and school, and teachers, and her real name, of which I am becoming increasingly fond. She continues to be elusive, however; magical, mysterious, and haunting.

If she is some sort of ghost, a spirit lingering between earth and hell, she is at least a ghost of a real human person who has suffered more in a short life than most do in much longer lives. I will not believe in a God who feels any less love for her than I do.

She now seems more pathetic. She was forced to grow up before her time, to become an adult hardly before she put away her dolls. If her aunt and uncle permitted her dolls. I wish I was holding her in my arms at this moment in my room here at the Latham.

I love her more than ever.

But I find it hard to remember what she looked like.

Both her family and her husband's family have left the neighborhood. Tomorrow I will try to learn where they might be. Even if I find them, however, I won't necessarily be any closer to Maggie—I guess I had better start calling her that now—than I was when I awoke from my dream, or whatever it was, in the Superstition Mountains.

I do not, however, intend to give up my search.

Brave young man, isn't he? And utterly unaware of the obvious truth that he will find Andrea King/Maggie Ward only if she wants to be found.

And is in a world where she can be found.

The next morning, Saturday, I ate a leisurely breakfast, read the comics in the *Inquirer*, deplored the Cubs' continued fall from grace, and set out again by cab for Saint Dominic's. I told my driver to meet me in front of the church at 4 P.M. It was a hot summer Saturday; lots of people would be on the porches or the door stoops or the streets, and I expected to be overwhelmed by waves of clues.

The image of waves reminded me of Lake Geneva and raised again the question of why I wasn't there, swimming in the lake, sailing in my father's cutter, and looking forward to a date that night with some lovely young thing who was prepared to adore the heroic naval aviator and listen wide-eyed to his description of learning how to fly a Phantom jet.

"We call it an FH-1, honey. 'F' stands for fighter, 'H' for McDonnell, and '1' means that it is the first version of this model. Understand?" Small kiss of reward if she does and of punishment if she doesn't.

This not unrealistic picture (it leaves out the likelihood that the young woman would want to look at furniture the following weekend) became more appealing as the hours of that hot August Saturday continued.

And I saw Maggie everywhere in her old neighborhood. Scores of young women with auburn hair and bouncing breasts were on the streets of Saint Dominic's, teasing, tempting, inviting. Fortunately for the peace of the community, I was able to resist the urge to speak to them.

She's not here, I told myself every five minutes. That girl is not Maggie. This is the last place you'll find her.

But the girl is cute, isn't she?

"Stop thinking that way," CIC demanded.

"Go away until you can come back with your automatic weapon," I replied.

The people of Saint Dominic's, being Irish, were willing to talk to the tall stranger with a Middle Western accent, despite the fact that his blue slacks and short-sleeve white shirt were a bit too expensive-looking for the neighborhood. The heat, the dust, the dense humidity, the impoverished atmosphere of the neighborhood did not inhibit their tongues. It was the same sort of environment I would encounter years later, with much lower temperature, in the west of Ireland on a week-end trade fair. They were more than willing to provide information about Anton ("Tony") Koenig and Howard ("Howie") Quinn and their families, lots of information, in elaborate detail and with as many illustrative anecdotes as I was willing to hear.

When have the Irish ever been reluctant to provide information?

But the information was useless for my purposes. Both Tony and Howie were described either as "hardworking" or "kinda dull." Howie was said to have a fierce temper and there were hints of black-market meat during the war.

"If you ask me, he got out of town not because of the girl but because of the cops."

"He had some friends who were friends of the big pols. They gave him a chance to vanish or go to jail."

As for Anton Koenig, a cop on the beat shook his head slowly. "He wasn't like us, Commander. Pretended to be quiet and thoughtful, but I think he didn't say anything because he didn't have anything to say."

That would never stop "us."

Both the women were described in varying degrees of hostility as thinking they were "better" than anyone else.

Young Andrew, I was told, was "very serious, didn't hang around on the street corners with the young hoodlums."

On the other hand, a sandy-haired kid who had been a gunner on a TBF whom I encountered in front of a corner drugstore confided that "Andrew was a jerk, sir. No one could believe that he'd be able to knock up that cute little kid. Musta got her drunk first. A lot of guys would have been willing to go after her, if they had a chance. Still would if she comes back. He caught it, didn't he?"

"On the *Indianapolis*, I think."

"Yeah? I heard he was transferred off before she brought the Bomb out to Tinian. A submarine guy a year ahead of me in school said he saw him repairing radar at Ulithi. Never did hear how he died, though. Something sort of mysterious. Is she coming back? Really hot stuff."

I wasn't sure and didn't tell the kid, who had no right to be alive, that I had a prior claim.

Ulithi was an atoll in the western Pacific, same meridian as Tokyo, which replaced Pearl Harbor as the Navy's advance base in the last months of the war. You could sit on the island of the *Enterprise* in that lagoon and see as many as ten carriers getting ready to go back to battle. It made you wonder—it still makes me wonder—how the Japanese thought they were going to win the war.

I pondered the possibility that Maggie's husband had been one of the technicians who tinkered with the *Big E*'s dubious radar.

"I don't know whether she's coming back."

"She was the kind of kid"—his worried frown deepened, as if he were wrestling with the ultimate meaning of human life, Jacob struggling with the angel—"you had to treat with respect if you had any sense at all. Know what I mean, sir?"

"I do and neither of us are in the Navy anymore."

"Yeah." The kid grinned. "Hard habit to break. You know, sir"—he laughed—"sorry, but what I mean is that you come back and you find that there are a lot of girls like her and you wonder what kind of an asshole you were for not noticing them before. They figure"—he sighed—"they're gonna straighten you out."

"And they probably will."

"You know it!" He laughed. "Good luck, she was a great kid. She deserved a lot better than what happened to her."

Dear God in heaven, she certainly did.

("That's right, darling," I told my fictional Lake Geneva date, to distract myself from the phantoms I was meeting on the streets of Philadelphia, "he was a gunner on a TBF, not a long-life-expectancy job in 1944. 'F' stands for Grumman, darling, so it's a Grumman torpedo bomber, not nearly as much a flying coffin as the TBD, the Douglas torpedo bomber that came before it, but not exactly a safe ride either. It was a good thing we made almost ten thousand Avengers, that was the name for the TBF; we ran through them pretty quickly. Do you want another beer?")

That was the most I was able to learn from anyone on the streets about Maggie Ward. She did not seem to be so clearly sketched in people's memories as her family and her in-laws.

"A sweet little girl. Very pretty. From a famous family that was in hard times, like the rest of us."

The cop who felt that Tony Koenig didn't talk because he didn't have much on his mind had the sharpest image of her. "She was a nice little girl, poor kid. She used to smile at me every morning and say, 'Hello, Officer Sullivan, how is your wife feeling today?' My missus has poor health, you see. I don't care what they say about her father, the Wards always had class and she did, too."

Indeed yes, officer, but where do they live now?

No one had the answer to that one. The Koenigs had left the neighborhood, it was generally agreed, because of the disgrace of the shotgun marriage; the Quinns one step ahead of the FBI. Andrew was dead. Maggie had given birth to a baby girl; she had mailed a few cards to her friends with that joyous news. No one knew where she lived now. Nor did they have any idea of where her family, or his, had moved.

The row house in which the Koenigs had lived was occupied by an Italian family of vast size, the mother of which fed me a plate of marvelous pasta and confessed that she had no idea where the Koenigs had moved. And couldn't have cared less.

"Very quiet people." She shook her classical head and its tightly braided hair in disapproval. "They don't say anything. Never have fun."

I could hardly decline the second plate of pasta, especially since I had not eaten a decent meal after our last dinner in Globe.

"You're too thin," she said. "Girls think maybe you have TB. You end up bachelor."

"Irish bachelor."

"Worst kind. Drink some more wine, make you feel good."

I left feeling very good indeed, deploring my inability to be instantly in Lake Geneva, my head light with Chianti, explaining to my date—who now had become a mythological beauty—the Navy's system of classifying airplanes.

"The F4F, dear" (I'd have my arms around her by now) "is, as I'm sure you understand, the fourth fighter plane produced by Grumman. It was called the Wildcat and was lucky to survive in a fight with a Zero. The F5F was a night-fighter version of the Wildcat, the plane that Butch O'Hare died in."

(I couldn't tell her about O'Hare field because that was Orchard/Douglas Airport in those days.)

"I flew an F6F Hellcat, our basic fighter, for the last two years of the war. We produced more than twelve thousand of them. It won seventy-five percent of our combat victories. It was not nearly as maneuverable as the Zero, but we liked it because it was sturdy and reliable and kept pilots alive. We had so much armor around us that the Japanese bullets literally bounced off our fuselages."

(I wouldn't tell her that nothing ever bounced off my plane because, medals or not, nothing ever hit my Hellcat.)

"The last aircraft I flew was the F8F Bearcat, a souped-up job that might have ended the war a year earlier if we'd had it in 1944. Great little plane and the last of the piston Grummans. The F9F is a jet, called the Panther. If I had stayed in, I'd be flying that in another year or two."

(And I wouldn't tell her, because I was not a major prophet, that I would be dodging North Korean and Chinese antiaircraft fire in my Panther.)

Through this long discussion of aircraft she would have listened with rapt adoration.

And I would not have realized that she couldn't care less about navy combat aircraft.

The woman I did marry finally made herself care; she

decorated our first apartment with photographs and paintings of navy aircraft. Then—it served me right—when I lost interest, she was hooked on airplane paintings.

God, as Packy says, is a comedienne.

But on that unbearably hot day in Philadelphia, forty years ago next month, I was not laughing.

I might never find Maggie Ward.

CHAPTER 23

I ENTERTAINED MYSELF WITH PLEASANT DISTRACTIONS about my imaginary but pliant lover at Lake Geneva, blended with self-pity because she wasn't in my arms at that very minute. Thus distracted, I walked the six blocks to the former Quinn row house, at the very outer limits of Saint Dominic's. I realized that if Andrea/Maggie had walked the shortest route to school, she would have passed the corner at the end of the street on which the Koenigs lived, a stoplight corner, where there would be a crossing guard. He could have waited for her there whether she wanted him to wait or not.

Saint Dominic's was a shabby neighborhood; the street on which the Quinns lived seemed the most shabby of all the row streets in the parish, near a suburban railroad track and a truck depot, beyond which there was a block of aging factories and then the docks. The street had slipped irreversibly in the direction of a slum.

I pushed the doorbell button. I did not hear a bell ring. I waited a moment and then knocked on the door vigorously.

"What's the hurry?" the young woman who opened the door demanded. "It's too hot to hurry."

She was tall and slender, with jet-black hair, buttermilk

skin, a ridge of freckles over her nose, spectacular legs, and a thin, delicate face—a "black Irish" beauty in white shorts and halter, with an accounting textbook in one hand, a radiant movie queen who transformed her slum setting into a background for hope and laughter.

I stared with an open mouth. So, I think, did she.

"Good afternoon," I said, trying to close my mouth. "I'm Jerry Keenan."

"I'm Jean Kelly," she said and returned my smile. "I'm studying for my summer-school exam at Saint Joe's. Would you like a glass of lemonade?"

Both of us had spontaneously turned on our Irish charm.

"I've just finished three glasses of Italian wine. I think some Irish lemonade . . ."

"Might make you sick?

"Might sober me up."

"I'll get it out of the icebox—we still have an icebox— the iceman comes every day. My parents and brothers and sisters aren't home, by the way."

"I still feel reasonably safe."

She laughed enthusiastically. "You talk funny."

"No, you talk funny." We both laughed together. I felt suddenly light-headed. I assumed that she did, too.

"You Navy?"

We had to talk about something besides our light heads and racing bloodstreams.

"Flyer."

"Helldiver?"

"I'm still alive, am I not?"

(The SB2C was a dive bomber, same name as the biplane in the movie with Wallace Beery, but even more dangerous because its tail tended to fall off in dives, a notable problem in a dive bomber. And a disgrace that kids were made to fly them. My wife refuses to permit pictures of the second Helldiver in her collection, just as she interdicts the Douglas Devastator—TBD. These planes were swept from the sky by the Japs at Midway; torpedo eight lost all its men but one in these crates. I'm not sure about her logic, but I agree with her sentiments.)

"Fighter?"

"Hellcat; squadron leader eventually, if that doesn't destroy your faith in the Navy."

My children, who lived through the Viet Nam disaster, find it hard to imagine that young people talked about where they were and what they did in the war as casually as they talked about where they were attending college. It was not that we were militarists. Some of us had more reason to hate war than the college protesters twenty years later. Unlike them we had seen our comrades die. But military service was part of our story, one of the episodes in our lives by which we identified and defined ourselves. It was an incident in our lives of which we were not necessarily proud but of which neither were we ashamed.

"I can believe anything about the Navy. But you *look* all right."

I didn't know quite what that meant, but I followed her to the kitchen. Sure enough, an old-fashioned brown wooden icebox. We'd left that behind in 1930. However, the house was pin neat and spotlessly clean. That didn't seem very Irish.

"I am mostly all right. But not totally all right."

That produced a cheerful laugh. Anyway, the girl was certainly not afraid of me.

A more leisurely inspection revealed long, slender legs, a narrow waist, spherical white breasts which her halter was not designed to obscure, and a smile that invited you to enjoy her loveliness.

What was that other girl's name again? The one I'm not searching for anymore?

"What year are you in?"

"Pre-freshman. I run an elevator in the Ben Franklin Hotel during the day"—she handed me the lemonade and led me back to the threadbare living room—"and go to school at night. I figure if I have a head start on the courses and get some good marks, they'll continue my scholarship."

Maggie would be the same age. For a moment I imagined she was Maggie. I was a half-inch away from taking her in my arms and smothering her with kisses. Instead I asked a dumb question, which I knew was dumb when I asked it.

"Why college for a girl, especially a pretty girl?"

"Everyone goes to college now." She waved a hand flippantly. "Even girls. And we get the best marks because we're smarter."

"And prettier."

"And just generally better."

We laughed joyously, young and happy with all our lives ahead of us. Then I turned serious.

"I'm searching for Maggie Ward," I said simply.

She put her lemonade on a coaster on the arm of her mohair-covered chair.

"I hope you find her." The twinkle had vanished from her deep-blue eyes. "Maggie is a wonderful girl. Are you in love with her?"

"I think so."

She nodded briskly, a possible flirtation turning into a serious business. "You have good taste. She's astonishing, and against terrible odds."

"I guess we're both members of the fan club. Do you know where she is?"

"I heard from her when Andrea was born, an instant love affair that was. She adored the kid. Then came a note at Christmas saying that the baby had just died. It was the first time I'd ever heard Maggie sound down. Then another note around Saint Patrick's Day. Wait, let me get it." She bounded out of the room, leaving a trail of inexpensive but tasteful lilac scent behind her.

"It's a strange letter," she said as she settled back into her chair, grim and somber. "Maggie was always a little strange, kind of . . . what's the word I'm looking for . . ."

"Uncanny? Ethereal?"

"Both words, I guess. She *knew* things, like she was plugged into another world. Anyway, listen. . . ,

"Dear Jean,

"I have more bad news, I'm afraid. Andrew has died too. I've lost my daughter and my husband in less than three months. His family did not even want the body. He's buried here in San Diego. I'm so numb that I cannot even weep. I probably never could love him, as you know, but I had become fond of him. He was changing and improving till everything went wrong for us. Again. I guess I was fighting those awful parents of his every day. I thought I was winning, but you can't win by yourself.

"Anyway, I miss him.

"I'm all alone now, free from Uncle Howard and Aunt Isobel, from my cute little daughter, and free from my husband for whom I tried so hard. Remember when I told you that someday I wanted to be free of all the obligations of the past and the present? Well, that day has finally come. And I discover that without obligations there is no reason to live.

"I am a very unimportant and useless person whom no one would miss. Maybe we're all that way. Maybe I just found it out at a younger age than most people.

"We will not see each other again, Jean. Do well in college, don't give up on Ralph, he has everything you want and need even if, poor dear sweet man, he doesn't know how much he's worth.

"I love you,
"Maggie."

"Ralph?"

"A boy. TBF gunner."

"Sandy hair, underweight, gentle brown eyes?"

"You got him." She blushed. "He's still kind of shook by the war. Lost a couple of pilots on his plane. He's going to school with me—because I'm there—but he's beginning to like it. You met him? He thought Maggie was wonderful too."

Poor Ralph. Probably figured he didn't deserve this intelligent bundle of loveliness. Probably he didn't, but which of us does deserve the woman who salvages us?

"So he said."

"This sounds like a suicide note, doesn't it?" The light-pink glow on her face suggested that we'd best not talk about Ralph. "Is she dead?"

"I don't think so . . . what did you do when you received this?"

"I had a return address from the card about Andrea's birth. I tried to find a phone number from Information in San Diego. They told me the apartment building at the address had been torn down. There was no listing of either Ward or Koenig which could have been her. I didn't know what to do, so I did what we Irish Catholics always do. I prayed for her. I still pray for her. Every night."

"Don't stop. . . . Do you think she might have killed him?"

"Maggie?" she exploded. "Don't be ridiculous!"

"Sorry. I had to ask."

"She had plenty of reason to kill the bastard." Jean was not mollified. "But you know her. Is she the killer type?"

"I think she's the victim type, the kind of woman that evil people enjoy hurting because she's so good."

"I can't see her killing anyone." Jean was not ready to drop her defense of her heroine.

"I agree." I shrugged. "Unless she was defending someone else."

We paused to consider that possibility. Jean then changed the subject.

"Are you sure she's alive?" she pleaded, her eyes misting.

You were important to these people, Maggie Ward/Andrea King. Did you know that? I wondered.

"A stubborn, hungry kid when she wanted to be." Jean Kelly folded the paper and placed it on the floor next to her chair. "He raped her, you know. Andrew Koenig, I mean."

"I didn't know."

"She was still sixteen, didn't know anything, her aunt

never explained sex to her. The nuns sure didn't. He came from the Navy, great big Joe War Hero, and wanted to screw her. She didn't know what it meant. So he showed her. She cried in my arms the next day."

"So she hardly could be said to have loved him?" My hands were wet, my throat tight. I wanted to kill him, but he was already dead.

"She was nice to him, because no one else liked him. When he talked about marrying her after the war, she listened politely but never agreed. I told her that he was a slimy little drudge and she said that she felt sorry for him. Maggie picked up strays—cats, dogs, birds, boys. Her aunt and uncle wouldn't let her keep the pets so she'd make sure one of her friends would give the poor creature a proper home. She should never have married him, but she felt she had to for the baby's sake. She even tried to love him, which is what Maggie would do. Poor kid. 'Scuse me. I gotta get a hankie."

My fists were clenched. I wanted to break something. Anything.

Jean Kelly returned, dabbing at her eyes. No makeup for this natural beauty.

"The nuns hated her, all except crazy old Patrice Marie, because her family had been famous—society pages of the papers and stuff like that when they were young. Her aunt hated her because her mother was pretty and she was ugly, and I mean ugly; a lot of the other kids hated her because the nuns like you if you hate the same people they hate. . . . You have nuns in school?"

"And priests in high school. Most of them weren't that way."

She nodded. "There's some great young nuns in class with me. Maybe the Church will change. Anyway, some of us got to know Maggie in grammar school and, Jerry Keenan, uncanny and eth—"

"Ethereal."

"Right"—she grinned—"ethereal she may be but she was also magic. Kind, funny, smart, always helping others . . . hey, are you another one of her strays?"

"I hadn't thought of it that way"—it was my turn to feel warm in the face—"but maybe I was. Maybe she felt sorry for me too."

Who took pity on whom in the railroad station with Bing Crosby singing "Ole Buttermilk Sky"?

"Poor Maggie was sort of a confessor for at least a dozen boys. I think it must have been those soft blue eyes. They poured their problems out to her and seemed to feel better afterward. Good thing, because all our real confessors could do was denounce 'immorality,' and you know what they meant by that."

"She certainly listened sympathetically," I agreed.

"You don't look like a stray." She evaluated me critically. "Not at all.

At our age, a little bit of flirtation was not out of order, even if we both had, more or less, other commitments.

"Do strays always look like strays?"

"Awful Andrew sure did. You see, the problem was his father. Dull and dumb, but stubborn. He pounded into his kid's thick skull that if a real man wants something badly enough, he takes it. You put a dope like Andrew in a barracks with guys who give him the business every night about being a virgin and you set up a rape."

"If he wasn't dead, I'd want to kill him."

"Calm down, Navy." Her eyes met mine and held them. "Men get killed in wars. Women get raped. It's not good, but it's not new."

"Please, God, never again." Had I invoked a God I did not yet believe in?

"Amen to that."

"Maggie was the leader of your bunch?"

"Sure was. Made us study and read and keep our noses clean with the nuns. And they never guessed what she was up to. She would have been class president if that old bitch Mary Regina had not gone to school with one of her great-aunts and envied her."

"So that's where it comes from?"

"The old bitch makes all the other nuns think like she

does. You see, the great-aunt was class president when Mary Regina wanted to be. So she got even with Maggie. From day one."

"Poor little girl, indeed."

"She was a tough one, Jerry Keenan. She took it all, never was mean or nasty back, and never gave in either. Till she got pregnant. To make it worse, she was really sick—all day, every day."

"Gallant?"

"Yeah." She winked. "Ethereal and gallant. And I hope not dead."

"I do too. . . ."

"Is she beautiful?" Jean Kelly picked up her lemonade glass and then put it down again. "She was pretty and I kind of thought that she might become a real beauty."

"Like yourself?" God forgive me, I couldn't resist it. Besides, it was true.

"Thanks." She smiled ruefully. "But not like me, like someone you'd see in the movies. Maureen O'Hara, you know?"

"Jeanne Crain?"

She considered reflectively. "That's better, a little bit more elfin face and maybe a more intelligent forehead than Jeanne. But just as lovely. Or will be soon, didn't you think so?"

I hesitated. "On her way to it maybe, but as my father once told me, some women either become great beauties or wither by the time they're twenty. Maggie could go either way. Depending."

"On what?"

"On what happens to her."

"She was the kind who survives," Jean said thoughtfully.

"She had to, didn't she? And by the way, you're not the kind who withers."

"You have a clever Irish tongue, Navy."

"That's what Maggie said to me."

"Did she really? That would not have been a Maggie comment two years ago."

"Would it have been a Jean Kelly comment?"

She laughed. "Hell, yes. So maybe the little brat was quoting me."

"You don't happen to know where her aunt and uncle are, do you?"

"Sure, I do." She leaned forward, resting her chin on her hands as if in thoughtful conspiracy, and thus revealed ample amounts of breast for my inspection. "We're supposed to forward anything that comes and not tell anyone, as if the FBI really cares about such small fish. I'm sure they don't know where she is, and they wouldn't tell you if they did."

I took a deep breath, steadying my concentration. "I'm looking for a needle in a haystack, lovely lady, searching for hints, any kind of hints about where she might be."

"They're in Florida, a place called Port Lauderdale, which I never heard of." She rose from her chair, being careful not to spill her lemonade, picked up my empty glass and left the room.

"Fort Lauderdale," I called after her, sighing to myself with both disappointment and relief.

"That's right." She returned, refilled lemonade glass in one hand, a small piece of note paper in the other. "*Fort* Lauderdale. You must have got good grades in geography, Jerry. I guess he runs a meat market down there too. Probably still has his thumb on the scale. Don't tell them where you found out about the address, not that it makes much difference."

"Thanks." I glanced at the address, put the paper in my shirt pocket, and attacked the lemonade.

"Do you think you'll find her?"

"Of course." I was not so confident, but I couldn't let this lovely young woman think that I was discouraged.

She stared thoughtfully out of the spanking clean window of the row house.

"There was a streak in her of . . . gosh, I don't even know what to call it . . . come on, Navy, you're good at words. . . ."

"Fatalism?"

"Worse than that."

"Despair."

"Right." She jabbed her finger at me in agreement. "Usually I would kid her out of it, but I was never sure that she wasn't going along just to keep me happy. She was always worried about what the dumb nuns called the 'unforgivable sin,' as though God's love can be limited."

Beautiful and devout too. Lucky, lucky Ralph.

"God has not done all that well by Maggie."

"He sent you, didn't he?" She cocked an appraising eye.

"On that happy note," I said as I rose from my chair, "I'd better ask if I can use your bathroom. It's a long walk back to my taxi after three glasses of Chianti and two of lemonade."

"First door on the left." She was brooding again, her head on her fist. "Dear God, I'd like to see Maggie again."

Need I say that the bathroom was spotless? Jean or her mother? Probably both.

"Your mother Irish?" I asked upon return.

"Sure . . . why . . . oh, you mean because the house is so clean. I guess we're exceptions in that respect. Don't drink, either."

I took her hands in mine and lifted her out of her chair. She looked away from me.

We were both silent for a few seconds, permitting the delightful chemistry of attraction, about which neither of us was going to do anything, flow back and forth. When you're young, some possibilities are better enjoyed if they can be remembered only as possibilities.

"Thank you, Jean Kelly. Jean Marie Kelly?" She nodded. "Of course it's Jean Marie," I went on. "Ralph is a lucky man."

She sighed softly. "Maggie is lucky too, and it's high time."

I touched her lips with mine.

I wanted to touch her flat, pale belly with my fingertips and knew that CIC was correct in loudly warning against such behavior. So I released her and walked briskly to the door. "Get out of here with class," CIC, absent for some time, interjected his opinion again.

"Go away until you can come back with your BAR," I replied.

But he was right: I had better not tarry.

"Good luck with Ralph," I said, shaking hands at the door.

"I'll shape him up." She smiled. "Never fear. Let me know if you find her."

I promised that I would, kissed her once again, and departed with a reasonable amount of class.

"Well," my wife would observe when I told her this part of the story, "at least you found out her name and address. That was better than you did with the might-have-been in San Francisco."

No special credit. She told me her name. And she lived at the Quinns' address which the nuns had given me.

And I would certainly never forget her.

Back at the Latham, I turned on the radio to discover that the Cubs were playing a doubleheader with the Phillies. They had lost the first game and were losing the second.

Naturally.

I couldn't phone the family because they were at Lake Geneva, where my father resolutely refused to install a phone. So, while I listened with one ear to the Cubs booting ground balls, I began to fill in my daily journal entry. Maybe it was the sexual chemistry between me and Jean Kelly, but that day's entry, now so faded as to be barely legible, does not embarrass me today.

> *The first impression I must put down on paper is the striking, humiliating, but not altogether unappealing thought that I may have been one of Maggie Ward's strays. She told me that she wanted to make love with me when she first saw me in the station. But did she find me desirable because I was a disenchanted young man on the way home from the wars, a boy who needed a touch of the warmth stored up in her big blue eyes?*
>
> *Whatever her own problems might have been, she would never have shared them with me unless she had first thought I needed her help. Afterward the mutual need between us became so demanding that it ran out of control.*
>
> *Did I force myself on her like awful Andrew?*
>
> *Certainly not. The love between us was passionate on both sides.*
>
> *And my dreams about the Yamoto and my shipmates have stopped. Now that I'm on track in searching for her, I'm sleeping peacefully. It*

almost seems that the nightmare at Clinton was the last of the nightmares.

My life started to turn the corner when I met her. Maybe the corner has turned completely now. Perhaps the horror at Clinton was an end and a beginning. Could it be that Andrea's—I should call her Maggie now—Maggie's role was to teach me how to love a woman and point me in the direction of becoming a writer instead of a lawyer, or in addition to a lawyer?

She was a brief grace sent to teach me how to live and how to love. Is that not enough?

No. I want her in my arms.

I paused and pondered what I had written.

Had Quixote found a mission for his life so easily?

Perhaps I had learned all that there was to learn from the pale, haunted young woman I had met and loved and lost. Ought I to forget about a quest that was probably hopeless?

The Cubs managed to load the bases in the first of the ninth, with one out. They were down two runs. All right, now's the turning point of the season.

I put my pen aside and listened intently.

By the way, what was the name of the American League club in Philadelphia in those days? No one knows? The A's, since then in Kansas City and Oakland.

I beat my grandchildren at Trivial Pursuit as long as sports is the subject.

Or war.

The next Cub batter struck out. And the one after that popped up to the shortstop. No runs, two hits, and no errors. Three men left on base.

Paradigmatic.

I called Delta Airlines and was told that they had a DC-3 flight to Miami and "intermediate stops" on Monday morning. I made my reservation and didn't ask what the intermediate stops were.

Then I returned to my diary.

She lied to me about two important facts. Her daughter did not die in a miscarriage. And her husband did not die on the Indianapolis. *In fact, he apparently died six months after the war was over. Moreover, she had an excellent reason to want to kill him, although both Sister Patrice Marie and Jean Kelly believe that impossible.*

But why lie to me?

I stopped my pen, or rather the Latham's pen, poised uncertainly over the notebook.

Maybe because she was afraid I wouldn't believe the truth.

I lifted the Latham's pen off the page again.
What is the truth?
I thought about that.

Something so horrible that she thought that she was poised between earth and hell.

What could that be?
I read over what I had written. It settled the question, as if there ever had been any doubt about it. I would not, could not, give up my search for Andrea King/Maggie Ward until I had an explanation. I might not find her. I had to know her real story. Then I could understand, I hoped, the strange experience that we had shared above Lost Dutchman's creek.
I went back to writing.

She seems like such an intricate and complicated person. How could a kid a little over eighteen be so elusive?

Maybe we're all that way. If someone were trying to hunt down the facts of my life, would he not decide that I too was a bundle of contradictions. Even in the family. Talk to Joanne and you'd learn about one Jerry Keenan, and then talk to Packy and I'd be a very different person.

The men and women in Saint Dom's remember her as sweet and pretty but indistinct. Ralph—the kid at the drugstore must have been Ralph, the lucky bastard—recollects her as hot stuff but still deserving respect. Jean Kelly, a bright, gorgeous, mature young woman, tells me

*that she was tough and ethereal and pretty and close to despair. For all
her own talents and resources, Jean worshiped her and depended on her.
She also tells me that Maggie played mother confessor to a group of boys.*

*She had a hard life, God knows. But she also had attracted good and
loyal friends. Yep, that was my Andrea. She had character. I guess I
knew that in Arizona. Not only tough, but strong.*

*And this is the "provoking little girl" that Sister Mary Regina
despised.*

Did you know any girls like her in high school?

*Sure, I did. I never made love with any of them. Never fought the
demons of hell for them as I did or imagined I did for her in the
Superstition Mountains. Would they have been like her under the
pressures she endured? Maybe. Why not?*

So it's not an impossible portrait, only a fascinating one.

*Which is why I am in Philadelphia in this August of 1946 instead of
Lake Geneva.*

"CIC!"

"Yes, sir."

"Didn't you tell me that she would always be part of my life?"

"I don't recall that I did, sir."

"Well, the guy with the BAR did."

"But that is true already, isn't it?"

*One tough, fascinating little bitch. Even if I don't find you, you'll be
carved on my memory and my conscience as long as I live.*

*But I intend to find you. Not just your secret, not just your story, but
you.*

*And then bring you home to the Butterfield dance (if not the
Harvest Festival, then something later). And never let you go.*

Never.

*It's your fault I didn't take on Ralph in a competition for Jean Kelly
this afternoon. Do you realize, Maggie Ward, what I'm giving up for
you?*

Well, I'll ask you someday.

So as the sun set and a touch of breeze played with the
curtain of my room at the Latham—no air conditioner but
"on the north side of the hotel, sir"—I admired my virtue for

not making a determined pass at Jean Kelly, considered the possibility of attending Mass the next day, and decided against it.

I would leave on Monday morning for Fort Lauderdale and her aunt and uncle whom I would like to strangle. I had no idea of what I would ask them or where I would search after what was certain to be an unsatisfactory talk with them.

I reconsidered my decision to stay away from Mass.

You could always pray "Dear sir or madam."

Or even "occupant."

When you were desperate enough.

CHAPTER

THE DELTA AIRLINES DC-3 THAT WAS SUPPOSED TO MAKE the run to Miami was out of service. So the three passengers scheduled to board in Philadelphia and the lone stewardess, a honey blonde with a wonderful Georgia drawl, were loaded on a Boeing 247D.

Of which my youngest daughter—the ineffable Biddy—said, when shown the picture in her mother's collection, "You'd have to be crazy to fly in something that tiny."

Such is the character of the 747 generation.

I'm not sure, however, that she was wrong. The 247D had seen better days, probably before the war; and we were buffeted by ridge after ridge of thunderstorms all day.

I wanted my good, solid, stable Grumman back the worst way. I also wanted to take the aircraft away from the idiot who was flying it, an impulse from which my wife has had to protect me intermittently in the course of our traveling together.

"Buy yourself a Gulfstream, dummy, if you want to play jet pilot," she tells me.

Note well the kind of woman she is: she says "Gulfstream" not "Learjet."

There were six intermediate stops between Philadelphia and Miami, of which I can only remember the first and the last—Washington and Jacksonville.

The other Philadelphia passengers were a honeymoon couple who had been married on Saturday—no other explanation for their lofty self-preoccupation was possible. So I had the blond Georgian to myself on the hop down to Washington.

Or she had me to herself.

There were two possibilities, I told myself as we bumped over the Washington Monument in downdrafts so strong I was convinced we were going to impale ourselves on it: either there had been a notable increase in the number of friendly young women available in the world during the past three weeks, or Andrea King, née Margaret Mary (Maggie) Ward, had pulled the blinders off my eyes.

Or maybe my dreams about Jean Kelly had poured high octane fuel on my already ignited lusts.

Drenched my bloodstream with more hormones, I'd say now. My virtue was strengthened, though not greatly, by the fact that in addition to listening to the Phillies on the radio the day before, I had taken in *Meet the Press*, *The NBC Symphony*, and *The University of Chicago Round Table*. On the first, a dullard named Joe Martin attacked Harry Truman for the "price-control mess," on the second, Toscanini conducted the Shostakovich Fifth; and on the last-named, two ponderous idiots talked about what GIs wanted out of education (a degree, but they didn't seem to realize it).

I didn't normally listen to symphonic music, but Maggie, as I was now thinking of Andrea, liked it. So . . .

They didn't have the ingenious custom of the mile-high-club then, the 247 could not make it to five thousand feet to save our lives, and there was not enough room in the single-toilet facility crunched into the back of the 247 even for the specified functions (at my height or any height more than that of a midget). But there wasn't much question about the Georgian's intentions.

It was flattering, especially when she gave short shrift to the other travelers who embarked and disembarked after we had jumped over the various puddles between Pennsylvania and Florida. As the nuns at Dom's would have undoubtedly said, the war caused a great increase in immorality. And, to quote Jean Kelly, you know what they mean by that. It was my impression, and still is, that immorality in that sense of the word has never been unpopular.

But, you will be happy to hear, I persisted in virtue.

She was, after all, a Protestant, albeit, she claimed, an Irish one.

And I was no longer Quixote, but Galahad on the quest.

The civilian airport adjoined the Naval Air Station at Jacksonville. I fidgeted nervously in my seat at the sight of the Phantoms and a newer jet, which I assumed was the Panther, on the tarmac. As we chugged up to the Quonset hut terminal, a flight of three Phantoms raced down the runway, stuck their noses firmly in the sky, and soared away, leaving their roar trailing behind.

For a moment I regretted my perfectly sensible decision to leave the Navy before I was hooked on jets.

You haven't left flying, I told myself, you've just left the Navy.

"Shore do make a heap of noise, don't they?" my blond friend observed.

That comment on the grace of the Phantoms scaling heaven confirmed my virtue.

I thought of the three students in my class who washed out, permanently, while we were in nearby Pensacola. Two of them collided shortly after takeoff—steering-control malfunction on one of the planes—and the other simply disappeared over the ocean.

Like Maggie's father, he never came back.

I was able to ponder their deaths with more objectivity than ever before. Maybe I was growing up, or maybe only becoming insensitive.

The commander of the NAS had been my captain on the *Enterprise* at the end of the war. When I was finished in Fort Lauderdale, perhaps I could come back here, pay my respects, and hitch a flight to . . .

To where?

Well, I could decide that later.

I evaded the persistent Georgian at Miami Airport, a small art deco (as we could call it now) terminal on the edge of the murky Everglades, and took a cab to the Waldorf Towers, an elegant hotel on the beach at Ninth Street (also art deco), where our family used to escape at Easter time. It has long since disappeared, to be replaced by one of the monsters of the late fifties, which in their turn are surviving now only on the courtesy of British excursion tours. Florida has become for the English what it was for us till the jets transformed the world: a haven of sun and warmth in the middle of winter (with no guarantees underwriting either sun or warmth).

When my kids ask what a 1920s Florida resort hotel was like, I tell them that it looked much like Al Capone's Florida home, which was celebrated earlier this year when WGN did the national con game about the walled-up chambers beneath the Lexington Hotel in Chicago.

It was paradise that oppressively hot day in August of 1946. Like the Arizona Inn, it had, thanks be to God, air-conditioning. (Noisy window units, but who cared?) I was weary from the flight and mildly sick from the day-long bumping in the thunderstorms. I turned on the air conditioner in my room and despite its noise promptly fell asleep. Ten hours later, when I woke up, I could not remember any dreams about blond Georgians or black Irish Pennsylvanians.

Which didn't mean that I didn't have any such dreams.

I ate a huge breakfast, swam in the ocean, and walked the beach, where I noted that the shorts-and-halter style affected by Jean Kelly was popular this summer. I applauded it and wondered whether it would be considered too immodest for Lake Geneva. I was pretty sure it would be.

Bikinis they were not. The shorts would be laughed off the beach today because they hid more thigh than they displayed. The suits were the equivalent of heavy girdles and bras legitimated for beach wear, graceless and ugly. But they did reveal a little bit more belly and breast than the one-piece suits. They seemed to invite you (if you were young and horny) to take the wearer in your arms and kiss her respectfully but persistently. For that time, they were perfectly delightful.

My eyes feasted on these lovely bodies and my imagination respectfully (more or less) undressed the most promising of them, including the occasional well-shaped mother in her thirties strolling the beach with a kid or two in tow.

Even fictionally naked, none of them compared with Maggie Ward.

I was reluctant to dress in my most conservative shirt and tie and be about my day's work. It would be much more pleasant to woman-watch on the beach. (I would have said girl-watch in those pre-feminist days, though the change of the name does not alter the pleasant nature of the activity.)

However, I turned in my laundry, ate an orange, and found a taxi driver who was prepared to drive me up to Fort Lauderdale.

In those days it was but a small suburb of Miami, hardly the place were the boys would be fifteen years later and then indefinitely thereafter at Easter. It was also so hot that Arizona seemed in comparison to be no worse than purgatory.

Quinn's Meat Market was beyond Fort Lauderdale off the road to Pompano Beach, on a side street halfway between the beach and the Inland Waterway. It was as shabby as the row house in Philadelphia, the most depressing store in a line of dismal shops on the first floor of a decrepit low-slung stucco two-story building, whose white paint, where it had not chipped off, had turned a kind of shoddy gray.

"Not much," the cabby observed, doubtless wondering what someone who stayed at the most discreet of the Miami Beach hotels was doing in this backwater dump.

"Hardly anything at all," I agreed, bounding out of the car as if, despite my sweat-soaked shirt, I were a competent and zealous government agent.

I was also furiously angry, more angry at the Quinns than

I was at the Japanese whom I had fought during the war. They had not done anything to me, but they had hurt my poor Maggie Ward.

The Quinns, standing together behind the counter as if united in fierce resistance to a hostile world, looked like an Irish caricature of Grant Wood's *American Gothic*, at the same time ridiculous and pathetically comic. Tall, skinny, rigid, bespectacled, he in a vest with a butcher's apron, she, astonishingly in the heat, in a dark-gray sweater, they watched my approach to the counter with a mixture of greed and fear. I was either a sucker to be taken or an enemy to be detested.

Ducks in a shooting gallery, more to be pitied than to be blamed, I thought. Then I remembered a vivacious little girl committed to the care of these monsters, who must have come into the world elderly.

"Do you want to buy something, sir?" he said obsequiously, hand on the butcher knife, which may have been the one that Maggie had used to threaten him.

Gutsy little tiger.

"Not especially." I leaned casually against the counter, glanced at the dreary chops in the display case and wondered if this part of Florida had no laws regulating the sale of meat.

"Well, what *do* you want?" she said in a dry, high-pitched voice.

"To talk a little," I replied, opening my wallet and flashing my officer's club ID card, which looked official enough to get me into Fort Knox. "About a number of things." I flipped the wallet shut and jammed it back in my pocket. "Black-market meat for one thing. Stealing from your niece's estate for another."

Bull's-eye. Direct hit. Target in flames and sinking.

"You're talking nonsense," he blustered, but all the starch went out of both their spines.

"Has that man finally come back to claim his sluttish daughter?" she sneered.

The shop smelled of an unhealthy mixture of Lysol and rotten meat. Even the sawdust on the floor looked old.

"I'll ask the questions," I sneered back.

I hadn't thought about the possibility that they might fear not only the FBI but Maggie's long-absent father.

"We didn't do anything wrong." He was surely the weaker of the two. "It costs money to raise a child—clothes, tuition, books. We sent her to a Catholic school."

"As a charity case," I fired in the dark again and again hit the target. "And then kept the money for school expenses. Don't try to fool me. We know everything."

"You won't be able to prove it in court," Isobel Phalen Quinn screeched. "You don't have any evidence."

I ignored her. "We know that you used to beat her with a belt, the one you're wearing, as a matter of fact; that you made sexual advances to her until she threatened to emasculate you with that butcher knife you're holding—"

"This is a carving knife." Hand and knife quaking, he tried to cut me off.

"Don't interrupt," I shouted. "We have enough to put both of you in federal prisons for the rest of your miserable lives."

"Shut up, you fool," she shouted. "Don't tell him a thing."

"What would a jury think"—I turned my anger on her—"of a woman who forced her sister's only child to marry a brute who had raped her, so that she could get rid of the child and have the child's money all to herself?"

They probably were misers, with lots of money, most of it Maggie's, socked away in War Bonds.

"It's not true."

"Ah, but it is," I proclaimed triumphantly. "All of it, and a lot more besides."

"What do you want to know?" Howard Quinn sighed in resignation. "We're simple, hardworking people. We don't have the money for lawyers."

"With all that money in government bonds? Don't try to kid me."

"What do you want to know?" Isobel was hysterical now.

"To begin with, where is she?"

I'd shot par for the first seven holes. I think, I told myself, you bogeyed that one.

"We don't know," they replied together, relaxing.

"She was always an ungrateful little chit," the woman continued. "After all we did for her, she never wrote us. We had to learn from our neighbors when her baby was born."

I teed up again. "The child to whom the inheritance should rightfully belong."

A chip shot away from the green.

"It's not much money, and with the way prices are going up"—the carving knife slipped out of his wet palm—"it won't be worth anything at all."

"You know full well that the little girl died. The question is whether you are responsible for her death."

"NO!" they bellowed together.

"We might have made some mistakes with the money" —he was melting into cheap lard—"we always tried to be fair, but we're not murderers."

Probably not. That would take more courage than they possessed.

"The father is dead, too."

"The United States Government is well aware of that fact, ma'am," I sneered. In truth, the government was not sure that he had ever existed, though his records were doubtless somewhere in a file in the "temporary" Navy Department buildings on the Mall in Washington. "We also know how he died."

That was hardly the truth.

"We don't know anything about it," her husband pleaded. "We don't even know how he died."

"Come now," I blustered toward a putt that would mean another par. "You don't mean to tell me that you raised the girl for eleven years and don't know the circumstances of her husband's death? You can't expect the government of the United States to believe that, can you?"

I missed the putt.

"She hated us because we tried to raise her to be a decent, God-fearing young woman," Isobel whined. "And she disgraced us and forced us to leave the community where we'd spent most of our lives."

"Really, Mrs. Quinn." This was an easy par-three hole.

"We both know better than that. If it had not been for some lingering goodwill toward Margaret Mary's father's family, you would not have been permitted by the Philadelphia police to slip out of town before the FBI arrested you."

Okay, I won the hole, but I wasn't going to win the match.

"We don't know where she is." He was sobbing. "If we did, we'd tell you."

I was sure he would.

"We'll see about that." I sneered again, hoping I looked like Paul Muni playing Al Capone. "We'll be watching your every move. And you'd better spend some of that money of yours on a lawyer."

I swaggered out of the store, breathing with relief the steamy salt air of the Atlantic Ocean.

I had beaten them into the ground, avenged myself a little on them, and felt rotten.

Ducks, indeed, in a shooting gallery.

And I had not eased any of Margaret Mary Ward's pain. Only God, should He really be, could do that.

And Maggie, my Maggie, was quite incapable of vengeance. She would have been furious at me.

I had learned that her childhood after her father's vanishing act had been even worse than I could imagine. So I had more respect for her gumption, for what I would call today her integrity.

There had to have been a gumption gene somewhere in the Ward past. Maggie had inherited it in all its purity and power.

Fine, it was nice to know that, though I could have surmised it without a flight to Fort Lauderdale.

But they didn't know where she was and neither did I.

I had expected such a result of my pilgrimage to the Quinns' meat market. Yet I was angry at myself, at the Quinns, at the world, and at whatever powers were responsible for the world, when I found that my expectations were confirmed.

I was not angry, though perhaps I ought to have been, at Andrea/Maggie for slipping away from me in the early morning hours in the Superstition Mountains and starting me on this dizzy, crooked pilgrimage. I would be angry at her later, but it didn't help.

"Any luck?" the cabby asked as I slammed the door of his 1937 Ford.

"What I didn't think I'd find out, I didn't find out."

I failed to add that I had no idea what came next.

Back at our family's favorite Florida hotel, I stripped off my soggy clothes, pulled on my swimming trunks, and swam at least a mile in the Atlantic, venturing out much farther than I should have because of my frustration and anger.

I read the papers—H. G. Wells had died, the Paris Peace Conference was fading, ships filled with Jews were running the British blockade into Palestine, and the Cubs had split a doubleheader on Monday—and tried to figure out what to do next.

I was at a dead end. As I had expected I would be. There was nothing more to be learned about Andrea/Maggie from those who had known her as a little girl and then as an emergent young woman in Saint Dominic's parish in Philadelphia.

I liked this Maggie Ward person, but I still had no idea where she was or where I should look next.

I phoned Delta Airlines and made a reservation for the flight the next morning to Jacksonville.

The admiral would bend regulations and put me on a plane to anywhere in the world that I wanted to go.

Fine. Where did I want to go?

Home to La Mancha? There surely would be a flight to Glenview.

No, not yet. There was still a month before law school began at De Paul or Loyola—if the latter was going to reopen now that the war was over.

I phoned home while I was pondering the problem.

Dad answered the phone. I told him I was in Miami.

"Are you really looking for a girl?" he asked, not so much upset as astonished.

"Trying to solve a puzzle."

"Where did the puzzle start?" he asked lightly.

"I suppose you could say"—I hesitated; the puzzle really was the death of Maggie's daughter and husband—"San Diego."

"Then what are you doing in Miami?" he asked, his voice patient as it always was when he felt his children were being thickheaded.

"I'm leaving for there tomorrow," I said. "Probably on a navy flight out of Jacksonville. I had to clear up some details first."

"We have a good contact or two in San Diego if you need it."

He meant political clout. That's what "contact" always means in our family vocabulary.

"Thanks. I may need it."

Amazing how much smarter Dad had become since I'd left for the service.

"San Diego," I wrote in my journal. "Where I probably should have started."

I thought about that.

"And I have no idea where I'm going to start when I get there."

CHAPTER **25**

I STARTED SEARCHING AT THE OBVIOUS PLACE, THE DEL Coronado Hotel (though it only became obvious to me when our FH-4 roared over it on its landing approach at the San Diego NAS). The flight time was a little less than seven hours, with two refueling stops and against a head wind. Despite the cramped quarters—the young Annapolis grad who flew the aircraft and I were virtually in one another's laps—and the uncomfortable crash helmet, I reveled in the excitement of the trip.

I told you that I wanted adventure.

I flew the second leg of the trip myself. The FH-4 was an easy plane to fly when you are at forty thousand feet. Taking off and landing were not so easy. I turned the controls back to the jaygee when we began our approach.

Withdraw your resignation, I told myself tentatively. You want adventure? Here you can have it.

CIC intervened. "And you want to endure the navy bureaucracy on the ground? Better you do what Maggie said and become a writer."

"Maggie is my woman, not yours."

Share and share alike.

I spent much of time there above the clouds thinking about her, puzzling over her story, trying to fit the pieces together in a coherent pattern. That was a mistake; none of us is coherent or consistent. Any simple explanation of the richness of a human person in a couple of sentences is prima facie erroneous. I've been married to the same woman for many, many years. I enjoy her in every way a man can enjoy a woman. I gave up trying to explain her even to myself long ago. She claims that she was too smart ever to try to reduce me to a couple of sentences. The reward of abandoning the search for understanding of a character, real or fictional, is that you are then free to enjoy.

So with poor Maggie Ward. The more I tried to piece together in a reasonable composite the various portraits that had been offered me in Philadelphia and Miami, the more elusive she became. And the composite sketch only overlapped partially the young woman I had met in the railroad station at Tucson and made love with in the bridal suite at Picketpost House.

Sister Mary Regina, Sister Marie Neri, Sister Patrice Marie, the people in the parish for whom she was a sweet and pretty little memory, Ralph, the Quinns, Jean Kelly—she was a different young woman for all of them. My own picture was most like Jean's, but there was something in each of their snapshots that seemed to apply and much that did not; even in Jean's warmly sympathetic portrait, I did not see the maturity or even the sophistication that Andrea King seemed to possess, a poise far beyond her years.

There were, God knows, enough traumas in her young life to demand rapid maturation as the price of survival.

And how did she survive? I wondered as our Phantom raced the sun toward the Pacific. Was not that the greatest mystery of all?

If she had indeed survived, a point about which I had not been sure since our first encounter in Tucson.

But even to be the kind of adolescent (teenager became a category in the late forties and early fifties) Jean Kelly had described was a remarkable achievement, given her life story.

I had not read, indeed probably not even heard of, Freud then, but I decided that her first five years must have been very happy and that her relationship with her mother and father and theirs with each other must have been deeply loving. One may have had weak lungs and the other weak will, but they produced a daughter with enough strength to survive and even to flourish.

At that moment I loved her with all the power and enthusiasm of which my young man's body and soul were capable. I wanted her. I would find her and save her.

Then, somewhere over west Texas or maybe even over southern Arizona where I had first met her, with the cloud layer a cotton carpet far below us and the sky a deep purple blanket almost at our fingertips, a strong memory of our first union at Picketpost returned, the image of her lovely young body as I removed the old-fashioned white nightgown seemed to be printed in full color on the sky.

I had to find her.

I can't claim that the Furies inside me had been extirpated. Rather they were chained by a more powerful force. The rest of the quest would be executed with controlled rationality. Quixote became Sherlock Holmes.

The question of whether she might not want to be saved became irrelevant.

As we landed, with a hard bump, I wondered briefly about her father. Were his bones rotting somewhere in a hobo jungle, his throat having been slit a decade ago for maybe a nickel or a dime?

Or had he been killed somewhere during the war? Maybe at Clark Field, where that monumental idiot Douglas MacArthur had his B-17s lined up in neat rows for the Japanese attack planes nine hours after he had learned that Pearl Harbor had been bombed?

And if Allen Ward was still alive, if he was making money again in the first bloom of postwar prosperity, how would he find his daughter? Assuming that he still cared about finding her.

If he was alive—and Maggie's instincts said that he was —he certainly still cared.

I lugged my duffel to the office of the NAS commandant and "reported" in.

"Like the jet, Jerry?" My first air-group boss grinned at me—coming out into the anteroom to shake my hand. "Want one for yourself?"

"When there's one with four engines, with enough room to breathe." I laughed back. "I'm not Navy, Tom, you know that."

"I sure as hell can't see you going to the Academy," he agreed. "Enjoy yourself while you're here."

Damn right he couldn't see me as a plebe at the Academy. I had little toleration for Fascism. It's a miracle I made it through preflight at Iowa City.

The skipper found a launch that was going across the bay to the mainland. After the long wait in the parking lot at Lindbergh Field, opposite the Naval Air Station, Roxinante was most reluctant to be called back into service. After considerable persuasion, she finally rumbled back into life. I collected some of my clothes from the BOQ and took the ferry over to Coronado Island. After the sweltering heat of Arizona, Pennsylvania, and Florida during the past three weeks, the alluring softness of late afternoon in southern California was like a comfortable bed with clean sheets in an air-conditioned hotel room—with a lovely maiden to caress your forehead and sing you to sleep in bed with you.

So much for fantasies, I told myself.

The Del Coronado, a great domed Victorian heap, stood at the edge of the beach, resplendent in its new coat of paint, a dowager with a new dress (even today it is still listed in the top twenty "charm" hotels of the world). It would be, I ignored my own prohibition of fantasies, a great place for a honeymoon.

I checked in, dumped my new supply of clothes in my room, and rushed for the ocean. Its warm, soothing salt tang revived me. Yesterday the Atlantic, today the Pacific, an easy achievement for the jet age. The cobwebs from the flight exorcised from my head by my swim, I donned my most-expensive-looking sport jacket and slacks and drifted casually down to the manager's office. After a few moments of Irish charm, hinting at great resources of wealth lurking somewhere in Chicago real estate, we were talking like long-lost friends about the wonders of the jet age.

He pretended to remember me from my previous times at the hotel—a major accomplishment, since I had never stayed there before. (Although I had on more than one occasion consumed a few quick ones in their bar.)

Almost indifferently, a bothersome request from my mother, to tell the truth, I inquired about a young woman who might have worked there during the last year, year and a half, a certain Margaret Ward.

"Yes, indeed." He smoothed his long, sleek black hair. "I remember the poor child well. She was a very likable kid. Came here . . . let me see . . . I should think about February of 1945, just a year and a half ago. We needed waitresses then because so many women were working in the war-production factories. She had no experience, none whatever, but there was something about her that made you want to give her a chance. She was intelligent and hardworking and very quickly became one of our most efficient service staff. Even when her, ah, condition became obvious, we kept her on as long as we could as a maid."

"Till late April, I presume."

"More like late May. We, uh, stretched a point in retaining her as long as we did because everyone was so fond of her." He shook his head. "I suspect she was below the legal working age too. Not, alas, beneath the age where she could be forced to marry some pig of a sailor. . . . Sorry, Commander."

San Diego at that time hated Navy almost as much as they hated Mexicans. Ironically, the navy people who settled there after the war became indistinguishable from the natives in their conservatism—and their hatred for Mexicans.

"Forget it." I waved off his embarrassment. "Let's stipulate that he was a pig before he entered the Navy. So that was the last you saw of her."

"No." He frowned. "She came back just a few months ago, a rather pathetic little waif. Let me check. . . ." He opened a record book and flipped through the pages. "It was the first week of April. She said that she had lost both her husband and her child. We simply had no room for her then. She seemed so worn and discouraged that I did offer to try to find her a position somewhere else and urged her to call me back in a couple of days."

"Were you able to find her a job?" My heart was pounding again. This might be the key that opened a lot of doors.

"As a matter of fact, I was. My friend, the manager of the Beverly Hills Hotel, was looking for a superior hostess for the Polo Lounge. Margaret would have been excellent. But she never called back."

"I see."

"It was"—he closed the book gently—"very difficult not to like her. So young and yet so poised and determined."

"So my mother said. Well, sir, I'll report home." I rose and shook hands with him. "I suppose she'll turn up. Thank you."

"Not at all, Commander. Do enjoy your stay. We are proud of the new Del Coronado."

"With reason."

He had been kind to my Maggie, so I forgave him for his slurs on the Navy. The San Diego locals doubtless had grounds for complaint. Hundreds of thousands of young men, about to go to war or returning from war, had invaded and on occasion seemed about to destroy their sleepy little paradise. They were much less of a threat to San Diego, however, than a Japanese carrier task force sitting two hundred miles off the coast would have been. The link between the presence of our Navy and the absence of theirs seemed to escape most of the local citizenry.

Better, I thought as I walked slowly back to my room, a hundred American air-crew drunks in your bar (and an occasional light drinker like me) than a like number of Japanese flyers yelling for sake and waving their swords.

I used a sheet of Del Coronado stationery for my notes; one does not write an unprepared entry into one's journal if one can help it!

1) January 1945. Philadelphia. Margaret Mary Ward and Andrew John Koenig are wed in a shotgun marriage in Saint Dominic's parish. Perhaps she is two months pregnant.

2) February 1945. San Diego. Margaret Ward (still using her maiden name) starts work as a waitress at the Del Coronado. When her pregnancy becomes too obvious, she is shifted to the back stairs and works as a maid. Leaves the Del Coronado in May. Her husband is at sea, probably at Ulithi. Possibly brought there by the Indianapolis.

3) August 1945. San Diego. Their daughter Andrea is born, probably early in the month. Andrew is most likely still in the western Pacific.

4) Between August and Christmas 1945. San Diego. Andrea dies. It is unclear whether her husband has returned. Probably he has.

(The most powerful military force the world has ever known virtually demobilized itself after the war. "The conflict is over, why aren't we going home," was the protest heard round the world. The government wisely sent us home as quickly as it could lest we mutiny and turn the world back to our former enemies. Those conservative historians who argue that Roosevelt demobilized rapidly as an excuse not to fight the Russians either were not around or cannot remember the riots of GIs demanding to be sent home.)

5) Between Christmas and March 1946. Possibly in San Diego, though that is not certain, Andrew Koenig dies.

6) April 1946. San Diego. Margaret Ward returns to Del Coronado, seeking her old job. Seems terribly depressed. Job is not available, but manager offers to find her another and asks her to call back.

7) July 22, 1946. Tucson. I meet Andrea King, as she is calling herself now, in the railway station. She tells me the next day that she is already damned, caught between earth and hell, and that she has committed unpardonable sins.

8) July 27, 1946. Superstition Mountains. She disappears after bizarre experience in ghost town.

I pondered this chronology.

There were two missing pieces that seemed to be important.

a) Where was she in the four months between her search for a job here and my meeting with her in Tucson?

b) When and how did her husband die?

There were, I told myself, answers to both questions and I would find them.

I did find them in the next two days. I wouldn't like either one of the answers. Not at all.

CHAPTER **26**

THE BUILDING THAT HOUSED THE SAN DIEGO *UNION-Ledger* in 1946 was as fusty and depressing in those days as the paper was, is, and, barring a miraculous intervention from extraterrestrials or the Deity, always will be.

They did have a public service bureau of a sort in a windowless room on the second floor. A woman librarian who was ancient enough to have come to California with John Charles Frémont, would, after complaint and negotiation, reluctantly permit you to read back issues, but only after you swore solemnly that you would not cut any articles out of the paper.

"We'll call the police," she warned, "if I see you so much as use a pencil to mark the paper. Vandalism must be stopped."

I endorsed this position enthusiastically and, having signed a document listing my addresses and bank-account numbers, retired to an even dingier corner where, under the light provided by a single 40-watt bulb, I began to read systematically the news of San Diego from December 15, 1945, to March 15, 1946.

The late President Roosevelt was very dead, but not forgotten. The *Union* insisted that he had staged the Pearl Harbor defeat to trick us into the war on England's side. It would have been a major achievement, I thought, for FDR to have so exploited the Japanese High Command.

It made me feel that I was back in Chicago reading Colonel Robert McCormick's *Tribune*, except that the *Union-Ledger* lacked the Colonel's madcap, solipsistic flair. It never hinted that its publisher won the First World War.

Four hours of reading old newspapers has the same effect on your sensitivities that retreat masters used to suggest cold showers would have on your "concupiscence" (an effect which in my case has never occurred): you begin to feel that if you read one more headline you will become a permanent zombie, capable of thinking and talking only in newspeak.

So I turned the page in the March 14 issue after glancing at the headline. And then turned another page. A tiny jab at the back of my brain suggested I had missed something important. I reread the last page. Nothing there.

Then the one before. This time the headline jumped off the page at me:

Wife Kills Sailor in Dispute over Dead Child

My fingers trembled. My stomach knotted. I did not want to read the story—halfway down the fifth page. Navy events were rarely front-page news now in the *Union-Ledger*.

> *Last night, police charged Margaret M. Koenig, 18, with the murder of her husband Andrew J. Koenig, 20, a radar technician assigned to the San Diego Navy Yard.*
>
> *Koenig either fell or was pushed from the window of their third floor apartment at 1225 Chatsworth Boulevard*
>
> *According to Lieutenant Wayne Manzell of the San Diego Police homicide unit, Koenig and his wife had been fighting about the death of their four-month-old daughter Andrea, who was found dead in her crib last December 20. Neighbors, Manzell said, reported that Koenig blamed his wife for the death of the child.*
>
> *"The first death looked kind of fishy," Manzell told the Union-Ledger, "but there was not enough evidence to justify a charge. This time we have a clear case of the woman shoving the sailor out of the window of their third-floor apartment over there in the Gateway district where all the navy people live."*
>
> *According to Manzell, neighbors also said that Koenig had been drinking heavily since the death of his daughter. "His body smelled," Manzell said. "He was pretty well oiled last night when she pushed him out the window."*
>
> *Margaret is being held without bail.*

I leaned back on my hard wooden chair and closed my eyes. Maggie wouldn't hurt anyone, they had said in Philadelphia. Yet she had pushed her husband out of a third-story window.

Possibly drunken husband.

Held without bail.

I would race over to the courthouse and bail her out.

CIC reappeared, on schedule: "Wake up, dopey, she's out of jail. That was months ago."

"Are you all right, young man?" The forty-niner woman

was leaning over me solicitously. A nice old lady despite her fustiness.

"Fine, thank you, ma'am." I opened my eyes and tried to smile up at her. "I'm resting my eyes after reading all these papers."

"Take good care of your eyes, young man, they're the only ones you have."

It is apparently a timeless proverb among the maternal half of the species. I've heard my wife use it often with our children. And now our daughters use it with their children.

"I sure will. Thank you."

I looked at the paper again. There was a picture of a young woman next to the story. Maggie, I supposed. If I had not noticed the headline I'd never recognize her. What had they done to her in prison?

I'd better get over there and bail her out before they did worse.

No, this is not Maggie since I'd seen her. It was Maggie before I'd met her.

I pulled my wits together. Maggie had been out of jail by early April at the latest because she had applied for a job at the Del Coronado. And the manager had not mentioned anything about murder charges. If he knew about them he would certainly have told me. But all he said was that her husband had died. Apparently the case had not made a big impact on San Diego. What difference did the death of one more sailor make in this city?

Thus reassured, I carefully worked my way through the *Union-Ledger* for the rest of March.

There was no further mention of the Koenig murder.

In Chicago the case would have been front-page news with pictures, interviews with neighbors, biographies of both participants, and breathless day-by-day coverage. But the *Union-Ledger* was fusty and dull, and uninterested in sailors and their families.

Their prejudice had made the ordeal easier for Maggie.

I drove back to the ferry and called my father from the Del Coronado. Without asking why, he assured me that he would call in an owed favor or two in the San Diego municipal administration.

So the next day I was sitting in the office of Lieutenant Wayne C. Manzell of the homicide squad of the San Diego Police Department. The central police headquarters in San Diego is built in California mission style—white stone building with a courtyard in the middle. Manzell's office faced the courtyard. Like all cop offices, the windows had not been washed for five centuries, the furniture had been salvaged from the last encampment of Attila the Hun, and the smell suggested that the men's room was next door, which it wasn't.

Adding to the stench was the aroma of Lieutenant Manzell's stogie, which could not have cost him even five cents. Prewar.

Manzell himself looked like the caricature of a Southern sheriff that would emerge in films of the fifties and sixties— a fat, bald, heavily jowled man who opened his mouth only to remove the cigar so he could spit.

He was polite enough to me, although his indifference to the "Koenig case" implied that I had disturbed a day that otherwise would have been devoted to thoughtful meditation, eyes closed, in the peace of his office.

"Yeah, I thought we had a sure murder-one conviction." He tossed the file contemptuously on his desk and placed his enormous shoes on top of it, as if to hold it down in a breeze.

There was no breeze because the windows were not opened and probably could not be opened. Your police windows installed five centuries ago are not designed to be opened.

"What went wrong?" I tried to sound sympathetic.

"Goddamn young DA couldn't see it. I says, she pushed him out the window. He says that there are witnesses from the adjoining apartments"—he pulled the file out from under his feet—"fucking CPO named Fred Weaver and his wife Magda who are willing to swear that he was drunk and beating her. Got drunk and beat her every night. Bitch deserved it, I says."

"Oh?"

"Hell, she killed the little kid too. Smothered it. Couldn't prove it. Never can prove those child-murder cases unless there are black and blue marks on the fucking kid, huh?"

"Yeah."

"Well, this Weaver couple and some of the other sailors in the building—that's all you got over there, you know"— he belched heavily—"fucking sailors and fucking marines— say he was shouting so everyone in the building could hear him that he was going to throw her out the window. Fucking marine coming in the front door—wooden building with paper-thin walls, you know what kind of shit the fucking Navy lives in—says that he saw him with his hands around her throat, shoving her out the window. She knees him in the gut and slips away, he loses his balance, and over he goes. A witness like that, says the young DA, and you're not even going to get a manslaughter conviction, not even when the defendant is Navy. Huh?"

"You disagreed?"

"Shit, it's no skin off my ass if another fucking sailor bounces his head on concrete. Funny thing, if he had killed her, we would have had an airtight case against him. Huh?"

"Yeah. Weird."

"Sure is. Anyway, the kid DA says that with witnesses like that we shouldn't even have brought the charges. I don't know what's wrong with kids these days. The war, I suppose. But since when doesn't a young DA want a murder-one charge. I think he has the hots for the little bitch."

"Cute?"

"Not as far as I noticed." He shrugged his massive shoulders. "Nice tits, if you like that sort of thing. You know what I mean, the kind you like to squeeze real hard till they scream, then a little harder so they'll remember you for a week. Huh?"

"Yeah." Someday I'll come back and emasculate you.

"But otherwise, I mean there was not much to her. Nothing else to get your hands on, huh? Anyway, you never can tell what you're gonna catch from one of them navy hookers, huh?"

"So you let her walk?"

"No choice."

"Too bad." I was about to ask him for the name of the assistant district attorney.

"Well." He belched again, massively. "She must have figured she was guilty anyway. Elsewise, why would she kill herself, huh?"

"Kill herself?" I felt as if I had walked into a meat freezer.

"Yeah, sure. Didn't you know that part of it? Took a walk in the Pacific Ocean, with her clothes on, and forgot to come back. One of the guys from the apartment building saw her, same fucking marine. Right straight out into the ocean, late in the afternoon, lemme see, of April 10. Body only washed up last month."

"You're sure?"

"Fuck, I don't know. We couldn't get any prints off the body. No one knows where she's from, so we can't look at her teeth. Anyway, who the fuck cares? It closes the file and that's that."

"I see."

With enormous effort, suggesting a man lifting a huge weight, he heaved himself to his feet and extended his hand. "Nice to talk to you."

"Did you send the body home?"

"Home?" he sneered. "Those fucking navy bitches don't come from anywhere. We released it to that CPO and his wife. What's their name?"

"Weaver," I said automatically.

"Yeah, they identified her. You wanna find out where it is, ask them. Course the Catholic Church wouldn't let them bury her in one of our cemeteries. Suicides can't be buried in consecrated ground, you know?"

"Really?"

Maggie Ward was dead. And buried in unconsecrated ground.

How then had I made love with her in the shadow of Picketpost Mountain?

CHAPTER 27

"YOU SHOULD HAVE SEEN HER, SIR," CPO FRED WEAVER said as he pounded the table. "Her face was swollen, both of her eyes were black, and her throat was raw from where he was choking her."

"And her poor little body was covered with black and blue marks," Magda Weaver chirped sympathetically, "from where he had beaten her before that day."

"I should have gone to his CO." The Chief shook his head sadly. "The Navy has enough trouble in this town without having a rating kill his wife."

"Or the other way around," I exhaled softly.

"*Well.*" Magda refilled my teacup. "Once the young district attorney saw what she looked like he knew he didn't have a case, no matter what that fat stupid lieutenant said."

"Your testimony was a big help too, I'm sure."

Fred Weaver, in neatly pressed khakis and with a soft Texas drawl, was the kind of noncommissioned officer who holds any military unit together. A man of medium height with a thin face, sea-blue eyes close together, crew cut with a twinge of gray in it, Fred and his ilk helped win the war by guiding twenty-year-old ensigns and jaygees through their first months of command. When you called him "Chief," you knew he really was the chief. Magda was a few years younger, perhaps late twenties, a pretty little canary person. Their two girls, middle years of grammar school, had obediently left the clean and orderly apartment when I arrived.

"I always said to Fred," Magda said as she settled herself in a wicker chair (in those days wicker was inexpensive furniture, the kind NCOs were likely to find in the semi-slum furnished apartments available to them off-base), "I always said I hope our girls grow up to be as sweet as poor Maggie.

She was such a lovely girl, and so good with the baby, sometimes like she was a doll and other times like a little sister, but always so careful. And little Andrea was such a good, happy little girl." She dabbed at her eyes with the tissue she had clenched in her tiny fist since we had begun to talk about Maggie Ward. "Poor children, they never had a chance."

"He wasn't a bad young man." The chief frowned, drawing his eyes even closer together, like the bright lights on a car. I wouldn't want to be a rating of whom he was suspicious. "Must have been smart or they wouldn't have sent him to radar school. But he wasn't, well, how should I say it, Commander, not too . . ."

"Quick?"

"That's it exactly." Chief Weaver nodded vigorously. "And always kind of suspicious, like he thought everyone was trying to trick him and so he couldn't really trust anyone."

"Not even his poor little wife, who tried so hard to make him happy when he came home in September."

"He decided to stay in," her husband continued. "Become career Navy. Not a bad deal. I've been in almost nine years now. In 1957 I'm only forty-two and I retire on half pay. What about you, sir? Are you going to try for regular Navy?"

"I don't think so," I laughed. "Crazy fighter pilots are not much use in peacetime, especially when they don't have a class ring from the Academy or anywhere else . . . you were saying, about Technician/First Andrew John Koenig . . ."

"I was about to say"—the chief smiled at his wife as she refilled his teacup—"that I'm not sure he would have made it in career Navy. If I had to do a fitness report on him, even before the trouble, I would have been obliged to say that a lot of the time he was surly and uncommunicative. Would do his job, but you could never tell when he'd come up with some crazy complaint about what the other men in his outfit were trying to do to him."

"Why, he was even suspicious of the poor little tyke when he came home." Magda clasped her hands angrily. "As if she wasn't his child and had no right to be in their apartment."

"Well, now, Mother, fair is fair." The chief raised his hand as if he were a judge passing sentence. "He turned around on that pretty quick."

"She turned him around," his wife fired back, "she was so pretty and so winning and worked so hard to please him. He even began to smile. But he never was very friendly with any of the neighbors, especially when we all had to move over here when they tore the old building down."

Thirty-year-old wooden apartment buildings, housing mostly navy personnel, were becoming a wasteful use of land on the harbor.

"I'm afraid"—the Chief bit his lip—"that he thought the move was part of a plot to get rid of him. It really wasn't, but since he didn't talk much to any of us, we never had a chance to tell him about this housing. I got him in here, in the apartment next door, when someone else canceled out. Otherwise he'd have had to move way out toward Chula Vista, and he didn't have a car either."

"He never even said thanks." His wife drew her lips in a tight line. "It was like we owed him an apartment."

The Weavers were practiced at telling the story. All I had to do was listen.

And resist the urge to weep with Magda.

"If she had more time, I don't know," the chief took over narration, "maybe she could have turned him around on a lot of things. She sure did have her work cut out for her, though."

"Babies die in cribs for no reason. They just stop breathing." Magda was wringing her hand at the terrible prospect. "You keep watching your baby to make sure she's still breathing, even though you know there's nothing you can do if she stops. You just want to tell yourself that it hasn't happened to you."

"Yet," I said quietly.

Magda smiled at me. "You do understand, don't you, Commander?"

"If I heard him say it once, I heard him say it to her a hundred times. 'If only you had been watching the baby . . .' "

"He never called her by her name, even though she was named after him," his wife jumped in. "Like that was some kind of trick too."

" 'If only you had been watching the baby,' " her husband persisted, " 'she'd still be alive.' "

"The doctor at the navy hospital where we rushed them did everything he could, but he said when little kids stop breathing like that, there's nothing you can do."

"He almost hit her when he finally came up from the Yards to the hospital." The chief shook his head sadly. "First thing he could think of when he rushed into the emergency room was to take a swing at her. Would have knocked her down, if I hadn't stopped him."

"Poor man." I didn't know why I said that. I hated the bastard. "Poor bastard" might have been better.

"He did hit her that night. We could hear him shouting and her whimpering. She never complained."

"The walls are pretty thin in these quarters." The chief blushed at the thought that they might have been eavesdropping. "You can't help but hear."

"And that terrible fat police officer who came around the next day asking his snide questions even though the doctor told him it was death from natural causes and there wasn't a mark on the baby."

"His exact words to me"—the Chief's knuckles were white—" 'if you navy shit want to kill your own kids, I don't give a shit.' "

"Charming man."

"The Navy has enough trouble in this town. Even then it was all I could do not to slug him in his big fat belly."

"I know the feeling."

"Another cup of tea, Commander?"

"Thank you, Miz Weaver, I have a weakness for Earl Grey."

"That's funny." She filled my cup for the third time. "Have another cookie too, you look thin. Like I say, that's funny, poor little Maggie liked Earl Grey too."

"I know."

"You knew her before this all happened?" The Chief cocked an eyebrow, a slight hint of suspicion.

The only completely honest answer was that I'd met her a month ago, long after she was dead. Obviously that wouldn't do.

"I knew her a long time ago. In Philadelphia, where she came from. I'm from Chicago, like I said, but our families were distantly related. My grandmother was a Maggie too."

Maybe my Maggie was right when she insisted that I ought to write stories.

"Oh, that makes it worse, doesn't it, poor man." Both Magda and Fred bought my tall tale. "Well, anyway, it was really bad for a while." Magda continued breathlessly, "He wouldn't let her talk to anyone and would come home drunk every night and beat her. During the day she'd sneak over to talk to me. The poor little thing was a wreck. She tried to pretend he wasn't hitting her. I don't think it made much difference, she was so worried that it was her fault the baby died. I mean, I guess I'd feel that way too, but . . ."

"Mothers worry," I said simply.

"Then it seemed to get a little better." The chief took up the story. "He didn't drink so much, except on weekends and the noise next door wasn't so bad. But, damn it"—he pounded the unsteady table again, shaking the artificial flowers on it —"if I'd only followed my instincts and talked to his CO or to the chaplain at the Yards . . ."

"Now, Fred." His wife raised a warning finger. "Don't go blaming yourself. You don't know whether it would have done any good. Probably wouldn't have."

"I suppose you're right," he said with a sigh. "You know what happened that night, don't you, sir?"

"Most of it."

"Things had been good next door for a week, maybe more. He even said good morning to me. Something went wrong at the Yard that day, I guess. He tied on a big one and came home roaring drunk. We all heard him in the hallway outside their apartment. He screamed that she was a killer and that he was going to kill her."

"He tried hard enough." Magda sniffed. "No fault of his that he didn't."

"Fortunately, sir, the man who saw what happened outside is a clerk at the judge advocate's office at the USMC Training Center. He tried to tell Lieutenant Manzell that Koenig was pushing her out the window, already had her halfway out. Then she squirmed away, he lost his balance and fell. Cracked his head like an eggshell."

We were all reverently silent.

"He wouldn't believe it."

"Wouldn't even listen. So Gunnery Sergeant Wendel found a really good lawyer that used to be in their office, a major, top flight. He talked to the assistant district attorney. . . ."

"A very nice young man . . ." Magda observed.

"Well, at least a man who seemed to be interested in justice. They let Maggie out after two days and dropped the charges the next day."

"I think that terrible man hurt her," Magda asserted. "Something ought to be done about him."

"I'm sure, Miz Weaver, that your husband and I can easily think of several appropriate measures. We live under the rule of law. Perhaps unfortunately."

I'd heard my father mumble that on more than one occasion.

"We buried Technician/First Koenig in the Catholic cemetery next to the little girl. The chaplain at the Yards said a nice Mass and preached a fine sermon. It seemed to pick the poor kid up for a day or two. Then she went into a stall. Like those zombies they're supposed to have in . . . where's the place, sir?"

"Haiti. Then, a couple of weeks later, she tried to get her old job at the Del Coronado back?"

"Heaven forgive me for it." Magda Weaver had abandoned her attempt to control her tears. "I told her she needed something to take her mind off her problems. And the pension money was held up, though the lawyer that Sergeant Wendel had found was working on that, too. So she needed money. When they turned her down it was like someone put out the last candle. If you understand what I mean."

"I do."

"The man over there told her he'd try to find another job for her, but . . . I don't know . . . it was just the straw that broke the camel's back."

"She cried herself to sleep that night." Magda wiped away her own tears, which were quickly replaced by others. "I held her in my arms, just like she was one of my own daughters, till she was sound asleep. I thought she'd be all right."

"Sergeant Wendel was driving up to the Marine Training Center early the next morning. There was a lot of fog but he thought he saw her walking along the bay by 8th Street."

"No place for a girl to be that hour."

"So he backed up and followed her. She just walked right into the bay. He shouted at her; she didn't seem to hear. He pulled off his shirt and trousers and went in after her. He lost her in the fog."

The Chief's voice began to crack. How much they had all loved my Maggie.

"We called the police and the Coast Guard." His wife saved him embarrassment. "They thought the bay would wash her up in a day or two. When that didn't happen, the Coast Guard said she'd probably drifted out to sea and we'd never recover the body."

"Then, when we'd given up hope," the Chief said, when he was in control of his emotions again, "Lieutenant Manzell called my wife; when was it, dear . . . ?"

"Five weeks ago. He said we could have our friend if we wanted her."

"His exact words, mind you, sir, to my wife, were that she wasn't very pretty anymore because the fish had made a meal out of her. Sergeant Wendel and I identified the body."

"You could be sure after all those weeks in the ocean?"

"As best as we could tell it was her, sir. It looked like

her. Who else might it have been? Same height and shape and age. Borne at least one child. All the details fit."

"We wanted to bury her with her husband and daughter; she had paid for the lot with her own money, saved from when she was working before the baby came." Magda Weaver sounded very tired. "The Catholic Church forbade the burial because the priest told us that suicides can't be buried in consecrated ground. So we chipped in and bought her a lot at the city cemetery up there by Balboa Park. Sergeant Wendel said that when the insurance money comes through we'll be reimbursed. Not that it makes any difference."

"The priest from the Navy Yard"—Chief Weaver spoke in hollow tones, as if the final words of the story were being uttered—"said some prayers at the undertakering parlor and gave a little talk at the grave. He seemed much more sympathetic than the San Diego priests."

There was not much more to say.

"When was the funeral?" I asked, not because I cared, but to ease the pain and the tension.

"Just a month ago," Magda Weaver said promptly. "July 21, 1946."

The next morning, Maggie Ward, using her daughter's name, had walked into my life in Tucson, Arizona.

CHAPTER **28**

IT WAS A SIMPLE INSCRIPTION ON THE SIMPLER TOMBSTONE:

MARGARET WARD KOENIG
MARCH 15, 1928—APRIL 23, 1946
MAY SHE REST IN PEACE

The late-afternoon trade winds were cooling San Diego and wafting in streamers of fog. In the distance, beyond the elegant greenery of Balboa Park, there stretched the blue waters of the bay and, disappearing in the fog and then briefly reappearing, the low-slung shape of Coronado Island.

A lovely view for my Maggie's last resting place, in its stark unpretentiousness; not quite a potter's field, but surely right next to it.

I was too shattered by the sight of that headstone to weep, to pray, to ponder. I knelt in the grass next to it and remained in a kneeling posture for a long time.

Why?

Why such a senseless life? Why such a terrible waste of talent? Why such a futile death?

Then I was angry at the Church. How could they know the state of Maggie's soul? Could they not have at least given her the benefit of the doubt?

In Chicago they would have, I told myself—a conclusion that Packy later confirmed. "Around here we figure that anyone who is so troubled that they would end their own life has to be incapable of serious moral reflection. That's the way the Romans figured, too."

But the biggest question of all: Why had this body, corrupted by many weeks in the ocean, appeared to me, alive and attractive, the day after it was laid to rest in this far end of the Municipal Cemetery?

Was it the same person? Was Andrea King truly Maggie Ward?

Who else could she be? Did not all the clues confirm that, even the Earl Grey tea?

Had her assignment been to recall me to my faith before she went to heaven? Was part of her purgatory the terrible fear that she was already in hell? Did she have to conquer that too?

It continued to be inadmissible that Maggie was damned. Had not I myself told her that God, should there be such, loved her as much as I loved her?

I would now add, as much as Jean Kelly and Sister Patrice

Marie and Fred and Magda Weaver and Gunnery Sergeant Wendel and Ralph Without-a-Last-Name?

"All right, Maggie," I promised her aloud there by her grave, "you win. I believe again. I don't promise that I'll bounce back into Mass next Sunday, but I'll make my peace with God because you said I should."

And that bizarre prayer brought me again a hint of the serenity I had felt the day before coming in on the FH-4.

I would never know what had happened on those strange, frightening, wonderful days in Arizona. I had loved and had been loved. That would have to suffice for the rest of my life.

It would probably be enough.

It would have to be enough.

Would I eventually forget her, as I'd forgotten my grandmother, the other Maggie, who died when I was a little boy, leaving only an impression of colossal energy?

No, this Maggie would be remembered with rich and full detail, in a memory that in time might turn from painful to bittersweet.

"You'll be part of me for the rest of my life, Maggie Ward," I told her.

Then I remembered the similar words of CIC, in his seraphic manifestation, at the Lost Dutchman's Mine.

No, I'd never forget her.

I actually prayed for her then, said the utterly Catholic words, "May Eternal Light shine upon her," rose from my knees and walked out of the cemetery and across Balboa Park, perhaps the most beautiful urban park in America.

Strangely, my numbness heightened my sensitivity to its beauty. The whole world, and especially this magnificent park, had become a warm blanket protecting my Maggie until we should meet again.

Twilight turned to dusk. A full moon inched its way over the mountains, turning the patches of fog into quicksilver dust that danced gently through the park. The full moon suggested the horror to me, as it would for the rest of my life. But the horror bound, locked up, restrained; only temporarily restrained, perhaps, and ready to break out at any time, yet sufficiently under control that I could admire the contradictory white forgiveness in the moonlight.

Only one other time in my life so far has the horror returned.

I found a Catholic church near the park. It was open, unlike most Catholic churches these days. Inside I knelt, not quite ready to resume diplomatic relations with the One represented by the flickering tabernacle light—a hint perhaps of the fragility and the durability of love—but ready to begin preliminary negotiations.

As if you can negotiate with God!

It seemed obvious to me that this crazy interlude in the first summer after the war—when most Americans were relishing a vacation and complaining about shortages—had to be put firmly behind me. Remember Andrea/Margaret Mary, yes. Benefit from my short interlude of love with her, I told myself, but do not become obsessed with trying to understand it.

The Adventure is over. The Romance is finished. The Woman has been won and then lost again.

Proceed with the serious business of life.

CIC for once agreed completely.

It was a sensible and reasonable reaction. In fact, its sensibility and rationality—as set down in my journal at the Del Coronado with the moon high in the sky over the quiet Pacific—astonishes me even almost forty years later.

It was a singularly ill-advised resolution and one that I would not be able to keep. And it was not the conclusion I ought to have drawn from my quest at all.

Perhaps I was too tired, too disappointed, maybe even too homesick to read the experience properly.

Or to note the hole in it, big enough for the USS *Missouri*.

It's twenty-four hundred miles, more or less, from San Diego to Chicago. If you drive eight hundred miles a day on Route 66 (may it rest in peace), you can make it in three days. In 1946 there was no interstate system (Biddy won't believe that there was ever a time when there was no interstate, just as she won't believe that there was ever a time when the Mass

was in Latin and young women her age wore girdles). To make
your eight hundred miles, you had to average forty-five miles
an hour for eighteen hours. If you took out a half hour here
or there to eat and maybe an hour or two to nap about midnight, you could cover the distance even in a 1939 Chevy in
a little under three days.

I turned off 66 (Ogden Avenue in Cook County) and onto
Harlem Avenue at seven o'clock in the morning; fifteen minutes later, Roxinante steaming and puffing, I pulled up in front
of our house on Lathrop, ambled into the kitchen and asked
my delighted mother for a double order of pancakes. I assured
my equally delighted father, before he buried his head behind
the Chicago *Sun* (no *Tribune* in our house), that I would register for Loyola Law School that afternoon, told an astonished
Joanne that I liked her hair blond, and challenged Packy to a
game of "Horse" on the backboard on our coach house.

The headlines in the *Sun* said that the Senate was about
to investigate the crazy racist senator from Mississippi, Theodore Bilbo; the government had issued an ultimatum to Yu-
goslavia demanding the release of survivors of two American
planes the Tito crowd had forced down; UNRAA director Fior-
ello La Guardia had fired an assistant who charged the Russians with using UNRAA supplies for political purposes. And
the Cubs had lost again.

> Home is the sailor, home from the sea.
> And the hunter home from the hill.

And the romantic home from the mountains.

Having forgotten, as you've doubtless noted, the most
important clue of all.

PART THREE

Maggie
Ward

CHAPTER 29

"HOW MANY DAYS OF COMBAT?" I TOWERED OVER MY FA-
ther in his "judge's" chair.

"I suppose you could say two weeks"—he squirmed
uncomfortably—"at the most."

We were in his "chambers," a room at the back of the
house paneled in thick oak, with deep maroon carpet, book-
shelves on every wall, and would you believe, a stained-glass
window. It was to that room I was called as a child whenever
I had violated some family rule, a more infrequent event than
I would have cared to admit to my own children lest they
conclude that Daddy was a creep.

My father was a big, solid Irishman, taller even than
Packy, with a build like a wrestler or a truck driver and a face
and a voice like an actor trained to play in Eugene O'Neill
tragedies, qualities that served him in good stead in the courtroom and on the golf course.

He was also a gentle and humorous man who never could
get over the wonderful joke of having a beautiful wife and
three children. He worked hard but relaxed easily and lived
into his eighties.

The only time I ever saw him angry was when Republicans won an election.

"And how many of your buddies died?"

"Three of them were wounded."

I had been called in for "consultation," as he always called it, when he heard from my mother that I had thrown the letter from the Navy Department in the wastebasket. Was I not perhaps forgetting the family tradition of citizen soldier?

"I don't have a wife to bring from Ireland," I snapped.

So it began.

Commander Jeremiah Thomas Keenan, USNR, Navy Cross (with star), having a problem readjusting to civilian life? Taking on his poor father in an argument about comparative war records?

What, me worry?

"And you rose to be captain?"

"First lieutenant." He was grinning. On the one hand he didn't like my decision to retire from the Navy in every possible way. On the other, good lawyer that he was, he relished his son's courtroom performance.

"And you won the Silver Star?"

"Bronze Star . . . I'll stipulate, counselor, that your war record is, ah, more extensive than mine."

"Wouldn't you say distinguished?" I was not to be appeased by his wit. My father was always most dangerous in his arguments when the wit took over.

"Distinguished? Well, now would you summarize it again?"

"Two years of combat, a squadron commander, came out the equivalent of an army light colonel, and two DSCs—Navy Crosses to us."

"Two?" He raised one of his silver eyebrows in surprise. "I didn't know about the second."

"I didn't tell anyone. The point in this cross-examination is that I know what war is like. I don't want any more of it. I don't want to make it easy for the government to start another war. . . ."

"You're not turning Republican on us, are you?" His handsome Irish face, red naturally and not from drinking, became seriously concerned. "You don't believe that stuff about Roosevelt getting us into the war just to save England?"

"I don't. And if he did, I wouldn't have blamed him. The Japs and the Nazis had to be beaten. Maybe the next enemy will have to be beaten, but not by me. And if you give old men a standing military of young men, they're more likely to start a war than if they have to rearm. No, Dad, I'm sorry. I'm not a pacifist in principle. But I saw too many fuck-ups to trust our leaders again."

"Maybe you're right." He did not want to continue the argument, in fact regretted starting it. "The public won't stand for another war—in this generation, anyway."

My father was seldom wrong in his predictions, and probably never more wrong than in that one. As my wife would later remark, if I had stayed in the reserves I would probably have managed to get myself killed and would have left her a widow with two children and another on the way. I observed that, as best as I could remember, she was not expecting in 1950, and was told that I would have doubtless impregnated her before going back to war.

She was angry at me (for several hours) over what might have happened, not ready to give me credit for having foreseen and forestalled it.

You can't win. The sooner you know that, the better off you are.

"Did you have a good talk with your father?" my mother asked anxiously, when I stalked through the kitchen to join Packy at the hoop.

It's harder to be objective about your mother. I don't think we ever realized how beautiful she was—long black hair turning silver, tall, durable full figure, sweet face, gentle voice, quick smile. My father loved her more intensely with each passing year. When he smiled at her Panglossian vagueness, it was never a smile of ridicule but rather of affectionate respect. He understood better than we did that beneath Panglossa there were shrewd street instincts that sized up others instantly and accurately, even if it was like pulling teeth to persuade her to share such an analysis with us.

"We had an argument and I won," I said churlishly. "But don't worry, Mom, I'll straighten out eventually."

That was her line to Dad, almost every night at supper when I did or said something boorish.

"He won't," Pack would chortle. "He's going to be a permanent problem of psychological readjustment."

"Patrick," my father would say in grim warning, as if any threat could repress my irrepressible younger brother.

On weekends, when Joanne was home from Barat, she would inform me that I was being "drippy," and I would retaliate by suggesting that she might try green rinse on her hair next week.

It was pretty hard to work up to a good generation-gap (as we would call it now) fight with my family. Mom was too gently vague and Dad too elusively shrewd. Packy was too much fun for sibling rivalry. The thickheaded Joanne was away at school most of the time.

I was also self-consciously aware that I was playing a role. I was indeed restless, frustrated, uncertain. But I also knew that I had cast myself into the part of the returned war veteran, indeed combat veteran, and so I was looking over my own shoulder watching myself.

That took some of the fun out of the game and also made me more careful about the feelings of others.

How much of the game was a real adjustment problem and how much Maggie Ward, damn her eyes?

I figured even then that I could only blame my reentry into civilian life (symbolized by "ruptured duck" discharge insignia on my flight jacket) for twenty-five percent, thirty percent at the most, of my problem. For all my good resolutions, Maggie was on my mind constantly.

She had been dead and buried in the tomb that morning I met her at Tucson. Damn it, she owed me an explanation.

So did He, especially since, even if I was ostentatiously avoiding Mass at Saint Luke's on Sunday, I had more or less reestablished diplomatic relations with Him.

I assumed that there would never be an explanation, but that did not stop me from demanding one anyway.

The principal target of my rage was Loyola Law School, in which I had enrolled because my father had attended De

Paul. The University of Chicago was not an option that would have occurred to any of us.

In 1946, Loyola moved from their old downtown headquarters into a "tower" building on Michigan donated by Frank J. Lewis. It was one of the wisest moves the Chicago Jesuits ever made. They were better prepared for the overwhelming influx of students than any other Chicago school; the University of Illinois was driven to teaching classes at Navy Pier.

Lewis Towers, once a hotel, had been a V-12, ninety-day-wonder midshipman school for Northwestern during the war, which turned out officers and gentlemen for the United States Navy in ninety days. The Jebs snapped it up in the nick of time. In 1946 the law school, closed during the war, opened with a first-year class of which I was a truculent and restless member.

I am convinced my son went to Yale Law School because I went to Loyola. I followed my father's example and did not reveal this knowledge to my son. My wife's threat to divorce me if I did, a threat not to be taken seriously in any event, was hardly necessary.

I suppose that the Deity whose existence I was now prepared to acknowledge, though only just barely, designed me to be a lawyer. I do not have a deep mind (my spouse disagrees, but I will let it stand), but my intellect is agile, my memory retentive, my tongue quick, and my self-confidence, in those days at any rate, was enormous.

Arguing the law is like flying an F6F, less dangerous but more intellectually rewarding. After the first week I knew I could breeze through law school with very little study and no anxiety. In a half hour of glancing at the books, I could absorb as much as many of my classmates would in five or six hours.

It wasn't fair, but whoever said life is fair?

My contracts teacher took a dislike to me during the first week of class. The feeling was mutual. If I couldn't fight with my father, and if God wouldn't fight back, Professor Hennessey was the perfect substitute for both.

"Are you with us today, Mr. Keenan?"

I try to tell myself that my recollection that he looked like John Houseman was the result of seeing *Paper Chase* many years later.

"Present, sir," I would snap back at him, as if he were a marine DI.

"Paying attention or scrawling your verse?"

"Both, sir. It's easy in this class."

Sometimes I was writing love poetry to Maggie, sometimes trying to sketch pictures of her—the face was fading already, the body was still clearly etched. My drawings, long since lost, were not, I am prepared to swear, obscene.

Not really.

"I see. Mr Keenan, what was your rank in the service, second lieutenant?"

"I'm retiring with a silver oak leaf, sir."

Slight awe in the classroom.

"And now you are a lowly first-year law student."

"I'll stipulate the law-student part, sir."

"I see. And what did you do in the war, Mr. Keenan? Sit behind a desk in San Francisco?"

He should have looked up my record before he got into a verbal battle with me. He was feeding me great lines.

"I flew an F6F, sir. Grumman Hellcat."

"I see. Very interesting. You are a decorated war hero, no doubt?"

The classroom was uneasy. A lot of professors need a goat to beat up on (the role my poor Maggie had played for the nuns at Saint Dom's).

"Is that appropriate matter for class discussion, sir?"

"Not necessarily, Mr. Keenan; but I feel that your classmates have a right to know what sort of distinguished fellow student they have. A purple heart, I presume?"

"Navy Cross with star."

Dead silence.

"Most impressive. May I make a suggestion?"

"I don't see how I can stop you."

"Why don't you forget about law and seek an outlet for

your natural heroic skills on the floor of the Chicago Board of Trade?"

"I might do that too, sir."

"Indeed. Now if you will explain this particular case, if you know which one we're discussing?"

The kid in front of me, an ex–tank commander from the ETO, pointed to the case in his book. I wasn't even on the right page. I faked my way through it and earned at least a draw in my responses to old man Hennessey's questions.

"A very interesting position, mister . . . or should I say Commander?"

"Suit yourself, sir."

"Well then, Commander Keenan, you argue an absurd position with considerable skill, but not enough to pass the exam at the end of the term, much less the bar exam. Too bad, you'd make an interesting crooked lawyer, but a lawyer you'll never be."

"Oh, I think I will, sir, but never a law-school teacher. I won't have to beat up on first-year law students to make up for my professional failures."

Gasp from the class. Then laughter.

It was like bombing the *Yamoto*. Too easy. I did become a law-school teacher—in addition to a number of other things in the profession, but I never did beat up on students.

I did beat up on poor Hennessey, however. He was a mean son of a bitch. I hated the Houseman character in the film. I even hated him in the Smith Barney ads on TV. He reminds me too much of Hennessey.

A few more run-ins and Hennessey left me alone. Found himself other goats to abuse.

So I stopped attending the contracts class. Fuck it all.

I hung around street corners with guys in the 52/20 club (the government paid you twenty dollars a week for a year if you were a veteran, just for doing nothing); drank more beer in a month than I had in all the years in the Navy put together; played basketball with Packy and his seminarian buddies (not all of whom found themselves a widow or a nun when the

Church started to change); shot pool at Fred's on Division Street in Austin a couple of nights a week; hung around some Loop bars; slept peacefully every night; and daydreamed that I saw Maggie's body in the sky. For example, when crossing the Chicago River at sunset on the wooden Lake Street El train, as the setting autumn sun would bathe the river and the buildings near it in a misty Indian-summer gold.

I dreamed about her and mourned for my lost love. I felt sorry for myself. I insisted in my diary that she was dead and I would not see her again. Yet I still looked for her every day in the crowds boarding the El train.

I also dated, mostly young women from nearby Trinity or friends of Joanne's from Barat. I heard Lawrence Tibbets in *La Traviata* and a recital by Gladys Swarthout at the Opera House, listened to George Szell conduct Mozart and Prokofiev at Orchestra Hall, watched Maurice Evans do *Hamlet* at the Erlanger, Joe E. Brown in *Harvey* at the Harris, the Laurence Olivier *Henry V* film at the Civic, Shaw's *St. Joan* at the Goodman, Lindsay and Crouse's *State of the Union* at the Blackstone, and Victor Herbert's *Sweethearts* and *Song of Norway* at theaters I did not note in my journal. Neither did I write down the name of the author of the latter. Edvard Grieg seemed to be enough.

I also began to take a mild interest in politics—enough to grind my teeth when I saw Harry Truman unable to keep the Democrats from going down to defeat in the 1946 congressional campaign. Some historians, most notably Robert Donovan in his excellent biography of Harry Truman, called the 1946 congressional election the "beef steak" election.

During the summer, when price controls were lifted, meat prices soared and livestock dealers rushed beef and pork into the marketplace. Then, when controls were reimposed in September, meat seemed to vanish from the stores of the country as the dealers and growers stopped shipping meat, confident that the prices would soon go up again.

Americans wanted plenty of meat at low cost and refused to choose between the two incompatible goals.

Truman played into their hands: tales of whiskey-drinking, poker-playing cronyism in the White House—characteristics which, as Donovan says, makes Truman attractive in hindsight—infuriated Americans then. He was nothing but a stupid clown. I don't suppose it helped that he didn't look much like a President.

(Incidentally, Dean Acheson, who was his Secretary of State, said that he had seen him drunk only once in the eight years of his presidency.)

There was also a growing sense that we had won the war and lost the peace. The world did not seem to be an appreciably better place. Roosevelt, it was widely felt, sold Poland down the river at Yalta (a position that ignored the fact that the Red Army had already occupied most of Poland), and Harry Truman had been conned by the clever Russians at Potsdam.

So blame Truman again.

My burst of cultural and political interests—unsuccessful attempts to escape from the ghost of Maggie Ward, if the truth be told—astonished my family, especially since on alternate nights I was hanging around street corners or shooting pool.

"Anything but study the law?" My father's faintly leprechaunish grin appeared hesitantly.

"Mom and Joanne want me to date nice girls," I replied like one who is put upon by the whole world. "I guess I can't do anything right."

The girls had a hard time figuring me out. I was polite, respectful, quiet, and gentlemanly. The last adjective meant that I normally made no passes and that my kisses at the end of a date demanded nothing in return. Some of them were frankly bored by the high culture (and to this day I'll argue that Victor Herbert was high culture); others pretended to like it to keep their date happy; still others were delighted that some "boy" would finally take them to an event they liked. All three groups would be lucky to be invited again.

The girls I would try on a second date were those who would admit honestly, "You know I've never been to anything like this before, but I could really get to enjoy it."

Which was my reaction too, I would confess.

"Why do you go to the opera, then, Jerry?" the nicest one of them all, Kate Walsh, asked after *La Traviata*.

My arm around her, as much as Roxinante's gearshift would permit, I told her the truth. Mostly. "A girl I knew in the service kind of made me feel ignorant because I didn't know about opera. She was right."

"Sounds a little nasty." She leaned against my arm.

"Not the way she did it."

"Did you love her?"

More points for you, Kate, for being up-front.

"Yes."

"What happened?"

"She's dead."

"Oh"—fingers to my jaw—"how horrible! What happened?"

"She drowned."

"Accident?"

"I don't think so. She . . . she was terribly discouraged about her life. With reason."

"Poor girl"—peck at my lips—"and poor Jerry."

"I haven't told anyone but you," I admitted, kissing her with more determination than any of the others. "Thanks for listening."

A good seduction routine? Sure, but I liked Kate too much to seduce her, even if I could have, of which I am not sure even now.

We did go out several more times, to hear Stan Kenton at the College Inn in the old Sherman House and Jackie Mills at the Rio Cabana as well as the Symphony. I fell half in love with her, but the other half wouldn't come. The problem was not that she was so different from Maggie, but that, despite her blond hair and pretty face, she was too much like her.

Maggie, possessive little ghostly bitch that she was, kept getting in the way.

Finally, after we had listened to *Madame Butterfly* in early December, our good-night kisses became torrid, a spontaneous hormonal reaction, I guess, of two young people who liked each other. My fingers found her breast beneath her V-neck navy-blue dress with the white collar.

"Who's Maggie?" she demanded, pushing me away gently. "The dead girl?"

"I'm sorry," I mumbled, angry, humiliated, ashamed.

"Don't be sorry, Jerry," she whispered as she touched my chin again, one of her favorite gestures. "I understand. But I can't compete with a ghost."

"You shouldn't have to." I would strangle that bitch Maggie Ward if I ever got my hands on her—in heaven or hell or purgatory or limbo or whatever.

"I like you," she said crisply. "And I could get to like you a lot, but . . ."

"I guess I need more time."

"I don't mean I won't go out with you." She smiled her marvelous imp smile. "You're too much fun and too generous and even too good at necking and petting to give up, but I don't want to get serious unless . . ."

Kate would have made the right man a wonderful wife. In fact, she did make the right man a wonderful wife. And they do go to the opera.

There wasn't a ghost of a chance in December of 1946 of me being that man.

The word "ghost" in that sentence was an accident. Or a Freudian slip, about which I did not know in 1946. But it describes my situation perfectly.

I was still haunted.

And the temper of the country was not much help. I began to think the wrong side had won the war.

The winter of 1946/47 was a mean time in America. Much of Europe was still only a half step away from starvation. And Americans, who still feared a return of the Great Depression, were becoming nasty because they couldn't buy all the things they wanted with the money they had saved during the war and were still making, especially cars and houses. We wanted two incompatible goals—more goods and stable prices. OPA was mostly dead, but it lingered on such important items as cars. The black-market price on a new car was twice the OPA price. ($2600 for a Buick, as opposed to the $1300 OPA price. If you wanted one of the tiny, crude TV sets, you could get one for a mere $350.) We had a double-market economy for several months—OPA and black, the latter being the supply-and-demand market. Many of us could afford to pay the black-market prices to buy our Oldsmobiles and our Philcos and our Kelvinators, which is why there was a black market; but we resented that we had to pay such prices, forgetting that a few years before, we couldn't afford such luxuries (now becoming necessities) at any price.

Everyone else wanted cars and beef. I wanted Maggie. As much as ever.

I still kept overlooking the most important piece of evidence and would continue to do so until it almost hit me on the head.

CHAPTER **30**

MAGGIE WARD WAS IN MY ROOM WHEN PACKY BURST IN. "I thought I heard that noisy machine at work . . . hey, that's not a mountain or a cactus! Some dame!"

I was watching my Arizona slides for the second time. On the screen was the only shot of Andrea that had not been ruined.

"The door was closed." I tried to be angry, a waste of time with Packy.

"Gosh . . ." He exhaled softly. "Is that the girl you were following, Jer? No wonder you're gloomy all the time. How did she give you the slip?"

My wife says that I idolize my brother Patrick because I

see in him characteristics that I'd like to have myself. If my blond (still), six-foot-four, broad-shouldered, witty, persuasive brother has ever had a moment of self-doubt, he cured himself before anyone noticed. It's lucky, my wife argues, that Packy is selling God and not encyclopedias. "Mind you, darling," she adds, "I like him too, but he'd be the first one to admit that you're the brother with depth."

Often I wish I could trade.

"Do you think she's prettier than Cathy O'Donnell or Teresa Wright?"

Sensing my despondent mood, Packy had dragged me off that afternoon to see *The Best Years of Our Lives* (which later won the Academy Award as the best film of 1946). It had made me even more despondent.

"They're pretty dames." Packy was eighteen, and in fifth year at Quigley, which combined four years of high school and one of college in a day-school seminary down on Rush Street, right next to Loyola Law School. "If they really let coeds into Loyola next year and they look like Cathy, it will be the end of vocations to the priesthood."

It was difficult to tell whether he was daydreaming about the young actress, unmistakably Irish-American, or my Maggie.

"She's gorgeous," he said wistfully.

"Cathy O'Donnell?"

"Your dame. Why did you let her get away?"

I almost told him the truth. The whole truth, not the partial truth I had shared with Kate.

"It's a long story, Pack."

"I bet it is; did you call her Dulcinea?" he continued. Then, focusing more closely on the details of the misty, impressionistic figure on the tiny screen propped up against my bookcase: "Does she have any clothes on?"

"No."

"Wow." He whistled softly. "I never thought you had it in you, Jer."

"Neither did I. And don't stare. You're going to be a priest."

"*That* has nothing to do with it." He whistled again. "Any more pictures?"

"No."

"It sure would be nice to have a sister-in-law like her around the house."

"It won't happen. It's all over."

"Sure?" He raised an eyebrow skeptically.

"Absolutely." I went on to the next slide.

He nodded, as if he understood, a movement of the head just like hers. "Let's have a game of twenty-one. You're not going to help yourself any by sitting here brooding about her."

"Not now, Pack; I don't want to help myself."

"You wanna brood?"

"Yeah."

"I guess I see the point." He glanced at the image of Gates Pass on the screen, as though Maggie were still there. "Are you sure it's all over?"

"She's dead."

"Oh my God . . . is there anything I can do?"

"Go practice your hook shot," I said gruffly, wanting his sympathy but not knowing how to respond to it. "I'll be out in fifteen minutes or so."

He left quietly. I went back to the picture of Maggie. It was not just my love that imagined you beautiful. Even my kid brother, with the tastes of a typical eighteen-year-old (seminarian or not), thinks you're gorgeous. I can't believe you're dead.

And you are more beautiful than Cathy O'Donnell or Teresa Wright or Myrna Loy or Virginia Mayo.

1946 was a great year for films—*Notorious, My Darling Clementine, Best Years, Brief Encounter, It's a Wonderful Life, Great Expectations, Till the End of Time, Two Years Before the Mast, Margie.* It was also a great year for new young actresses, with the emphasis to meet the spirit of the times on wholesomeness instead of glamour. Rita Hayworth, Linda Darnell, Betty Grable, Virginia Mayo, Lana Turner were being succeeded by Donna Reed, Jeanne Crain, Mona Freeman, Gail Russell, Diana Lynn, and Teresa Wright and Cathy O'Donnell.

They were too much for me because they all reminded me of Maggie. The wholesome domesticity between Jimmy Stewart and Donna Reed in *Wonderful Life* drove me out of the theater before the film was finished (Packy told me how it ended). I didn't want domesticity yet; not exactly. But I didn't exclude it either, did I? I was good with kids wasn't I, even with the winsome little Ryan punk with his Pratt & Whitney roar?

I wanted romance and adventure, didn't I? How could I identify my Maggie with these suburban-housewife actresses?

The answer was that romance and domesticity, adventure and a family—Maggie Ward seemed to promise them all.

When I was thinking about writing this story, I bought videotapes of the great '46 films to see if they were as good as I remembered them.

They were not. Even classics like *Notorious* and *Clementine* were not as smooth and professional as contemporary films. And the others were hokey. But the young actresses were still beautiful.

My heart ached at the young Donna Reed, recently dead from cancer, and a striking promise of my own mortality.

Every day after our birth, my wife noted while the tape was rewinding, is pure gift. For her and for us. There were tears in her eyes too.

Both *Best Years* and *Wonderful Life* were, however, fascinating portraits of the time after the war. In both cases the heroes built homes for people. Fredric March (who won the Academy Award for best actor) and Jimmy Stewart fought with reactionary bankers to make loans to returning service men. Dana Andrews, decidedly overweight for a B-17 pilot, said that all he wanted was a home in the suburbs and finally went to work for a company building houses. He told Teresa Wright that it would be years before he made much money. Like any loyal lover of a returned vet, she replied, in effect, that it made no difference.

They both were confident but uncertain.

That was 1946.

The two films were not left-wing critiques of American

society. Both believed in the "American way"—hard work, ambition, expansion of opportunities, jobs for everyone. The "baddies" were those who wanted to return to the old rigid anti-expansionist spirit of the Depression. Bankers, in other words.

Who was going to win?

Like Fredric March and Dana Andrews and Jimmy Stewart and their lovely housewives-to-come-home-to, the films were betting on expansion. But uneasily.

They didn't realize that the expansionist energies were so powerful that even the bankers would soon be swept along. Willingly.

That's forty years later. *Best Years* oppressed me then because it made me feel ashamed of myself. Unlike Fredric March, I did not have to work for anyone. Unlike Harold Russell, I still had both my hands. Unlike Dana Andrews, I was not burdened with a faithless wife and a job as a soda jerk. I was a spoiled rich kid, isolated from the experiences of my own generation.

All right, I didn't have women like they did, not yet. But there was a plentiful supply of those, too, some of them, like Kate, of the highest quality.

But I had no good reason to feel sorry for myself.

"Packy," I asked on the El the next day, "what can I do to help poor people?"

He looked up from his Greek book. "Huh?"

"I want to help the poor."

"Invest in low- and middle-income housing," he said promptly.

"I saw the film too, remember?"

"And listened to Dad and Ned. You want some direct experience? Well, there's always the Catholic Worker house up on North Avenue. A bunch of vets run a soup kitchen every night for skid-row people."

"Communists?"

"No. A woman named Dorothy Day founded the movement. She was a Communist who became a Catholic. Wrote a book called *From Union Square to Rome*. I have a copy somewhere. Radical, but Catholic."

"Like us."

"Not even remotely." He laughed. "What's her name?"

"Dorothy Day, like you just said."

"No, dummy, the girl on the slide."

"Maggie. Or maybe Andrea. Hard to tell."

"Maggie? Like Grandma? That's a free ticket in this family. What do you mean, 'maybe' Andrea?"

"It's a mystery, Pack. I'll explain someday."

"I go up there to the Catholic Workers a couple of times a month," he said as we left the El station at Forest—the end of the line. "Want to come?"

"Why not?"

It was time, I told myself, for some kind of political activity.

We had lost the election. It was a sure defeat before the ballot boxes opened. Gallup predicted, accurately enough, that the Republicans would win control of the House and possibly the Senate. They also, to my father's horror, won control of Cook County. The Kelly-Nash-Arvey machine, as it was called in those days, lost every race on the county ticket. A man named Elmer Michael Walsh (my father claimed that he didn't really exist) defeated Dad's good friend, State Senator Richard J. Daley, in the race for sheriff.

Time chortled that the political tide of history had been turned and that the Democrats would be out of power for the foreseeable future. The *Daily News* announced the "End of the Machine" in headlines that would be repeated many times over the next forty years.

In fact, 1946 was the only time in the last sixty years that the Republicans won both houses of Congress. They are not likely ever to do it again.

And the report of the machine's demise was premature, as it was many times later.

The media, particularly the Luce journals, discovered that they could not control the outcome of elections save perhaps in reenforcing the way people already felt two years later, when "Fighting Tom" Dewey was turned back by Harry Truman, who also swept back in a Democratic Congress.

Two events had taken place: the final lifting of price controls and the conversion to peacetime economy had opened the cornucopia of consumer goods, and people discovered, without knowing it yet, the concepts of "real wages," or "lifestyle"—prices went up but income went up more.

And Truman earned for himself the reputation of being a tough, feisty man, especially by fighting the unions, and especially later that winter by fighting the universally despised John L. Lewis of the United Mine Workers, who was trying to improve the "real wages" of the miners and of other union members so they could deal themselves into the prosperity that was emerging. It was only common sense that, if the industrial workers were going to buy the consumer goods necessary to sustain prosperity, their wages had to go up.

But that common sense was not evident to a President who desperately needed a victory over someone and a press and public who needed someone to blame for the "slowness" of the postwar recovery—anything short of instant conversion from planes to automobiles, refrigerators, radios, and homes was too slow.

Everyone seemed to be on strike—bus drivers for fifty days in Chicago, airplane pilots, construction workers, copper miners—but no strike was a better target than the coal strike, welcomed by management, which saw a chance to let the government break the union. Truman sought an injunction against the strike on the grounds of a national emergency because the country was still technically in a state of war. Brownouts were ordered in the cities to conserve coal, railroad schedules were cut to the bone, someone banned Christmas-tree lights, headlines told of seventy thousand jobs being lost in Chicago and that the recovery might be delayed or permanently impaired.

Every frustration in the country was turned on the miners and their dark, foreboding president.

Few blamed the mine owners, who would not negotiate in good faith; or the government, which by interfering in the collective bargaining process excused the owners from negotiation.

The courts sustained the injunction. The union was fined heavily. The strike ended. We had lights on the Christmas trees. Truman had proved he was a bigger man than John L. Lewis. And the nation, having done in the miners, reveled in its victory over men who, as my dad said, had the toughest and nastiest job in the world.

Most historians on that era will tell you today that there was no justification for the injunction, that the Supreme Court, as always following the election returns, had violated the Constitution, and that, in a crowning irony, the mine owners the following year, riding the boom then like most everyone else, gave Lewis and the miners virtually everything they wanted.

The coal strike of 1946 revealed the dark, peevish underside of what my generation now calls the postwar world, just as the McCarthy (Joseph, not Eugene, I have to say to the younger generation) episode would emphasize it again a few years later. Having clawed our way, as we thought, with our fingernails to the beginnings of a better world than we had thought possible during the Depression, we resented those who might share it with us and those who seemed to challenge it ever so slightly. If the unions had been destroyed by the anger of 1946 or by the subsequent Taft-Hartley labor law, a largely ineffectual attempt to repeal the Wagner Act (my father called T-H hell for unions, purgatory for management, and heaven for lawyers), working men and women would not have had the money to join the rest of us in the demand for more consumer goods, the boom would have busted and the depression would have returned.

I was giving some of my attention to politics. I was wondering about Kate, worrying about Maggie, pondering what I should do with my life. Still, it was hard to live in our house and not learn a lot about politics from listening to my father talk to—"lecture" might be a better word—my mother, and from his occasional conversations with a much younger lawyer, Ned Ryan. In later years when I began to study seriously, more or less, that period, I was pleased to find that the instincts and prejudices that I had picked up at home were fundamentally good ones.

You must not judge the postwar era by the '46 election or the coal strike or the McCarthy witch hunts. Truman *was* reelected. McCarthy was swept from power in 1954 when the Republicans, having won the Senate back in 1950, lost it again to the Democrats. He never had, not even at the height of his popularity, the support of a majority of the American people. The unions did survive. Higher education for women and for blacks did win almost unchallenged approval.

The expansiveness, the optimism, no, I'll use the right word, the *hope* of 1946 was too thin to permit many of us to be tolerant.

That would take another quarter century.

Ned Ryan was a West Sider who had committed the unpardonable crime of moving to the South Side when he came home from the war with the Medal of Honor for fighting off a Japanese battleship at Leyte Gulf with a broken-down DE squadron.

"While you and your friend Bill Halsey"—he would wink at me—"were way up north chasing carriers without any planes on them."

Ned was short and my father was tall. He was thin and my father was hefty and solid. His hair was black, turning silver already, my father's was silver turning white. But they were both Irish political lawyers of the old school (a school to which I belong, I am happy to say, and my own son after me): shrewd in the ways of street politics, heavy with political clout, impeccably honest, and politically liberal.

They both were especially unhappy about Daley's loss.

"Has anyone ever said he took a thing?" my father demanded.

"And how many state senators courted their wives by attending the opera?" Ned asked.

"What would you say of a navy flyer who takes a girl to the opera?"

"Would it be a sign of true love?"

I ignored their winks. The family loved Kate.

"And how many politicians read Dickens to their children at night and history books to themselves after the kids fall asleep?"

"How many know that Dickens is anything but the name of a street on the North Side?"

"And who Goethe is?"

They both laughed. They pronounced the German poet's name as it is to this day by the Chicago Irish, "Gay-thee."

"Well, don't they say he'll not die in the State Senate anyway?"

"Is that what they're saying?"

The "they" in these conversations were never specified.

There was a pause while Dad refilled both their glasses and went into the kitchen to fetch me another beer.

That's right, he got it for me. I do the same for my sons. And daughters.

Sometimes, anyway.

"They say Russell Root"—Ned sipped his small glass of Jameson's, straight up—"will run against Ed Kelly next April, now that the machine is dead."

"Do they now." My father preferred single malt Scotch. "Well, I hope so. But do they say that it will be Ed again? Hasn't he had his turn?"

"Don't you hear that?"

"Why should I be hearing that?"

I was playing with Ned's two-year-old son Johnny, a cute, wide-eyed little punk with a fey smile.

"Well, would you be hearing," Ned went on, "I wonder, that Jake Arvey is thinking of running Marty Kennelly on a good-government ticket?"

"Don't they say that Major Douglas is our good-government man?"

"But wouldn't he make a grand senator?"

"Is that what they're saying?

"And what do you think of Marty Kennelly?"

"Doesn't everyone say he's an honest man? And wouldn't an honest man make a fine mayor?"

"Even if he's so honest that he doesn't know all the ways to be dishonest?"

"And would leave the city to the gray wolves?

"And isn't that what the gray wolves want?"

I made a paper airplane for Johnny and threw it into the air with a great roar, not at all like a Pratt & Whitney, if the truth be told.

"And who will he be facing in 1948 with Major Douglas running for the Senate?"

"Would we be so lucky to get that little fella from New York again?"

My father sighed. "Do you think we could ever be that lucky? Would the American people ever vote for a man with a mustache who looks like a doll on a wedding cake?"

"They never would," Ned Ryan ended the conversation as Johnny threw the plane back to me with a roar that did sound remarkably like a Pratt & Whitney.

My father was never more right in a prediction.

Ned is still alive. And his son, Father Blackie to all, is the rector of Holy Name Cathedral. He still throws paper airplanes at me. My wife and I have an apartment in his parish (in addition to our house in River Forest. "Why go home when you're downtown at nights?" she asks not unreasonably; besides, apartments in the Near North are useful for orgies). When he sees us coming he makes an airplane out of the first Catholic publication on which he can lay his hands and whooshes it at us with a sound still very much like a slightly asthmatic P & W.

You may think I made up the question-laden dialogue between Dad and Ned Ryan, as my son the priest (Jamie) says Saint John made up most of the great lines Jesus has in the Fourth Gospel. But I did not.

I wrote it down that night. I'd begun to write stories.

She will haunt me the rest of my life if I don't.

And if I do.

It was Maggie haunting me, I'm sure, that forced me to ride on the El with Packy that night to find out what the Catholic Workers were up to.

We had three cars at the house—Dad's old Lasalle, a twin of Ned Ryan's, Mom's new white Olds convertible (in which with her perfectly groomed silver hair and well-maintained figure she attracted considerable attention, which flustered and pleased her), and my Roxinante. Still, in those days we routinely used public transportation. The El was a quick and convenient way to ride downtown or to Loyola and Quigley. Who needed a car? On an elaborate date with Kate, I'd clean up Roxinante and pick her up in the car; but neither she nor any other girl would complain about an El- or streetcar-ride to a movie or a nightclub.

Cars were nice, particularly on weekends, but you didn't need them yet.

My memory of the El rides in 1946 are shaped by two images—darkness and worried faces.

The whole year indeed is "dark" in my recollection. Perhaps I was used to the relatively equal length of day and night in the tropics or to year-round daylight savings time during the war, with yet an extra hour of "war" time added during the summer. Or maybe I had been spoiled in sunny San Diego and had forgotten about the dreary Chicago winters.

Or possibly my life was dark because a light had gone out of it.

And the faces on the El—so many grim, anxious, worried faces of working men and women—some black, mostly white, faces worn out permanently by the anxieties of the Great Depression, faces in which the budding national optimism had yet to make an impact, faces that would haunt me for the rest of my life.

You don't see such faces anymore except in the housing projects and in the first-class sections of jets on Monday morning and Friday afternoon, the faces of salesmen and executives for whom the rats in the rat race are running too fast.

On the El during those dark late afternoon rides, I vowed

I'd fight poverty and fear in the life that was still ahead of me. I don't know whether I've won any of those battles, but I didn't quit either.

Beyond River Forest there were only two suburbs that mattered—Maywood, a working-class community to the southwest, and Melrose Park, an Italian-American town to the northwest. Farther west there was only forest preserve, farmland, and an occasional town, and eventually the string of small municipalities strung along the Fox River Valley.

There was, I thought that night as I read Dorothy Day's memoir *From Union Square to Rome,* a lot of land out there that could be filled up with houses. Maybe I could invest in the future and in homes for vets like Dana Andrews by buying some of that farmland and making it available for construction.

The next day, on a pay phone from Loyola, I called the trust officer who handled my money and told him to put it all in land west of Chicago, "where homes can be built."

He congratulated me on my wisdom and assured me that I would make a lot of money.

I thought about his remark when I had hung up. I didn't want money. I wanted to cooperate in the building of houses in which families could live in decent comfort.

It was the best investment decision I ever made, even with my insistence that we would only sell to developers who would build "good homes." And I had been reading a Catholic Worker book when I made it.

There were a lot of ironies in the fire in 1946.

In the meantime I went a couple of nights a week to the Catholic Worker "house of hospitality," helped in their soup kitchen, read their paper, argued their positions, and learned firsthand about poverty, incurable, helpless poverty.

It meant I missed Fred Allen and Bing Crosby and Bob Hope (not Jack Benny, because he was on the radio for Jell-O on Sunday night), but I didn't miss them very much.

Kate came with me sometimes and was even better at kindness to the poorest of the poor than I was.

"I'm learning more from you, Jerry Keenan," she said as

she hugged me fiercely one night, "than from all my professors in college put together."

She didn't pull away from my hand on her breast—outside her dress, of course.

I am falling in love with this lovely girl, I told myself, and it isn't fair to her. She's willing to take the risk of competing with a haunt, but she'll lose.

Until I get the damn haunt out of my head.

I was confident that the damn haunt was not in hell and would never go there. Purgatory? What had she done to deserve that?

So what was left?

Can't you leave me alone? I demanded.

The vets, a few years older than I was, who had founded the Chicago Catholic Worker house, were not pacifists like Dorothy Day. They hated war as I did, maybe not as much because I was the only one of them who had seen combat. Politically they were liberal Democrats, as I was—and surprised to find that someone from River Forest might, on a few issues, like unions, be more liberal than they were. Religiously they were disenchanted Catholics, the two leaders former seminarians who had attended Quigley before the war and had been active in a Catholic Action movement called CISCA in the thirties. One of them went on to edit a pervasively snide and snobbish Catholic (mildly) left-wing journal. The other later worked for *The New York Times*, wrote Kennedy's Houston speech on religious liberty to Protestant ministers, which probably won the election for him, was active at the Second Vatican Council, and left the Church to become an Anglican after the birth-control encyclical in 1968. He still wanted to be a priest, it was said, and the Anglicans would ordain him. He died a deacon, just before his ordination to the priesthood.

In 1946 I would not have imagined such an event. At that time, I could have seen him becoming a Communist or an atheistic socialist like Michael Harrington (also a product of the Catholic Worker movement), but an Anglican?

As Packy put it, "Will he become a Republican?"

I learned a lot from the Catholic Workers in the postwar

years, most notably the connection between my religion, to which I was returning as slowly as possible, and my political instincts.

Was Maggie Ward really responsible for awakening this social concern, which remains with me to this day? After all, she had never discussed social problems with me, and she might even have been, God forbid, a Republican.

Loving Maggie, even if only for a day or two, had opened up my soul to the world and made me sensitive to emotions of which I had never been aware before she squirmed her way into my life. I would never be the same.

CIC or the seraph or whoever was right. She would be part of my life forever, even if I could never again take her to bed with me.

Eventually, I told myself, she will be only a pleasant and inspiring memory, not a sexual obsession. In the long run.

As Lord Keynes had said, though I didn't know it then, in the long run we'll all be dead.

I also met Dorothy Day, who was, as the Catholic Worker people insisted, a saint. The only other person like her that I have ever encountered is Mother Teresa, and the only way I can describe both experiences is to say that they were encounters with radiant goodness. Humans qualitatively different from the rest of us.

I expected to be pushed toward agreement with her own vision of the movement. In fact, we hardly discussed the Catholic Worker. And I did not have to defend my affluent background, as I did with some of the Chicago movement members. I don't remember much of what we did talk about, except that it was about God and service to others. Miss Day led by example and inspiration, not by indoctrination. It is the way with saints.

One sentence does stand out, and I didn't have to write it in my journal or in the pile of little dialogues I was recording: "It does not matter where we come from or who we are. It only matters who we become by the ways we love others."

I quote that dictum often to my kids, even today. I ask my wife if I am boring them. "Certainly not," she replies, hugging me passionately, which she is apt to do at odd times, even when we're fighting. "They're telling it to their kids too. And if it does bore them, too bad for them. They should hear it anyway."

On the ride home that night on the Lake Street El at Halsted, I could have sworn I saw Maggie on the opposite platform. Seeing her again was like an explosion, like ice floes breaking apart. I left the train at Loomis, crossed over to the opposite platform, and rode back to Halsted. The young woman who I thought was Maggie was still waiting on the platform. Not Maggie, not even pretty.

Idiot, I told myself as I descended the stairs and crossed over to the westbound platform. Lovesick, haunted idiot.

(It was quicker to ride downtown on the subway and hike from Forest Avenue at the end of the El ride to our house than to take the North Avenue streetcar straight west. I am convinced that there are still North Avenue streetcars wandering west, even though buses replaced them decades ago.)

It was a great year for songs, *Carousel* and *Brigadoon* had both spawned hit tunes, "Don't Fence Me In" and "Swinging on a Star" were still popular. "Tenderly," "Come Rain, Come Shine," "The Gypsy," and "Doing What Comes Naturally," were the songs of the year in addition to those I've already mentioned. The songs wore better than the films, some of them became standards as the years went on.

"Tenderly" was our song—Kate and mine. It made me wonder whether Maggie and I had a song which was ours.

"Ole Buttermilk Sky" in the train station?

The Cook County Forest Preserve District had thoughtfully maintained Thatcher Woods on the west end of River Forest, just a block away from Trinity.

The night after I met Dorothy Day, with "Tenderly" playing softly on one of the music stations, I was kissing Kate's naked breasts in the front seat of Roxinante, ignoring the restraints imposed on me by the gearshift.

There were pretty, fresh young breasts, all the more delectable because I was sure that I was the first man to see them naked or to kiss them.

Caution and maybe fear finally stopped us.

And my inexcusable comparisons between her breasts and Maggie's—the ghost was a jealous lover.

"I guess we should stop." Kate sighed and rearranged her straps (two sets, because the slip was a more extensive garment in those days) and her satin cups. "You are quite good at this sort of thing, Jeremiah. I'll always have pleasant memories of how good it can be."

I zipped up the back of her dress. "I'm sorry if I went too far."

"Nonsense," she said briskly. "I didn't try to fight you off, did I?"

"No."

"I can't think clearly," she said as she turned off the radio, "with that song playing."

"I'm glad."

"So am I." She laughed. "But we should think clearly for a minute."

I knew what was coming.

"We are becoming, I believe the word is"—she laughed again, not in the least nervously—"involved with one another."

"You've noticed that?"

"I have." She touched my jaw. "And I don't mind in the least. I am not in any rush to marry—"

"First date that hasn't talked about furniture."

"Be quiet, please." She put her hand over my mouth. "On the other hand, we are both kidding ourselves if we think we're not stumbling in that direction."

"Those are supposed to be my lines." My mouth escaped from her hand, but was quickly recaptured.

"I think I could probably go to bed with you," she went on calmly, "with less guilt feelings than you could take me to bed. That's not the point. The point is that we are both sufficiently Irish Catholic as to figure that we'd have to marry. Right? Don't answer. Just nod your head.

"Okay. I could get ready to marry if it came to that. Could you? Just shake your head. See? It's not only that you have to resolve your Maggie problem. You also must figure out what you're going to do with your life. Stop struggling." Her eyes turned teary. "You shouldn't try to settle that question just because you find that you're stumbling into marriage, right?"

I nodded agreement and she released my mouth.

"So I'm not saying we'll break up and I'll certainly not let you out of taking me to that Benedictine ball—"

"Bachelors and Benedicts," I corrected her.

"Right. But nothing steady or nothing heavy from now on, are we agreed?"

It was a breakup, a friendly one. And we would date occasionally. But the romance was over.

And I felt like a prize fool. How can anyone give up an intelligent, generous, lovely young woman like Kate because of a haunt?

But give her up I did.

Well, I thought to myself that night, if I do go to confession on the law-school retreat—which started the next day—I wouldn't have to confess that I was still in the "occasion of sin." As if someone like Kate were really in God's mind an "occasion of sin."

I had learned a few things in my pilgrimage away from the Church and back. Like who God was.

And while I still didn't much like Him, I had to admit I was caught in the chance metaphor I had dredged up from my unconscious in Globe to persuade Andrea that she was not damned.

God felt about me the way I felt about Maggie. Or even the way I felt about Kate.

"That is flattering," I told Him, "but You sure do have a strange way of showing Your love."

It would seem even stranger after the bombs the retreat master dumped on me, a retreat which, incidentally, nearly caused my expulsion from law school.

CHAPTER 31

I ALMOST FORCED THE JESUITS TO THROW ME OUT OF LAW school.

Then I never would have met Father Donniger, the priest who told me that my experience with Maggie Ward was "not at all unusual, my very dear one."

The rules said that everyone in the university must make an annual retreat—a rather pathetic attempt in retrospect to maintain a Jesuit influence in a school that was being overwhelmed by an influx of students the Jebs had never anticipated.

The "spiritual exercise" became a game in which administration and students matched wits. The students usually won. The administration's techniques for checking attendance were ingenious, but not as ingenious as the students' tricks for evading attendance. Priests in general and Jesuits in particular have displayed as long as I can remember remarkable abilities at getting into no-win situations with young people.

I would not play the game. Religious devotion, I told the Dean, a layman, and the "Regent," a Jeb, ought to be a matter of free choice. Virtue, I quoted a passage from Thomas Aquinas that I had picked up in first-year college, results from the repetition of free acts. They had no right to attempt to impose it, and their abuse of student freedom was counterproductive: the retreat was doomed to failure before it began, no matter how good the retreat master.

"It's our school," said the Jeb, "we make the rules, you keep them or you leave."

"I think the courts might hold differently," I replied curtly. "I can see the headline, 'Navy Pilot Expelled from Law School over Retreat.'"

"It won't come to that, I'm sure," the Dean, a nervous

little man with no hair on his head and a rubicund face like my father's, pleaded. "No one else protests, Jerry. I'm sure you'll change your mind."

"Fat chance," I snarled at him.

I would like to persuade you that as long ago as 1946 I was a defender of the civil liberties of students, a cause I would later join with better legal preparation. I would also like to persuade you that I was anticipating by a decade and a half or so the opening up of Pope John's window in the Catholic Church.

In fact, as I'm sure you've guessed, Quixote had found another windmill with which to joust and thus distract himself from the lost Dulcinea.

Both the Dean and the Regent knew my father. They were aware that he was sufficiently a radical Irish Democrat actually to go to court to defend the religious freedom of his son, even though he thought the son was a damn fool for refusing to go on the retreat. The Jebs were not sensitive to PR in those days, but the Dean was, especially since the law school was in the midst of a fund-raising drive—that was the beginning of the time when universities were *always* in the midst of fund-raising drives.

He proposed a not unreasonable compromise: I would agree to attend. They would agree not to demand my attendance card after the first session.

"If you feel compelled in conscience," the Dean said uneasily, "to stay away from the other sessions and thus override your agreement with us, we will not be able to enforce the agreement."

"You will, however, attend all the sessions." The Regent didn't like the Dean's compromise.

"I'm not a Catholic anymore," I insisted with little regard for the facts.

"Everyone benefits from a weekend devoted to God, no matter what their faith." The Regent sounded like a braying farm animal when he preached, as he was at that moment.

"I don't have any faith, and I don't believe in God." I wondered if Maggie's ghost was listening. "And I won't go to your retreat. When was your last retreat, Dean Rochford? If students must make retreat, why not administrators?"

"You be at that retreat," thundered the Regent, "or we'll expel you."

"See you in court, Father." I walked jauntily out of the Dean's office.

Why did I show up at Lewis Towers—across from the old Chicago Water Tower, which seemed an eyesore in those days and not a precious historical landmark—the first weekend in December for the retreat?

Kate made me.

"If ever I saw a stupid son of a bitch who needed a retreat, it's you," she said with the timeless authority of an Irish-woman when she sees the spiritual welfare of her man in jeopardy. "Of course you'll make the retreat."

So that was that, even if we did break up, more or less, between the conversation and the retreat. Maggie's spirit did not need to come back to haunt me.

The law-school retreat was not exactly what Saint Ignatius of Loyola had in mind when he designed his *Spiritual Exercises*. We did not go off into a quiet place in the country. Rather, we rode the El or the streetcars down to Lewis Towers, where we attended class every other day of the week. We listened to the retreat master's conferences in the small and stuffy chapel and then were supposed to wander around the building or the streets outside in silence. Then we were expected to return home, avoid our girlfriends or our wives and the radio and newspapers, and devote our "free time" to prayer and reflection.

Nor did we dedicate thirty days to our "spiritual renewal." Rather we participated in one conference on Friday evening, returned Saturday for three more conferences, and concluded on Sunday with Mass, two conferences, and the final "papal blessing" (which was supposed to prepare us for instant heaven should we die on the way home).

The final conference, Benediction of the Blessed Sacrament, and papal blessing were timed nicely to coincide with the Bear-Cardinal game, the most important annual conflict between the South Side and the rest of the city, dwarfing the springtime "city series" between the Cubs and the Sox.

The returning vets on the Bears might have been a pale shadow of the great 1942 team, but they were still good enough to have clinched the Western Division title three weeks before the season was over. Nonetheless, a victory for the Cardinals would prevent mass suicide on the South Side, so the game was of enormous importance.

And we would be imprisoned in the Lewis Towers chapel.

The Jebs always showed a wonderful sense of timing. Like the United States Navy, they did things their way. Regardless.

Father Donniger was an odd duck, a tall, broad-shouldered German farmer from Kansas who taught theology at the Jesuit Seminary in Saint Mary's, Kansas. He looked like an aging and withered Gary Cooper, an illusion fostered perhaps because his voice sounded like Cooper's with a smoker's hack.

Most of the retreat was devoted to "sins of the flesh," rather a distortion of the genius of the *Spiritual Exercises* of Saint Ignatius but common fare for the time at retreats for Catholic men and boys. If we were not married, we were not supposed to enjoy women at all; if we were married, we were supposed to enjoy other women not at all, and our wives as little as possible.

No one had told Father Donniger that two-fifths of the law-school students were married men. So we were warned repeatedly against "those sins of the flesh popularly known as necking and petting."

"I wish we had time for even a little necking and petting," a married student whispered in my ear. "It was more fun before we were married."

By our age in life we were immune to the Church's diatribes on the subject of sexual play. We might confess it before receiving Communion, much like a hockey player would sit patiently in the penalty box after a rule infraction, but we didn't intend to stop, mostly because it was almost impossible to stop even if we wanted to and we didn't want to. Nor did we think we would be damned to hell for all eternity because we "fooled around" a little bit. Or a lot.

"Better that they should insist on play after marriage," my wife remarks bitterly, "than denounce it before marriage." Even today that is an apposite observation.

After his ritualistic denunciation of "sins of the flesh," however, our Kansas farmer talked about the proper "attitude toward and treatment of women" with discernment and a sensitivity I have rarely heard from any man. Even the married students sat up straight and listened carefully.

"When you think, my dearest ones, you have been more gentle and tender with a woman than you ever believed possible, that you have become a paragon of consideration and affection, I tell you, my dears, on that day you will only have made a poor beginning in responding to their legitimate emotional needs."

I had absorbed some such wisdom from my father's relationship with my mother, learned it practically in my glorious few days with the lost Maggie Ward, and had grown, though not much, in the exercise of this wisdom in my dates with Kate. But the aging Jebby was the first man who ever put these insights into explicit sentences for me.

"If you are not willing to abandon your harsh, aggressive male instincts and approach a woman with complete concern for her longings and desires, you are unfit ever to marry a woman. You can take it, my dears, as an absolutely certain law of nature, that it is impossible to shower a woman with too much undemanding affection."

"Right," my wife would agree emphatically later when I told her about the retreat.

Father Donniger was preaching this excellent wisdom at a time when most retreat masters still thought women were traps designed by the devil to lure men's souls to destruction.

When he warned of the dangers of the sins of the flesh, commonly called necking and petting, I ostentatiously scribbled erotic poetry, whether about Maggie or Kate I no longer knew because they were becoming identified. When he talked about tenderness with women, I listened carefully—only pretending to write poetry.

Father Donniger was talking about what my son Jamie

calls "sexual affection as communication," though I'm sure he would have been horrified by the terms. Indeed, his discussion of the care and treatment of women (he wouldn't have used those words either) never mentioned sex, almost as though tenderness and sex were utterly unrelated subjects.

"I can hardly wait to get home and try this on my wife," the married vet whispered into my ear again. "It makes the Bear-Cardinal game look dull."

"Heretic," I whispered back. But I was thinking of Kate too. And of how much I had learned about women and about love and about life at the Picketpost House.

Father Donniger told us after the first conference that he was available for "consultation and direction" in an office on the floor below the chapel, "any hour of the day or night, my most dear ones."

The "dear" stuff, Packy assured me on Friday night, was Jesuit novitiate talk. "In Europe, where it's all done in Latin, they call each other 'carissime,' which is, as I'm sure you realize, the vocative case and the superlative mode of the adjective 'carus,' which means 'dear.' It's a lot less objectionable in Latin. They use the literal English translation here. I guess the Jebs become accustomed to it, and don't know how dopey it sounds."

"I would use a stronger word." ·

Anyway, on impulse I blundered into his office after Mass on Sunday while the rest of the law school was eating stale rolls and drinking coffee so strong that it could have floated the *Enterprise*.

I spilled the whole story of Andrea King/Maggie Ward, understanding as I poured it out—effectively told, wasn't I going to be a storyteller—how badly I had wanted to tell someone about what had happened.

"Remarkable, my very dear one," he said as he beamed enthusiastically, "you are to be congratulated. You are among the very fortunate."

"I certainly would not want to be responsible for her damnation, Father." I had expected the usual fierce confessional denunciation that exorcised some of the guilt you felt that you might have used the girl—which you probably had. How dare he not provide me with the guilt release I wanted.

"I wouldn't worry about that." He waved a dismissive hand. "Human weakness is such that God readily waives punishment on sins of the flesh."

"Huh?"

"Let me ask you some questions, my dear." He leaned forward eagerly, his pale-blue eyes sparkling behind thick horned-rim glasses. "You tell me your plane was never hit by enemy fire. Could the reason have been that you knew the instant before where the enemy fire would be?"

"Uhm . . . well, now that you mention it . . ."

"And you know the instant beforehand when a professor is about to ask you a question in class?"

"Sometimes."

Poor Hennessey.

"And you admit that you knew the young woman"—he rose triumphantly from the chair behind his standard Jesuit-issue late-medieval desk—"was a ghost as soon as you saw her?"

"Well . . . I did have that reaction."

"Doubtless you are not as sensitive to these matters as she is," he said as he began to scribble on a square piece of scratch paper—a neatly cut quarter of a sheet of mimeograph paper, "but, like her, you are open to influences and power we only dimly understand."

"Is she alive or dead?" I almost screamed at him. "Will I ever see her again?"

"Hmn . . . ?" He handed me the paper, on the reverse of which there were duplicated notes, in Latin. "Here is a list of books by Father Thurston, which may be of some help to you. He has made quite a study of these matters and has followed closely the research done at Duke University."

"Is she alive or dead?" This time I did scream. "Will I ever see her again?"

"My very dear one"—smiling benignly, extending his arms as if in benediction—"doubtless she is alive and doubtless you will see her again . . . either in this world or the next, who can say."

"Is she in hell?"

"Even you don't believe that is possible, my dear." He continued to beam cheerfully at me. "Good angels don't come from hell, do they? And surely she was a good angel for you, was she not?"

"I committed sexual sins with her!" I wanted to disagree with this intolerably merry man.

"We must denounce sins of the flesh for many and good reasons, my dear." Again the dismissive wave. "But I do not think God was very angry at either of you. You both were young, you were lonely, you needed affection and love; God had other goals for you both, surely he was tolerant of what almost inevitably had to happen in pursuit of those goals. He delights, to tell you the truth, my dear, in using crooked lines, even very crooked lines, to draw straight."

"What picture is he drawing for me?" I demanded hotly.

"Who is to say, my very dear one, who is to say?"

"What happened out there, Father?" I felt myself slump back in my straight-backed wooden chair (also standard Jesuit medieval-torture issue). "What the hell happened?"

"Before I entered the Society, my dear," he said as he put his hands behind his head expansively, "I was trained as a physicist. As a philosopher and now a theologian I have always had some slight interest in these diverting little events. So other members of the Society from other provinces and occasionally even a prelate of the Church will consult with me on such phenomena."

"We're not the only ones it happened to?" I was disappointed, to tell you the truth.

"You know Hamlet? More things under heaven, Horatio, than your philosophy dreams of? We live, my dear child, in a universe filled with wonder. My colleagues in physics are now ready to admit that ours is a mysterious and open cosmos which we will never completely understand. The more we know about it, the more we know that we don't know. You and your Maggie share acute perceptive faculties, you were both under enormous strain because of recent events in your life, you stumbled into a place where there were powerful, what shall I say, residual traces of evil. You did battle with that evil. Perhaps you did not win completely, but surely you did not lose."

"No," I said firmly. "They didn't beat us."

"So you may have to fight them again, more likely in this world than the world of imagination, which is also a real world, my dear."

"I'm kind of dizzy by now, Father. I don't think there are many men who would believe my story."

"Well." He beamed enthusiastically. "I did not sprinkle you with holy water, like that poor Irishman, did I? They drink too much, you know."

I was prepared to forgive him his stolid German bigotry.

"You know of other people to whom this has happened?" I still couldn't accept the fact that we were not unique, a fact that was now encouraging.

"That is why I did not sprinkle you with holy water. Yours is a most reward—most interesting case, but, my dear, the forces of good and evil which lurk in our cosmos, of construction and destruction, are locked in combat, in a war in heaven." He scribbled on another sheet of paper. "Always we are involved in that war, on some rare moments of peril and grace, much more explicitly than is normal."

"I see." My heart was pounding. This dialogue would be written down during the next conference. It was too good to miss.

"This is the name of an English author, unfortunately too little known in our country. He has written a novel called *War in Heaven* which you might find helpful."

The name on the paper was "Charles Williams." He is still too little known.

"Should I keep on searching for her, Father?" I asked at the door of the small, stark office.

He shook my hand energetically in his massive Teutonic

paw. "I should perhaps advise you, my dear, to forget her and get on with your life." He smiled as if blessing me. "I know that such advice is futile and perhaps even incorrect. You will never stop searching for your Maggie Ward. She is a suggestion of another world, a touch of the numinous, the wonderful, the surprising. One never forgets such hints of grace as long as one has a hunger for the numinous. No, you will always search for her."

Maggie Ward as grace, how about that!

For a moment I could imagine him with wings, a five-star admiral's uniform, and a BAR cradled in his arms.

Even in 1946 the Church and the Jesuits were not nearly so rigid as many of us thought. A complex, faintly daffy man like Father Donniger could be an angel of freedom for a haunted young man—even if he could not promise that the haunting would ever end.

In the next few days I devoured the books of Herbert Thurston, S.J., and Charles Williams. I found that there was a reasonable explanation, as outlined by Father Donniger, for what had happened in the Superstition Mountains. Reasonable, if not altogether rational.

My pain over the loss of my Maggie did not abate, but now it did not seem a lunatic pain.

The retreat master's words on tenderness caused me to be more tender and hence more passionate with Kate.

His words on the continuing search for Maggie Ward caused me to accept her decision to break up.

On Sunday, December 8, 1946, I went to Mass and received Holy Communion for the first time in two years, much to the delight of my parents and my siblings. I had already started to turn my dialogues into little stories.

The week before, as I found out the next morning, when I came down off my retreat high, the Cardinals had beaten the Bears 35-28.

December 15 would be the playoff with the hated New York Giants. It would be a day which, for many reasons, I would never forget.

CHAPTER 32

THE WEEK BEFORE THE BEARS PLAYED THE GIANTS, I SAW Maggie Ward in a snowstorm on Maxwell Street.

Maxwell Street was what we would call today a flea market in the heart of the first West Side Jewish "ghetto" (described a little later in the sociological classic by Louis Wirth), a middle-eastern bazaar a few blocks west of the Loop. You could buy almost anything your heart desired—clothing, food, jewelry, furniture, appliances—in its wood and canvas sheds and on top of upturned wooden crates on the curbs and in the gutters. The only provision was that a buyer must be prepared to haggle over the price with the seller, often a frail old man in a battered cap that made him look a little bit like an ancient Leon Trotsky. You would ruin a bearded Maxwell Street merchant's day if you accepted his asking price. The hard-fought bargain was the heartbeat of Maxwell Street life.

I could afford to buy my clothes at Marshall Field's or order them made to my specifications from a tailor. Neither was nearly as much fun as a couple of hours of glorious haggling with the shrewd old merchants of Maxwell Street, whose beards and accents I often suspect were carefully maintained as essential components of the game.

I had decided in early December that my clothes were not "funky" enough, as my kids would have said. The appropriate style for a vet was GI surplus—khaki slacks, an "Ike" jacket with an insignia from another outfit, a fatigue shirt, combat boots, and maybe a Wehrmacht great coat for the winter.

My San Diego civilian sport clothes were distinctly unfashionable.

I argued with CIC that it was all right to accept the fashion self-consciously as long as I bought my new apparel on Maxwell Street. He did not dispute the point.

I found everything I wanted on that December day with

thick snow flurries and an ominous gray-white sky that threatened blizzard. I hoped it would be a fierce storm because I hadn't seen a good Chicago blizzard in three years.

When the flurries finally turned into a storm, I was trudging away from Maxwell Street on the already slippery sidewalks, my treasured new garments draped over my arms—you expect gift wrapping, maybe? I was not quite certain where I had left Roxinante. I finally found her on Halsted Street. Just as I was unlocking the door, I saw the woman, waiting to board a Halsted streetcar, at the corner a quarter block away.

I tossed my purchases into the backseat of Roxy and ran to the corner, knowing in the back of my head that I was playing games with myself, just as I had in my wild race around the West in August.

I reached the red car as it began to move, grabbed the handle on the running board, and pulled myself up to the platform. My heedless momentum pushed several elderly Polish and Jewish women shoppers into the conductor, who dropped a handful of dimes he was putting in his money changer on the wet platform. (Fare was seven cents at the time.)

"You'd think he was chasing a girl," a Jewish woman remarked to a Polish woman.

"Ain't it?" the other replied.

"Her name is Maggie," I told both of them with what I hoped was my most pleasing smile.

"So why shouldn't a young man chase a girl?"

"Ain't it?"

I apologized to the irate women, picked up the dimes, apologized to the furious conductor, paid my own fare and, feeling like the proverbial bull in a china shop, shoved myself into the main section of the crowded car and toward the motorman's platform in the front.

There were only three young women in the whole packed mass of humanity, one of them remarkably attractive with a round face, high cheekbones, Slavic fashion. She smiled, more in amusement than in offense, at my intense stare.

"I'm sorry," I mumbled.

"Not the right one?"

"Worse luck for me."

She laughed, but, virtuous young person that she was, she turned her head to inspect the blanket of snow that God was dropping on our city.

I got off the front of the car at the next stop and fought my way through the wind and the stinging back to Roxy. I'd made a fool out of myself. Worse than that, I knew I was making a fool out of myself when I was doing it.

All my life I would pursue her, Father Donniger had said.

Twenty-five years from now would I still imagine that I saw her in, say, the Piazza di San Marco in Venice?

I started my Chevy and told myself that the only thing worse that could happen would be for the Bears to lose to the Giants on Sunday.

It was not an especially good year for Chicago sports fans. The Cubs had gone into the first phase of their half-century tailspin. Notre Dame had achieved nothing more than a 0–0 tie in its first attempt at revenge against Army for its wartime humiliations by the service academies. Ray Meyer was trying to put De Paul together after the loss through graduation of George Mikan. Mikan in his turn was trying to break his contract with the Bears so he could join the Minneapolis Lakers (ever wonder, young folk, where the LA franchise got its name?). The Hawks were not much. The Cardinals had beaten the Bears, but they weren't worth much either, although they had great young talent and rumor was it that Charley Trippi would play for them next year. (And the Cards, known happily in the precincts of Comiskey Park as The Big Red, would field the greatest backfield ever—Trippi, Elmer Angsman, Pat Harder, and Paul Chrisman—and win their only championship.)

The Illinois basketball team, called the Whiz Kids when as five freshman they had won the championship, were back but their fire was gone. The Chicago Rockets in the new All America Conference—engineered by the sports editor of the *Tribune*—were both an athletic and financial disaster. The new conference had, however, skimmed off some of the best talent of the prewar Bears on whom age and service had also taken their toll. We had easily won the Western Division, but the Giants had robbed us of championships at other times, most notably in the famous Gym Shoe Game of 1934 (after a 13-0 season).

It was a lot easier to worry about Sid Luckman's passes than to worry about making a fool of myself on another streetcar.

The All America Conference, dominated in its brief existence by the Cleveland Browns with Otto Graham's passing arm and Lou Groza's toe, was a flop. The Browns, the Forty Niners, and the Dallas Colts were absorbed into the NFL (the last, who had been the New York Yanks and the Boston Yanks, would later become the Baltimore Colts and finally, in total ignominy, the Indianapolis Colts.)

The world struggled on, unpromisingly. Europe was in desperate financial trouble. Communism was threatening Greece and Turkey. Phil Murray had been re-elected president of the CIO, but a Communist faction led by general counsel Lee Pressman dominated the board. There was a brief leftist general strike in the San Francisco Bay area. The Baruch Plan for international control of all atomic weapons was rejected by the Russians. *Ma Perkins*, the last of the Chicago radio soaps, decamped, like Phil Donahue forty years later, for New York. General Marshall had returned from his failed peace mission in China. Rumors persisted that Harry Truman was about to resign and turn the country over to the Republicans. In the State Department, Dean Acheson was preparing memos that in February would lead to the Marshall Plan for the financial salvation of Europe and the Truman Doctrine for the defense of Greece and Turkey—twin schemes that would save Europe but make the Cold War official. The travel sections described how you could spend a week in Miami on ten dollars a day. Walter Winchell sounded more glum each Sunday night before the *Dear John* radio program. You could fly to New York for $32 on United Airlines, which would also deliver airmail editions of *The New York Times* to you every morning. The *Times* had just revealed that many German rocket scientists had secretly been spirited out of Europe and were working on American projects, including one Werner von Braun. Princess Elizabeth was reported to be "virtually" engaged to some Greek Prince—and down the drain went my chances to be Prince Consort in England!

Finally—some things never change—the Celtics were dominating professional basketball.

A picture on the front page of every paper in the country summed up the mood of the nation: a grimly determined woman standing in front of a bus, staring down an angry bus driver. He had slammed the door in her face. Like everyone who ever experienced such rudeness from public transit, she felt the impulse to stop the bus from moving. Unlike the rest of us, she acted on the impulse, walked in front of the bus and refused to move unless the driver opened the door. Neither would give in. The standoff lasted for hours, till the bus driver was replaced and the woman, name unknown but a national heroine, stalked away.

Irritable times to be haunted by the memory of a pretty young woman whose picture I stared at, door to my room locked to fend off Packy, every day.

I hadn't started to think about Christmas shopping; law school was insufferably dull; baiting Hennessey was no longer fun; I missed Kate only a week after breaking up.

What was there left besides the Bears?

Pro teams in those days carried only thirty-three players. Center Bulldog Turner played linebacker on defense, quarterback Sid Luckman and halfback George "One-Play" McAfee played safety on defense. At the end of an eleven-game season in mid-December they were all pretty battered. How could we possibly win? Especially in cold weather?

The weather turned mild, the snow melted, and win we did, not gloriously but effectively, 24–14. The key play was a touchdown run by Luckman—the last of the Jewish quarterbacks—called "twenty-two bingo keep it." Today we'd describe it as a quarterback draw.

So the Bears began their downward slide, winning only one more championship (also against the Giants) until a crazy, complex, courageous Mick named Jim McMahon emerged

forty years later, our first effective quarterback since Luckman.

After the game I turned off the radio in my room and
settled down to the stack of mail—I was carrying on a cor-
respondence with many of the men in my squadron and with
the widows and parents of some of those who had died. Because I was the "old man," I was supposed to be a source of
wisdom. I would let the mail pile up for a week and then
organize myself for the agony of replies. On Saturday I had
opened the envelopes and stacked the folded letters in a neat
little pile. I then threw away any envelope that didn't have a
return address, lifted my small Underwood portable to my
rolltop desk, and began work on the first letter.

I had typed responses to the first two letters, opened the
neatly folded third item on my stack, and stared in astonishment at its contents.

I must have gazed at it a long time. Later, when Packy
bounded in from a pre-Christmas choir practice at Quigley,
he found me holding an unmarked sheet of lined notepaper
in one hand.

And eleven ten-dollar bills in the other hand.

CHAPTER **33**

"THERE'S ELEVEN BILLS HERE." PACKY HELD UP THE MONEY.
"Your ghost girl pays interest."

I had told him the whole story of Andrea/Maggie, leaving
out only the details of our lovemaking—lest I shock his youthful, seminarian ideals. Or make him think less of Maggie.

"I prayed at her grave," I muttered, still overwhelmed.

"She does look a little ghostly, to tell the truth," he said as he picked up the enlargement I had made of the slide, "but gorgeous ghostly. And you slept with her . . . as I said, bro, you astonish me! Make me kind of envious too."

"You're going to be a priest!"

"Doesn't mean I give up fantasies." He turned the picture to consider Maggie's misty bare shoulders from another angle. "Well, I suppose we have to find her, right?"

"We can't find her, Pack," I said wearily, schoolmaster to slightly retarded student. "I told you she's dead."

"Ghosts don't return loans"—he waved the money at me—"with interest; loan-shark rates, too. Let me see . . . you gave her the money in August, no, she took it from you in August, this is December, four months . . . that's forty percent per annum. You ought to be ashamed, bro"—he laid the money respectfully on my rolltop—"of exploiting the poor kid. Think of how many houses she had to haunt to make that money."

"She's probably a waitress somewhere."

"A haunted restaurant? I can see the ads: 'Ghoulish Goulash, served by the prettiest ghost girls this side of Transylvania. Bring your own garlic.' "

"Packy, it is not funny," I said, but I was laughing too. "I prayed at her grave."

"Someone benefited by your prayers, but not Maggie or Andrea or whatever her name is. I think I'll picture her as Maggie, you wouldn't fall so heavily for an Andrea. . . ."

"I did."

"Only because she looked like a Maggie." He considered the enlargement again. "A spectacular Maggie at that. No wonder Kate couldn't hold your attention."

"She's dead, Packy. She's haunting me."

"Baloney." He shook his head impatiently. "I don't care what happened in those weird mountains or what grave you prayed at, these worn ten-dollar bills are as solid as gold, even with inflation. She's alive somewhere and findable. What's the postmark on the envelope?"

"Postmark?" I tried to focus my attention. . . . If Maggie really were alive . . .

"Sure." Packy snorted impatiently. "Every letter mailed in the United States has the name of the post office from which it is sent, usually smeared and almost illegible, but we'll make it legible and start searching there."

"And I'm Don Quixote!"

"Shape up, sailor. Where's the damn envelope?"

"I threw it away." I rose from my desk chair, still disoriented and confused but beginning to hope.

"You did what?"

"I didn't notice the money till today. I tossed the envelope in my wastebasket"—I searched frantically under the desk for the wire basket—"yesterday afternoon."

Empty.

"You know Mom, a wastebasket with waste in it is as bad as an idle mind—both are the devil's workshop. I suppose you didn't notice the postmark."

"I didn't pay any attention. . . ."

"Well." Packy leapt enthusiastically to his feet. "The garbage pickup isn't till tomorrow morning. Let's go out back and find her envelope." He glanced at the notepaper. "It'll be cheap stationery, she's obviously been saving her nickels and dimes to pay you. More and more do I like this Maggie Ward. She's certainly too good for you, bro."

He rushed out of my room and banged down the stairs, like the overgrown adolescent ox he was. I straggled along after him, not caught up yet in his enthusiasm and not sure even that I wanted to renew my madcap pursuit of the elusive Maggie.

Still, I joined Packy in the chill, damp mid-December dusk as we hunted for an envelope that may have been mailed from beyond the tomb but had also certainly been sent through the United States Mail.

We had no trouble finding my little stack of white, beige, or red-and-blue-trimmed, 5-cent airmail envelopes. But none of them seemed to be from Maggie. I rushed back into the house to find the letters so we could match them.

"Bring a flashlight," Packy yelled after me.

"Whatever are you and your brother doing out there in

the garbage can?" my mother asked hazily as I ransacked the kitchen for a flashlight with batteries that worked.

"An envelope from a ghost."

"Oh." She considered my reply judiciously, spatula dipped in cake frosting in her hand. "Well, wear a jacket, don't catch cold."

I grabbed my Ike jacket and Packy's Quigley basketball jacket and flashlight and, letters stuffed in my pockets, raced back to the alley. The adrenaline was pumping in my blood now. Packy's enthusiasm had infected me. The chase was on.

"Hurry up, Don Quixote," Packy demanded as I rejoined him, "the game's afoot and we haven't a second to lose."

"Wrong book."

"I'm not so sure." He began to sort the letters and the envelopes into matching piles. "You better do this, Jer. I don't know these people."

It took a few minutes. Every letter was matched with an envelope. Left over was Maggie's little piece of lined note paper.

"Damn the bitch," I shouted, "she's taken the envelope back."

"Great." Packy pounded me on the back. "You're entitled to be angry. But in River Forest we don't permit ghosts, and certainly not in our garbage cans. Did you tear it up, by any chance?"

"I might have." I tried to remember, shivering now from the cold. "I don't usually . . ."

"Let's look for scraps of white paper." He shoved the flashlight at me. "You hold this and I'll go through the mess again."

"I'm not sure that it's worth it." The beam of light was shaking as my hand trembled in the cold. The weather forecast said the temperature would drop to zero tonight. It was already dropping.

"Hold the damn thing still." Packy was arranging several pieces of paper like a jigsaw puzzle. "This look like it?"

It was the right size and had the right feel. "I think so."

"Now to find the postmark. I hope you didn't tear it in half. Where the hell is it?"

We dug back into the heap of garbage searching for a few scraps of white envelope paper.

"I think this might be . . ." I held up a tattered bit of white.

"Aha." Packy grabbed the scrap and my flashlight. "Oh my God! Look at this!"

The light was shaking in his hand too. But while the substation number was illegible, there was no doubt about the rest of the postmark:

December 13, 1946. Chicago, Illinois.

CHAPTER

"WE MUST GO ABOUT THIS SYSTEMATICALLY, WATSON." Packy, who was enjoying himself altogether too much, it seemed to me, was seated at my rolltop, pencil in hand. "The girl has class, you say, despite her dime-store stationery. She has some experience waiting on tables. She works in elegant places like the Del Coronado and the Beverly Hills, so the first spots to investigate in Chicago are the quality restaurants in the best hotels—Pump Room, Empire Room, Boulevard Room, Beach Walk—and the top nightclubs—Chez Paree, College Inn, Rio Cabana, Latin Quarter, Vine Gardens, maybe even the Trianon and the Aragon. Would she maybe be a Chez Paree adorable?"

"She's supposed to have a wonderful singing voice, but I can't see her dancing in skimpy clothes."

Pack glanced at my photo, which I had made from the

slide, from which he had a hard time averting his eyes. "I won't contend the point," he said with a wink. "But I suppose we can write off the Silver Palm and the 606 Club."

He tapped his pencil thoughtfully. "Why do you think she chose Chicago?"

"Because she is a clever little bitch." I wanted to see her again, but I was very angry at her. "Right under my own eyes is the last place I'd look."

"And yet she'd be close to you."

"I guess I'd like to think that's part of it." I buried my face in my hands. Why had I ever become involved with the tiresome little wench?

"If she's that clever," Packy continued, so consumed by the excitement of playing detective that he was oblivious to my ambivalence, "she'd probably avoid the places where you might show up with a date—College Inn, Chez Paree, Aragon. We'll try the hotels first."

"A wig, glasses, makeup—she never wore it—might fool me if I wasn't looking for her."

"Is she that smart?"

"Very smart. And very scared. And, I guess, very confused."

"How old did you say she was?" Packy picked up the photo.

"Eighteen, and, Packy, stop ogling that picture. She's my girl."

He thought that was an outrageously funny remark. "Finders keepers, bro." He turned the picture over, face down. "But I'm only looking for a sister-in-law to take care of you when I go off to the Big House next September."

He grimaced, not liking the prospect of the seminary at Mundelein at all. With good reason.

"I wonder if the family will like her," I mused, still not quite ready to organize the search. Or rather, to listen to Packy's plan for organization.

He turned over the photo. "She's crowded a lot of living into eighteen years, hasn't she?"

I nodded. "A lot of tragedy."

"They'll like her," he said confidently. "She's Irish, she's Catholic. . . ." He hesitated. "My God, Jer, she is a Democrat, isn't she?"

"I didn't think to ask . . . probably. She must be."

"You didn't ask?" My brother stared at me in disbelief.

"I don't think so."

"You certainly must have been in love!"

So Quixote and Sancho began their pursuit of Dulcinea in the bitter December cold before Christmas of 1946.

Or maybe it was Holmes and Watson in pursuit of the game that was afoot.

Dad was puzzled about this sudden joint social life of his two sons, but he only let us know that he had noted it. Mom observed that wasn't it nice that the two boys were getting to be friends again.

We tilted at all the windmills in the Loop and the Near North Side (as Tower Town was now being called) in search for the dubious Dulcinea.

We were sorting through a haystack. Suppose that, for example, the day we sortied to Chez Paree on Fairbanks Court between Michigan Avenue and the Lake, and listened to Sophie Tucker and Bobbie Breen, it was Maggie's day off. Or suppose that she had decided not to be a waitress. Or suppose she had been passing through Chicago when she mailed the eleven ten-dollar bills—paying loan-shark rates, as Packy had commented. Or suppose she was working in a suburban speakeasy turned gambling resort.

Suppose a hundred other possibilities. Once you're on the chase, it becomes an end in itself.

Our technique varied. Usually Packy was the advance scout, peering into the restaurant or the nightclub over the maître d's head in search for a plausible Dulcinea. He would then report to me in the lobby or outside in the bitter cold where I would be waiting. If there was someone inside who might be Maggie, we would bribe the maître d' to find us a table and investigate more closely. At the Pump Room of the Ambassador East, I actually called the young woman with the crisp auburn halo "Maggie" and made her very angry indeed.

Packy cooked up a wonderfully sad story about a woman lost in the war to win her over to our side.

We listened to the music of Dick Jurgens, Art Kassel, Lawrence Welk, Ted Mills, and even Sol Perola at Colosimo's, the Outfit joint out on South Wabash where I was sure Maggie would not work more than one day.

"Who knows what a young woman on the run would do?" Packy enjoyed the revue at Colosimo's more than I thought a seminarian should.

We listened to swing, jazz, and even waltz music. We met some pretty and friendly girls, with whom Pack was very cautious, as a seminarian ought to be.

"I'd get thrown out if the rector knew I was here." He dismissed his caution with an easy laugh. "Talking with a girl would mean excommunication reserved personally to the Pope."

A couple of the young women would have been interesting date and even courtship material, if I were not chasing and being chased by a will-o'-the-wisp.

"Why do you shut up when they try to be friendly?" I asked my brother.

"I don't want to pretend to be anything I'm not. Strictly off limits for those whose proximate goal, as we say in philosophy class, is husband, home, and family."

"Fair enough."

I hate to confess it, but we had a great time on our search. Good music, presentable entertainment, pleasant companions, the excitement of a quest with a brother whom you admire. The only problem for Quixote and Sancho was that we did not find Dulcinea.

We even investigated, very briefly at Packy's insistence, the Silver Palm. "It would be a perfect hideout," he argued.

He was disgusted by the show. I—God and the Feminist Movement forgive me—was both repelled and attracted.

None of the admittedly lovely young women, I insisted in my head, was as beautiful as my Maggie.

They were not, however, ugly.

"Let's get out of here," my brother insisted after the first number. "I think those poor kids are being used."

"By their own choice, but okay. I told you Maggie wouldn't be in a place like this."

"Let's try Ireland's," he suggested.

Ireland's was a steak house more or less around the corner on Broadway, a legendary steak house, I would add, for a long, long time.

"That's not a bad idea." I rose from the table with him. "It's classy and yet not on the beaten path exactly."

There were more nightclubs in Chicago in those days because there was no TV. And fewer restaurants because not very many people could afford to eat out often and because the pleasures of expense account living had yet to be invented.

We both demolished mammoth steaks, drank a couple of beers (not strictly legal for my brother, but he was rarely carded), enjoyed discussing the prospects for our various teams next year, and had another entertaining evening.

But no Dulcinea.

So, despite the alluring images from the Silver Palm that continued to swirl in my head, we returned home to River Forest the Saturday night after the Bears victory discouraged.

"As I said, Pack"—we were sprawled in his room, drinking yet another beer—"we're in the haystack. What if she was passing through on a train, remembered me, and threw the money in an envelope?"

"And just happened to have the right address?"

"Suburban phone book."

"What if"—he sucked on his beer bottle, no cans then—"what if it really is money from the 'other side'?"

"That's always a possibility. Remember what Father Donniger said."

"In principle." He set the bottle down on top of his Greek dictionary. "That's always a possibility, a final duty required by Saint Peter before she gets in the front door."

"Or the Blessed Mother before she gets in the back door."

"That girl is not the back-door type . . . oh, damn!" He

jumped up enthusiastically. "We made a terrible mistake! We forgot the most obvious place of all!"

"What's that?" All I wanted to do was to finish my beer, go to bed, and dream of the lovelies from the Silver Palm.

"The Camellia Room at the Drake!"

"Sweet-sixteen parties and golden-wedding anniversaries?"

"What better place for our Maggie? No passes, classy clientcle, pleasant if dull setting, and little chance to find a single war veteran, under thirty anyway, sitting at your table. And they hire attractive young women who look like they're finishing their college courses. Ideal! Lemme think. Yeah, they do serve late breakfast on Sunday mornings. Let's give it a whirl! Eight o'clock Mass at Saint Luke's, then we whip down Chicago Avenue and pretend we are really high-class tourists. Wear a tie, bro, and no Ike jacket or Wehrmacht coat."

He dashed to the phone, dialed a call and carried on a conversation with someone at the Drake Hotel.

"No waitresses? Are you sure? Only men? Even during the war? But . . . yeah, I see." He hung up. "Damn!"

"No waitresses at the Camellia Room?"

"I guess they'd defile the black and white tiles and the fake camellia trees. . . . I have the feeling Alexander Dumas would not be amused."

"Alexander who?"

"Dumas. Fils, of course. The illegitimate son of Dumas pére. The Frenchman who wrote the book *La Dame aux Camélias*. You know, the book on which *La Traviata* is based. Hey, is this broad literate?"

"To put it mildly."

"Well, that's good. Anyway, I'm frustrated. That would have been the perfect place for her . . . our own little Lady of the Camellias."

"She likes operas," I said.

"Yeah. Well, that won't help us find her. . . . Wait a minute. I have an idea. I bet she's in the Lantern Room, right next door. That's a classy place too. Then she gets first shot at the

Camellia Room, when they let waitresses in. Okay. I know they have a late breakfast too. It figures."

It didn't figure at all. It was rather a wild shot in the dark. I protested that I wanted to sleep late, but Sancho would hear none of it.

"Get thee to bed, the game's afoot and we need our sleep!"

I protested weakly against this mixture of literary references but did indeed get me to bed. And dreamed not of the girls of the Silver Palm but of Maggie Ward.

Dressed like a girl at the Silver Palm.

My nightmares seemed to have been left behind at Superstition Mountain. I couldn't quite remember when they had stopped; but apparently, save for occasional reruns when, to tell the truth, too much of the drink had been taken, my war dreams had submerged. For the moment.

"The drink being taken," as anyone who is Irish knows well, is more than a couple of beers. My wife contends that it rarely happens with me, not because of any inherent virtue but because I fall asleep.

The sermon at Saint Luke's the next morning was about "being home for Christmas"; the priest welcomed home all the vets who had not been home last year and reminded us that at Christmas home was wherever love was.

A proposition with which I was fully prepared to agree that morning. My reluctance to charge the windmill at the Lantern Room had been swept away by a great tidal wave of hope. Maggie Ward would be home for Christmas, I was convinced. Home meant River Forest.

Where, I told myself, she belonged.

Hope does not mean certainty; every other minute I doubted the common sense of the hope of the previous minute. As I drove carefully down slippery Chicago Avenue, dodging around the occasional poky streetcar, I hid my enthusiasm from Packy behind a mask of pretended sleepiness.

He was not fooled.

"This is going to be it, bro; she'll be there. A Maggie Ward belongs at the Lantern Room, in the middle of all that pink and green and the nice old ladies and the wide-eyed tourists and the giggly high school girls."

"There aren't many tourists a couple of days before Christmas," I said with a pretense at sourness.

We parked in the lot where the John Hancock Center is now and hiked down Michigan Avenue against the north wind to the Drake. The Magnificent Mile was not magnificent yet. State Street was still "that great street." North Michigan was still a kind of a gap between the Loop and the Gold Coast. Before the Bridge was built in 1920, Pine Street, as it was then called, was a neighborhood of breweries and soap factories. Then, after the Bridge was opened, it began to expand slowly with the construction of the Wrigley Building and Tribune Tower, which stood as sentinels on the riverbank. At the north end the Drake and the Palmolive Building (with its Palmolive beacon designed to guide planes across the Lake—the Lindbergh beacon before he became identified with the political right) told you that you had arrived at the Gold Coast. In between there were a few hotels that did not compare with the Palmer House or the Stevens, but were useful for proms, one- and two-story buildings with shops that were beginning to be fashionable, parking lots, the Fourth Presbyterian Church, and an occasional apartment building, like the gracious old queen mother, 900 North Michigan.

Cardinal Stritch could have bought the block east of Quigley Seminary just before the war for a hundred thousand dollars. In 1946, Saks Fifth Avenue opened a shop in what had been a record store on that site and is now the Crate and Barrel. The Magnificent Mile had begun, as anyone who thought the Depression might not last forever would have guessed.

Even now the Drake is a stately old hotel, not at all a place to be ashamed to admit is your Chicago address, despite the proliferation of luxury neighbors all around—Mayfair Regent, Ritz-Carlton, Tremont, Whitehall, and soon Four Seasons. It was, as I pointed out to my wife on our wedding night as we rode up to our suite, the only hotel I knew that had couches in its elevators. She wondered if that was a suggestive remark. We laughed at that comment all the way to our door.

If it was not on our list of windmills in 1946, the reason was that it was a bit too formal and stiff for the youthful trade, the unmarried young men and women and perhaps the recently married, who would soon spill over from the Loop into the new night-life district that was beginning to take shape on Rush Street.

Perhaps you looked forward to living in an apartment in the Drake when you retired. You might entertain important guests from out of town there. You might bring your family for supper there on special occasions, particularly when the children were partially civilized, so they could experience a touch of gracious living. You might well spend your wedding night there—as my wife and I did. But it was not a place you went to be entertained.

Packy and I ducked in out of the cold through the Walton Street entrance, checked our overcoats and climbed up the stairs to the massive oak-beamed lobby, which always seemed to me to be ready for the arrival of the Queen Empress. Today it was the Queen Empress at Christmas: the lobby was festooned with wreaths, colored lights, and a massive Christmas tree.

Humbug, I thought bitterly to myself—I was in the unhopeful minute.

"Come on," Packy urged me. "It's exactly the same food as the Camellia Room and you get a view of Michigan Avenue. And they have waitresses, pretty young ones, as I remember."

"You go in and check it out," I told him.

"What are you going to do for breakfast?"

"I'm not hungry. She's not there, I feel it in my bones. Check it out, then come back and we'll go over to the Pearson or some less elaborate place and have a cup of coffee and a piece of toast."

"With jam?"

"Don't be an idiot! Now check it out."

"All right, all right. These jobs can't be rushed."

Packy disappeared into the refined pastels of the Lantern Room in which soft music from a violin and a piano mingled with the discreet clinking of silverware and china.

I found a comfortable chair at the other end of the lobby and resolved to sleep for a few minutes. I closed my eyes, but my heart was thrashing away too rapidly for me to keep my eyes shut, much less snooze.

Packy stayed in the Lantern Room for at least a thousand years.

The bastard was eating breakfast.

Finally he emerged, all six feet four inches of handsome, virile blond. With a grin on his face as wide as Lake Michigan.

He glanced around the lobby, searching for me. Then he caught my eye and lifted his thumb upward in a sign of victory.

It can't be true.

"She is even more beautiful in person," he raved, "than in your picture, even if she is fully dressed. You think at first, well, she's okay, pretty even, but nothing to brag about. Bring her home to Mother for Sunday dinner, fine, but don't boast to the guys at the corner about her. Then you take another look and you know you're watching undiluted radiance."

"How do you know it's Maggie?" I demanded frantically.

"Huh?" He seemed surprised at my question. "Oh, that's easy. I asked her what her name was. Sure enough, it's Maggie."

CHAPTER **35**

"Let's get out of here." I turned and walked rapidly, no, ran toward the steps to the lower lobby.

"What?" Packy trailed behind me, Sancho dragging the unwanted lance.

"I don't want her to see me." I ran down the steps, jumped in front of an elderly man, and plunked our checks and a dollar bill—a massive tip in those days—in front of the hat-check girl.

"I don't think she will rush out of the Drake, to tell you the truth." Sancho was decidedly in no hurry.

"I'm taking no chances." I tossed him his coat and slung mine over my shoulders. "Let's hurry."

Outside, the wind howling at our backs, I searched for the question that had been hammering at my brain and found it again.

"How did you find out her name?"

"That was easy." Sancho/Sherlock was rushing to keep up with me. "I spotted her as soon as I entered the room. You could hardly miss her. She seemed to be working the tables by the window, overlooking Michigan Avenue—that's where you put your best waitress—and so I saw a family leaving a table and I asked if I could have it because I liked to watch people walking against the wind and the hostess thought I was kind of funny and so I got the table."

"And?" We were already at the parking lot.

"And this lovely young thing smiled at me and said good morning and asked what I wanted. I said orange juice, pancakes with maple syrup and bacon—two helpings—and tea."

"While I'm starving."

"But Watson," he protested as he jumped into the car. "Quick, turn on the heat. As I was saying, Watson, the game was not only afoot. She was right there. So she brings me my tea and I smile politely, not flirtatiously, mind you, and thank her and she smiles again."

"I bet not flirtatiously." I used too much choke on Roxy who, in protest, refused to start.

"So she does an excellent job of feeding me my breakfast and I smile again and ask her if her name is Patricia Anne. She blushes a little—boy, her skin is pale, isn't it? But she's luminous when she blushes. And she says I'm miles away. I say that I like to try to link up Irish-American names with Irish-American faces and would I win a bet with Mary Louise."

"Saints preserve us, as Mom would say."

"Well, they may have to from that young woman. She

blushes even more and says maybe I'm getting a little closer. I have one of the two names right. So I try Mary Anne and am rewarded with a laugh, a happy-enough laugh, though her eyes looked tired. Okay, says I, what about Mary Margaret?"

"Is she being taken in by this?"

"Mostly. When she comes up to the table for the first time, she looks at me kind of dubiously like she has seen me before. But by the time we're playing the name game, she's convinced I'm far too handsome and charming to be any relation to this drip Jerry Keenan . . . try the car again."

Roxy, as cold as we were, decided it was time to get out of the lake winds. We chugged dubiously down Michigan Avenue and turned right onto Chicago Avenue.

"She tells me I'm doing pretty well but I have the names in the wrong order. I leap in and say, right, Margaret Mary, Peggy for short. She is horrified. She hates the name Peggy, it is so common. No, she's Maggie. I observed that it's a very pretty name and certainly not common in Chicago as far as I know save in the *Herald Examiner* comics, but I thought it was a common name in Brooklyn. Now she pretends to be really hurt. Brooklyn, she insists, is a VERY common place. Boston, I guess. Not at all. Nose slightly up in the air—we're enjoying the fun now—Philadelphia!"

"Brilliant, Holmes."

"Elementary, Watson. Now would you please turn on the heater?"

"All right, all right." I wasn't at all cold. "How did she seem?"

Packy considered carefully. "When she was serving me she was, how to put it, 'professional' I guess is the word—friendly, hiding behind a mask. Then, when we began to joke, she became very animated, the kind of woman you'd want to pick up and carry out with you."

"*You* would." I skidded to a stop in front of a red light at Halsted.

"Nope. Anyone would. Then, when I said good-bye and left, I stole a fast look at her eyes. Sad, lonely, haunted. God knows with reason. But . . ." He hesitated, drummed his fingers on the ice-coated window on his side of the front seat, and spoke very slowly, "But, Jerry, she's no ghost. She's alive and she wants to live."

"She said that to me at the Arizona Inn."

"Why the quick getaway?"

"I have to figure out what I should do."

"Bring her home for Christmas. I bet she has nowhere to spend the day."

Wasn't that what I planned to do?

"I don't want to make any mistakes."

"It's not my game, but I thought mistakes were inevitable."

"I've fouled up before with her. I have to figure out what comes next."

"Sancho only carries the lances, his is not to reason why. But you've been searching for this glorious dame since August; you find her, and then you run."

"Damn it, Pack, I said I have to plan my tactics."

"It's hesitant tactics like that which almost lost the war for us, Commander. What has happened to those good old navy instincts?"

I had to admit it was a fair question.

Loyola was closed for Christmas vacation. I should have been studying for exams. Instead I thought about Maggie all day Monday, December 23, carefully, shrewdly, dispassionately. What had happened to my instincts was an inexcusable misinterpretation of Father Donniger. Maggie was still in pain. I must be careful not to hurt her more.

What I finally did that evening was what I should have done the day before, but it was more carefully planned out and hence inadequate.

About seven-thirty, I looked into Packy's room. He was reading Chesterton's *The Everlasting Man*.

"I'll see you later, Pack."

He glanced up. "No spear-bearer tonight?"

"I don't think so."

"Good luck."

"I may need it."

"I doubt it. If you don't brighten up this house with her on Christmas Day, I may never forgive you."

"I sure as hell intend to try."

I waited in the lobby of the Drake till the restaurant closed, collected my Wehrmacht coat, which, over my pinstripe suit, made me a different person and hung around near the door the help at the Drake used to exit. I pulled my stocking cap down over my ears, partly for disguise, but mostly to keep warm. I waited for several millennia, though my watch said it was only a half hour. Several other young women left the hotel, but I was restrained this time—no staring into astonished faces. I would know Maggie's walk.

And I did. She walked briskly, as the cold demanded, but also as if she were carrying a heavy burden in addition to the small purse and paper shopping bag.

She crossed Michigan on Walton, walked by the 900 North Michigan apartment building and, scarf pulled tightly around her head and thin cloth coat buttoned to the top, hurried through the cold and lonely darkness across Rush and State and Dearborn, around the top of Bughouse (actually Union) Square in the shadow of the Newberry Library to the Clark Street car stop.

I walked twenty or thirty yards behind her, trying to silence the hobnaillike thump of my combat boots on the snow. But Maggie didn't seem to be listening, either because she was too tired or because she had made her peace with the dangers and refused to worry.

It was a long wait for one of the new, streamlined Clark Street cars, which had already been named, not inappropriately, Green Hornets. I huddled in the door of the library, noted that we were again under the light of a full moon, and tried to keep my fingers from falling off.

Maggie reached in her shopping bag, produced a book, and under the streetlight on Clark Street on December 23, no, it was already Christmas Eve, 1946, calmly read while waiting for a Green Hornet.

When the car finally came, she closed the book around

her finger, paid the conductor the required seven cents, walked halfway up the almost empty car, sank wearily into a seat.

I followed her, again noisily and clumsily, sat a couple of seats behind her, and strained my perfectly good aviator's eyes to see what she was reading.

Carlo Levi. *Christ Stopped at Eboli.*

Unquestionably an intellectual. Now if she only proved to be a Democrat.

We got off at North Avenue, crossed the street, and boarded the ancient red streetcar that would branch off from Clark and go up Lincoln. It was much colder inside the car than in the toastywarm Green Hornet.

Maggie was too absorbed in her book to notice the highly suspicious young man who was following her.

There were only two other people in the car—aged cleaning women returning from their jobs in Loop office buildings. I felt sad for them too. But, unlike my Maggie, they probably had families with whom to celebrate Christmas, not merely painful memories.

The car moved rapidly through the winter night. We crossed Halsted, then Fullerton, and chugged by the grounds of McCormick Theological Seminary. Maggie returned Carlo Levi to her shopping bag, walked, a little less briskly, to the front of the car, and spoke to the driver. He stopped at the next corner, Sheffield, just north of Wrightwood. I moved to the center door. Maggie got off and turned automatically up Sheffield. I followed behind her as an Evanston El train roared by on tracks behind the two apartment buildings on our right.

Now the neighborhood is at the heart of near-northwest-side yuppiedom. Then it was a German and Swedish ethnic community, not quite yet picturesque, fading off into the edges of poverty, but still stable and safe, though perhaps not perfectly safe for an eighteen-year-old girl in the early hours of the morning. The northernmost finger of the Chicago fire had reached into the neighborhood, eliminating all but a few of the wooden buildings. The sidewalks were raised later as part of the city's struggle out of the swamp of mud on which it was built, but first floors below ground level and second-floor entrances remained as relics of the swampy days at the turn of the century. Even many of the post-fire stone three-flats with pointed roofs, evidence of the German influence, had second-story entrances.

Then it was an ugly neighborhood, now we think it has character.

Halfway up the block, Maggie turned into a wooden pre-fire three-flat. She climbed up the stairs, opened the second-floor entrance, and went in. That meant she lived on either the second or the third floor. First-floor residents would walk down to the entrance on the old ground level below the sidewalk.

My brain roaring with a noise louder than a thousand El trains, I walked by the house, turned short of the corner of Shubert Avenue by a church which, I noted, was Saint George's Greek Orthodox, returned quickly to her three-flat, and climbed the slippery wooden steps. There were four apartments on the third floor, small, small flats. Next to one of the doorbells, neatly printed, was the name for which I had been searching since August—"M. M. Ward."

I must have hesitated five minutes, shuddering with the cold, before I worked up enough nerve to push the buzzer.

"Yes?" she replied promptly, still wide awake.

"Andrea King?"

Total silence.

"Or should I say Margaret Koenig?"

More silence.

"Would Maggie Ward do?"

"Go away."

"I will not, even if I freeze to death."

"I don't want to talk to you."

"You don't have to talk to me. I must return some money to you."

"Money?"

"I don't take loan-shark rates. You only owe me a dollar and a half interest. I figure I'm entitled to a fifty-cent service charge. So I have eight dollars to return to you. I don't want it on my conscience when I receive Communion at midnight Mass tomorrow. No, tonight."

The buzzer rang.

CHAPTER 36

THE DOOR OPENED SLOWLY, A PIQUANT ELFIN LITTLE FACE peered around the corner, over the chain. When the face saw me it exploded with more joyous light than all the Christmas trees in Chicago put together. I would remember that joy in the disappointments of the next month and for the rest of my life.

Oh yes. Your rating, Michael, Seraph, Wars in Heaven, was right. So was Father Donniger.

Quickly the face turned somber, annoyed, displeased at the interruption.

"Here's your eight dollars, Maggie. Should I call you that?" I asked humbly. "I'm not sure what name to use."

"How did you find me?" She didn't take the eight dollars.

"Postmark on the envelope."

The little-girl face squinted in a skeptical frown.

"The United States government always tells you with a stamp on an envelope from what town or city a letter is mailed."

"Really?" She seemed impressed. "I suppose that terribly good-looking boy is your brother after all."

"He's older than you are."

"He's still a boy," she sniffed.

"You didn't answer my question. What name should I call you?"

The door opened a little more. She was wearing a heavy,

dark-blue chenille robe. "Maggie is my real name. I've given up lying." Guilty pause. "I never used to lie. I'm ashamed of myself for lying to you. Forgive me."

"Sure."

"Your brother is very clever." Her jaw jutted up as contentiousness returned. "It was only afterward I realized how he had tricked me."

"Will you take the money?" I extended my hand to the crack between the door and jamb.

She considered me dubiously. "I suppose you want to come in."

"If I may, but it's not necessary."

"I can't leave you standing out there in the cold. I suppose I could make you a cup of hot chocolate."

"I'm trustworthy, Maggie. Reasonably trustworthy."

"No sex." She opened the door a quarter way. "I've given that up too, just like lying."

"I don't have it on the mind at the moment."

She opened the door all the way and stepped aside to permit me to enter. "I know that." She laughed briefly. "I think I might be more flattered if you had it just a little bit on the mind."

I'd won the first phase of the battle. Tonight the only goal was a promise that she would come to River Forest for Christmas dinner.

Poor little girl child—so lovely, so badly hurt, so confused and uncertain. Proceed slowly and gently, Quixote; this is not a windmill to whack with a broadsword.

Well and good, but still you were a damn fool for not carting her off to River Forest that night.

Underneath the robe, she was wearing heavy pink pajamas to keep warm in the chilly if bravely cheerful cave in which she lived. It was a single room with a small kitchen alcove, and a tiny bathroom without a shower or a tub. An old-fashioned coal heater, converted to gas, occupied one corner of the room; there was a sealed gaslight fixture on the wall. A bed, a table, a dilapidated mohair chair, and a paperboard wardrobe constituted the furniture underneath a ceiling bulb in another old gaslight fixture. Piles of books lined the walls, and a stack of notebooks rested against the chair.

My kids would not believe that such an apartment could exist in Chicago outside the slums, but in the middle 1940s there were tens of thousands of such places without central heating and shower or tub. They were modified "cold water" apartments, with a toilet and a washbasin installed in a crudely partitioned little compartment, but the bathtub was in the next apartment or one of the others on the floor. You had to ask permission to use it, and perhaps pay for the hot water. Maggie was more fortunate than most who lived in such places because there was surely a shower for waitresses somewhere in the bowels of the Drake. A mile or two farther south in the Polish neighborhood between Division Street and North Avenue, there were still outdoor privies and buildings without bath facilities whose residents had to use the public bathhouses that the city provided (one of which was made famous in a Saul Bellow novel). Even after the war, many Chicagoans thought themselves fortunate to find such a cave in which to live.

It was easy for social critics like Pete Seeger a few years later to make fun of the "ticky-tac" suburban houses that were to spring up on the fringes of most of the cities of the country. But Seeger was a rich kid who went to Harvard. He never lived in a cold-water flat. So he never knew the joy of having for the first time your own bathroom and separate bedrooms for the different members of the family.

Like many other women in such places, or worse places, Maggie had done her best to make it look bright and comfortable. The coverlet on the bed, turned down now, was a bright floral print, the inexpensive throw rug a bright green, a miniature Christmas tree with a single string of lights glowed on the table next to a small crib set. A bright picture of sun and beach was tacked to one wall and Raphael's Madonna smiled benignly from a print on the other panel of wall space. Crowded, cold, and uncomfortable, the apartment was nonetheless impeccably neat, a stern warning that its occupant would tolerate neither disorder nor nonsense.

Some women, my wife says, not without contempt, have order in their homes and nothing else.

"I'll turn up the heat," Maggie said as she bent over the stove. "Can't have you freezing to death."

"At least it's not coal," I said, leaning against the wall and wondering if I would be asked to sit down.

"Those poor men." She leaned against the opposite wall. "It would be impossible to pay someone too much for that kind of work."

Aha, a Democrat. One problem resolved.

We stood motionless and silent, two cautious animals warily waiting for an advantage.

Maggie seized the initiative. "You've returned to the Church?"

"You can't leave it, can you?"

"And you're writing?" Back firmly erect, hand at the top of her robe, Maggie was playing the Mother Superior role like one trained to it for years.

"Yes, S'ter."

"Hmff," she sniffed. "I'll believe it when I see it."

I laid my still unclaimed eight dollars next to her tree. "And you, Maggie Ward, have you got around to admitting that God gives us second chances?"

The starch went out of her back and Mother Superior was replaced by a novice caught stealing cookies.

"God keeps giving us second chances as long as we live." She bowed her head. "A young man taught me that in Arizona."

"Well, he did something useful in his life then."

"I'll make you that hot chocolate. . . ." She turned toward the kitchen alcove. "Sit on any chair you want."

I moved aside a copy of *Henry Esmond* and a notebook and sat on the edge of the chair.

"I made it with milk," she said, returning with two steaming cups. "You still look haggard."

"And you still look thin, but unbearably beautiful."

She flushed, opened her mouth to, I think, thank me, and was interrupted by a ringing telephone.

She dived behind the chair and pulled out the phone. "Yes? How was the train ride?" Her eyes flicked toward me and then away and then back again. "And your family? Good. Naturally I miss you. No, I really couldn't come. They need me at the Drake on Christmas morning and I promised. Certainly we will celebrate New Year's Eve together. No, not scared, just a little tired. We're shorthanded these days. Yes. Thank you. I'll talk to you tomorrow. Good-bye."

A rival, eh? Well, that should make life interesting.

"Don't look at me that way." She stood defiantly next to her bed. "Why shouldn't I have a boyfriend?"

"I like competition."

"I'm not sleeping with him . . . it's . . . it's not really serious."

"But he calls you from his parents' home, where he has gone for Christmas vacation, at one o'clock in the morning, on a phone he's probably paid for?"

"It's none of your business!"

"What's his name?"

"Wade McCarron and he's about thirty and he works at the Board of Trade and he's from Nashville and he's a nice man and I'm *not* sleeping with him."

"If your mind reading tells you that I think you are, it needs repair. Stop looking guilty, sit down, and drink your hot chocolate."

Anytime a Chicago mick loses to someone from Tennessee, he has quit before the competition started. From the look of sympathy in her enormous blue eyes I was willing to bet that Wade McCarron was one of Maggie's strays. I could beat any stray, especially one from Nashville, Tennessee. That I might also be a stray was not relevant.

Obediently Maggie sat on the edge of her bed. "Whom did you talk to?"

"Well, let me see." The hot chocolate was delicious. I

wondered if she would make seconds if I asked politely. "Sister Mary Regina, Sister Marie Neri, Sister Patrice Marie, a guy named Ralph . . ."

"Ralph Nolan," she murmured automatically. "Jean's Ralph. How is he?"

"Jean's trying to shape him up."

"She'll do it too. So you talked to Jean too?"

"They both love you, Maggie."

"I know," she said sadly. "I let them down. Who else?"

"Isobel and Howard Quinn, the manager of the Del Coronado, Lieutenant Wayne Manzell, a lovely man, I might note, CPO Fred Weaver and his wife Magda, Gunnery Sergeant Wendel . . . I guess that's all."

"A real Philip Marlowe." She stared at the floor. "You missed the manager of the Beverly Hills Hotel, but I guess he doesn't matter."

"My brother Packy is the detective. He'll tell you I'm not even a very good Watson."

"He's a very attractive young man, looks like your mother. You look like your father."

"What!" I put my chocolate cup on the floor.

"Anyone can ride the Lake Street El to River Forest and walk down Lathrop."

"You could have been caught!"

"Only if you were searching for me. And in Denver you didn't find me even then. Or," she added triumphantly, "the other day on Maxwell Street."

Lost both those, Commander.

"I see you everywhere, Maggie," I said sadly. "I think half the young women on the street might be you."

"I'm sorry." Her eyes glistened and she extended a hand tentatively in my direction. "I know what it's like. I think I see my father in most of the men his age on the street. I didn't mean to hurt you."

"But you did get caught." I reached for her hand, but she pulled it back.

"I didn't know about postmarks."

"You wanted to get caught." I picked up my nearly empty hot-chocolate cup.

"That's what my psychiatrist says . . . here, let me make you more."

"Your what?"

"My therapist. He says that superficially I came to Chicago because I thought you'd never look for me here, but really because I wanted to be close to you, especially if I needed help, and that deep down I wanted to be caught." She shrugged wearily. "I guest Dr. Feurst wins that one."

"Dr. Feurst?"

"He's short and funny and old," she spat out defiantly, "and has a long white beard and he thinks I'm cute and a little crazy and I don't sleep with him either. I don't sleep with anyone. I'm a mess and I have to straighten my life out and get an education. So I work and go to school and study and see Dr. Feurst and date Wade once a week. Okay?"

"I came here, Maggie, to return eight dollars, not to argue with you. I'm glad you're seeing a doctor and going to school and I wonder if you are serious about that second cup of hot chocolate?"

"I'm sorry." She bounced off the bed. "I'm still being selfish."

I joined her in the tiny kitchen, so close that I smelled the faint Lily of the Valley scent she was wearing. If she was reading my mind then, she knew that sex was on my mind, powerfully on my mind.

Slow down, Commander.

"Despite my awful lies"—she stirred the powdered Ovaltine into my cup of warm milk with more determination than was necessary—"you know all there is to know about me, don't you, Commander?"

"It would take a lifetime to do that, Maggie, and I'd probably only have made a start."

She turned abruptly away from me and strode back into the room. "I mean you know about Andrew and the baby . . ."

"And your suicide."

"Even that? How can you know all those things and give a damn about me?"

Despite the hot chocolate, I felt a cold shudder run through my body. Was she admitting that she was dead?

Dead women don't seek out funny old shrinks with long white beards. Do they?

Her tears had begun to flow. I could put my arms around her, console her while she cried in my arms, and then make love to her. I stopped myself at the last minute.

CIC intervened to recommend me for a good-conduct medal.

"Your daughter died a natural death, your husband fell out a window when he was trying to strangle you. You're not a murderer, Maggie Ward. I'm sure Doctor Feurst says the same thing."

"How do you know?" she demanded, haughtily dabbing at her eyes. "How do you know what I felt when I pushed him? I wanted him dead. I wanted to be free of him. I wanted to start my life over again."

"So you tricked him into trying to strangle you?"

The second hot chocolate was better than the first. Or perhaps I was only enjoying the glow of my good-conduct recommendation. Both my virtue and my tactics were operating according to plan.

"Of course not," she said, huddling down into her huge chenille robe.

"Gunnery Sergeant Wendel said you slipped away at the last minute and he lost his balance and tumbled out the window."

Maybe I should try to take her hand again.

"Don't you dare," CIC warned sharply.

"He didn't tell the truth exactly. I pushed Andrew, real hard, he lost his balance, and I shoved him again."

"Deliberately intending that he fall out the window and land on the concrete?"

"No, I didn't think . . . but I didn't care. I just wanted him to stop beating me. I wanted to be free from him. Forever. I was glad that he hit his head." Her voice rose to a near hysterical shriek.

"And terribly sorry too."

"That's right. I mourn him every day. Poor boy, he meant well and he was nice a lot of the time and he tried." She was bent over, sobbing into her folded arms. "Doctor Feurst says I must learn to accept my own responsibilities and ambivalences. That's a good word, isn't it?" She peeked up at me. "Ambivalences?"

"Maybe." I didn't want to argue with her because that would do no good. "Maybe it was like a dogfight. I didn't want to kill the poor Japanese fellow. He was not my personal enemy. After it was over, I hoped he had survived, though their planes weren't built for survival like ours were. I was sorry he was dead, but I was glad I wasn't dead and glad he wouldn't get a chance to kill me again that day."

"That was war," she said as she sat up again, "not a family fight."

"In both cases, the goal was survival." I was really knocking out the long line drives. All I had to do was to keep my hands and arms under control. "I agree with Dr. Feurst: I know why you feel bad, and even why you feel guilty, but you are not a killer, Maggie Ward, much less a murderer."

"He was not a bad boy, really." She shook her head sadly. "He tried hard. His parents were such terrible people. . . ."

"You tried hard too, Maggie. You did your best to be an appealing and satisfying wife."

"And scared him. I thought he'd like a wife who would be . . . well, kind of a whore in the bedroom. After a while he did like me that way some of the time. And so did I, God help me. Then, when Andrea died, he only enjoyed it if he would hurt me and force me. If she had lived . . ."

"They crippled him for life, Maggie, he could never have survived any major crisis; it wasn't your fault. . . . Doesn't Dr. Feurst agree with me?"

"He keeps asking me whether I think what happened to Andrew was my fault. He won't tell me what he thinks."

"And your answer?" I leaned forward, as if to pray she

would say something that suggested she was ready to absolve herself.

"In my head, I know it was mostly not my fault." She pointed to her skull. "But here"—she gestured to her chest and her gut—"I've not caught up with my head."

I was about to applaud her wisdom when the apartment was shaken by what seemed to be a massive Christmas Eve earthquake and a roar that sounded like a hundred Pratt & Whitneys.

"Don't be afraid; it's only the El," she laughed. "Your great Chicago institution. I kind of like it. I think it keeps me company."

I waited for the rolling apocalypse to pass and returned to my argument.

"Whatever your lovely chest and belly might say, I didn't learn anything on my Philip Marlowe quest—and I appreciate the reference to Raymond Chandler. By the way, I do think there's a bit of the Humphrey Bogart about me. . . ."

"You're sexier," she insisted, giggling through her tears.

"If I am, the reason is that I've had a good teacher." Heroically I ignored both the hint in what she had just said and the appealing flame on her face. "As I was saying, all I've learned on my tour of windmills makes me admire Maggie Ward more than I did in the bridal suite at Picketpost, if I didn't know her proper name then."

"That's when I knew for sure that God would give me another chance, that I wasn't damned. Thank you, Jerry. You're a sweet man." She touched my cheek and then pulled away her hand as if I were a hot stove. "Are you sweet enough to understand what I mean when I say I need time to make something out of myself and my life, maybe a long time? Please," she pleaded, "try to understand."

"Sure, I understand what you're saying." I emptied my hot-chocolate cup. "I think you need to keep seeing Dr. Feurst. I definitely think you need to go to school and read all these books." I waved at the piles all around the room. "But I won't accept the notion that you are not an extraordinary and special young woman right now. I'll give you time. I'll even understand that you think you need a long time. But I want you, Maggie Ward, and I intend to have you. Is that clear?"

Brave talk, huh? From a coward.

"I need time," she begged. "Time to be free, to live, to do something with myself and my life."

I put my hand over her mouth, taking a leaf from Kate's book. "Be quiet, woman. As I said, you have your time. I won't push you or hurt you. But I also won't stop loving you. And, having found you on this cold Christmas Eve morning, I am not about to let you run away from me again. Your Denver maneuver is no longer acceptable, is that clear?"

She hesitated and then nodded her head slowly.

"Furthermore, I refuse to believe that after a certain point, in the not too distant future, you cannot better fight the demons of your past with someone else's intimate and loving help. Is that clear?"

I removed my hand. She was a stove too. Sizzling hot despite the temperature of the room.

"You really are writing, aren't you?" She grinned wickedly. "Your speeches are much more literate than they were last summer."

"And you, young woman, are just what Sister Mary Regina said you are—a provoking little bitch!"

She ducked away toward the end of the bed and then realized, with some disappointment perhaps, that I wasn't going to seize her. "I bet she didn't say 'bitch' . . . and, lest you really try to throw me over your knee and on Christmas Eve too, yes, I understand what you're saying. So everything is clear between us."

"Clear, Maggie, but uneasy."

"*Very* uneasy."

"Two points before I let you get some sleep in your lonely bed." I ticked it off on my finger: "What about your suicide? How come I knelt at your grave in San Diego last summer and pleaded with God to grant you in the next world the peace you did not find here?"

"What?" She leapt out of the bed in terror. "My grave?

I'm not dead, Jerry. Really I'm not. I mean I thought when the waves kept rolling me back to shore that I was dead and that God didn't want me yet. Even in Tucson when I saw you, I still felt, well, kind of mostly dead. I was so depressed. My parents, little Andy, Andrew, they didn't want me back at the hotel ... I was worthless. So I tried to kill myself, and well"—she was pouring out the story now, perhaps with more emotion than even to Dr. Feurst.

"Don't you dare," CIC repeated his warning, "or I'll take the good conduct medal away."

"Well ... I suppose I had a kind of nervous breakdown ... 'yah, a small, werra small psychotic interlude,' Dr. Feurst calls it.... I was walking around in a daze"—she turned crimson—"until a very sweet boy ... "

"Young man. Packy is the boy."

"Young man ... woke me up. I knew I was alive. And God had thrown me back from the waves not because He didn't want me but because He did."

She was glowing now with happiness and hope. This is not going to be easy. "CIC, are you a seraph now?"

What else?

"Sergeant Wendel saw you walk into the water. He tried to swim out to save you. He couldn't find you. The police and the Coast Guard searched in vain. Several weeks later a body washed up on the shore. The Weavers, brokenhearted and I suppose wanting a decent burial for you, were convinced it was your body. The chaplain from the Navy Yard said a few prayers at your grave. So did I."

"For some other woman"—hand on her face in horror. "Poor thing ... why ... but that's not up to me to judge, is it? And all the time I was up at the Beverly Hills working as a hostess, until someone from San Diego remembered me from the picture in the papers when ... when Andrew died and they had to let me go. Oh, what terrible things I've done! How can the Weavers ever forgive me."

"One phone call will do it and make their Christmas. Jean Kelly too."

"I can't . . . I'm so ashamed . . ."

"You were not yourself, and"—I was CAG One—"you will call them tomorrow, Maggie Ward, and that's an order. Understand?"

"Yes, sir, Commander, sir." Her smile of adoration struck at the foundation of my resolutions.

I rose from the chair. "They love you, Maggie Ward. They understand and they are eager to forgive."

"I'm being forgiven by everyone this night before Christmas Eve," she said thoughtfully. "I don't deserve it."

"Probably not," I agreed. "But that doesn't make any difference. And by the way, it's after midnight so it's now officially Christmas Eve. Which reminds me, there is a condition for my forgiveness for the merry chase on which you led me."

"A condition?" She grinned at me warily.

I strolled toward the door. Casual, relaxed, confident.

"Yep."

"And that is?" She followed me, also casual—and cautious.

"My second point, previously listed but not described." I ticked my second finger. "You are to eat Christmas dinner with us tomorrow evening. Otherwise my brother, that terribly attractive boy, as you call him, will disown me for life."

"No."

"Yes."

"No."

"It's an order."

"I said no and I mean no."

"I'll come and take you by main force."

"I'm working in the morning."

I was standing in the corridor, my foot firmly in the doorway. "I can eavesdrop on phone calls as well as the next person. I followed you home from work tonight without you noticing me, didn't I?"

"Yes," she admitted grudgingly.

"Pack is a very strong boy. You won't even make it to Bughouse Square before we kidnap you."

"You wouldn't dare."

But she wasn't sure.

"We would."

"I'd love to come, Jerry." She smiled sadly. "I'm afraid to, but I'll come anyway."

The face lighted up in the Christmas-tree smile.

"That was a quick change."

"I promised I'd stop lying. Besides," she whispered, teasing a weak spot she'd found, "your brother is so cute."

"Provoking bitch. What time should I pick you up?"

"I'm working. I'll take the subway and the El."

"I'll pick you up."

"No."

"Yes."

"You won the big argument, can't you let me win the small one?"

"I don't understand, but okay. Don't try to run out on us."

"I keep my promises now, Jerry. At least I try. I'll phone you when I leave work—I can get away by twelve—and if you want, you can meet me at the Merrion station."

"Go to Forest, the next stop, the end of the line."

"All right."

"Promise?"

"Scout's honor." She crossed her heart. "Aren't you going to kiss me?"

I touched her lips very lightly. "Merry Christmas Eve, Maggie Ward."

"Same to you, Jerry Keenan. And a Happy New Year."

I paused. "About that I have not the slightest doubt."

I did.

"Jerry," she called after me as I walked down the first flight of steps. "One more thing."

I walked back up. "You want to be kissed again?"

"No. I mean yes, but that's not why I called you. There's one more detail that you missed."

Were we going to talk about Clinton? I hoped not. That

difficult conversation should wait till after the joys of Christmas.

"Okay."

"It's about the Beverly Hills. You see, the nice manager at the Del Coronado said he'd call, and then I tried to kill myself like a little fool." She made an impatient face at her own stupidity, not ready to administer self-absolution yet. "So when I got out of the water and dried off, I got my suitcase out of the locker at the bus station and rode up to Los Angeles and they hired me anyway."

"I kind of assumed that."

"Well, as I said, they fired me when they found out about the charges against me in San Diego. The manager there liked me too . . . managers seem to like me. . . ."

"Everyone does but your aunt and uncle and those ugly nuns and a girl named Maggie."

"So he recommended me for a job in Tucson."

"At the Arizona Inn."

She nodded miserably. "I wanted so much to spend a little bit of time with you that I lied horribly. I told myself that after you dropped me off in Phoenix I could take the bus back to Tucson. I'm so ashamed."

"And I'm inordinately flattered." I cupped her chin in my hand and kissed her again, with a little more insistence this time. "I don't think a woman has ever wanted to spend any time with me, much less such a beautiful woman. Merry Christmas."

"If God forgives"—tears again—"as easily as you do . . ."

"And a Happy New Year." I closed the door firmly. "And a hundred more of them."

Not a bad beginning, I told myself, as I strode down Sheffield Avenue under the full moon. Not bad at all.

But the horror was only chained, not destroyed.

CHAPTER 37

I WOULD HAVE SAID THAT MAGGIE WARD TOOK MY FAMILY like Grant took Richmond. But Grant took Richmond only after several years of combat and only with the help of Sherman's armies coming up from the south. Maggie captivated my parents, brother, and sister instantly and without any help from me.

I was willing to help; I wanted them to like her.

She didn't need my help. After a few moments she knew it and raised a supercilious eyebrow at me, so that I knew she knew that she could do without my assistance in winning over these easily won people.

"Margaret Ward, this is my mother, Mary Anne Keenan."

"You have such a beautiful home, Mrs. Keenan, and an even more beautiful family to match it."

"My father, Thomas Keenan."

"My son tells me that you're from Philadelphia, young woman, but that you're still a Democrat."

"The Wards were voting Democratic, several times every election day, when the Keenans were living in trees."

Dad grinned happily. "I bet we vote more often than you do."

"My sister, Joanne."

"Your dress is lovely, Joanne."

"Uh, thanks . . . I like yours, too."

"And my brother Patrick, generally called Packy."

"Sancho!"

"Dulci!" He lifted her off the ground, swung her around in space, and kissed her mightily.

"Hey, she's my girl."

A flight of daggers flashed at me from her eyes. She was no one's girl.

The hell she wasn't.

"I did bring you a present." We had seated ourselves in the living room for a drink before dinner. Maggie had asked for a "small glass of sherry."

Not only modest in her green knit two-piece dress (which left no doubt about any of her curves) and witty and polite but also refined.

"I bet it's in that package."

"May I give it to him?" she asked my mother with great respect.

"By all means, dear. I'm sure we're all dying of curiosity."

I opened the package, with fingers that perhaps shook a little. It was a soft, hand-tooled Florentine-leather notebook binding, in elegant maroon, with a fountain pen and holder attached.

How many cold nights in her flat had it cost?

"Someone as important as a retired commander should have a proper notebook for his journal."

"What about a lowly law-school student?" I kissed her forehead. "Thanks, Maggie."

"A lowly law-school student who is practicing to be a great writer," she said severely.

"I didn't know you were going to be a writer, dear." My mother seemed surprised, but no more so than if I had announced that I was going to a Black Hawks game.

"Time we have a writer in the family." My father, like Packy, couldn't take his eyes off my pretty friend.

"Didn't you buy her a present?" Joanne demanded with her usual subtlety.

"Were you expecting a Christmas present, Maggie Ward?"

"Yes."

"Oh." I feigned dismay.

"Don't tease her, darling."

"I don't mind." Maggie leaned back in her chair, completely confident.

"Well, let's see what we can find here behind the tree." I rummaged around. "Do I have something left over? I wonder what's in this box. Well, let's take a chance. Do you want to open this one, Maggie?"

I handed her a narrow, oblong box.

"Beast." She placed it on the arm of her chair.

"Open it."

"Should I?"

"Or we will," Packy exclaimed. "Jer has never given a girl a Christmas present before."

"Well . . ." She clawed the wrappings off frantically. "I'm not very curious, am I? . . . Oh!"

"What lovely pearls," my mother said. "You have excellent taste after all, Jerry."

"Perfect for this particular girl," my father agreed.

"A double string," a wide-eyed Joanne gasped. "They must be really expensive."

Patrick: "Put them on her, dummy."

So I removed the pearls from their cushioned box and, with as much ceremony as if I were crowning a queen, draped them around Maggie's lovely neck. She sat passively, hands folded, without words for the first time since I'd known her.

The pearls were too much. She shouldn't take them.

But she wasn't going to refuse them either. "They're beautiful, Jerry." She kissed my cheek. "Thank you very much. . . . And, Tom, may I have another tiny sip of sherry."

Even before we began to eat the turkey it was clear that Maggie was not a quiet waif whom we had invited out of the abundance of our compassion to share Christmas dinner with us. She was rather an intelligent little imp who could not be restrained from being the life of the party.

It was all an act, a brilliant performance by a skillful actress. In fact, she was a wounded and troubled young woman, fighting desperately to stay alive. But stubborn, strong-willed, proud girl child that she was, she would prove to the Keenans that she was as poised as they were and maybe a little more so. It required enormous effort and afterward she would suffer from emotional exhaustion. She'd probably cry all the way home.

All right, if that was the price, she'd pay it.

Dear God, how much I loved her courage.

Mom quickly became "Mary Anne." As in, "Mary Anne, what beautiful china!"

"Where did you go to college?" Joanne blurted out at the dinner table after grace.

"I'm taking classes at the YMCA College between dinner and supper," she replied calmly. "I work at the Lantern Room at the Drake and I just walk over there. I think next year some of the faculty will start a new university. They might call it Roosevelt. So it will have to be good, won't it, Tom?"

"Absolutely."

"A waitress?" Joanne's lip curled in disbelief.

Packy's expression said that he wanted to strangle her, which was exactly how I felt.

"I think I'll be able to make up my high school work by summer"—Maggie speared a piece of white meat—"and be eligible for a scholarship."

"You didn't graduate from high school?"

My mother, who usually pretended that Joanne's crudities didn't exist, stirred uneasily.

"I was married in my junior year and went to San Diego with my husband."

If you promise that you're returning to your habit of telling the truth and you are Maggie Ward, you tell the truth.

"You're married!"

Calmly Maggie scooped up a chunk of dressing. She knew that such questions would arise and was prepared for them. "He died in an accident while he was in the Navy."

Ah, but you don't tell any more of the truth than you have to tell. My heart melted with sympathy for her pain.

But the questions had to be answered eventually.

"Thank God you didn't have any children!"

"My baby daughter died in her crib." Maggie put down her fork. "The doctors said she was born with something wrong in her breathing."

"You poor kid." Joanne reached out and held Maggie's hand. "You're really wonderful!"

Packy rolled his eyes. For once the middle child had done something right.

"Thanks, Joanne." Maggie gripped her hand in return. "So are you," she choked, "all of you."

"A toast." My father raised his glass of white Chablis. "To Margaret Ward, a young woman from Philadelphia, but still a Democrat, who brought us much extra merriment on this merry Christmas. May we see her on many more Christmases yet to come."

"Hear! Hear!"

Maggie lifted her glass in return, the fingers of her other hand unconsciously on her new necklace.

"Thanks to all the Keenans," she replied, eyes glistening, "for sharing a merry Christmas with me."

The dinner continued cheerfully, the major crisis surmounted. Maggie, the ingenious little witch, had turned a liability into a powerful asset. If I didn't capture her for all future Christmases I'd be in enormous trouble with my family.

She wanted to be captured, but was afraid of captivity. Understandably. All the close relationships in her life had been mangled. Every happiness had been snatched from her grasp. She was wise to proceed cautiously. Perhaps I ought to have a word with her doctor to make sure that I did not stand in the way of rapid progress to self-confidence.

"Jean Marie Kelly says hello," she said, smiling triumphantly at me during a lull in the conversation. "Ralph Nolan gave her a ring at midnight Mass. Astonished her completely."

"She took it, I hope."

"Snatched her hand away so he couldn't change his mind."

"Jean Marie Kelly?" My mother treated every new name as if it might be a club member from Butterfield whom she ought to know and didn't.

"A friend of mine Jerry met last summer."

"Jerry is resisting the marriage craze of the moment," my father observed, tilting the wine bottle in her direction.

"I can't say that I blame him," she said, offering her glass for more wine. "Though he is getting a bit long in the tooth, isn't he?"

"How old are you, dear?" Mom needed all the demographic details. "Twenty-one?"

"Nineteen in March, Mary Anne." If you are committed to the truth, you are committed to the truth. "I just look older."

"Younger," Packy insisted. "Child."

"Your parents?" Mom wanted to fill out all the details.

"Mom died of TB when I was five. Dad was a lawyer like you, Tom. He sort of disappeared into the Great Depression."

"Dead?"

She hesitated. "I'm not sure. Deep down inside me I hope he's alive. But maybe I'm only fooling myself."

We were silent for an awkward moment. "Maggie sings." I rushed in where angels fear to tread. "Maybe she'll sing with us after supper."

"I'm out of practice."

My dad raised his glass in semi-toast. "So are we all. Mother plays the piano, Patrick and I do the violin, Joanne breaks the rules by being rather good on the cello, and himself pretends to strum on the bass."

"You never told me that!" She turned on me accusingly.

"When you hear me, you'll know why."

"Grandma Maggie was a fiddler, among other things," Packy informed her. "So we're a little bit more cultivated than the other Chicago Irish."

"Which is why we don't live in trees." My father smiled at her. "At least not when we have guests from Philly."

So Maggie joined our Christmas consort, which was not nearly so crude as we pretended. Her light, slender voice soared over our accompaniment, and after "Silent Night" and "Gésu Bambino" she assumed, as if by right, the role of consort director.

I took some pictures of the rest of the consort with my new flash attachment that night. Maggie stands out, not because she was a good five inches shorter than any of the rest of us, not because she had somehow elbowed her way into the center of the family, not because she looks so young, not even because she was incandescently lovely, but because of all the happy faces, hers is the happiest.

Only when we played and sang "White Christmas"—the most popular song of the Second World War—did her eyes mist. Too many painful Christmases past.

But the happy smile in the picture says that she thought the worst was over, that the demons had no more power over her.

In that she was mistaken.

At the end of the evening we almost had a fight. I insisted I would drive her to her apartment. She insisted that she would take the El.

"Maggie Ward"—Dad settled it—"forget you're an Irish-woman just once and do what you're told."

Her jaw jutted up in preparation for rage. Instead she merely grinned at him. "Yes, Tom."

"The day I married my wife, my new father-in-law"— Dad was launched on one of his favorite anecdotes—"took me aside and said that I was marrying a very strong-willed woman but that he had found an absolutely certain method of keeping her under control."

"And what is that?" I asked eagerly, wishing he would keep the advice short so that we could depart for our honeymoon hotel.

" 'Always give her whatever she wants.' "

We all laughed dutifully.

"He doesn't always." Mom, who somehow was always flattered by the story, provided her standard reply.

"Seems sensible advice to me," my darling said with a perfectly straight face.

"We'll see you at the Christmas Dance, dear." Mom kissed her good-bye as we were leaving.

"Christmas Dance?"

"Why, at Butterfield!"

Is there any other?

"I haven't been asked."

"You will be," my father predicted.

"Well?" I asked as Roxy slithered down Lathrop.

"Let me cry first," she said, reaching in her purse for a handkerchief.

"Be my guest."

She pulled out of the tears in a few minutes. More would be shed, I was willing to bet, before the night was over.

"Thanks for waiting." She wiped her eyes. "Now about your wonderful family, much too good for you, I was afraid they were going to lock me up in the basement. They must really be convinced that they have an old-fashioned Irish bachelor on their hands."

"They like you, Maggie. You were worried that they wouldn't like you at all and now you're worried that they like you too much."

"I do the mind reading," she said irritably.

"Jean Kelly painted me a picture of Maggie Ward, the natural leader and the life of the party. Now I've seen it confirmed."

"Did you go to bed with Jean Kelly?"

"You're changing the subject." I turned toward Harlem. "And certainly not. Jealous?"

"She was enthusiastic about you. You thought of going to bed with her?"

"I'm a healthy adult male. I repeat, are you jealous?"

"Certainly not. And I'm not going to the dance either."

"Yes, you are. You're dying of curiosity."

"I am not . . . besides, I don't have a dress."

"We'll buy you one at Marshall Field's."

"You will *not*! I am not your mistress."

"You're the woman I love."

"That doesn't entitle you to buy me clothes."

"It does too. Anyway, I have a precedent. Remember Steinfeld's?"

Pause.

"I'll make a deal with you."

"All right."

"I'll go to the dance at Buttercup . . ."

"Butter*field*."

"And you," her voice lowered to a conspiratorial whisper,

"you agree not to bother me for the next . . ." hesitation as she calculated the longest possible time she could demand, "the next six months."

"What . . . ?"

"I need—"

"Time."

"Right."

"The competition . . ."

"Is not serious. *Please* . . ."

"Can I talk to Dr. Feurst?"

"Well," she considered my counterproposal, "I don't see why not. He'll tell you I need time too."

"Then it's a deal."

"Fine . . ."

"What's the matter?" We turned down Fullerton Avenue, which was almost empty of cars.

"You agreed too easily."

"I'm a reasonable person. I understand that you need time. Besides, have I ever violated a promise to you?"

"No . . ."

"All right."

"But there is always a first time, isn't there, CIC?"

"Yes, *sir!*"

When we turned north on Southport Avenue, Maggie broke the long silence. "I really was okay tonight?"

"What do you think?"

"Dr. Feurst will accuse me of not wanting to admit that your family liked me a little. You're not objective, but you're probably more objective than I am."

"I guess they liked you, but just a little."

I felt a light blow to my arm. "Only a little?"

"Well, maybe a little more."

Another blow, imperious this time. "*Tell* me!"

"You may quote me to Dr. Feurst as saying what you know full well to be the truth yourself, provoking child. They adored you."

"I don't understand why."

"That's besides the point. You will, in view of your promise not to lie, quote my exact words to Dr. Feurst: You know full well they adored you."

Pause.

"Well?"

"All right"—sigh—"I suppose I *have* to."

Poor girl child, still unable to accept your own goodness. Well, we'll change that, Dr. Feurst and I.

I turned right on Diversey from Southport and right again on Sheffield and stopped Roxy in front of her apartment building.

"Can you leave the heater on for a few minutes of conversation?" she asked briskly.

"Sure." I took my hand off the ignition key and rolled the window down an inch, so we would not risk carbon-monoxide poisoning. "Do you want to neck?

She shoved my arm away firmly. "You've been so proud of your restraint, you don't want to ruin your record now, do you?"

Back to the mind reading.

"All right." I sighed with noisy patience. "What's on the agenda?"

"Why I deserted you in Arizona."

"Oh."

"You remember that awful wind and the storm and the terrible smell and the thick rain clouds? And how we were both knocked against the car and you hit your head on the door?"

"Was that what happened?"

"I lost consciousness for a few minutes too—the heat and the exhaustion and the emotional strain, I guess. And, more than anything, the shock of discovering I was really still alive and getting another chance whether I wanted it or not."

"We didn't go back to the buildings?"

"I woke up and it was dark and you were twisting and turning next to me as if you were having terrible dreams. I tried and tried and couldn't wake you. But finally you settled down into a peaceful sleep, so I thought you were all right and then . . . well, I panicked and ran. Then," she turned away, embarrassed and ashamed and lovely, "I thought you wouldn't mind if I borrowed some money. I promised to pay it back." She looked up at me, fragile and shy. "And I DID pay it back."

"With exorbitant interest."

"I wanted to get away from that terrible place and from you and from everything in the past and start again. I know that's silly because it was you who gave me my new beginning, but I was terrified of you—still am, I suppose—so I had to run."

"Did you have any dreams?"

She thought about the question. "I suppose so. I was so tired I don't remember them. And I have a harder time remembering dreams than you. Your friends who died and Andrew and the baby were all jumbled up. And I think there were demons coming to get me, but you chased them away and so I woke up and ran away from you."

"I did?"

"You certainly did." She nodded vigorously. "That's the most important part of the dream. You and some other nice person saved me."

"Only a dream?"

"No, silly." She shook her head impatiently. "The dream told me what had already happened. You saved me in the . . . well, un-dreamworld just like in the dreamworld. So naturally I was afraid of you and had to run away."

"I don't get that part. Why were you afraid of me?"

"I was afraid that I loved you so much that I would hurt you like I hurt all the others. Maybe even worse than I hurt them."

"That was dumb."

"I don't think so," she said stubbornly. "Anyway, I dragged my suitcase into that town . . ."

"Tortilla."

"And I told them that there was a man asleep by a car up near Clinton and took the bus to Apache Junction and another bus to Globe and then the train to Bowie and El Paso."

"I thought you might do that."

"And I worked there to make some money and then took

the Denver and Rio Grande to Denver, where you almost caught me, and then the Burlington to Chicago."

"I see."

"And now I want to apologize for running away from you when you were unconscious and maybe hurt and needed my help."

"But you didn't want to hurt me."

"That's different."

"I don't see how."

"Maybe hurting you in the future sometime was what Dr. Feurst calls a neurotic fear. Leaving you by the car was cowardice."

I still didn't understand and I thought she didn't either.

"It's all right, Maggie. You were badly confused. So was I."

"I'm so ashamed." She turned away. "So ashamed."

I kissed her forehead. "Don't be. It's all right now. . . ."

"Do you think that what happened was that the evil or maybe the possibility for evil in both our souls sort of . . . well, combined for a little while?"

"Your guilt and my violence?"

She was silent for some time. "Something like that."

"Could be. . . . By the way, who was the other good person in your dreams?"

"He was"—she frowned in mystification—"a big blond man in a fancy navy uniform with a gun in his arms and a wild grin on his face. He was on our side. Somehow, as I said"—she seemed to be trying to recall the images—"he and you saved me."

"I see."

"I don't know who he was"—she kissed my cheek—"but I know you did save me." Her hand touched the happy spot where her lips had rested. "And you are the sweetest man who has ever lived."

With that admirable exaggeration she pushed open the door on her side of the car and raced up the steps to the apartment door.

I did not try to follow her.

During my return to River Forest, I was less happy than

I should have been. I had tracked down Maggie Ward. She had been an immense success with my family. She had provided a reasonable explanation for the war in heaven by the Lost Dutchman's Mine, combined with Father Donniger's wisdom it was the best explanation I was ever likely to get—an intense fantasy interlude shared by both of us that reflected a war in heaven which had already taken place. We might not have won the war, but at least we hadn't lost it.

And she was convinced that I and my seraph friend had saved her. "Hear that, CIC?"

No answer. Not working on Christmas in peacetime?

Or off somewhere singing with the rest of them?

Why, after this highly successful forty-eight hours, was I uneasy?

Because she was such a complex and powerful young woman, much more than the pale, fragile girl I had met in July in the railroad station? A strong and still badly confused and troubled refugee from horror and death?

Because the recovered Dulcinea was both less and more than the girl of my dreams?

Because I dimly realized that for all the success of my tactics, my strategy was still unfocused, perhaps dangerously so?

Or because, under the waning Christmas full moon, I was not convinced that the war in heaven was finished or that I would win it?

Maybe it would never end. Maybe my eternal purgatory would be to be always close to victory and always doomed to have it snatched from my hands at the final moment.

Grim thoughts at the end of a merry Christmas Day. But as I would find out shortly after the first of the year, prophetic thoughts.

CHAPTER 38

"I WILL NOT WEAR THAT DRESS." SHE POINTED AT IT AC-cusingly, an outraged and violated vestal. "It's too . . . revealing."

"You'll look lovely in it, dear," the elderly saleswoman said as she smiled benignly. "You have the perfect figure for it."

"Try it on," I ordered.

"You make me try all these dresses just so you can ogle me," she hissed in my ear as she slipped off to the dressing room.

"You're the most provoking young woman I've ever kept."

Her jaw jutted skyward, but her smile illumined half of North State Street. Despite her contentiousness, Maggie was reveling in our shopping expedition to Marshall Field's two days after Christmas.

"She is so lovely," the salesperson gushed. "You're a lucky young man."

"If I don't mind a lifetime of arguing."

"She's just joking because she's embarrassed."

"I know."

"It is too revealing," Maggie insisted when she returned wearing the dark-red dress with a low neck, white trim, and a white belt, its straps, such as they were, designed for her upper arms and not her shoulders. "I'm almost naked to my waist."

"Not quite."

"If fits you perfectly, dear. We won't have to do any alterations. If you need it for tonight . . ."

"We'll take it." I handed her the charge card.

"No," Maggie begged.

"Yes," I commanded.

It was a dialogue we'd been having all morning. I was winning.

"Are you sure it isn't too . . ."

"Revealing? For someone else, maybe. But it's perfect for you, Maggie. I wouldn't risk embarrassing my mother or myself or you at Buttercup, would I?"

"Butter*field*, silly! And I'll have to buy a new . . . new foundation garment."

"You look fine."

She crossed her arms protectively. "I'd be arrested if I appeared in River Forest like this."

Women's fashions in 1946 demanded thin waists and slim, boyish hips. If your well-preserved figure, like my mother's, happened to be in the classic mode, you were forced to don undergarments which, while not as constraining as the steel-boned, laced-up affairs of the pre-1914 era, nonetheless imposed all kinds of unwanted pressure on your flesh. With the return after the war of off-the-shoulder dresses, especially formals, the corsets encased you from breast to hip in restraints that barely permitted breathing. Even young women with nearly perfect figures like Maggie were still obliged, in the name of a blend of modesty and fashion, to encase themselves like that, especially if they were baring their neck and shoulders.

"I won't argue with you about proprieties, Margaret Mary," I told her as we approached the corset department, "but you looked wonderful in that dress."

"I did not."

"We bought it."

"To keep you happy. Give me the charge card. I don't want you hanging around the corset department. You might embarrass the women."

"And myself." I gave her the card. "I'll meet you at the Walnut Room for morning tea."

"All right."

"What color is it?" I asked as she strode into the tearoom, unloaded her armful of packages on the chair next to me, and collapsed into one across the table.

"It matches my face when you stare at me that way."

"You'd be a lot more angry if I didn't stare at you."

"I'll be embarrassed all night, Jerry; I'll be practically *naked*."

"We should be so fortunate to have that happen. Besides, you'll have a lot more clothes on than you did at Picketpost."

She closed her eyes and tilted her head backward in sensuous recollection. "That was so long ago. Did it ever happen? Certainly it did. You saved me then, Commander; you started in the railroad station and you finished by that terrible mine, but Picketpost . . ." She opened her eyes and smiled at me lovingly. "That's when my second chance began."

"Whenever you want, we can do it again."

"I need—"

"More time." I was beginning to hate the refrain.

"I'm sorry." She touched my hand. "I wish I didn't."

I was not altogether sure I believed her. Maggie now was just frightened of strong emotions.

"Are you sure I won't look common and vulgar?" She gripped my hand suddenly. "Everyone will be staring at me and I'll embarrass you and your—"

"Margaret Mary." I held her hand fiercely. "Stop that this instant. Why shouldn't everyone stare at you? You'll be the most beautiful woman at the dance. But they will think not that you're vulgar or cheap but appealing and modest. You saw the girl in the red dress with the white trim and the lovely bare shoulders with the pretty breasts, which are covered just enough, in the mirror. You know she'll never be common or vulgar, no matter what the nuns or her aunt and uncle said."

"I'll *feel* common and vulgar." Despite her fears she wolfed down a scone as if she had not eaten in two years. "I'll feel that I'm disgracing your mother and father."

"No, you won't, and that's an order."

"Yes, sir, Commander, sir."

"You are going to wear my pearls."

"*My* pearls." The imp's glint appeared on her face, the most charming of all her many expressions—except adoration for me. "And distract people from my cute breasts? Don't be ridiculous."

"They are cute, all right, but you are basically an imp and a tease and a troublemaker, aren't you, Maggie Ward?"

"It took you a long time to figure that out, didn't it?"

"If you don't wear our necklace, I'll tie you to the flagpole on the seventh green and leave you there all night."

"I wouldn't dream of not wearing it, silly."

"And now, finish off that plate of scones and your Earl Grey tea."

So we finished our tea and shopped for stockings and shoes and perfume. Laden with packages, Maggie was ready for the "Buttercup" Christmas dance. She insisted on riding home on the subway and the El. "You need a haircut," she informed me, as we left Field's through a Wabash Avenue entrance. "I will not be seen at this high-toned dance with a man whose crew cut is beginning to curl."

"It's not high-toned, Maggie. River Forest is not Lake Forest; we're strictly middle-class Irish with a little bit of money. We don't know how to be high-toned."

Suddenly, despite the post-Christmas crowds on Wabash, she leaned her head against my chest and began to sob. "I'm so ashamed of myself. I'm such a dope."

I held her close, welcoming any physical contact that fell within the rubrics of my strategy.

"I love you, Maggie."

"I know." She continued to sob. "And I love you. You're so wonderfully sweet." She touched my face, as if to make sure it was still there. "You've been kind and good and generous to me and I've acted churlish. . . ."

"The nice thing about your kept woman being a literary woman is that she uses such fancy words as 'churlish.' "

"I *love* being your kept woman," she wailed, "and I'm so afraid of it that I act like a clod. . . ."

"Not quite so literary."

"Be quiet." She poked my arm. "Let me finish."

"All right."

"Thank you for the pearls and for the dress and for all the

other things. And thank you for being kind and sweet and thank you for Christmas and the Christmas Dance and everything."

"My pleasure, Maggie Ward." I held her in my arms until her weeping stopped. And a little longer for good measure. "I didn't take it seriously, you know. I mean I knew you were grateful and that most of the things you were saying were sardonic humor."

"Sardonic?" She lifted her tearstained face. "And I use big words. . . . Do you really know that I am grateful with every bit of feeling I have?"

"Yes, Maggie. And I'm grateful too. My new life began in Arizona just as yours did. It's a two-way street."

She nodded, that quick, comprehending gesture of understanding and agreement that so fascinated me the first hour in Tucson.

"I should go home now and do my hair."

"And I should get a haircut . . ."

"Or I'll leave you on the seventh green. And that's an order."

"Yes, ma'am, Admiral, ma'am."

"Silly." She kissed me and turned away, back toward State Street and the subway.

Mercurial. Chameleon. Unpredictable. Delightful. Haunted.

What happens after the dance?

I'll worry about that after the dance.

As all our family confidently expected, it was Maggie's dance. If she was shy or embarrassed or felt cheap or common or vulgar or out of place, she gave not the slightest hint. Rather, she accepted the admiring glances like an absolute monarch accepts the adulation of her subjects.

"Philadelphians," my father said as he shook his head in astonishment, "don't have that much class."

"An exception to prove the rule?"

"Most probably," he agreed. "You don't mind if I dance with her?"

"So long as Mother doesn't."

He eyed me as if I were an opposing counsel. "She won't, as long as you dance with her."

That night The Club was a glittering tribute to the first year of the postwar world, a hint of affluence yet to come. It smelled of evergreens and champagne, red and white decorations sparkled on the walls, Glenn Miller music urged the elegantly clad bodies to sway gently back and forth. The war was over, peace had begun, and prosperity had finally come around the corner.

As luck, or perhaps a comic Providence would have it, the first person we met inside the club was Barbara Conroy.

"Barbara, this is Margaret Ward; Maggie, this is—"

"So you're the young widow from Philadelphia Joanne Keenan is raving about. *Well,* all I have to say is that you're welcome to him. Maybe you can do more to make him a man than any of us did."

She turned and stalked away from us, a triumphant, if slightly foolish, harpy.

"You were lucky you didn't marry her" was Maggie's only reaction.

"I'm sorry if she bothered you."

"Not in the least," she said and laughed. "To tell you the truth, I don't even feel sorry for her."

"Don't you ever dare become that overweight, Margaret Mary Ward."

"Angela is my confirmation name, if you want to be absolutely formal. . . . I couldn't become that overweight even if I wanted to."

In my arms on the dance floor, smelling of the lilac scent I had picked out and wearing my pearls and our dress (so she had ruled, in a burst of generosity, they were to be assigned), she was relaxed, light as a summer breeze at the end of a hot day, and utterly trusting.

"Is that you beneath all that armor?"

"A compressed me"—she winked—"but a happy me. I don't know why we women put up with such terrible fashions. Next time I'll take your advice."

I did not make an issue of "next time," but my heart did a slow, lazy spin of delight.

"Look at your mother," she continued, "she has a wonderful figure. She shouldn't have to be bound up in one of these terrible corsets."

"I agree."

"I bet they made love while they were dressing for the dance."

"Maggie Ward!" For the first time she had genuinely shocked me.

"Well, certainly, they made love. Look at the way she glows and he looks so pleased with himself. They'll do it again after the dance. I think it's cute."

"No privacy at all from your dagger eyes."

"I can't help what I see. And what's wrong with seeing it anyway? It's not only cute, it's beautiful. I even knew it with my parents when I was a little girl. I mean, I didn't understand what they did, but I knew they were very pleased with each other. Dr. Feurst says that's one of the reasons I . . ."

"Survived?"

"Uh-huh. His exact word."

"My husband wants to dance with you," Mom said as we passed them on the dance floor.

So we exchanged partners for the rest of the dance.

Though more fully armored, my mother was as light in my arms as Maggie, and even more radiant. Unless my untrained nostrils were deceiving me, she was wearing the same scent. Her short silver hair gleamed in the light of the dance hall, as did the jewels on her neck. Her strapless maroon gown emphasized her classic beauty, and the skin of her back was Irish-linen smooth. I held her close, her eyes level with my chin, her ample breasts solid against my chest.

She did not seem in the least upset by the intensity of emotion she must have felt in me. On the contrary, she relaxed against me in snug contentment.

Maggie Ward, I told myself with more than a trace of love-besotted incoherence, had opened to me the possibility of enjoying the beauty of all women and even of recognizing the unquestionable attractiveness of my mother.

If I was not careful, this Maggie Ward person would unmake me and then remake me completely.

"I am honored by the two most beautiful women in the room during the same dance."

"I know you're not going to let that lovely child get away." She smiled imperceptibly at my compliment. "She needs you so much. Just like I needed your father."

"Maybe I need her as much as he needs you."

She actually blushed. "You'll never find another girl like Maggie Ward."

"I know that."

My head was whirling—too much emotion, too much revelation, too much beauty. We finished the dance in silence.

I brushed my lips against hers, lingering for a fraction of a second.

"I hope Maggie matures into a woman as lovely as you are, Mom."

She was mildly flustered but not displeased. "You'll have to keep her around for a quarter of a century to find out, won't you, dear?"

Score one for my gorgeous mom.

"Tom is cute," Maggie informed me when the dance was over. "No wonder you're such a nice boy."

"I'm overwhelmed with compliments."

She patted my hand. "And I am having the time of my life, as you surely know without having to read my mind."

Just then we encountered Kate.

"Kate, this is Maggie Ward. Maggie, this is—"

"Maggie!" Kate's eyes flooded instantly. "I'm so happy, so very, very happy." She embraced my date enthusiastically. "I'm so looking forward to getting to know you."

"Me too." Maggie rose to the occasion and gave no hint of surprise.

"What . . ." Maggie began when Kate and her date drifted away.

"I called her Maggie when I was kissing her good night after a date. Then I told her that you were a girl who had died."

"The poor thing," Maggie said as she drew back from me, "how embarrassing, and how nice of her not to mind." Then she returned to me, even closer. "No, poor Jerry, to be in love with such a drippy ghost." She touched my cheek again. "Poor sweet Jerry. It would not have been a mistake at all to marry her."

"My intentions are elsewhere."

To which she did not reply but only danced serenely in my arms, humming the waltz music along with the strings of the orchestra.

In the car after the dance, she sobbed all the way back to her apartment.

"Don't pay any attention to me, Jerry," she begged during a temporary intermission in her tears. "It's not your fault. It was a wonderful night. I loved it all. Just a crazy"—she began to cry again—"nervous reaction, like the other night. Silly Margaret Mary Ward has to pretend to be the life of the party and wear herself out."

"It's all right, Maggie, I understand."

I walked her to the door of her building, guiding her arm as she tried to negotiate the stairs up to the second-floor entrance on new-fallen snow with our Marshall Field's high heels. I kissed her good night, firmly, as appropriate for an important date, but no hints or requests for a prolongation of the evening.

I was hoping nonetheless that such an invitation would be issued.

Foolish hope.

"Remember your promise."

"Yes." I had forgotten it completely.

"I know your phone number. I'll call you when my life is better organized than it is now. But don't wait for me."

"That's not part of the promise."

"Yes, it is." She ducked inside the door and slammed it. I heard her dashing up the old stairs.

I was not particularly troubled as I drove home. There were two alternatives, about which I did not want to think on the pleasant pink cloud that I had brought with me from the dance floor with Maggie so light in my arms:

Either I would keep my word and let her drift out of my life. Or I would pursue with relentless determination and demand that she marry me and permit me to finish what I had begun with her. And vice versa.

"I hear she was sensational," Packy greeted my return. Seminarians didn't attend such worldly, women-infested events like Christmas dances. "I didn't think she'd work up enough nerve to risk going."

I told him about my promise.

"Do you intend to keep it?"

"Absolutely not."

Packy smiled approvingly. "All's fair . . ."

"In love and war."

The mention of war may have been the reason I dreamed about Rusty and Hank that night.

But the old dreams returned the following night too.

CHAPTER

I should have charged into the Lantern Room and carried her off?

I should have listened to the message in her smile at the door of her flat and ignored all other messages?

I should have accepted her at her word that she was in Chicago because she wanted to be near me?

I should have realized that the only reason for her to walk down Lathrop was that she wanted to be caught?

As my friends in New York would put it, what can I tell you?

Yes to all four questions.

Moreover, I could have acted on such responses without ever dishonoring Father Donniger's wisdom on how to treat women.

As is transparent to me after six decades of life and doubtless to you after a hundred and twenty thousand words, I am a bit of a Hamlet.

Put me in a situation where there is no time to think, where I am constrained to act on instant instinct—air combat, a courtroom, the floor of the Board of Trade, an attack by a nasty panelist at a professional meeting, the final phase of negotiations with a publisher—and I'll perform superbly. Give me time to think and I'll very likely think too much. Perhaps I was searching for Romance and Adventure in 1946 because I was looking for a life in which I could rely on instinct instead of thought.

Perhaps it is a result of growing up in a family that seems to have flourished not only economically but emotionally. Maybe I've never been hungry enough, in a number of different senses of that word, to take chances when there is time to reflect on them.

This thin-bloodedness, if you will, is my tragic flaw, and I've had to contend against it, with varying degrees of success, all my life.

It is precisely at those times when I begin to see all sides of a question and stumble into the endless and bottomless swamp of analyzing the questions to death, that the demons begin to return, in one form or another, and the horror becomes partially unchained.

In Tucson, when I offered to buy breakfast for the pathetic little serviceman's widow, at Picketpost, when I compelled her to perform my sexual initiation, I was acting on instinct and acting wisely.

That night at the door of her apartment, when I did not lift her into my arms, chenille robe, flannel pajamas, and all, and cart her off to River Forest, I was acting reflectively and stupidly.

Even my wife, who has insisted through the years of our marriage that I am too hard on myself, admits the validity of my self-analysis. Characteristically, she defends me against it.

"You're a thoughtful man," she argues, "so you think. What's wrong with that? Maybe you do worry too much sometimes, but that's part of being you. I prefer that sort of man to someone who is merely a bundle of conditioned reflexes. And if that girl really wanted you, she ought to have known that she would have to take the final step toward you."

In any event, as the first postwar year turned into the second, I was deeply involved in analysis and reflection *in re* Maggie Ward.

Maggie would not join our quiet family New Year's party. She had promised the night to Wade. I drank too many beers, far too many, and woke up in time to listen to the Rose Bowl game.

Illinois beat UCLA 45–14. A Big Ten victory—that will show you how long ago 1947 was!

The next morning I actually rode the El down to Loyola to spend a couple of hours in the law-school library, studying civil procedures. After lunch I strolled over to the Drake to talk to Maggie. My rival was with her.

He was a jerk.

Wade McCarron was about thirty, taller than me, broad-shouldered with receding blond hair and a developing potbelly. Like many other big men who are beginning to go to seed because of an excess of food and drink and a deficit of exercise, he compensated by sucking in his gut and pushing out his chest.

Maggie introduced us in the lower lobby of the Drake, without a flicker of emotion. We established that Wade was from Tennessee, had served in the Marines on Guadalcanal and Iwo, rising from the ranks to become a bird colonel, and that he had made a lot of money on the Board of Trade. We also put on the record his dislike of navy flyers who had done nothing to support his troops on the ground.

"The young lady says she doesn't want to see you anymore, fly-boy," Wade McCarron informed me. "If I were in your position, I'd pay attention to her."

I didn't take him seriously. He was a crude blowhard, a pathetic loudmouth. At most he was another one of Maggie's strays.

"Where did you folks spend New Year's Eve?" I asked, pretending that we were engaged in a casual, friendly conversation.

"Colosimo's," Maggie said coldly. "It was very interesting . . . and you made a promise," she added coldly. "I told you that I didn't want to see you anymore and you agreed."

"Typical spoiled navy brat," McCarron snarled. "I won't warn you again, punk."

"I have an appointment with Dr. Feurst this afternoon," I said to Maggie, ignoring her escort's silly bluster.

"I gave you permission to see him." She wouldn't look me in the eye. "I've kept my promise; why don't you keep yours?"

"Because he's a no 'count hound dog, hon," the ex-colonel informed her, in a voice that had taken on a mountaineer's accent. "He needs a good whupping."

"I will not stand here while you two men humiliate me with your tough talk, I do not intend to be late for class." Maggie stalked away.

"First you get whupped, worm." He tried to sound mean. "Then you get killed. Clear?"

"I'm terrified." I turned on my heel and walked out. Maggie had a certain taste for losers. What was she up to?

I pondered that during the brief walk back to Loyola and concluded that she thought Wade was safe because she would not fall in love with him and I was not safe because she was already in love with me.

I fed a stack of quarters into a public phone in the Lewis Tower's lobby. My friend at the Bureau of Personnel told me enthusiastically that they were much better organized now. I rejoiced with him and posed my new question. He must have had the material on his desk: no officer named McCarron had fought on Iwo. And after a few seconds' search he added that no one with that surname had been on Guadal either.

I thanked him, told him to forget about Andrew Koenig and check on a recruit named Wade McCarron from Tennessee.

Maggie's current stray was not only a loudmouth, he was a phony.

That fact did not make him any less dangerous, a truth that should have been self-evident.

I worked out the scenario in my head as I ambled down Michigan Avenue to the 50 East Washington Building, even then an aerie for shrinks. Dr. Feurst, however, was not an eagle but an elf, a Jewish elf from the Schwarzwald, a bald, vest-pocket Santa Claus with a propensity to massacre English syntax as his laughter indeed shook his belly like a bowlful of jelly.

"Ya, gottdammit, vatdahell, young fella," those phrases in various orders served as punctuation marks for his discourse. "She vill neffer get over vat hast been done to her. Vat you dink? Psychological problems are like da common cold? Vatdahell?"

"I shouldn't try to persuade her to marry me?"

"Vatdahell, young fella." He pounded his belly as if he were weak from laughing at me. "Gottdammit, absolutely not, nein?"

"Absolutely not what?" I did not want to like this mad little character, who even put his finger next to his nose when he talked, as did the real Claus.

"Gottdammit, vat's wrong vit you, young fella? Don't you understand plain English? You should absolutely not abandon your—ha!—chase of da young voman? She make fine bride, nein?"

"She won't recover from the, uh, traumas of her life, but I should still try to marry her?"

"Iss contradiction? Gottdammit? Iss attractive, iss smart,

iss brave. Vhy not marry her? So you don't have any problems, ya?"

"As I understand you, Doctor"—I was laughing with him now, despite myself—"you're saying that Maggie's losses will always be with her and will always shape her personality, but they won't prevent her from being a good—and happy—wife and mother?"

"Gottdammit, young fella, vat else I been saying all dis dime, nein? Except she vant them get in da vay. Iss always possible. Iss healthy young voman, ya? But can do unhealthy dings, nein?"

"She loves me, I dink, uh, think. No, I know she loves me. But she wants time to work out her problems with you and to attend college. . . ."

"Vatdahell, young fella, you make wife stop seeing me?"

"No."

"Gottdammit, you make her stop going school, stop ruining pretty eyes on all dem books?"

"Certainly not."

"Zoooo?"

"Sometime maybe but not indefinite?"

"Vhy you keep repeating vat I already say? You vant be celibate like brother? Ha! So you don't vait forever, ya, nein?"

"I see." I didn't, but I should have.

"Zoooo, gottdammit, you someday make her choose like mature, pretty young girl, ya? But don't manipulate . . . iss werra bad, werra terrible, nein?"

"Manipulate?"

"Yah, sure. Gottdammit. Misses father, nein? Nice man, veak man, ya? She takes care of veak man. You iss not veak man. Don't pretend you can't live vitout her, gottdammit?"

"Yah."

"Freedom!" He leaped to his feet, an elf celebrating liberty. "Ve must all respect everyone's freedom. Dat is vat you fought for, nein? Even the freedom to make our own mistakes, gottdammit, young fella. So you respect her freedom even to make her own mistakes, even tragic mistakes. Yah? Nein?"

"Don't exploit her sympathy and let her make her own

mistakes." That's the wisdom with which I came away from Dr. Feurst's office.

Unexceptionable wisdom. After decades of trying to practice the granting of such freedom to those I love, I know that such a grant is not incompatible with pressure on the beloved, up till the very last second. I suppose I should have known it then. Perhaps I did not want to. Perhaps having found Dulcinea, I was now discovering that I didn't want her. Certainly the notes in my journal that night, so different from the two conversations I wrote in my story notebook—housed in Maggie's Florentine-leather Christmas present—suggest that I was beginning to think that she was not, after all, worth the candle.

But first I must record the third conversation, the only talk my father and I ever had about sex.

We met by accident at the Lake Street El station. The temperature had risen to the upper twenties, a promise perhaps of spring still far away. We walked home down neatly shoveled sidewalks and past snow-covered evergreens and Christmas-lighted windows—no picture windows in River Forest.

"Are you in love with that little girl from Philly?" he asked abruptly in his "friendly witness on the stand" courtroom manner.

"I think so."

"Are you going to bed with her?"

It was the first hint I had ever heard from his lips that men and women engaged in such activity.

"No . . . I did in Arizona."

"That's an important part of marriage," he went on, as though my previous reply had no effect on his line of questioning. "More important than the priests and nuns seem to know. It gets even more important as the years go on. Not less, despite what you might have heard. At least it should."

"I would hope so."

He glanced at me with a satisfied smile. "It isn't easy. Women aren't prepared . . ." He sighed. "Neither are men, for that matter."

"Margaret was married before, you know."

"I'm not sure that makes much difference. Under the circumstances."

"She's a remarkably determined young woman."

He glanced at me again, understanding my answer to mean that Maggie had proved a promising bedmate in Arizona.

"It's a thing you can't afford to let yourself give up on. Women's needs are different, but not completely different. You need patience and persistence. The persistence is more important, especially when you find yourself tiring of patience and try to persuade yourself that sex isn't important because there are other glues holding your marriage together—kids, home, plans. Then you really have to be persistent. And not worry about making a fool out of yourself. It's like hitting a home run with the bases loaded and two outs in the ninth."

"I understand."

"Some people are more fortunate than others. They establish patterns early. But still they have to keep at it."

"I understand."

"Your mother is a remarkable woman," he continued, his eyes darting nervously. "I'm sure you see through the mask of vagueness she wears sometimes."

"Sure." I hadn't seen through that mask very often.

"Most of our friends think I am the dominant one in the family." He shoved his hands firmly into the pockets of his overcoat. "You doubtless perceive the truth—that she is the stronger of us two and influences me far more than I influence her."

"Certainly." I had not perceived that at all.

"Even in this matter," he stated, turning an even darker shade of red, "while I may have been the more, uh, forceful at the beginning, we have reached a certain balance now; indeed I sometimes think to myself—though I would never say it directly to her—that even here she is in fact often the leader."

I often ponder that revelation when folks who grew up after 1960 think that they have discovered for the first time that women like sex.

"I understand."

"What do you understand?" he demanded irritably.

"That you and Mom have a great sexual relationship."

"Do you? I wondered whether kids notice. . . ."

"Oh, yes." A lot of pieces of a puzzle that I had never noticed before fell into place: the closed bedroom door on Saturday mornings, sounds of muffled laughter, smiles over secret jokes, extra affection in a "good-bye" kiss in the morning or a "hello" kiss in the evening. All part of the ordinary environment of our life, no more requiring special explanation than did breathing.

Good for them, I say, even forty years later.

"The matters of the, uh, bedroom can hardly be kept totally secret," he murmured, averting his eyes from mine, "they do tend to pervade the rest of life"—he laughed nervously—"don't they? Yet you can hardly talk about it, much less explain it to your children, can you? Or ask them if they comprehend the, hmmm, intensity that is involved and the way it soothes other . . . problems."

"Even Maggie noticed."

"At Christmas?"

"At the dance."

He laughed, both embarrassed and complacent. "The young woman would be burned as a witch in another century."

"Definitely."

"She's precious, son. A gold mine."

The Dutchman's mine?

"She's had a rough life for one so young."

"All the more reason to tread carefully. And be patient."

We had arrived at our Dutch Colonial house, so the conversation was over. Sex had been mentioned explicitly, once and by me. But my father had pretty much told me the story of his marriage-long love affair with my mother. I loved them both at that moment as I had never loved them before.

"Dad . . ." I blurted.

"Yes?" He sounded irritable again, displeased that the awkward topic had not been finished.

"Well . . . if my wife is as beautiful and wonderful as

yours"—Maggie Ward had loosened my tongue—"I don't think I'd be able to keep my hands off her either."

His bushy white eyebrows shot up in delight. He pounded me on the back.

"You indeed are my son." He laughed. "Never a doubt."

Did he add "And be persistent" at the end of the conversation? Given his own fondness for Maggie Ward, I can't believe he did not. But I didn't record it in my story notebook.

And did he recount our conversation to Mom, perhaps in bed that night? Then I didn't think so. Now I'm certain he did. And I'm sure they both laughed at me, quietly and affectionately.

As I consider my record of this conversation in the now dry and cracked "storybook" Maggie Ward gave me for Christmas in 1946, I am convinced that my mother and father are together again, still deeply in love, in heaven or, as my son Jamie the priest puts it, "in that which is to come." I still ponder their lifelong love affair. What rhetoric, what vocabulary did they have to talk about their love? Or did they talk about it? And how did they know at the beginning of their romance that they were well matched? Or did they?

Were they just lucky? Or was there some instinct that possessed them both?

"You can't figure out everything," my wife says. "You were the lucky one to be born from such a marriage."

Amen to that.

My journal that night was devoted entirely to the pros and the cons *in re* Margaret Mary Ward.

The cons were pretty strong.

She's eighteen years old, the age of a freshman in college, a girl who would have graduated last June from Trinity. If she had grown up in River Forest, I would not date someone that young, no matter how pretty she might be. She is erratic and unpredictable and heavily burdened by the losses in her family. They are not her fault, but she will still bring them with her to marriage. As Dr. Feurst said, she will

*mourn for them as long as she lives. She is a fascinating lover, but I
must not permit sex to blind me to the problems she has.*

Dulcinea sought is much safer than Maggie Ward found.

I did not add what was also the obvious truth: her vitality
and determination, her sensuality and passion, scared me.

That night I dreamed again about Hank and Rusty and
the other men whose bunks were empty after missions on
which I had led them.

CHAPTER

THE NEXT MORNING I WAS SUFFICIENTLY UNCERTAIN ABOUT
the conclusion in my journal to leave the Loyola library long
enough to corner Maggie at the Drake and invite her to go to
the movies that night.

"We've never had a proper date," I argued.

Perhaps I wasn't sure I wanted the found Dulcinea anymore, but I wasn't quite ready to give her up yet either.

"I'm working." She gestured at the nearly empty Lantern
Room—its red walls and black screens in a less dignified hos-
telry than the Drake would have suggested that it was a bordello (not that I knew about the inside of a bordello).

"I thought we might see *The Razor's Edge,* it's one of the
top ten."

"You made a promise." She continued to arrange silverware without looking at me.

"Or *Open City. The New York Times* listed it as one of
the ten best."

"I *said* you made a promise." She banged a fork into place.

"Yeah, but I didn't intend to keep it. All's fair in love and war. . . . speaking of war, *Razor's Edge* is about the trials of a war vet. It might help you to understand me."

"I've already seen it with Wade." She bustled to another table. "I can't imagine a vet more different from Tyrone Power than you."

"I'm better-looking?"

"Please, Jerry, my boss is giving us dirty looks."

"*Humoresque? Road to Utopia* with Bing and Bob?"

"*No!*"

"I remember the way you smiled at me when you opened the door to your apartment. . . ."

"*Please!*"

"All's fair—"

"This is neither love nor war. You're becoming tiresome."

So I went to *Open City* by myself that night, after finishing my review of civil procedures. I encountered Maggie and Wade as I was coming out of the old Studio on Chicago Avenue, replaced now by what Biddy calls the "Needless Markup" (Neiman Marcus) Building.

"Jerry, *please!*"

"I'm innocent!" I pleaded. "How would I know you were coming here?"

"You're asking for it, fella." Wade was playing his tough-mountaineer role to the hilt.

"It's a free country, hillbilly," I snarled back.

It might have been wise for me to tell him what I knew about his war record then. I guess I didn't want to embarrass Maggie.

We both loved one another. Each of us wanted out of the relationship for reasons of our own. But neither of us was able to let go. Maggie, to give her credit, was better than I at acting as if the affair were finished.

"Leave him alone, Wade; let's not be late for the film because of a man who won't keep his promises. . . . And I repeat, Quixote, this is neither love nor war."

"Don't worry about him, hon." Wade glowered at me. "He'll leave you alone."

"Anytime, hillbilly."

I shouldn't have said that.

"She is afraid to risk herself," I wrote in my journal that night. "We come to the moment of truth and she doesn't have enough truth."

But Jerry Keenan was not afraid to risk himself at the last minute, not at all.

Loneliness and sexual need force most lovers out of those moment-of-truth fears. Wade McCarron was her insurance against such a surrender to the fate of our species.

He was more dangerous than I realized.

He and his thugs caught me the next night, in a snowstorm, just outside the Forest Avenue El station. I was as unprepared as Admiral Husband E. Kimmel had been at Pearl Harbor.

The thugs held me while McCarron beat and kicked me.

On one track of the dual-track tape in my head, I was back in the Dutchman's ghost town, fighting off the demons. "Take that, you fucker, and that," McCarron repeated with monotonous lack of imagination. "And that, fucker, and that."

Only he wasn't McCarron anymore; he was Jacob Walz, the Dutchman.

I remembered that McCarron had promised a beating the first time and death the second time. So I wasn't going to die, unless he overdid it by mistake. Only it wasn't McCarron, it was the Dutchman and two of his demons.

Where the hell was Michael, seraph?

I kicked at Walz, missing as he ducked, but he kept his distance. I kept kicking until the pain became too much. I then merely endured, thinking of the souls in purgatory, as I had been taught to do in the dentist's chair.

And of the place in hell to which I would send Wade McCarron, no, Jacob Walz.

Even after my defensive kicking had been routed by pain, he was careful not to get too close. So I kept all my teeth.

Groin, stomach, chest, face, McCarron pounded away relentlessly. But not very skillfully. He was, I thought contemptuously as I struggled with the two hoods, a powder puff.

Too much time in the saloons in Phoenix talking about your lost mine.

But given enough time, even powder puffs can hurt you.

"Looka that, boys, he done vomited on me. Fucking rich fly-boy got no manners. Mebbe I should teach him some." His fist crashed into the side of my face. I tasted the sharp, salty tang of blood.

Never let a Zero get on your tail with the sun behind him.

I'd find him in one of those Phoenix saloons and beat the shit out of him in a fair fight.

Finally they dropped me in the snow, a mass of undifferentiated pain. Blood was pouring out of my mouth, I could hardly see through my swollen eyes. I was curled up in a fetal position now to protect myself from more blows.

You want to take the girl off to hell? Sure, you're welcome to her. I don't want her anymore.

McCarron, a real hero, kicked me viciously in the back. "You're lucky, fucker, we didn't kill you. Next time you won't be so lucky."

Next time you won't get behind me in the sun, hillbilly.

I lay there in the falling snow for a long time. I could freeze to death, I told myself, if I did not stand up and move. But the snow piling up on top of me seemed to be a soothing blanket. Why fight it?

There would be no one in the Forest Avenue station at this hour. Someone might stumble over me on the street. A car might come by. I could hobble to Oak Park Hospital, almost a mile away.

It never occurred to the winner of two Navy Crosses that he could also push the doorbell of the nearest house.

I decided that no friend of Maggie Ward's would send me to God's judgment seat before my time. So I chose Oak Park Hospital.

Or was it Apache Junction? Or were they the same?

And where was the guy in the fleet admiral's uniform?

I struggled to my feet and tried to straighten up. A dagger of pain raced through my chest and gut. I fell back into the snow.

All right, dummy, you don't try to straighten up; got it?

I tried again and collapsed again into the snowbank.

The third time I made it.

No thanks to you, you fucking specialist in wars in heaven.

Many light-years later, covered with blood, bent over in pain, and compulsively shivering from the cold, I stumbled into the emergency room at Oak Park Hospital (the secular name chosen long ago so as not to offend Protestants). Sister Mary Norbertine, who had been present for my birth, stared at me in horror. "Jeremiah Keenan, with whom have you been fighting?"

Fucking nun would say "with whom."

"The Dutchman. Next time he won't get behind me in the sun."

"I'm going to tell your mother, young man." She gently led me to something that might have been an operating table. "You're too old to get into fights."

"Especially when I lose. Next time I'll win."

CHAPTER

I HID THE *TRIBUNE* WHEN I HEARD MY FATHER'S VOICE IN the hospital corridor.

General Marshall might replace Jimmy Byrnes as Secretary of State because the President had grown weary of Byrnes's propensity to act independently. The State of the Union message had been a flop. Bernard Baruch and the other American delegates on the Atomic Energy Committee of the United Nations had resigned in frustration because the Russians did not want to negotiate—being busy, as it later developed, building their own bombs from plans stolen by Klaus Fuchs and Julius Rosenberg. Dean Acheson, who would be later denounced as soft on communism because he said he would not turn his back on Alger Hiss, was designing plans to save Europe (for which he would still later be denounced as an architect of the Cold War). Europe was in desperate need of saving as coal shortages forced the suspension of industrial production in many countries. Film Daily voted *Lost Weekend* the best picture of 1946. Ben Hogan won the Los Angeles open.

And, like Ray Milland in *Lost Weekend*, I wanted a drink, a nice big, soothing drink to kill the pain.

"Feeling better now?" Dad's voice was relaxed, his face tense, his fists clenched.

"Yeah." I tried to sound bored and casual. "No major damage except some loose teeth and two black eyes."

"And bruised ribs and kidney and badly cut lips and some internal bleeding."

"A few aches and pains. The bleeding has stopped, by the way. He wasn't much of a puncher. If it wasn't for those two hoods . . ."

"They're on their way to other jobs in Cuba." Dad flipped open a small spiral-ring notebook. "A friend of mine talked to a friend of The Waiter's. It'll be a long time before those punks seek a little extra money on the side. . . ."

For those of you who don't know the history of the Chicago Outfit, The Waiter was Paul "The Waiter" Ricca, Capone's successor, or rather Frank "The Enforcer" Nitti's successor (the real-life Enforcer did not fall off a roof as claimed in the film about "The Untouchables").

"Sit down, take off your hat and coat, stay awhile."

He grinned crookedly. "There's a lot of your grandfather in you."

"I don't drink as much."

"Mr. McCarron's Cadillac, bought, I suspect, on the black market, was towed away from LaSalle Street by the police today despite the bribe he had given to the beat cop to park in a no-parking zone." He ticked off the line in his notebook.

"Funny thing, his was the only car on a street of illegals which was towed away."

"Really?"

"Really. It was found that he has several moving violations for which he has not put in a court appearance. So he couldn't even drive the car away from the police pound. The federal government is interested in his tax returns. He has been suspended from trading because the governing board wants to take a look at the ways he made money on pork bellies during the meat-price run-up."

"Funny thing. I bet they're not looking at anyone else."

"Now that you mentioned it." Dad smiled cheerfully. "There are a number of other things which might happen if he doesn't get the message."

"He's not very bright."

I thought about telling him of McCarron's threat to kill me. Navy Cross winners don't admit that sort of thing, do they?

Not if they're damn fools.

"They tell me he's certain to get himself hurt eventually. He spends a lot of time over at Colosimo's telling everyone what a big war hero he was and pushing people around. Sort of person who likes to talk about his friends in the mob but who doesn't understand any of the mob rules."

"A bit of a nut."

"He'll find himself in Dutch with the Outfit if he pushes the wrong person around, even if he does it after a few drinks; the son-in-law, say, of some higher-up."

We let that hang in the air for a moment. The Outfit was strongly committed to the preservation of the family.

"Speaking of his war record, I don't think he was ever at Iwo or Guadal. Almost no one was in both battles. And my friends at Navy have no record of a Colonel Wade McCarron. They're checking up on him."

I told him the name of my contact and he jotted it down.

"That could be a big gun if we need it."

"He's a bit of a nut," I repeated.

And I let him get behind me in the sun.

Damn fool.

"What about the girl?"

"Maggie? Lay off her. She's a nice girl." My ribs hurt whenever I became too enthusiastic. "She had nothing to do with it."

"Why's a nice kid like her hanging around an overgrown punk?"

"Maggie has a fatal flaw. She collects strays."

"It could be really fatal if someone in the Outfit decides to go after him."

"Nothing in her life has prepared her to have much judgment about men." I rested my head on the pillow. "Save in one case."

"Are you finished with her?" His pencil was poised over the notebook. Maggie might be on her way out of town on the next train.

"I don't think so, Dad. Anyway, she's not involved in this mess."

"If you say so." He flipped the notebook closed. "I hope you're not having any crazy ideas about going after this punk by yourself?"

"Who, me?" I asked innocently.

"Let me do it my way." He eased the notebook into the inside pocket of his double-breasted gray jacket. "The idea is to remove the danger, not to get even."

"Right."

"When are they going to let you out?"

"When Sister Mary Norbertine is ready to forgive me for getting in a fight."

We both laughed. I stopped quickly because of my aching ribs.

"They want to keep me here another day to make sure nothing starts bleeding again. I suppose I'll be home the day after tomorrow. Mom brought the torts book so I could study for exams. I'll start in on that tomorrow morning, when they stop giving me this magic-dream medicine."

"Don't get addicted."

"No danger of that."

Not when the Dutchman and his crowd lurk on the periphery of your morphine-induced dreams.

After Dad left I returned to those dreams. They were soothing, the way I later learned the last stages of oxygen deprivation, before your brain begins to be damaged, are soothing.

Much later, the corridors were dark, I was aware of someone else standing at the doorway.

"Sister Mary Norbertine said I could come in if I didn't wake you." Maggie looked like a fifth grader, scarf pulled down over her head, coat collar turned up, as she stood at the door.

My heart flooded with love. And desire.

"I won't tell."

"I'm sorry."

"I don't look very impressive, do I?"

"It was my fault."

"Thanks for coming, Maggie. Your voice kills pain better than drugs. Sorry I can't get out of bed. Sister Mary Norbertine would kill me if I tried."

"I'm responsible."

"And I wasn't even nicked during the war, funny, isn't it?"

"I caused it."

"Maggie, this has to stop." I lifted my head off the pillow. The dagger shot through me again.

"Don't hurt yourself," she said as she rushed toward me. "I'll be good. I promise."

She meant it, poor girl child.

"You have this bad habit of picking up strays, young woman." I gingerly eased my head back into its proper place.

"Strays? Oh, you talked to Jean Kelly; I forgot."

"Two bad choices. One good one."

"Who's the good one?" She sounded puzzled. I wished I could see her face in the dark.

"Modesty prevents me . . ."

"Oh, you're not a stray, Commander." Now her laugh was cheerful. Young. Loving. "Not at all. Different class completely."

"What class?"

"Men who keep me. Buy me clothes. Lacy underwear. Nylons. Take me to nice places and nice dances. Spoil me completely. I never felt sorry for you."

"Uninitiated twenty-four-year-old?"

"You didn't need to be taught anything, Jerry." Her voice was a soft caress. "You knew how to be sweet to a woman. All you lacked was experience. I felt a little sorry for you because you were lonely and guilty and looking for adventure, but not really sorry. You definitely don't fit into the category Jean would call 'strays.' "

"What category then?"

" 'Sweet' and 'cute' are the only adjectives I want to use in a hospital room at night with you all bandaged up."

Well, that was clear enough.

"I hope you're finished with your latest stray."

"I certainly am." She sounded offended that I even had to ask.

"Promise me something?"

"Anything, Commander."

"Only sweet and cute boys from now on. No more strays."

She giggled like a thirteen-year-old.

"What's so funny?"

"You sound so much like Dr. Feurst. . . . 'Ya, ve vill haff no more of dem fellas, nein? Only nice boys from now on, like dat poor luffzick sailor boy, ya?' "

"I am not lovesick. . . ." I stopped laughing because of my aching ribs.

"I should leave. I either provoke you or make you laugh and you hurt either way."

She made no move to leave, however.

And we were joined by Sister Mary Norbertine.

"You did wake him up, dear, didn't you?" She did not sound the least bit angry. "I knew you would."

"She didn't, S'ter." I defended my woman.

Oh yes, she was my woman again. Definitely. I would write that down in the journal as soon as I had a chance.

"Don't listen to him, S'ter. I did too."

"Well, I don't know, Mary Margaret, whoever marries this young man will have her work cut out for her."

"Yes, S'ter," Maggie agreed docilely. "But he's not really bad. If you know what I mean."

"Getting into a fight at his age. I don't see why a nice young woman like you would want to visit him, Mary Margaret."

"Margaret Mary, but don't call her Peggy."

They both ignored me. Maggie had made another conquest.

"He can be very sweet, S'ter," she purred. "And he means well. You know what men are like, especially if they're Irish."

So it went. I wondered after Maggie left whether Sister had come to my room to forestall too much intimacy. I doubt it now. She merely wanted to know, womanlike, whether I appreciated how fortunate I was to have an adorable little girl like "Mary Margaret" care about me.

The next day they took me off painkillers and let me walk around a little. In that era, before health-care inflation, hospital stays were long and leisurely affairs.

The next evening I was studying contracts, without too much interest, when my friend from the Bureau of Personnel called.

"Hey, Jer, I talked to your father yesterday. Couldn't find him today. He told us you were having trouble with this phony McCarron. I wouldn't doubt it. He's a bad actor. A general discharge from Pariss Island. Taking money from young recruits in crooked gambling, picking on civilians in bars, beating up a woman who walked out on him. Charming and personable crook at first. You know the type. Doctors call him a psychopath or something like that."

"Beating up on women?"

"She wasn't a whore either. Girl he met at the USO. She wouldn't press charges, or we would have had a general court-martial. Don't turn your back on him."

"I did once." I struggled out of bed, ignoring the sudden jabs of pain. "I won't do it again. Send photostats to my dad, will you? Thanks."

I was half-dressed when Packy showed up.

"Where you going, hero?" He frowned, dangerously.

I told him where and why.

"I'll come with you."

"It's my fight."

"Why did we beat the Japs?"

"We had more planes and ships than they did."

"Exactly."

"It's my fight."

"It's your car too. I drove over in it. But I don't think you can drive it to North Sheffield."

"You win."

"Let's go."

I should have asked the man at the Bureau of Personnel how quickly Wade McCarron went after women who turned him down.

His attack on me suggested he moved quickly.

CHAPTER 42

PACKY AND I SAT IN THE CHEVY AND WATCHED THE LIGHT on the third floor of Maggie's old three-flat.

"It looks peaceful enough," he said dubiously.

"I'm not taking any chances." I hurt, I ached, I was in agony. Every ice rut that Roxy hit on our ride from the hospital had been a reprise of my beating.

I wouldn't be much good in a fight.

Unless, I told myself with true Navy Cross heroism, I had to be.

I glanced at my watch: nine-thirty.

"I'm going up there."

"Is she home from work yet?"

"Maggie wouldn't waste the electricity."

And she's still saving money because of the cost of my maroon leather notebook.

"You can't go alone."

"You're the reserves. Give me five minutes and come up after me."

"Police?"

"What can they do? We have no evidence against him."

If I had known just how dangerous the night would be, I would have called the police instantly.

I struggled painfully out of the shotgun seat of Roxy, took a deep breath, decided inhaling was a mistake and hobbled up the unshoveled wooden staircase to the door of the three-flat.

I put my finger on the buzzer, hesitated, and tried the door. It was open.

Someone else had come before me and left the door open. There were four other apartments. . . .

Don't let him get behind you in the sun this time.

I slipped through the door and climbed quietly up the steps. At first, each step sent a new shot of agony through my body. Then, as the adrenaline began to flow, I forgot about my aches and pains.

I paused on the third floor landing. Someone—male—was shouting in Maggie's apartment.

"Go get Packy," CIC advised me. He was right about how you won the war. Quantity, not quality.

He might hurt her.

I crept closer to the door.

"That peckerwood is trying to destroy me. They took away my job. They took away my car. I'll kill them all."

Maggie's reply was muffled.

"He's your friend. You're part of the plot. The peckerwoods are always scheming to get me."

So I pushed the door open.

Maggie was cowering near the stove. He was holding the collar of her chenille robe in his hand. Her hair was a mess, BUT there was no sign that he had hit her yet.

Thank God.

"Well, Colonel McCarron," I said genially, now aware again of all my aches and pains, "nice to see you again. Haven't seen you since your general discharge at Parris Island. Phony."

"I'll kill you," he thundered.

"You seem to have lost your hired thugs. I hear they had to take a little trip to Cuba. Too bad; it will be a fair fight this time."

"I'll kill you!" With a brutal shove, he sent Maggie flying across the room and against her bed.

"I doubt it very much."

But I wasn't sure. I had no experience in either American boxing or Japanese martial arts with a badly injured body. Well, I would soon find out what it was like.

"Get out of here!" Maggie yelled furiously. "I don't want you stupid men fighting in my apartment."

She pushed McCarron toward the door, as if she were a bulldozer and he a pile of dirt. "Get out! I don't want to see either of you ever again."

"The young lady wants us to leave, peckerwood." He leered evilly at me.

"Fine with me."

"I'll take care of you and then come back and see if she's any good in a quick rape."

"Lock the door, Maggie."

"You think that's gonna stop me, peckerwood?" He chuckled. "I'll break that door right in."

The smell of gin, and a lot of it, wafted toward me. Jacob Walz always drank too much before a fight. That would make it easier.

I let the Dutchman get behind me again. I tried to hobble down the steps quickly to stay ahead of him.

"Running, huh, peckerwood?" He was bumping and weaving above me. "Can't run fast enough to get away from old Wade McCarron. I'm going to tear you apart with my bare hands."

I didn't look behind me. I must get to ground as quickly as possible so I could turn and face Walz on an equal footing.

I almost made it.

On the wooden landing outside the door of the second floor entrance, he lunged after me. I dodged to the side of the platform, not quite quickly enough.

He landed on me with the full force of his large, fat body and sent me tumbling down the full flight of slippery stairs.

Battered, breathless, bleeding from my mouth again, and with shudders of pain echoing and re-echoing through my body, I lay on my back in the snow on the sidewalk. The Dutchman rushed down the stairs full speed, prepared to stomp on me with both feet.

A Zero in the sun.

Behind him the demons were screaming for my blood.

Just as he jumped, I kicked him in the gut and twisted away. Screaming like an injured rhinoceros, he sailed over me and tumbled into a snowbank, now doubled up in pain of his own.

So now we're on even terms. And you're outnumbered, even if you don't realize it.

I'm not sure what I would have done next. Probably picked him up and dragged him off to the local police station. I hurt too much for a sustained fight.

He rolled over, pawed in his coat pocket, and pulled out a small silver revolver, a twenty-two, probably, I noted as I watched it emerge, small and deadly like a water moccasin sliding around a tree stump.

That's how the Dutchman had killed Meisner, his partner. And the Mexicans.

"I'm going to blow you apart, peckerwood."

He was too drunk to aim properly. On the other hand, he might get lucky.

I spun on my left foot, and with a clumsy imitation of the proper martial-arts kick, swung my right foot toward his gun hand.

I missed his hand completely but connected with his shoulder.

It was enough to send the gun spinning into the snow.

And turn me into a raving maniac.

Threaten my woman, would he? Try to take her away from me, huh?

Not in this caveman's district, Jacob Walz. Not here.

I forgot my own injuries. I forgot decency and honor. I forgot to worry about how I would explain eventually to the police. The horror of the Lost Dutchman must at last be ended. I didn't want his gold, but he wasn't going to take my woman away from me. Not now or ever.

My fists, remembering enthusiastically the skills from my days on the Fenwick boxing team, slammed into his chest, his gut, his face with exuberant glee. I beat him to a bloody mess.

Even now I don't feel much guilt.

He fell into the snow a couple of times. I dragged him to his feet and pounded away again.

Finally I tossed him into a snowbank.

Two of the Dutchman's hired demons tried to grab me. With a sharp swing of my shoulders I sent them into the snowbank too.

"I'm outnumbered, CIC; where are you with your BAR when I really need you."

Suddenly he was there.

"That man assaulted my brother, officers, with a gun. There it is. It's the second time he's attacked him. I'm Pat Keenan, a Quigley seminarian, this is my brother Jerry. He won two Navy Crosses in the war and this slacker who was thrown out of the Marines tried to kill him."

Not Pat Keenan. That was not Pat Keenan. That was a fleet admiral with wings.

"What year did you start at the Q?"

"Forty-two."

"Pete Grabowski. I was there in thirty-nine. Did you have Clarkie?"

"Sure did."

"He flunked me out. Just as well, my wife says. Hey, this gun is loaded. Mean-looking son of a bitch, isn't he?"

"My brother was escorting him from a young woman's apartment where he'd made improper advances. Then he pulled the gun."

"Sure looks that way to me; but how come you didn't help your brother."

He wasn't my brother. He was Michael. Seraph. Specialist in wars in heaven.

"Does he look like he needs any help?"

CHAPTER 43

FOR THE NEXT COUPLE OF DAYS I WAS HIGHER THAN A PHANtom jet.

During the war I would return from combat, avoid looking at the empty places in the wardroom, plunge into my bunk and sleep as if I'd been drugged. In later years I smoked pot a couple of times with no discernible effect. Exercise does not give me a high.

Physical violence, however, sends me into orbit—which disproves my wife's contention that I am not a violent man.

I talked, I chattered, I babbled, I ranted. Most of what I said was incoherent to others. Poor Packy could not understand why I thought he was Saint Michael. The police wondered why I called Wade McCarron "Walz" much of the time. My father, understandably, wondered about the "gold mine" I claimed to have won. Sister Mary Norbertine fetched the hospital chaplain when I raved about demons.

The cops were persuaded that the mixture of pain and painkiller from my previous battle with McCarron and my memories of wartime experiences made me temporarily "nervous." The hospital chaplain recommended a Florida vacation. The law-school dean suggested a semester off.

I replied that I had routed the demons in a fair fight and the girl was now legitimately mine. All mine.

Not that I had made any attempt to call her and claim her. Andrea King, as she was again, lived in the same world as the Dutchman and Michael.

Finally I crashed with a thud, became morose and depressed, was released from the hospital—with a warning from S'ter to stay away from there, for a few weeks, anyway—and went home to study contracts and torts and civil procedures.

Today I am still uncertain. Both the incidents were real, both were related to my search for meaning in life, both were part of my quest for adventure and romance, both involved Andrea King, whatever might be her current name, both were part of an ongoing conflict between good and evil that we haven't lost yet.

And both hinted that if I continued to be involved with Andrea King, I'd have all the adventure and romance I wanted: the Dutchman and the seraph would always lurk just around the corner, waiting to renew their war in heaven for the possession of her soul.

After I collapsed from my violence-induced high and began to ache again, I concluded that studying civil procedures was a lot easier.

I was even respectful to Professor Hennessey.

With a little more self-restraint, Wade McCarron could have gone a long way. In small-town and rural America in the early years of the century, such men, sociopaths we'd call them now, were not dangerous because everyone knew their reputations since first grade and no one trusted them. The mobility caused by the war gave the Wade McCarrons of the country a larger stage on which to perform and greater freedom to escape punishment.

Maggie, an isolated young woman deprived of her own roots, was the perfect victim for such a man.

He had overreached, as such men always do, sooner than many of them. Now he was finished in Chicago. He was held without bond for forty-eight hours in Cook County Jail on charges of illegal possession of firearms, assault and battery, assault with a deadly weapon, and attempted murder. His seat on the Board of Trade was revoked because he had obtained it under the false pretense that he was a combat veteran. The federal grand jury was considering conspiracy charges. The IRS was taking a hard look at his tax returns.

He jumped bond the day after he was released. No one tried very hard to find him. He was killed in a barroom fight in Juárez, Mexico, the following summer, a lost soul in whose character conscience had been misplaced. I tried to feel sorry for him and did so in my head. In my gut I still remember the muzzle of the little silver revolver waving unsteadily at me, like a snake ready to strike.

Maggie Ward—into whom Andrea King was again dissolving?

I had won her in a fair fight, had I not?

Sure, but, if it's all the same to you, can I return the prize?

Or so I thought as January shivered toward February, the exams drew near, George Marshall became Secretary of State, and "I'll Dance at Your Wedding" surged to the top on the Saturday-night *Hit Parade* radio program.

Even the song didn't bother me. Whose wedding?

Me date?

Don't be silly! I'm finished with women!

That is not, however, how the Good Lord—or Lady Wisdom, as my son Jamie (the priest) calls Her—has designed our species.

So, almost without realizing it, I found myself, on the Sunday before the exams, boarding the Lincoln Avenue street-car at North Avenue.

I glanced fretfully at the handful of people on the car, more afraid, I think, that she would be among them than that she would not be there.

I saw her halfway down the car, bent over a book. My heart exploded with relief and love. "She's yours, after all," CIC informed me; "you won her in a fair fight, didn't you?"

Right!

I sat next to her and removed Mauriac's *The Vipers' Tangle* from her mittened hand.

"Good afternoon, Maggie Ward. I thought I'd remind you that I won you in a fair fight."

Her shooting-star smile lit up the streetcar, the grimy gray North Side and most of the rest of the cosmos. Then she turned it off just as quickly, twisted away from me toward the window, and buried her face in her mittens.

"I'm so ashamed."

I took possession of her tough little jaw and twisted her face back toward me.

"I don't care whether you're ashamed. . . ." I tilted the jaw upward. "I don't quite mean it that way, Maggie. I hurt when you hurt, but I won't permit it to get in the way."

"I deserted you," she said helplessly. "Just like I did in Arizona."

I hadn't bothered to think about that.

"He would have hit me and raped me and maybe murdered me. You saved me. And I threw you out of my apartment too. And I didn't come running down the stairs to help you." Her eyes filled with tears. "I didn't even look out the window to see what was happening. Well, not at first."

"And when you did?" I continued to resist the pressure of her chin, which wanted the worst way to collapse to the floor of the streetcar.

"I thought I saw you on the ground and then I flew down the stairs"—she snickered despite her tears—"with a carving knife in my hand."

I couldn't help myself. Public conveyance or not, I kissed her. "Butcher knife?"

"No." She shook her head vigorously. "This time it was a carving knife. And I saw your adorable brother talking to the police and you stalking around like you were Achilles or some other warrior who had won a battle and I laughed and I cried and I ran back upstairs and put the knife away."

"Adorable, huh?"

The picture of Maggie Ward, in blue flannel pajamas, heavy robe trailing behind her, rushing into battle with an enormous knife clutched in both hands was worth the price of admission.

Okay, Seraph, maybe there's three of us now.

"Well," she said as she blushed, "not as adorable as you. And not nearly as sweet. But," she rushed on, eager to put all her guilt on the table and learn whether absolution was still possible, "I realized that I had betrayed you again and was so ashamed that I didn't have the courage to visit you in the hospital or even call you on the phone. I thought I might never see you again."

"Did you really?" I put one hand on either shoulder.

"No, I really didn't. I knew I'd see you again. I just couldn't wait."

"And my adorable brother Packy, alias Michael the Archangel, kept you informed, every day, on my hospital progress."

"I heard, secondhand, every one of Sister Mary Norbertine's sermons. Packy loves you almost as much as I do."

I put my arm around her and drew her close. "You are direct when you make up your mind, aren't you, Maggie Ward?" I placed François Mauriac back in her hands. "Finish your book."

"I'm forgiven?"

"The issue is irrelevant. I won you. . . ."

"In a fair fight. I know that, Aeneas, but . . ."

"But the violence which you have already experienced in your life dispenses you from any obligations other than self-preservation when you're threatened with more violence. I don't feel betrayed, Maggie."

We left the streetcar at Sheffield and walked, hand in hand, through the old German neighborhood, stronghold of the German American Bund just before the war, though, heaven knows, most German Americans were as opposed to Hitler as the rest of us.

The German-American Cardinal put it succinctly: "Hitler was an Austrian paperhanger, and a poor one at that."

The first mid-winter thaw was upon us. Dirty snow was melting under a disapproving gray sky; streams of water were frantically seeking a direction in which to flow. Patches of

black and naked front lawns had begun to appear. The smell
of rain hung threateningly in the air. Nature and humankind
both knew it was a joke, a false alarm, an ingenious and perhaps mean-spirited trick. Tonight or tomorrow night a sudden
freeze would sweep the city and convert it into a massive
skating rink. The next day a blizzard would cover the dangerous ice with a deceptive blanket of snow.

And once more the poet's prediction about spring following winter would be proved wrong. In Chicago anyway.

Key in hand, Maggie angled her jaw toward the heavens
on the outside landing at the door of the building, "I'm not
letting you in to express sorrow or gratitude."

"Are you letting me in?"

"Silly. I'm letting you in—"

"Do you think you can keep me out?"

Lips pursed, she considered me thoughtfully. "Probably
not, Finn."

"Who?"

"Finn MacCool, Irish Achilles, berserker . . ."

"You got me perfectly."

She inserted the key, turned it, and struggled with the
door. "*Anyway*, I'm not letting you in for any of those silly
childish reasons which I would not want to have to confess
to Dr. Feurst when I see him tomorrow . . ."

"Let me." I pushed the door with my shoulder. It sprang
open easily.

"Men *are* useful." She acknowledged my ceremonial bow
and preceded me into the stairwell.

"Rarely," I agreed. No demons. No ghosts, no memories
even of my war in heaven here.

"You're not letting me finish." The stairs were dark, but
I could imagine her eyes flashing dangerously.

"Finish then." I extended my arm around her waist and
pressed my fingers lightly against her well-armored belly.

You'd be fired at the Lantern Room if you did not wear a
girdle.

"I'm making it unnecessary for you to break the door
down, Jeremiah Thomas Keenan, because . . ."

"Aren't you going to finish?"

"Because"—she gulped—"I can't live without you."

When Maggie makes a gift of herself, she does it with ribbons and fancy wrapping paper and nothing held back.

I tightened my arm around her.

"Funny thing. I know what you mean. Which is why I spent a perfectly good Sunday afternoon before exams watching Lincoln Avenue streetcars."

She opened the door to her apartment without any help from me, slipped out of my arm, tossed aside her coat, and turned up the gas heater. "No point in freezing."

"I don't plan to freeze." I hung up her coat and mine in the paper-thin wardrobe.

Maggie watched with troubled blue eyes. "Sometimes I think you are too sweet to be real."

"Because I hang up coats?" I closed the door of the wardrobe. "That's the way my mother raised me."

"She's a dear . . . Should I make you some hot chocolate?"

"Just what I wanted."

"Hmff." She strode into the kitchen alcove as if the three or four steps put a vast distance between us.

I followed after her. She kept her back to me as, fingers unsteady, she measured the spoons of Ovaltine into two chipped mugs.

She's scared, I thought. So am I. We're both driven by energies that we do not control.

"What about time, Maggie?"

She turned on me, surprised. "I'm not working tonight, the Lantern Room is . . . oh . . ." She paused as her face flushed. "You mean the time of which I needed more . . . like my correct sentence structure?"

"Literary women speak correctly. And, yes, I do mean that time."

"I'll always need time." She cradled one of the mugs in her hand. "I'll always have to struggle with what happened to my family, both families, I guess. That shouldn't have any effect on how I feel about you."

She waited uncertainly for my reply.

"Your milk is warm enough now."

"Huh? Oh ... does it make any difference to how you feel about me?"

"What do you think? ... Be careful with that milk."

"I won't spill it ... I think it ought to, if you had any sense. But ..." She filled my mug and presented it to me triumphantly. "If you don't have any sense, there's nothing I can do about that, is there? Would you take this into my drawing room, sir? I think I have some chocolate cookies here in the cabinet."

"Nothing like a chocolate orgy." I chose the edge of the bed, leaving her the mohair chair.

"Yes, there is." She curled her legs under her and studied me, waiting for my reaction.

I thought it ought to be both realistic and hopeful. I tried for the right words and ended up with, "I love you, Maggie."

"Yes, but ..."

"But nothing. Yes, I will have another cookie. Your life has been different from that of the Rosary freshmen I wouldn't date this year because they are too young and giddy. The result of what you have suffered and survived is that you are more attractive rather than less attractive. I don't mind a little extra fragility, because there is a lot more strength."

Her eyes misted. "You are unbearably sweet."

"Sister Mary Norbertine doesn't think so."

"Yes, she does. She told me so. Even"—she laughed—"if you do get into too many fights."

"Enough talk, Maggie Ward." I finished my hot chocolate, wolfed down another cookie, and stood up. "I've waited long enough."

She rose also. "Me too."

I took her mug out of her hands, put it carefully on top of a stack of books, and consumed her in my arms. It was our first real kiss since Arizona, more slow and elegiac than passionate. A lot of mistakes and missteps were forgiven and dismissed.

An El train roared by, stirring us out of an embrace that might have lasted forever.

"Did we start that earthquake?"

"You get used to them. I hardly notice anymore."

"There are certainly enough pleasant distractions in this apartment."

She rested her head against my chest. "Too long . . ."

"Much too long."

I helped her out of her navy-blue sweater and dark wool skirt, a project that required much tugging and pulling and giggling and brought to mind shattering pleasure. I had to tug and pull some more and overcome hysterical giggles as I struggled with the thick winter underwear she was wearing over her bra and girdle and which were a delight to tug away.

"It's cold in here," I protested as she began the same task with my clothes.

"It takes time for the stove to warm up. Why don't we jump into bed?"

"Will it be warm there?"

"Isn't that up to you, Sir Lover?"

Still partially clad, shivering from the cold that had not yet been exorcised from her apartment, and laughing happily, we dived under the covers of her harsh, narrow bed and clung protectively to one another.

The uniquely human aspect of human sexuality, my son Jamie the priest tells us authoritatively, is its quasi pair-bonding dimension. Satisfying human sexuality differs from the sexuality of the other higher primates in that it disposes the couple, without any conscious intention on their part, to more sex. Their bodies are disposed, not fated, mind you, or genetically programmed, merely inclined to combine again.

"Tell me about it," his mother says patiently. Jamie prepares to tell her about it until he realizes that she is using the expression in its teen-talk sense. He grins sheepishly, knowing that Jamie the priest can do nothing really foolish in the eyes of his mother.

My body and the body of Maggie Ward were certainly inclined to combine again. It is perhaps true that we were not programmed genetically to make love that afternoon, but our freedom of choice, as we clung to one another, sharing warmth and hope, was severely limited. To put it mildly.

She was wearing my turquoise pendant. Fingers on the top of her breasts, I lifted it off her chest. "I should have given you a ring."

"I wouldn't have taken it."

"If I'd had the nerve to buy it, I would have had the strength to make you take it. And then you couldn't have run."

"I'll never run away on you again," she promised.

"I won't let you try."

It was an exchange of vows which, however well-meant, was not altogether binding. Not yet.

There was no need to hurry, no rush to finish what we had started. The warmth of each other's bodies on a damp, dreary afternoon was enough pleasure for the immediate moment.

"Not as luxurious as Picketpost, is it?" Maggie's fingers caressed my chest. "Tell me if I hurt you. I keep forgetting that you were banged up, despite the traces of those distinguished black eyes you had."

"If you bump one of those bum ribs, you'll hear the yell."

"Not as comfortable as Picketpost, is it?"

"More commonplace." I was kissing her neck and throat. "And ordinary. Two lovers relaxing with each other on a gray Sunday afternoon in a dull city."

"Exciting city," she reproved me. "I hope there are many such damp, gray Sunday afternoons."

"There will be hundreds of them, Maggie, thousands."

Maggie broke the spell of elegy first. "Please love me, Commander. It's been so long."

Gently I unhooked her white bra and removed it with ceremony and flourish. "I'm getting to be an expert. . . ." My voice trailed off in awe as I beheld her beauty. A little waif child with glorious breasts—invitation, challenge, comfort, demand, quest, home.

"Not as good as I used to be?" she asked dubiously.

"Better than ever." I brushed my lips against both wonders. "And, Maggie, you're so thin and frail."

"Four pounds under Picketpost." She sighed. "I think that will change now."

"Skin and bones." I touched her ribs.

"That all?"

"A few more things too." I touched each nipple, already firm and ready for me.

She groaned and tugged at my shorts. "So you're naked first. I've won."

"Hold still, you clever little imp." I pinned her to the bed and, with no help from my squirming prisoner, pulled off her recalcitrant satin girdle. I paused to consider the results of my labors.

"Your evaluation, Commander?" She stopped struggling and uncertainly offered herself for my scrutiny.

"Well." I pretended to ponder and inspect with the palm of my hand her breasts, her belly, her thighs, her delicious rear end. "Dulcinea continues to have the fresh, budding body of a young girl, but now a girl who is rapidly maturing, as predicted, into an exciting, no, wrong word, awesome woman."

"Impressive," she moaned, her body stretching in anticipation of pleasure.

"Did Finn MacCool have a woman?"

"Etain."

"Fine, because he is about to become a berserker again."

"That is the general idea." She dug her fingers into my hair. "Isn't it?"

So once more and, as I thought, finally and definitively, I took possession of my Holy Grail.

"What would have happened," I asked when we had finished the first round and, covered now with sweat, were lying side by side, immensely pleased with ourselves, "if, the first night I appeared here, I had peeled off those absurd flannel pajamas and done the same things I've just done."

"Some silly preliminary resistance, maybe," she responded promptly, "but same final results. Which doesn't mean that you made a mistake."

"I've been a bit of a dullard."

"And I've been a little fool."

"I still love you."

"And I love you too, Commander."

We silently enjoyed our joint self-satisfaction.

"Why so quiet?" I finally asked.

" 'Silence is the perfectest Herault of joy, I were but little happy if I could say, how much?' "

"Shakespeare?"

"Who else, silly. *Much Ado About Nothing.*"

How many women can quote the Bard after they make love with you?

I pondered that thought as I feel asleep.

"No," Maggie said suddenly, as if making a decision of enormous importance, perhaps to enter a contemplative order of nuns, "you don't understand at all."

"What don't I understand?" I asked sleepily.

"What you do to me." She squirmed around so that her head was resting on my stomach, her eyes looking up at me. I ran my hand down the curve of her back and rested it on her butt. "You don't have any idea at all."

"Maybe not," I admitted.

"Like all men," she continued, launching into a classroom lecture, "you think you are the only one who is physically involved. You don't understand that from the first moment in that railroad station, body and soul and whatever else there might be, I wanted you, needed you, had to have you." She kissed my belly. "I'm not hurting your poor ribs, am I?"

"Not at all." I patted her rump. "Continue, please."

"It was not just that you're cute, though you are," she said as she caressed my torso playfully from top to bottom. "Or that you're unbearably sweet, though you are that too." She touched my cheek, the symbolic action which every mention of my alleged sweetness seemed to require. "I saw a handsome man that morning in Tucson who was also a good man."

"A good man with bad intentions?"

She was now kissing my body, every inch of it, a new technique which effectively guaranteed that, except for moans, I would remain silent. "Even your 'bad' intentions were sweet. I hadn't known many good men in my life who were also strong and brave and terribly passionate. If I was dead, and I was pretty sure that I was, you'd bring me back to life. Then the dam burst." She drew my hand around to the thick wet swamp between her thighs. "The modest little convent girl who learned to play whore to please her brutal husband and unintentionally awakened herself sexually wanted to strip off her clothes right there in the station and take you into her body. I told myself that I ought to be ashamed of myself, and I covered up pretty well, didn't I?"

"You sure did."

"I was obsessed before we finished breakfast." She was kissing me, passionately, demandingly, indeed obsessively. "I don't think I'll ever get over that obsession, Jerry Keenan. I know I don't want to."

"It's all right with me," I gasped.

"And I'm so afraid." She paused in her ministrations.

"Of hurting me? Stop worrying about that."

"You don't understand, my darling . . . dear God, I love you . . . you're so strong and good, I'm afraid you'll destroy me with your love."

"Wait a minute." I restrained her lips with one hand and one of her hands with the other, prolonging my delicious agony. "What are you saying?"

"I may win the verbal sparring matches some of the time"—she squirmed to be free and return to her work—"but if I give myself to your love, I may stop existing. I don't care anymore. I have to trust you."

"Huh?"

"Let me go, you beast; if you're going to annihilate me with your goodness, I should at least enjoy it . . . that's better."

Now her demanding lips were everywhere. And I was going to annihilate her?

"I understand, Maggie."

She suspended her attack on my loins and peered into my eyes, blue daggers knifing into my soul. "You do! Oh, Jerry, you do! How wonderful! Okay," she whispered, returning to her destruction of my sanity, "I *do* trust you."

I was trapped all right, but I didn't mind in the least.

She threw back the blanket and knelt above me. Like a new postulant sacristan holding a chalice, she took possession of my most tender parts.

"Maggie," I groaned in protest.

"You're so beautiful," she began to kiss her chalice, slowly, sweetly, reverently.

"I think I'm being raped," I gasped.

"You don't seem to mind."

"You'll drive me out of my mind." I cupped a firm breast in either hand and felt the full-blooded nipples challenge my palms.

"So you lie there," she said, suddenly very angry at me, "thinking you've found your Holy Grail who's going to keep adventure and romance in your life till you're eighty at least. And you're wrong. I found my Holy Grail, right here in my hands, my sweet, good, passionate"—she drew a deep breath—"terrible, beautiful man." Still holding her prizes, she straddled me. "Of whom I'm terribly afraid and whom I adore, and I found him before you found your silly old girl grail."

"Wonderful!" I howled, as I eased her into position above me, and then imprisoned her breasts again, this time crushing them in response to her pressure on me. "Would you admit that maybe we both found the grail that God wanted us to find?"

"Don't distract me with academic questions," she insisted, very gently lowering herself on me, her body wet now with eagerness for mine. Then she paused. "If God loves me as much as I love you, then I am really frightened of Him. Isn't that marvelous?"

I could hardly, in the circumstances, disagree, could I?

"I love to do this to you," she shouted triumphantly and stretched out over me.

An El train roared by as she screamed repeatedly in exuberant joy. Maggie was right about the Els: after a while you hardly noticed them.

Father Donniger had told us only half the truth. If you are infinitely tender with your woman and almost obsessively concerned with the intricate details of her pleasure, she may on occasion—no guarantees—turn into a ravenous aggressor who will drive you to the outer reaches of ecstasy. I would learn that truth again in the years of marriage from my wife, who especially delights in the drive-the-man-to-ecstasy game after we've had a quarrel. Especially in the forced intimacy of hotel rooms.

Thus Maggie Ward conquered me that damp gray day in 1947 as our bed became drenched with sweat of two hungry, twisting young bodies and winter temporarily melted at our window pane and El trains thundered in the background.

Afterward, still naked but now all shy and modest, she cuddled herself in my arms and fell asleep, a single unexplained tear on either cheek.

I thought my quest was finished. Maggie Ward was now mine, beyond any possibility of being lost again. And I, God knows, hers.

A prediction that was about as accurate in its prophecy as my father's prediction that there would not be another war in our generation.

CHAPTER 44

FIRST THERE WAS THE AUTO ACCIDENT.

A drunk in a brand-new Buick piled into me in the darkness at North Avenue and Harlem, a crazy, dangerous corner because all the north-south streets jog at North. As the massive car raced through the stoplight and appeared at my window like a B-24, I'm sure I shouted "Maggie!"

At least I tell myself that's what I shouted instead of something irreverent like "Shit!"

It was dark for a long time. When I finally woke up, the sun was shining and Maggie, Mom, and Sister Mary Norbertine were staring down at me, all too much like mourners at a wake.

"Doesn't he look natural," I murmured. "Sure old Tom Smyth does a wonderful job with a corpse. Course he was a young man."

S'ter: Always was a smart aleck.

Mom: You frightened us, dear.

Maggie: Go back to sleep. Then open your eyes and ask where you are. Don't you ever go to the movies?

Me: My girl won't go with me.

S'ter: She has better things to do than to waste her time with the likes of you.

Me: I agree.

Maggie: I might make an exception.

I had suffered a concussion and some new bruises on my ribs. I was lucky to be alive.

Roxy was in the car-equivalent of Oak Park Hospital, receiving a total rehabilitation.

Oh, yes, I was very lucky to be alive.

And the law-school exams were two days away. Were my scrambled brains capable of answering a single question?

"I'll knock them cold," I told Maggie. "Most lawyers have scrambled brains anyhow. And will you stop looking at me like the accident was your fault? You didn't run into me with a brand-new Buick, paid for, I'm sure, with black-market money."

"If you hadn't come to see me, you wouldn't have been hurt...."

"That kind of argument is hereinafter completely forbidden; do you understand that, Maggie Ward?"

"The accident did scramble your brains."

"Not the rest of me. Now would you stop distracting me

with your lovely body and permit me to get back to the much-less-interesting subject of contracts?"

The exams did not seem too difficult. After the last one I declined my classmates' proposals for a drinking bout and, my head still aching and my body still hurt in many and odd places, stumbled home for what I hoped was a good night's sleep.

I had just pulled the covers over my head and turned off the lights when Mom called up: "Maggie's on the phone, dear."

I dragged myself into the hallway and picked up the phone.

"Sorry to wake you, Jerry. Something very strange has happened."

"What?" I asked, feeling my stomach turn uneasily.

"My father is here. He's still alive."

CHAPTER 45

"Château Lafitte, Maggie? It's prewar." Allen Ward removed his rimless glasses and laid aside the wine list. "I'm sure you'll like it." Glancing at me, he inquired, "Ever had any of it, Gerald?"

God forgive me for my answer, true as it was.

"My father put away a pipe of it in 1935."

I don't think Allen heard me. Or, if he did, he dismissed my response as patently false. No Chicagoan could possibly have enough knowledge or money for so provident an action.

He filled both our wineglasses and then put the bottle aside, some distance away from his own upturned glass.

With considerable flourish, Allen had escorted us to lunch at the Pump Room in the Ambassador East Hotel.

Movie stars in transit from Los Angeles to New York used to ride in limousines from one railroad station up to the Pump Room for lunch and then back to another station to continue the trip.

It beats the Pancake House at O'Hare.

Not to make the scene in the Pump Room (where a young ex-football player named Irv Kupcinet was already jotting down items for his column) was somehow to be déclassé.

Unless you were a native Chicagoan.

It was hard to dislike Allen Ward. Handsome, witty, urbane, he was short and dapper, youthful in appearance and manner, almost an elder brother to Maggie, a kind of Irish Thomas E. Dewey, although his mustache was trim and slender like the rest of him. You had to look at the lines around his darting brown eyes and then into the haunted eyes themselves to get a hint of years of hobohemia and alcoholism and then wartime combat in the Red Arrow Division from North Africa to Germany.

He had plans for his rediscovered daughter in which I did not fit. It would be, I thought with some relief, entirely her decision. There was nothing I could do, one way or another, to affect her choice.

So soon out of a woman's bed was I ready, not without smugness, to be quit of her.

"I'm rebuilding the old family house at Cape May," he said as he filled my glass again. "Maggie will spend her summer vacations from Bryn Mawr down there. You'll certainly be welcome to visit us on one of the long weekends next summer, Gerald."

"Jeremiah. Prophet."

"Major prophet," Maggie added as she watched her father's every move, dagger eyes probing relentlessly. Her reaction to him was unreadable.

"Usually known as Jerry."

"Sometimes only Commander."

"It's been too many years, Maggie." He put his hand on hers. "But give me time and I promise you I'll make up for it."

"That isn't necessary, Daddy," she said, face expressionless, "we must be friends in the future and forget about the past."

"We can do so much more for her back home, Gerald." He turned to me, not having heard anything that Maggie or I had said. "Schools, social contacts, debutante balls, friends, a renewed family heritage of which she can be proud. Maggie will become one of the great women of the city, as was her mother"—his voice choked—"before her."

"I imagine we could find a place for her in Chicago, too."

"Her heritage is not really middle class at all"—he leaned forward and spoke in his favorite tone, an intense whisper—"I don't want to sound like a snob, and God knows six years riding the rods cured me of any of that, but Maggie's family is one of the oldest Irish families in the country. That's a priceless heritage."

"And we were painting ourselves blue and living in trees." Maggie's lips parted in a small smile.

"I've been lucky. I should never have survived the thirties, much less the war. Only three men from my company survived from beginning to end. And it was only luck that I didn't gamble away the suburban land which has restored our family fortunes. My new wife is a wonderful woman. And now I've finally found my daughter. God has given me a second chance. I intend to make the most of it."

He used the word "luck" but he meant "merit." By sheer willpower and hard work he had overcome the dirty tricks fate had played on him. Yet he was surely sincere. And, with the help of one of the early AA groups he'd beaten the "creature"; his wartime record was impressive; and his profitable land sales during 1945 and 1946 indicated that he was at least a quick businessman, if not a profound one.

Like many others who were fortunate enough to ride the wave of prosperity in the postwar years, he would take credit for having caused the wave.

"I have very good news for you, Maggie." He beamed proudly. "You're about to become a sister. Your stepmother, a young woman as pretty as you but in a different way, will present me with a child in the very near future. I'm sure you'll love both mother and son."

"Son?" Maggie flicked an eyebrow.

"Well, I'm hoping for a son to balance the family. But another daughter would be just as sweet a gift."

Out of one eye Maggie had been watching the Pump Room waiters. She seemed to approve of their professional skills. "I'd like to have a little brother or sister," she murmured.

Allen had told us about his life since he had vanished in an alcoholic haze from Philadelphia. He had not asked about Maggie's life. Did he know he had been a grandfather for a couple of months? Probably not, and he probably didn't care.

He was a pleasant, shallow, self-centered man who had discovered a reincarnation of his adored wife. He would expiate his guilt to the wife by showering the daughter with all that his family had lost—and in the process hardly notice the daughter as a distinct person.

He had earned the right to undo the past, had he not? Who could deny him the pleasures of rebuilding the Ward family world?

Had Maggie forgiven him for abandoning her?

Instantly in her head anyway. "I know what it is like to go mad from loss," she had whispered in my ear in the plush lobby of the Ambassador East. "He tried. He wasn't strong enough. He seems much stronger now."

Whether Allen Ward would survive more tragedy seemed to me to be problematic. However, he might not have to. His run of good luck might continue.

What did Maggie think in her heart? The adjective "major" before "prophet" was a hint. If she made a decision in her heart, I would win. If she went with her head, he would win.

And probably her head would mislead her. But who could say for sure? It was no longer a choice between life and death but between two kinds of life, either one of which might be a mistake.

No longer a war in heaven, but merely an earthly choice.

Or perhaps it was a more subtle phase of the war and hence more dangerous.

"I'll never forgive myself for deserting Maggie." He addressed himself to me, but he was talking to her. "But I think I can make it up to her. We'll both refute the doomsayers who thought the Wards had lost their guts, won't we, Maggie?"

She dipped a bit of fillet into béarnaise sauce. "I think you've done that already, Daddy. But it would be nice to have the world in all those old pictures come to life again."

"For your mother's sake."

"Yes, for Mom's sake."

"You look so much like her, almost a twin sister."

I read in a book the other day that children of alcoholics have to "guess at what is real." It seemed to me to explain much of Maggie's problem. At eighteen, almost nineteen, the daughter of an alcoholic, she was still trying to determine what was real.

I showed the passage to my wife. "Surely that was the poor thing's problem," she agreed. "Too bad she didn't understand it then. Your relationship with her might have been quite different."

"Do you have a family, Gerald?" Allen turned to me.

"Oddly enough, I do. A father, a mother, a brother, and a sister."

Maggie's daggers, angry now at my irony, shifted to me.

"And your father works for the city?"

"He's a lawyer. My mother is a musician. My brother is studying for the priesthood. My sister is still in college. I'm a bum."

"I'm sure you're not." He laughed easily, working hard at impressing Maggie's young man with his friendliness. "And you were in the service? Or were you too young?"

"I flew an F6F." He had been told that at least twice before.

"Jeremiah was a commander and received the Navy Cross twice." Maggie was still watching my reactions instead of her father's.

"Navy Cross?" He frowned. "Is that like the Bronze Star?"

"DSC," Maggie said evenly.

"Really? Well, that's impressive. But don't you think it

would be better for Maggie to come home and attend Bryn Mawr or even Immaculata? They have so much more to offer than the, uh, YMCA College."

So much for my decorations.

"I think Maggie ought to do what Maggie wants to do." Damn it, girl, smile at me when I say the right thing. "And make up her own mind where home is. We do have some decent higher educational institutions around here. There's my alma mater down on the Saint Joe River, which won the National Championship this year, and Saint Mary's across the road. . . ."

Maggie's lips had parted slightly. I did amuse her, but mildly.

"Maggie can attend whatever college she wishes," he said as he hugged her. "It's been such a long time, however, I'd like to have her close to home. But money is not a problem anymore, thank God."

"It's nice to be able to choose," she said guardedly.

Her father was, after all, pathetic. If I were in his position, I would want the same thing. Please, God, I would not be so unselfconscious in my manipulations.

"Gerald." He turned to me, man to man. "Will you tell her that she should quit that terrible job? She no longer has to lower herself. She need not ever work again. And she certainly doesn't have to wait on tables."

"Well, Allen"—I pretended to think about it but I had been saving up this line through the whole lunch—"I've only known Mag since last July, but I've known her as an adult a little longer than you have. I wouldn't dream of telling her what to do. The Irish genes run true in your daughter. No one tells her to do anything."

"Not twice." Maggie seemed to be choking back a laugh.

Point, no, several points, for the Navy.

Should I have been trying to do more than score points?

Impress Allen Ward? He was impressed only by the fervor of his own dream.

Make him look bad to his daughter? Sure, and duck when the tornado hit me.

Argue my case against his, my dream against his dream? To what purpose? Maggie would make up her own mind.

Too easy on myself? Obviously. I could beat up a psychopathic rival with a gun in his hand. But how do you go about routing a slightly pathetic father passionately pleading for a second chance?

Looking back, the only way to have done that would have been to occupy the same bed with Maggie every night of the week. As lover first and then as husband almost at once.

A husband can beat a father, even a sadly hopeful father. For a chaste, and indeed dispassionate lover, it is more difficult.

Anyway, as I told Maggie that night, I couldn't make her decision. And I wouldn't.

We were parked in front of her building on Sheffield. Snow was flurrying around Roxy's reconstructed windshield.

"You think he's a weak man," she said and jabbed an accusing finger at me.

"If you're reading my thoughts again, you're not reading them accurately."

"You think he's a snob."

"I think he is a man with a desperate dream to undo the mistakes of his past and recreate a lost, lovely world."

"Would you do the same?"

"I wouldn't use a daughter in service of my dream."

"What would you do?" she demanded hotly.

I put my arm around her, tentatively. She did not fight me off, but neither did she relax into my embrace.

"When I have a daughter that age, I hope I listen very carefully and sensitively to what she says she wants. I hope I don't make the mistake of imposing my dreams on her dreams."

"That's a very clever answer."

"I'm a very clever fellow." I drew her closer.

"You were laughing up your sleeve at him."

"So were you, Maggie Ward, only you hid it better. Major prophet, indeed."

She giggled. "Younger people always laugh at older people."

"I won't tell my daughter what to do and I certainly won't tell her mother what to do."

"Meaning me?"

"Meaning you."

"That's a proposal?"

I stirred uneasily. "No, it's an assumption."

"It lacks validity until the proper formality has taken place."

"I quite agree."

"Will it take place?"

We were grinning like a pair of idiots.

"Yes. I imagine it will."

"Oh. When will it take place?"

"In about fifteen seconds if you'll give me a chance."

"Take thirty."

"I propose"—I thought I might do rather well at this even though I hadn't planned it—"to take off a year from law school now that I've passed the first-semester tests, find myself a wife—lovely, passionate, pliant—and wander around the world with her for a year, making love and seeing sights, in that order. . . ."

"Really?"

"Really. Then I propose to come back home, return to law school, send my wife, presumably pregnant by then, back to whatever school she wants to attend, keep her in it till she graduates, and maybe figure out together with her some purpose in life."

"Ah. Interesting. You will have to find a woman to whom this is appealing."

"I've found her. So I'm asking her to marry me."

I took her in my arms and kissed her soundly.

"I'm not surprised," she murmured contentedly.

"You thought I had it on my mind?"

Neither of us said anything. Maggie drew away from me. Two damn fools, we both lost our nerve at the same time.

"He needs me, Jerry; poor sad little man."

"He has a new wife, pretty in her pictures, not much older than you are."

"If he can't leave behind his guilt, he may destroy that marriage too."

"It's your responsibility to exorcise that guilt?"

"Isn't it?"

"I don't need you the way he does, Mag." I began to marshal the facts for my closing argument. "My survival is not in doubt now. Maybe it was in Arizona. . . ."

"Not even then," she said fervently.

"We'll stipulate that. I merely want you. I can live without you if I have to, but it will be a dull, gray life by comparison. I won't plead need. Only passionate desire and powerful love."

"I don't doubt either." She patted my hand. "I guess I have to make a decision, don't I?"

"You can love us both, darling," I said. "Each in our proper way."

"You could come to Philadelphia, couldn't you? Become part of our world?" She grew angry at me as she thought about it. "Why is it only one way? Why do I have to become part of your world?"

"Do you really think I would fit into your father's plans?"

"Why not?" Her jaw jabbed upward.

"Think about it."

She did.

"You'd always be Gerald. 'My daughter's husband. Nice man. Plays a good game of golf. Not much substance. From Chicago, you know. But she's fond of him. I had hoped for someone from a better family. . . .' "

"You'd hit me if I said that."

"I know." She laughed sadly. "I don't have any illusions, Jerry."

"Is there anything more I can say?"

"No. I guess not. I'll need some time . . . not like the last time I needed time, which meant till the day after the Last Judgment. A few days?"

"Take as long as you want."

"In that, ah, contract you offered me . . ."

"Yes?"

"You implied a, uh, formalization of our liaison. . . ." I kissed her again.

"Damn literary woman."

"In the near future."

"As soon as the banns can be announced. Sooner, if you want." I touched her breast protected by coat and sweater. "Is that a problem?"

"The sooner the better." She moaned softly. "If we do it."

"I'll do my best to make you happy, Maggie."

"I know that. I don't doubt my happiness."

"Don't doubt mine."

"I'll try not to."

I thought I was an odds-on favorite.

I should have either taken her home to River Forest or spent the night in her apartment. Either way I would have had a yes by the next morning.

I thought about it briefly as she huddled in my arms. She would not resist either strategy. But I figured that I ought to be noble. I should permit her to make her choice free of the pressure of intense emotions.

I should not win the battle with her father by proving that I was a more effective lover than he was.

It was a stupid decision.

CHAPTER 46

I TALKED TO HER EVERY DAY. WE FINALLY SAW *OPEN CITY* together, necked and ate popcorn during the film. She absorbed popcorn and passion in equal amounts. I received my grades, ninth in the class. Maggie earned As in both her courses, much less a surprise, I told her. I did not press her for a decision. I assumed that I had won. I assured her that we could come back to America at various times during our *wanderjahre* as she called it. A month at Lake Geneva.

I even surreptitiously reserved a date at Saint Luke's on the Saturday before the beginning of Lent.

I also, being a prudent man, registered for the second semester.

I came home from Loyola on registration day, nervous and frustrated from my encounter with the bureaucracy, still aching from my bumps and bruises, hopelessly in love, and in a black mood because I did not quite fully possess my beloved yet.

Joanne was home on her mid-year vacation. I greeted her churlishly and stomped upstairs.

A quarter-hour later she knocked on my door. "Are you decent?"

I was lying on my bed, disgracefully decent. "What's up?"

"Maggie called a couple of hours ago. She's taking the Broadway Limited to Philadelphia. Her stepmother had a little boy. The baptism is Sunday. She wanted to say good-bye. I didn't know she had a stepmother. Is she going to stay in Philadelphia?"

"Probably."

"Are you going to live there?"

"In Philly? Certainly not."

Trust Joanne to delay an important message, I thought, remaining immobile on my bed.

Well, the decision had been reached. I'd lost. Too bad. I felt relieved. Nice girl, but too much, really, when you stopped to think about her rationally.

I wonder what Kate is doing tomorrow night.

I seemed to hear some strange noise. Not exactly flapping wings, but . . .

Rumors of angels?

"Get off your fucking ass and go get her."

"For an angel you have a very dirty mouth."

"You forget that you imagine me as a fleet admiral. So I use salty language ... I said go get her."

"I don't want her anymore."

"I told you that we'd put a lot of work into her."

"So what?"

"We made her a good lay to attract you, moron. She's special, very special."

"You could call me asshole. It's a word senior officers love."

"I don't want to shock you. I said—"

"I know what you said. So you made her a good lay to capture me. So what? Why don't you take care of yourselves?"

"You took the theology courses. You know we can't act without human cooperation. That's you, asshole."

"Find someone else, moron."

"You like losing your woman?"

"Doesn't make any difference."

"Bullshit."

Then I realized I didn't like losing. Period.

Pilots, man your planes!

I bounded out of bed, grabbed my flight jacket, rushed down the stairs and out into the cold January air. I piloted a protesting Roxinante at flight speed down Washington Boulevard to Union Station.

It was a clear late-winter afternoon. A waning full moon had risen above Lake Michigan. The demons were still there, lurking for the time they would be unchained.

If I remembered the schedule correctly, the Broadway Limited left in fifteen minutes.

Union Station was a great heartless smelly cavern even in those days when it was jammed with people. Like the station in Tucson, its aroma was a mix of stale water, human sweat, and diesel fuel, but all in much larger quantities.

A stinking cemetery, I thought, as I raced through it toward the gate from which the Broadway left, for dead hopes.

Would she be on the train already?

Or would she be waiting for me at the gate?

She was waiting.

"Sorry, Mag," I said breathlessly, "I was late getting home and Joanne muffed the message. Congratulations on being a sister!"

"Allen Richard Ward." She beamed. "Six pounds five ounces, mother and child doing nicely now. The little guy had some bad moments, so they baptized him on the spot. Sunday they're going to fill in the ceremonies at the hospital."

"Tell you what." CAG One was flying on instincts now, fogged in and forced to trust the words that sprang to his lips, "Cancel your reservation, come out to River Forest and have supper with us, and you and I can fly down there tomorrow on United and spend the weekend. You can call from home."

She was tempted. Oh, God in Heaven, was she tempted.

"I bought a one-way ticket, Jerry."

"Easier to cancel."

"They need me, all of them. I talked to Irene, my step-mother; she needs me worst of all."

"You can do both, Maggie Ward," I insisted as I held her upper arms, gently but firmly. "You can do anything you want. It's only a couple of hours by plane. We'll have the money to make it possible to spend time in both cities."

"Philadelphia is my home, Jerry."

"Were you ever as happy there as you were at our place on Christmas?"

"That's unfair," she bristled.

"All's fair . . . and don't tell me this isn't love because it is."

"I've made up my mind."

"Change it."

The conductor was shouting " 'll 'board!"

"Why?"

"For me. You love me. Don't try to pretend you don't." My grip on her became tight, fierce.

"You're breaking my heart."

"No, Maggie Ward. You're breaking your own heart. And mine too."

The conductor shouted again. The Broadway Limited was making chugging sounds, impatient to begin its mad race to

Paoli and Thirtieth Street and then on to Pennsylvania Station in New York.

"Let me go, Jerry," she begged. "I have to be on that train."

But she didn't struggle.

"No, you don't. We can fly there tomorrow."

"I want to be on that train. Please."

"You're saying no to me?" I released her. "You're ending in one railroad station what began in another?"

Clever shot. She hesitated.

"I have to, Jerry. I have no choice."

"Don't give me that. You do too have a choice."

"I must run." She turned to the gate and lifted her bag.

"It's a no to me, Maggie Ward?" I called after her.

Inside the gate, she turned to face me again and nodded.

No, Jerry Keenan. Thanks, but no thanks.

Well, I'd tried and that was that.

Her face a mask of pain, she lifted her hand in a half-wave, and then, lugging her familiar heavy bag, rushed to catch the impatient train.

I turned away and walked slowly through the massive cavern. I heard the Broadway Limited begin to move.

A broad-shouldered person in a trench coat with a gray fedora pulled down over his forehead glared at me with sad blue eyes.

You could fold wings up under that coat.

I ignored his sad eyes.

The Broadway Limited was bearing Maggie Ward out of my life. January 22, 1947. Six months to the day. Six months—I glanced at my watch—four o'clock in Tucson; six months and nine hours.

Her guilts and my hesitations had won.

EPILOGUE

MY WIFE RETURNED THE MANUSCRIPT OF THIS STORY WITH her usual spelling and punctuation corrections and her usual comment, "I don't see how a man can become a distinguished jurist and a successful writer and not be able to punctuate."

I had long ago given up defending myself, since no defense was ever accepted.

Further comments on the substance of the story were always available on request, but the unwritten rules that guide our peaceful coexistence is that we comment on the professional work of the other only when asked.

Heaven help me, however, if I should fail to ask!

So I asked at the lake the following weekend. We had the cottage to ourselves, the children and grandchildren blessedly busy in other activities. Even Biddy the water sprite.

We lay side by side in bed holding hands. Outside, the full moon flickered on the rippling waters. The horror was still chained, but as always still ready to break loose.

"What did you think of the new book?"

"I liked it a lot." Squeeze of the hand. "Best yet, maybe."

Who worried about *The New York Times* after that review.

"I don't sound too garrulous?"

"You sound like a man looking back on his youth with

perspective and respect. And a little wisdom, but not oppressive wisdom."

Well.

"What didn't you like?"

"I think you make yourself look like a nerd at the end."

"Nerd?"

"Well, maybe only a wimp. A man who quit when he shouldn't have quit."

"I see. . . ." Now the next question in our scenario: "How do you think I should end it?"

"You're too hard on yourself." She ignored the question until she had finished her sermon. "I've told you that all along."

"Without much effect."

"I didn't say that, but you are still too hard on yourself . . . why don't you have him look at the sad eyes of that big blond trench-coat being once again and then chase the train just a moment too late. It pulls away before he can catch it."

"Then?"

"Well, then he walks back to the terminal and there she is waiting at the door of the platform. He rushed by so quickly that he didn't see her."

"Uh-huh."

"She looks shy and kind of frightened and all tired out and he says something real intelligent, like why didn't she get on the train, and she says she couldn't and might she please have just one more chance, and he says a couple of thousand, and she says one will do for the moment; then, though there is no reason to think he has to revert to caveman behavior, he picks her up and carts her off—his choice of words—to Roxinante, his car, you know."

"I know."

"Then he has to return to pick up her suitcase, about which he'd forgotten. She waits in the car, because she has nowhere else to go and, with her just one more chance, no desire to go there, anyway. And maybe she's found that being 'carted around' is sexually interesting."

"Heavy suitcase."

"Right."

"You don't think the reader will know that all happened. I mean, I kind of hint . . ."

"Not if you don't tell her."

"Or him."

"Or him," she agreed.

"Yeah." I thought about it. "I could end it that way."

"You'd be much nicer to him if you end it that way."

"It might work. What about her? Am I too hard on that dreadful girl?"

"I don't think so, poor confused child. How many times do I have to tell you that you always romanticize women?" She touched my cheek. "That's all right. You're sweet." Her fingers remained, softly caressing. "Very sweet." The caress became more tender. "Always have been."

"That's nice to hear."

"I suppose," she said with a sigh, the drawn-out martyr's protest that usually accompanies her schemes to do what she wants to do, "you're planning on that orgy I promised if you finished your book?"

"You've been reading my mind, Maggie Ward"—I drew her close to me—"since that day when we heard Bing Crosby sing 'Ole Buttermilk Sky' in the railroad station forty years ago next week."

Still mystery, still gift, she yielded herself to me. But not without the last word.

"It was Hoagy Carmichael."